. . . .

51st DIRECTIVE

A NOVEL

MICHAEL AGLIOLO

FACT:

The **National Security and Homeland Security Presidential Directive 51** (sometimes simply called "Executive Directive 51"), created and signed by President of the United States George W. Bush on May 4, 2007, is a Presidential Directive which claims power to execute procedures for the continuity of the federal government in the event of a "catastrophic emergency." Such an emergency is construed as "any incident, regardless of location, that results in extraordinary levels of mass casualties, damage, or disruption severely affecting the U.S. population, infrastructure, environment, economy, or government functions."

The unclassified portion of the directive was posted on the White House website on May 9, 2007, without further announcement or press briefing.

INVISIBLE

Chapter 1

'I *should have stayed invisible'*, Brian told himself. *'God knows I tried'*. But that wish had died a long time ago.

Zigzagging through D.C.'s crowded streets, Brian made his way to the blue mailbox in front of the post office. Maybe there was still time to stop what he'd helped set in motion.

He checked both sides of the street before sliding the letter through the mail-slot.

Instinctively slipping his hand into his coat pocket, Brian touched the MK-23 semi-automatic pistol his brother had given him on his 50th birthday. The two and a half pounds of precision black steel had been his constant companion for the past couple months. It felt as cold as his soul.

The smell of fried chicken from the Shake Shack he'd just passed reminded him he hadn't eaten, another one of the side effects of being hunted. He moved a little quicker as he headed to his car.

The digital clock on the dashboard read 11:56 AM. Four minutes to get to the meeting area, four minutes to make up his mind.

Turning left onto Pennsylvania Avenue, then left again into the backstreet alleyway at the end of the block. Brian turned off the engine and waited for the signal. The taxi at the far end blinked its headlights twice then slowly pulled alongside his car. The tinted window in the back seat of the cab rolled down. A pair of cold gray eyes stared out at him, the same dead eye's he'd seen too many times before. The man was wearing Army fatigues. He always wore fatigues. *'The same shit as usual'*, Brian thought.

Silence filled the empty space between the two vehicles as Brian handed over the 64-gigabyte memory device and waited for the soldier to slip it into the air-gapped laptop and punched in the MX-7 password. The encrypted files came up on the monitor, casting a green light in the man's eyes and re-enforced the evil Brian felt every time he'd encountered the soldier.

Brian realized he was holding his breath as he waited for the last file to open before finally letting it out into the stink of the alleyway.

The DBAN software he'd embedded into the files began to infect the root directory on the laptop. The monitor went dark as the hard drive crashed.

"What the fuck!" the soldier swore, his eyes now reflecting the black screen.

Brian thought about pulling his gun from his coat and ending the man's life. The idea felt irresistible as it crossed his mind one last time, but it was pointless, this was the end game. Too many had already died, a lot more would follow if he didn't act.

"Go to Hell," Brian shouted at the soldier, "and take the general with you."

The laser dot from the soldier's Smith & Wesson flashed across Brian's left eye before coming to rest on his forehead.

'God, if only I could have stayed invisible'.

"Straight to Hell," Brian repeated just before the silenced twenty-two-caliber bullet tore through his incredible brain.

"You first," the soldier whispered before telling his military driver, "Get me out of here."

The taxi idled back to the main road and turned right, the quickest way back to the Pentagon.

•••

ERICA

Chapter 2

"**S**he's a 'he'," Jake reminded his two buddies, as they funneled me into the boy's bathroom at my Virginia Beach Junior High School.

"And you're a fat asshole," I yelled back and did my best to knee Jake where I knew it would hurt him the most. But he just turned sideways. Nothing was going to stop him from finding out for himself.

When Jake pulled down my pants, all three boys jumped back two steps like what they saw might be contagious.

Turns out this wasn't the last time my privates were going to intimidate someone.

I have to admit at age twelve I did look like a boy: tall, skinny with short dark hair, not a curve on me. Hell, my name's Erica. Leave off the 'a' at the end, and I was your buddy Eric.

After school, I told my older sister what happened. She clued me in that it wouldn't be the last time guys would try to take my pants off. Then, she told me why.

In the next twenty minutes I passed from a tall, skinny girl who looked like a boy, to a tall, skinny girl who'd just found out what's percolating.

Apparently, as guys,,that girls veill Jake and his two pals stared at me as I walked by at lunch the next day. I stared back until they looked away.

I haven't lost a stare-down since.

I'm 31 now and still tall. But the 'skinny' has been replaced with the 'thing' that makes some guys lose the ability to hold a thought while contemplating the geography between my eyes and my ankles. I call it the 'five-second checkered flag scan,' one long eye-fuck from head to toe. No pit stops, no penalty flags, just riding around the track until they cross the finish line. It used to be funny, now I can set my watch by it.

My sister and I inherited our looks from our mom, along with her 'take no prisoners' attitude, but the DNA gods decided to bless me with my dad's blue eyes and his desire to be in law enforcement. I've discovered that men can't handle brunettes with sky-blue eyes. They also have trouble with the fact I'm an FBI agent, at least that's what my ex-husband told me when I threatened to arrest him for being a jerk. I've always wanted to be a cop. My dad and two of my uncles were cops. My dad used to bring his squad car home at night and park it in our driveway. Nobody drove fast on my street, ever. He'd let my sister and me sit in it and pretend we were calling for 'backup'. *"There's a 211 in progress, requesting assistance, code 2."*

One time I accidentally hit the wrong button and reported a burglary in progress at our address.

That was a fun evening.

At night my dad hung his uniform over a chair in his bedroom. When he became police chief he had to wear a suit, I didn't sleep as well, but by then the seeds were in the ground. I was going to be a cop one way or another.

After college, I applied for the Clandestine Service Program with the FBI. The background checks fared pretty well. It didn't hurt that half my family were cops. My I.Q. test came in at 139 and the powers that be at the FBI decided I'd make a pretty good analyst. But analysts gather information and assess threats to our country. I didn't want to assess 'em, I wanted to arrest 'em. So I turned down the analyst assignment and applied to be a field agent.

Fortunately, my dad had taught me how to handle a gun as I came into puberty; pretty sure he was sending a message to the boys in my high school.

The three straight 'gun range' titles on my application found their way through the bureaucracy and landed me at Quantico for five months of training. That got me moved from analyst to field agent.

My first assignment had me working in the Chicago FBI office; tough town for a gal with attitude. After getting shot at twice they decided my lifespan would increase by a couple of years if I transferred to the Washington D.C. office. I made the move two years ago.

Everything was working out fine until two weeks ago when I got sent to the FBI basement to pay for my sins.

I AM DEAD

Chapter 3

Today's the fourteenth day of my 'attitude adjustment'. I'm spending it on 'mail duty' on the bottom floor of the FBI headquarters in D.C.

According to my boss, FBI Bureau Chief David Gilliam, the 'attitude adjustment' was necessary if I wanted to keep getting a paycheck. He wasn't angry. I could tell by the way he tried to hide his smile.

I guess I could have handled the situation a little better. But hell, I didn't even pull my weapon on my 'intoxicated co-worker' two weeks ago. He should have read my personnel file before saying what he said to me at his 'retirement party'. Like I mentioned, my mom taught us 'not to take any prisoners'.

Seven more days of this nonsense and I'd be back in my office on the eleventh floor.

I was settling in at my desk when Ron Collins rolled his mail cart to my station. Ron's three years younger, and three inches shorter, than me. Handsome, naïve, and has been trying to wisecrack his way to asking me out for the past week.

"Ah, if it isn't Agent Erica Brewer," Ron announced as he parked in front of my desk, "Sent from high above to schlep with us mortals here in the lowest levels of FBI hell." He proceeded to give me the 'five-second checkered flag scan'. One long eye-ride from head to toe. No pit stops, no penalty flags, just riding around the track until he crosses the finish line. It used to be funny, now I can set my watch by it.

"You have no idea how I love it when you look at me like that," I whispered. "Makes me crazy inside." He tried to match my stare but surrendered like Jake did in the seventh grade.

Ron tried to come up with a snappy comeback, but his brain was in full lockdown mode and could only manage another 'body scan'. I glanced at my watch and started counting. Five seconds later he walked away.

A stack of mail sat on my desk. The top letter came from someone named George. No last name, which wasn't unusual. George believed he was duty-bound to express his outrage at the FBI 'listening device' he'd found in his bedroom drawer. George included a photo of the device, which I thought looked a lot like an eraser from a number two pencil.

The Discovery Channel's documentary on government listening devices had kept complaint letters like this one rolling in. I had to admit George made several good points about the FBI playing God. I found his threat, 'if we didn't stop trying to listen in on his personal life, he'd defect to Pakistan and join a terrorist group', both compelling and ill-advised. He didn't leave a return address or a phone number. Too bad. I wanted to tell him I'd join him if I didn't get out of the mailroom soon. I stamped it 'level one' and put it in the "out" pile.

The next was a single page letter, folded into three sections, addressed to F.B.I Chief David Gilliam.

In the last couple of weeks, I'd read nearly three hundred letters. This one was handwritten and stopped me in the first three words:

I am dead.

The first bombing will occur Thursday the 24th, which will confirm this note is real.

Our military is fractured, lives are at stake, no one in the government can be trusted, not even the ones who are dead.

My death will have occurred on Wednesday the 22nd in an alleyway off Pennsylvania Avenue. Once this is confirmed, it is paramount that a hidden flash drive be located and the contents examined. The proof of what I am saying is disclosed in the encrypted drive. Any attempt to open the file without the following passcode will destroy the information it contains.

Passcode: Wtq9zYcZ>/baW~VwMn77ogHqwQ=

Only my brother knows where to find this flash-drive. Unfortunately, many will die before its message is decoded. God help us. B.M.

Hoaxes were the rule in letters like this. But this had my gut churning. I re-read it.

I'd been fooled once before by someone claiming to be in possession of secret information about the Russian government. They gave dates and locations of secret drop zones. I passed it up to level two. It turned out to be a high school kid with a great imagination. I had to sit through a lecture from my boss. Wasn't going to let that happen again.

I dialed the Washington police homicide department.

"This is agent Erica Brewer with the FBI, authorization code A555 delta 119. I need confirmation on a possible homicide at 14th and F Street, on the 22nd of this month. Can you confirm the victim's name?"

"Hold please." The line was quiet, no music thank god, but Eric Clapton's 'I Shot The Sheriff' would've been a hoot. A minute later a man's voice came on the line.

"Agent Brewer this is Detective Marco, I worked the case you're inquiring about. I can confirm we responded to a murder on the date and location you mentioned. The victim's name is Brian Mitchell, age 57; unmarried, lived at 2299 Oak Street apartment #5 in D.C. His brother, Steven Mitchell is en route from California to claim the body."

The detective remained quiet for a moment before adding, "the victim had a Heckler & Koch MK 23 on him."

"Thank you, detective," I replied. "Can you fax the death report to this office?"

"Yes, ma'am."

I hate it when I'm called ma'am.

"One more thing Detective, you hesitated for a second before reporting the victim carried a Heckler & Koch MK23. Why the pause?"

"The MK23's not your typical civilian weapon. It's a Special Forces sidearm, the one we used in Afghanistan. Caught my attention is all."

I thanked him for his time and disconnected.

I typed the victim's name and address into our database. The man's I.D. file cued up on the screen.

To be honest, I've used this database a couple of time before going on a first date. Helps a gal decide if she should bring her gun.

Our murder victim was an average looking middle-aged white male. A salesman for Delta Pharmaceuticals based in D.C. No military service, never married, and no prior arrests. This was a guy living the day-to-day thing until someone decided to put a stop to it.

I leaned back in my chair, chewed a fingernail, weighing my options. I re-read the letter for the fifth time. The guy knew he was going to be

13

murdered. He also wrote 'many will die'. Hoax be damned, my gut wasn't letting this one rest. I put the letter in a red folder and headed for the elevator.

The doors opened, three men stood stoically inside the carriage. I stepped in and stood in front of the one on the far left, the tall one with the handsome face and a mustard stain on his tie. Next stop, the eleventh floor.

I felt a soft embrace on my shoulder from Mister Mustard. I froze, looked out of the corner of my eye at the other two men standing with us. They were oblivious, staring straight ahead at the metal elevator doors. Mustard's hand moved slowly down my side toward my hips. I coyly reached back, slipped my fingers around where his wedding ring should have been. He let out a long sigh and moved his hand. Part of me wishes I could have pulled my gun and aimed it at his crotch, but we'd already been on two dates and I decided to cut him some slack. Besides, I didn't have my weapon. It's locked in my gun safe at home. Not a lot of call for it in the mailroom. The elevator doors opened, my grumpy special friend pushed passed me gently, turned left toward his office without looking back. I turned right and crossed to the end of the hall, I stood in front of the door a moment, gathering my thoughts. A gold plaque fixed on the door read:

:: FBI BUREAU CHIEF : DAVID GILLIAM ::

"Is he in?" I asked his secretary as I walked into the reception area, closing the door behind me.

"Yes, he's just about finished with the head of security, shouldn't be more than a couple of minutes." I was still standing when my boss's door opened and two men walked out of his office.

"Miss Brewer," said the older of the two, Allen Sanchez, the Head of Security, as he approached me.

"Mister Sanchez," I replied with a friendly smile. I've always liked Allen Sanchez, a good man. But the younger man with him, I hadn't seen before. I could tell in a pair of heartbeats he was going to do the five-second walk down to my legs and up again. I was tempted to look at my watch and count the seconds out loud but I waited for him to finish.

He tried to hold my gaze when he got back to my eyes, so I stared until I could see his eyes shake. He turned away, but not soon enough. Stepping blindly, he bumped into his boss standing in the doorway. "Relax Mike," Sanchez told him and gave me a surprisingly sincere smile. "She tends to do that to folks." He waved and walked on. "Nice to see you, Erica."

"Nice to see you too, Allen."

Beside us in his doorway, Gilliam cleared his throat. "To what do I owe this pleasure?" he asked. I'm sure his approval was hidden somewhere beneath that stoic glare.

I handed him the red file I brought with me. "Think you should see this, Boss."

"This better be good," he said, waving me into his office, "Or I'm going to believe you don't like it in the mail room."

I smirked. "I love it down there. In fact, I'm considering asking for a transfer. Permanent like. Imagine how good it will look on your expense account, my GS-10 salary doing the job of a GS-5. Works for me."

He held the door open, pointed to a chair.

Gilliam, he lets me call him 'boss', had worked his way up the FBI hierarchy the hard way, first as a field agent, then through the ranks all the way to the FBI's Washington Bureau Chief. A job he's had for the past 12 years. Rumor has it he'd been offered the Secretary of Homeland Security position but had quietly refused. He's sixty-two years old and looked every year of it. His hair has thinned but his stomach hasn't. Married to the same woman for thirty-five years, he has two daughters with families of their own. I like him. More importantly, I trust him. He's the one who recruited me from the Chicago office. Told me I had the brains and guts to work in the counter-terrorism unit.

"Okay," Gilliam told me, opening the folder, "let's see what you're using to get out of the mailroom this week." Nodding his head slowly as he read, he raised his glasses, shot a glance at me. "What makes you think this is real?"

I picked up the next piece of paper in the red folder, showed it to him. It was the info I had gotten from Detective Marco. "MK-23. It's a special sidearm the military used in Afghanistan. That's what caught the eye of the cop who gave me the report. He thought it was strange someone never in the military would have one."

Gilliam read the letter again. "Tomorrow's the 24th. Our victim says a bomb is going to go off tomorrow but doesn't say where. Also says 'no one can be trusted. Doesn't give us much to work on."

He slid the letter back in the envelope, placed it in the open folder in my hand. "Not much we can do here Erica" and gave me a reassuring nod. "But I can see why you brought this to me."

I set the report on his desk and pointed to the name of the cop I'd spoken to. "One thing we could do, let me talk to this Detective Marco again. See if there's anything else at the crime scene that might tell us something."

Gilliam gave me a little smile. "Mailroom getting you itchy?" He drummed his fingers on the file. "Any letter that leads with 'I am dead' has my attention. Go ahead and talk to this detective and let me know what you find out." He pointed his finger straight toward the basement. "And finish out your week down there." The same finger turned to point towards the door. "Now go."

<u>MARCO</u>

Chapter 4

A s I left my bosses office heading back to the mailroom, I paused in front of Anthony Hayes's office. Tony's the head of our Operational Technology division and the guy I'd stood in front of in the elevator. I was about to knock when I heard him say, "Come on in Erica."

How does he know it's me, the little shit, every time…?

I walked in and closed the door.

"Nice try in the elevator Tony," I muttered. "But you're married and what happened before I knew you were still married is not going to happen again."

"We're separated," he told me. "Been separated for a year, do I have to wear a sign on my shirt saying 'separated' when I ask a woman out?" He looked at me, his dark eyes locked on mine.

Damn those eyes, they were why I said yes to going out with him in the first place.

We'd only been out twice, but the chemistry had been hard to resist. My divorce, two years ago, had started to fade into the background and my hormones were making a comeback. Tony almost talked me into letting him into my apartment after our first dinner date. His eyes, my re-energized libido, a couple of glasses of Pinot Noir and I'd been pretty close to violating the prime directive.

On our second date he told me he wasn't divorced, only separated. I hit the emergency brake and the evening ended.

"Separated means still married," I reminded him. "I don't have a lot of rules. In fact, this might be my only one, but it's a rule I don't mess with." I changed the subject, "How'd you know it was me standing at your office door before I even knocked?" I asked. He'd done it several times in the past. "How do you do that?"

"I have no idea," Tony answered. "I can see a little shadow under the door, but I have no idea how I know who it is. I just kind of feel it. Comes in handy sometimes."

I replied, "I'll bet it does." Tony's the head of the surveillance division. "Look, Tony, I came by to tell you no more elevator stuff. I'm sorry, I have no business telling you what to do in your life, but I'm still working out my own stuff, okay?"

"Yeah, I get it," he mumbled, looking at me with those eyes as I left his office.

When I'm not 'doing time' in the mailroom I have my own office at the end of the hall. I thought I'd make sure my name still graced the door.

Everything was like I'd left it, messy. I put my feet on my desk and looked over the top of my shoes at the city eleven stories below. My computer, which gives me access to about everybody in the country, beckoned me to log in.I'm pretty sure most Americans hate the idea that I can run a detailed search to find out almost everything about them. I get it, I'm not crazy about the intrusion either. But predators are out there hunting innocent people, and along the way it's become necessary to have folks like the FBI find these dirtbags and put them somewhere they can't hurt the innocents. So we hunt the hunters, lock the criminals in cages and when necessary, track down the killers. Sometimes I use a computer, sometimes I use my 40 caliber Glock 22.

I ignored my computer for the moment and called Detective Marco at his precinct. He agreed to meet at 4 PM at his office.

With a few hours to waste before then, I fired up my computer and dove into some research. The semi-automatic Heckler & Koch held a 12-round magazine specifically designed as an offensive weapon for Special Ops combat forces. A civilian version called the Mark 23 used a 10-round magazine. I noted this in the case file.

The letter had mentioned an encrypted flash-drive with a boo-by-trapped password. I called Shreya Aswini, our best

bureau's computer specialist and my best friend. We worked a couple of cases together when I first got to Washington, gone out a bunch of times for drinks at The Fat Angel Restaurant. There's nothing like Russian vodka and Sicilian pizza to jumpstart a friendship.

Shreya can drink. I can do shots with the best of them, but this woman has an empty leg. She also has a big brain, a beautiful face and stands five foot two in heels. How did such a little body hold so much alcohol? We chatted it up for a minute before I gave her the encrypted number from the letter and asked if it sounded authentic.

"Reads like a ColdFusion MX7 strong encryption function," Shreya told me. "If you make a mistake inputting the password all of the data on the drive vanishes and there's no getting it back."

"If I get my hands on this flash drive, I may need you to work on this with me," I told her and added, "Be a good idea if you typed in the password."

"It'll cost you a gin and tonic," she said. I could hear the devilish grin on her lips through the phone line. "And some chicken curry."

I agreed to her terms, hung up, and gave my office one last look of longing before meandering back to the mailroom. Ron Collins stayed away from me while I read more letters to our beloved FBI and ate a bag of popcorn and a Granny Smith apple, my version of a home-cooked meal.

At 3:30 I headed to the precinct. Traffic in Downtown D.C. between 2:30 and 7 PM was stop and go-slow. Mostly stop.

I drive a black '69 Chevy Super Sport. Paid thirteen grand for her, put another ten in the engine and now she gets me where I'm going quickly. I've gotten stopped a couple of times, mostly by cops who want to check out the car. I can tell they want to frisk me too, but things change when I show them my FBI credentials.

I got to the police station a few minutes early and found Detective Marco's office on the third floor. His door was open. He had both feet on his desk and I could hear him laughing into the phone. He saw me in the doorway, pointed at a wooden chair, smiled as I sat, and gestured to his phone. 'One second,' he mouthed to me as whoever was on the other end of the line continued.

"Yeah, well you should believe me. I can cook pasta sugo, Mom taught all of us. Okay, right, no problem. I'll be there with enough for ten. What about Uncle Jim? Okay then, enough for thirteen. See you then. Yep, bye."

He hung up and stood. "Sorry about that, my nephew's birthday party is this weekend. I'm Detective Marco, you must be the agent I spoke to about the murder?"

"FBI Agent Erica Brewer," I replied.

"Right, nice to meet you."

He walked to a metal file cabinet, pulled out a file and handed it to me. "I'll be right back, take a look at the last page," He left.

He returned with a plastic evidence bag. "Thought you'd want to see these," and sat back behind his desk waiting for me to finish the report.

"Pasta sugo, what is that?" I asked, closing the file.

He laughed and glanced at me. Marco was handsome, his smile sincere. He was about four inches taller and maybe five years older than me. His dark eyes were flecked with green, like the glass marbles my sister and I used to play with on the front porch. He hadn't shaved and the stubble masked a small dimple on his chin. A slight scar on his forehead above his left eyebrow broke the symmetry of his face, giving him a bad boy look. He wore a black shirt tucked into a pair of black slacks that matched his hair color. A wisp of grey was making its way north above his ears. The holster around his left shoulder had a Glock-G22 in the saddle, same as mine. Not sure why, but someone using the same gun made me trust him a little bit more. A strange reason to trust someone but anything bridging the gap between cops and the FBI is a start.

"Pasta sugo is spaghetti with meat sauce," he told me. "That's what we call it in my family."

I looked at the plastic bag on his desk. It contained a wallet, a cell phone, a few bills, and some credit cards, but no gun.

Sam saw me looking. "This was all the victim had on him." He gestured towards the pile of evidence. "The wallet had a couple hundred dollars in it, a driver's license, three credit cards plus a cell phone. We didn't find any evidence of a struggle. The gun in his coat pocket is locked in the evidence room."

I opened the bag and looked at the driver's license. "Has anyone in your department searched the man's home?"

"Yeah," he told me and crossed his arms, "I checked out his apartment, found a personal phone book and located his brother's name and number. I made the call and notified him about his brother's death. He's flying out tomorrow to claim the body. Sounded pretty broken up."

"How about his phone, anyone checked out who he'd been talking with?"

Sam replied, "Not yet," and had a question of his own, "Can you tell me why the FBI's so interested in this guy, how do you folks even know about him?"

"We received a letter from the man you found, a letter addressed to my boss."

"To your boss?" Sam repeated and ran his hand through his hair. "Can I see the letter? I'd like to see if anything might shed some light on our vic."

I gave him the usual FBI B.S., "I'm afraid not, we're still checking on a few statements he made."

"Anything in the note I can tell his brother? He seemed pretty upset."

"I can't," I said, remaining cordial. "It's the usual FBI BS. Analyzing. Assessing."

My attempt at humor was lost on him. He gave a sympathetic smile, trying to appease me. My hands were tied, he knew it. He was pushing, but not too hard, sensitive to the bureaucracy.

"Did the letter mention his brother." He asked.

It was my turn for a compassionate smile. "Unfortunately, it's all I can say for now." I wanted to tell him and he knew it. He lowered his eyes and nodded, alleviating the pressure. I was grateful. "I'd like to speak to Mitchell's brother when he arrives," I said. "Can you let me know when he gets here?"

I could tell Detective Marco wasn't happy, but he managed a cordial smile. "Of course."

I smiled, courteous. "Nice meeting you detective." He extended his hand, but before I could take it, I remembered something. "One more thing Detective, you mentioned the gun he used, the Heckler & Koch MK 23. Was the magazine a ten load or twelve?"

"Twelve."

We shook hands. "Good luck with the pasta," I told him as I headed for the door.

"You t--" His phone rang.

I nodded, let him answer the phone. Closing the door quietly behind me, I heard Marco call out. "Agent Brewer, hold up."

I went back in, curious. He slammed the phone back onto its desktop cradle. "Our murder vic's apartment building is on fire. My dispatcher says there are three fire trucks on the scene. It's still burning but under control."

My fingers clutched the car keys in my pocket. "I'll follow you," I said. "So drive fast."

I called my boss as I pulled out of the parking garage and brought him up to speed on what I'd found and where I

was going.

"Lucky you," he said. He knew I'd rather get a root canal than go back to the mailroom. "Keep me posted."

I flashed my FBI credentials to get past the police lines at the apartment building. The fire was out, but the building was still smoldering. I saw Detective Marco talking with the fire chief. I made my way over to them.

The Chief was saying, "...about two hours ago, they..." He stopped mid-sentence and looked at me.

"This is FBI Agent Brewer," Marco told him. "She's looking into the same case I was telling you about."

"Do you know where the fire started," I asked.

"In the basement," he replied, glancing at my legs.

"The fire worked its way to the first floor," he said as his eyes moved to my waist. He folded his arms over his chest and took a long look at my second story. "My investigators are looking into it now, should have an answer later today." Finally, looking at my eyes, he concluded: "I didn't see any structural damage to the foundation, the building looks good."

Damn straight. I stared at him till he looked away.

Sam asked him, "Which apartments were closest to the origins of the fire?".

"Numbers two and three," the Chief answered, excusing himself to take a call.

Sam looked back at the building before telling me, "Our victim lived in apartment number four,"

"That was my arson detail," the fire chief said, re-joining us. "He confirmed the fire started in the basement next to several discarded oil cans and engine parts. It looks like whoever was working in the basement was careless. My guy's still investigating, I'll get their final report in the morning."

"Can you send over the report when it's done, chief?" Sam asked. He turned to me. "You want one sent to your office, Agent?"

I nodded and we exchanged cards, "Can I go inside and take a look around?" I asked.

"You'll have to put on a fire suit and mask or wait till tomorrow when all the smoke has cleared."

I'm wearing a black Pencil Skirt with a white top and knew the fire suit would require me taking off my skirt. "I'll come by tomorrow," I told him.

I nodded to Sam, taking out my car keys. "Thanks for letting me know about the fire."

Walking back to my car, I knew something wasn't right. Too many coincidences were popping up. A letter telling us he was going to be murdered, a military weapon, and now a fire? Coincidence?

I sure the hell hope so, the letter claimed there'd be an attack on Thursday.

Today's hump day.

Touché

Chapter 5

I headed home. Got to my apartment, took off my shoes and threw them into my bedroom on top of a pile of wadded up clothes. I'm not the neatest gal you'll ever meet.

I'd gone shopping two days earlier. I grabbed a hunk of cheese, a bag of chips, and poured a glass of wine into a tall beer mug. Plopping down, I turned on the Wizard's game.

The Warriors point guard drove the lane and dropped in an uncontested ten-footer. "Get a center who can play some D," I yelled at the TV.

By nine o'clock I'd had enough excitement, took a shower and climbed into bed. Somewhere deep in my third R.E.M. cycle, my cell phone vibrated.

My boss's name came on the screen. I'm a smart aleck in the morning and answered. "It's 6:45 boss, my letter opening time isn't until 8--"

"A bomb exploded," he interrupted. "Ten minutes ago in front of the White House. Someone threw a backpack over the fence. Nobody's hurt, but the White House is shut down, the President's in the bunker and there's a manhunt for the person caught on the surveillance cameras."

Gilliam's voice turned grave. "Get your butt over here. You're off mail duty till further notice."

I dropped my pajamas on the floor, did a 'cold water' wake up splash in the sink and got dressed. I took my Glock from my gun safe. I hadn't needed it in the mailroom unless you count the times I wanted to shoot myself out of boredom.

I made it to my office in twenty minutes where the bombing report sat on my desk. I read it and called Gilliam's office.

"You're expected at the White House Secret Service offices," Gilliam told me. "Report to Agent Howard Decker. He's in charge of the investigation. He'll be the first to know when the bombing suspect is identified." He paused, took a breath. "Let's keep Mister Mitchell's letter to ourselves for right now. Report directly to me on my cell. It's going to be a shit storm over there so work your way around it."

My boss had it right, the White House was harder to get into than a Victoria Secret store on Christmas Eve. Barricades on Pennsylvania Avenue kept traffic as far away from the crime scene as possible. D.C. Police were walking the area with bomb-sniffing dogs.

My credentials were checked, they held my weapon at the door and made me walk through the body scanner twice. I smiled at the guy running the equipment. He smiled back.

I'd been to the White House several times on business and I knew my way to the Secret Service office. I was directed to the man in the back of the room, a phone to his ear. I made my way his direction, watched him hang up the phone.

"You're Agent Decker?" I asked.

"Thanks for reminding me," he replied. "You're Agent Brewer from the FBI. Been expecting you. Please follow me." He waved me behind him.

Walking swiftly, he led me through a large open area where twenty or so agents were talking on their phones. Everyone was packing heat, looking the part. I could smell the testosterone.

We stopped at a large screen in the front of the room. Decker pushed several buttons on a keyboard and the surveillance footage of the bombing came to life.

A time stamp read 6:33 AM EST. The footage was grainy but I clearly saw several people standing in a small group in front of the White House gates, near the North Lawn. A man using a cell phone was taking a photo of the group. Another man, about five feet from the group, wearing a dark hoodie and sporting a black backpack, faced the White House. I watched him remove the backpack, put his hand inside for a few seconds, and throw it over the fence. He sprinted out of the frame. A second surveillance camera showed the same person running across Pennsylvania Avenue. A third camera showed the individual coming toward the lens, running closer, closer. The camera shook for a second and Decker paused the video.

The image froze. The black hoodie covered most of the perpetrator's face. Decker pushed another button, the person continued running, finally turning left at the corner where the cameras lost him.

Decker informed me, "We've got the group he was standing with in the conference room."

"We know it's a him?" I asked.

"That's what everyone in the group said. None of them admit to knowing him. They say he slipped into their group as they were approaching the fence. Our surveillance cameras confirmed their statement."

Decker pushed a couple more buttons and the video ran backward until it shows the same guy, head down, approaching the group.

The Secret Service would confirm his height after they did a comparison measurement with the fence, but I pegged him at six feet. He wore dark jeans, a black T-shirt, and black tennis shoes. Nothing unusual. This guy knew everything was being filmed, he wasn't going to be wearing a nametag.

I looked back at Decker, "What kind of explosives were used?"

"We found traces of C4. It looks like a timed detonation. The bomb exploded twenty-six seconds after it hit the ground. My guys are working the area, we'll have a complete report within an hour."

"Can I talk to the group?" I asked him.

"Sure, follow me."

He led me to a conference room. Four women and three men sat at the table. They grew quiet as we walked in. "This is FBI agent Brewer," Decker announced. "She'd like to ask you some questions."

Decker walked out of the room and closed the door.

Two of the men did their version of the five-second-eye scan, so did one of the women. The rest looked down at the table.

I scanned the room. They were tourists hoping to get a look at the White House and now they were in it, being held by the Secret Service as suspects in a terrorist attack.

I'll bet that wasn't in their tour guide's sales pitch.

I decided to talk with them as a group before singling out any individuals. "Have any of you seen the guy who threw the bomb over the fence before today?"

"No," they all said at once like they'd been practicing.

"How many of you knew each other before today?" Five hands made their way in the air.

"We're from Detroit," one of the five said and pointed out the others. "We're here with a tour group. We've been friends for years."

From Detroit, I thought. Now there's a motive to want to blow up the government.

"How about you two?" I asked the remaining two men.

"I didn't know anyone before today," one of them told me. He kept scratching his forehead, eyeing the exit. The other guy shook his head 'no', and looked back at the table.

"Who was at the fence first, you folks or the guy with the backpack?" I asked.

One of the women in the group answered, "We were there for a couple of minutes before we asked this guy," she pointed to one of the men, "to take our picture. That's when the guy you're looking for stepped to the fence, hardly noticed him until he started running up the street."

"How about you," I asked the last guy. "When did you join the party?"

He kept his head down, wouldn't make eye contact.

"I walk by here every morning," the guy muttered. "Sometimes I talk with the people looking at the White House. Gives me something to do."

"You ever see the guy with the backpack before," I asked him.

"No, but I said hi to him today."

"You see his face?"

"Maybe a little, he had on a hoodie covering most of it. He turned away from me, so I left him alone."

"If we get an artist in here, can you describe him?"

"Don't know, I could try. Do I get paid?"

You got to love the guy's patriotism. Someone throws a bomb at the White House and this guy wants a royalty check.

"No," I told mister 'do I get paid', "all you get is a ride home sometime today, but you can hold out for the money if you want, I'm sure it won't take longer than two or three days before the government gets the okay to fund your 'startup'. Someone will find a place for you to sleep at night while they do the paperwork."

I walked over and opened the door. Decker saw me and came over.

"You got a sketch artist?" I asked. This gentleman would like to lay down a description of our perp, and he's going to need a place to sleep for a couple of days while you negotiate a 'finders fee'."

Decker looked at me like I'd been drinking, which was starting to sound like a pretty good idea.

"I was just asking," the guy muttered under his breath, "I'll do it for free."

You got to love America, the land of the free, home of the 'if you pay me', I'll be brave.

"I'll get a sketch artist," Decker told me. "You want to talk to these folks any more today?"

"Not today, but I'd like a copy of the surveillance footage you showed me and I'm assuming you're going to be checking the footage for the previous couple of weeks, see if this guy in the hoody has been checking out the area."

Decker fixed me with a stare, "It's being done right now, we'll let you know if we find anything," and handed me his card.

"Nice meeting you Agent Brewer."

"Yes, it was," I replied. "Thanks for reminding me."

Touché.

ANNEXATION

Chapter 6

The door to General Wallace's office was already open as he made his way out into the expansive hallways of the Pentagon. It was time to meet with the President at the White House.

The four star general had managed to move the meeting from the Oval Office to the President's private study. He hated the President's office as much as he hated the liberals who controlled congress. The round room made him nauseous - no corners, no reference points. But it was the closed doors that put him over the edge. He felt trapped. Claustrophobia on steroids.

Showing his credentials at the White House gate, the general was met at the front entrance by the President's Chief of Staff and escorted to the President's private study.

These were the last few months before the President's final term in office would transition him from the most powerful man in the world to a tax-paying citizen.

The two men had met eight years earlier at the beginning of the presidents first term. They'd found themselves alone in the kitchen at Camp David. It was a late evening and neither man had been able to sleep. As they talked they discovered each other's deep hatred, anger, and contempt with the liberal wing of the opposition party.

Both men found in the other a compatriot willing to use the power they'd acquired to save the 'greatest country ever to bless this earth'. The President ended the conversation that night by telling the general, "Come see me if you ever foresee the liberals taking over the country."

Two years before the end of his second term the President's approval rating had fallen below forty percent. The writing was on the wall. The left was gaining momentum. The nation was reversing course, turning away from the ultra-conservative direction the President had imposed the previous years.

The frontrunner of the liberal wing for president was gaining momentum. The candidate was running on a promise that had rocked both men to their core.

The annexation of Mexico.

Just like Puerto Rico, the candidate claimed, Mexican citizens would be given freedom of movement between the two countries. Mexico, the fourteenth largest economy in the world with its rich deposits of oil and natural resources would energize the flagging economy of the United States.

The candidate had convinced the nation that annexation would give our government the authority to wipe out the cartels and remove the corruption that permeated the Mexican government. The money to complete the annexation would come from gutting the half trillion dollar military budget.

A landslide victory would give the presidential winner a mandate to carry out his promise. The polls showed the majority of Americans had agreed and the new liberal Congress was ready to move ahead with the candidate's plan if he was elected.

The President and General violently disagreed with the candidate's crusade. For the past eight years, the president had done everything he could to close the border, claiming the hordes of refugees were infiltrated with terrorists, criminals, and subversives. Decreasing the Pentagon's funding would relegate the United States to third world status, the general argued. Without an act of courage it would be the end of everything the two men believed in. This candidate and the liberal congress would steer the country into a death spiral.

It was time to do what the founding fathers had done. Stand up to the enemy, destroy them, and lead the United States away from the liberal minefield.

No matter the toll, America must be saved.

Their revolution to save their country was about to commence. The General knew it and with the President at his side, they had the guts, guns, and God to get it done.

They weren't alone. Patriots recruited by the General were ready to die for the cause. Most would.

Fate had opened the door to stop the liberal uprising. Water damage from a broken pipe during the holiday recess had necessitated a twelve-foot area in the ceiling of Congressional office number H-131 be replaced. Three of the general's loyal soldiers from the US Army Corp of Engineers oversaw the reconstruction.

Sixteen pounds of colorless, odorless Sarin nerve gas was smuggled into the construction area in a portable acetylene welder tank and slid under the insulation alongside the ceiling joist.

The gas could be released into the ventilation system in the House chamber using a multi-digit binary code activated by the President's encrypted cell phone.

Evidence had been planted that would point to Iran as the terrorist nation behind the attack. War would be declared. The President would enact Presidential Directive 51 and take complete control of the legislative, executive, and judicial branches of the government. General Wallace would be appointed Chairmen of the Joint Chief of Staff, overseeing all branches of the Military.

The time had come for the soft to die. America would close its borders, turn off the liberal agenda at every juncture, and re-establish the United States military to its rightful place as the most feared in the world. The liberal cancer killing the country would be carved out in a single stroke. The pain would be great but the nation would endure. It would be primal survival of the fittest, and General Wallace damn well knew who the fittest were.

The general opened the encrypted files on his air-gapped laptop and brought up the timeline. He knew the information by heart as he briefed the president on the final details.

The joint session of Congress was set for a week from Monday night, at 9:05 PM Eastern Time. The newly elected British Prime Minister had been invited to address both houses of Congress as a show of unity against the rising terrorist attacks crippling Europe. The General and the President would escort the British Prime Minister to the chamber doors. Both men would narrowly escape the disaster, removing them from any suspicion.

All inside the enclosed Chamber would die, including the

Presidential candidates. The election would be suspended. Directive 51 would be declared. The President would oversee a nation in crisis. Yes, Wallace thought, closing his laptop, many would die. Some had already fallen. The soldiers who oversaw the reconstruction of the ceiling had already died in a roadside bomb after returning to Afghanistan. Other co-conspirators had experienced similar fates - fatal heart attacks, car accidents, and a few unexplained deaths.

The President and the General stood and shook hands, each man holding the eyes of the other. They had gotten this far by living up to the sacred promise they'd made to each other.

Trust no one.

•••

NOT YET

Chapter 7

I drove back to work, headed straight to the boss's office. Two people were already waiting but Gilliam called me in first. Nothing like a bomb threat coming true to let you cut in line. I closed his door and stood in front of his desk.

Pushing up his sleeves Gilliam ordered, "Debrief me on what the Secret Service gave you."

I took a seat and gave him all the details.

Gilliam pulled out our murder victim's letter, spun it towards me as he put it on his desk. He pointed to the first line, 'The first bombing will occur on the 24th.'

"The 'first attack' implies there will be more. Plus our murder victim's apartment building caught on fire."

I added my two cents, "Too many coincidences. Are you going to bump this to the next level, get Homeland involved?"

"Not yet," he cautioned and pointed back at the letter.

The next line read, 'no one can be trusted'.

Gilliam explained, "Let's keep this between you and me for a little longer. This is still pretty thin. Get in touch with Detective Marco and see when the brother of our victim is coming. You need to be there when he arrives."

"I'll check with the fire department too," I added, "see if I can take a look inside our victim's apartment."

I tried not to show any enthusiasm and asked, "Does this mean I'm out of the basement?"

Gilliam scowled and waved his hand for me to get going. The look on his face told me I was poking a lion with a stick so I made the right choice and left, heading to my office.

The eleventh floor had lots of personnel coming and going. As I walked past Tony's office, I heard him say, "Hi, Erica". His door was shut. How the hell does he know?

I made a couple of calls, one to Detective Marco, left a voicemail requesting a callback, the other to the fire chief who gave me the okay to inspect the inside of our victim's apartment.

I'd brought a change of clothes, low-key and comfy. I slid into a pair of baggy jeans, a pullover sweatshirt from my alma mater, and my running shoes. I tucked my hair under my well-worn Washington Wizards basketball hat and headed over to the apartment building.

A D.C. fire truck sat out front where four firefighters were busy doing cleanup work. I recognized a couple of them from the day before, I'm pretty sure they didn't recognize me. My clothes look like I'd just gotten off a farm truck.

I showed my ID and one of the guys walked me to apartment four.

"What are you looking for in here?" he asked. "The fire started in the basement."

"Yeah, I know, just want to look around," I told him, and added, "Anything that gets me out of the office."

He smiled and opened the apartment door.

We gave each other the 'ain't it great to work for the government' look. "I'll take it from here," I told him and closed the door behind me.

The fire hadn't damaged Mitchell's apartment, but a ghoulish odor hung thick. Fires don't discriminate, they burn everything they touch and the combination of plastic, old furniture, bed frames, and everything else people collect came together to make 'the smell from hell'.

The place looked a lot like mine, two bedrooms with hardwood floors, white walls and messy. I stepped carefully around a pile of books on the floor and made my way into the guest bedroom. It looked like a computer store with everything connected to an ATX electrical supply.

This guy was ready for a power outage.

I turned on one of the computers. A serious looking password request kept me from going any further. I turned it off and looked around. Three separate stacks of books rested in the corner. Most were engineering manuals on writing code. Only one was titled Pharmaceutical America. It reminded me to take a look in his bathroom medicine cabinet. Too many free drug samples have caused a lot of folks to take their own lives.

I started looking around for the memory stick he'd mentioned in the letter. I doubted it'd be lying around easy to find, so I climbed in deeper.

Opened every drawer, cabinet, and box in the place.

Looked in the refrigerator, the freezer, even in the Cheerios box.

I ate a handful and put the box back.

I did an FBI search without making the place messier than it already was. Respect for the dead and no search warrant made me take it easy on the place.

The apartment had a sliding glass door which opened to a small patio. As I slid it open, a black cat ran past me and made a dash for the kitchen. Blackie started meowing, serious meowing, like feed me or I'm going to eat you kind of meowing.

The cat didn't seem to care if it knew me, just wanted me to open the refrigerator. So I did. No milk. I closed the door, remembering I'd seen a bag of Friskies, grabbed a soup bowl and filled it. The cat practically climbed my leg to get to it. Using my FBI skills, I concluded that Mister Mitchell owned a cat.

Unfortunately, that's all I'd learned about Mitchell. I checked the rest of the cat food bag for the memory stick. Nothing.

I ate a hand full.

Just kidding.

My cell rang. Caller I.D. showed it was Detective Marco calling me back.

"Thanks for calling me back Detective. Things got a little more urgent after the bombing this morning. Can you tell me when Mister Mitchell's brother is due to arrive?"

"This afternoon, landing at Andrews Air Force Base. I'm scheduled to meet him at the coroners at three."

"Okay to meet you there?" I asked. "This case has moved up several notches."

"The letter again?" Marco asked. "What does it have to do with the bombing and when do I get to see this letter?"

"I'll run the question by my boss before I see you at the coroner's later today."

"Please do," he replied and hung up.

The cat finished eating and started doing the cha-cha in front of the sliding glass door. I opened it and Blackie gave me a soft meow before rubbing against my leg and walking out.

"You're welcome," I said and closed the door, making a mental note to tell Mitchell's brother about the cat.

The drive back to my office was quick. That's what you get when your foot touches the gas pedal of a 397 big block with dual four barrel carbs.

I called my boss from the office and told him I hadn't found much at the apartment, but would be meeting Mitchell's brother later this afternoon at the coroner's office. Asked if I could show them the letter?

"Not yet," was all he said.

I looked over the police report again. The brother's name was Steven R. Mitchell, his address was listed in Oceanside, California, I Googled his name. Turns out Mister Mitchell is Marine Colonel Steven Raymond Mitchell, age fifty-five, Commander of the Marine Corps base at Camp Pendleton. I read his bio on Wikipedia.

A photo of the Colonel came up on the screen; it was easy to see a strong resemblance to his brother's photo. Both men were tall, big boned, like football players. The Colonel was wearing his marine uniform in the photo with medals pinned to both sides of his coat. I almost saluted the screen.

The colonel's bio revealed he'd flown jets in the first Iraq war. His plane had been severely damaged on a mission. He and his navigator were forced to ditch their plane into the Persian Gulf. He'd been awarded the Distinguished Service Medal, the Combat Action Medal, and been promoted up the chain of command. For the past five years, he'd been base commander at Camp Pendleton, in charge of over 160,000 military and civilian personnel.

I closed the colonel's file and read the note one more time: "Only my brother knows the whereabouts of the flash-drive. When my identity is discovered, he will know where to look."

"Many will die before this message can be decoded."

"God help us."

I'm pretty sure Colonel Mitchell would be asking questions I couldn't answer.

High-ranking military men who have control of air-launched missiles and nuclear weapons don't usually take kindly to 'I can't tell you,' for an answer.

I was beginning to miss the mailroom.

<u>COLONEL</u>

Chapter 8

The Coroner's office was located a few blocks from the Metropolitan police station. I'd managed to stay out of the building as both a visitor and a customer until today.

I've sat through a couple of autopsies during my FBI training so this wasn't my first venture into the 'belly of the beast.' But being around dead bodies in the morgue doesn't put me in a great mood.

I'd changed my clothes back to my official FBI 'look' before leaving the office and made my way to the morgue reception desk. They asked for my credentials.

"They're expecting you in Lab Three," the receptionist told me. "Take the elevator to the basement floor. You'll need to put on scrubs before entering."

Great, I'm going back into the basement again.

I found the lab and saw two men through the observation window. I put on a light blue unisex pullover scrub and a hair net and tied a white air mask over my nose and mouth before knocking on the glass. One of the men waved me in.

42

Unfortunately, this had been a busy week for the morgue, a line of bodies lay on gurneys along the walls. Washington D.C. looked like a popular place to die.

Both men stood beside a body covered with a white sheet.

As I approached, Detective Marco introduced me, "Colonel Mitchell, this is FBI agent Brewer, the woman I told you is looking into your brother's death."

We nodded at each other.

"I'm sorry for your loss, Colonel," I told him.

He stood there silent. Even with a mask over his face, I could see his pain.

"I've explained your interest in this case," Marco told me.

The colonel glared at me and barked, "I'd like to see the letter my brother wrote, Agent Brewer."

That didn't take long.

I glanced over at the detective before answering,

"I'd like to show it to you, Colonel, but at this time the decision's, not mine to make. I will pass your request on to my boss the minute we're done here …" *Should I call him Sir, or Colonel, or Mister Mitchell?*

I wanted to be respectful, but some men are easy to read. They're used to being in control. Before you know it they'll be telling you what to order for lunch.

But I'm getting ahead of myself.

I decided to go with 'Sir.'

"Sir, it's important to ask if you know where your brother would have hidden a memory device? In his letter, he indicated you would know where to look."

"What is this about Agent," he demanded. I could see a vein pulsating on his forehead.

His military voice washed over me, my vocal cords started to tighten, along with a couple other parts of my body. "This is about national security, Colonel."

I was done with calling him 'sir'. Plus, I don't like it when parts of my body tighten up without my consent.

"The memory device," I repeated. "Do you know where your brother may have hidden it?"

"Yes," he whispered, "I do," and walked out of the room.

I stayed next to the body alongside Detective Marco.

Marco hesitated for a moment before saying, "He's pretty busted up, the colonel's been around a lot of death in his profession but when it's your brother…"

Giving the body one last long look, we walked out of the morgue.

We removed our scrubs and found the colonel in the main reception room looking out the window.

As we approached, the colonel turned to face us. His body language had changed, his shoulders bent forward, his head angled downward.

"When Brian and I were kids," he murmured, "we used to hide stuff from our parents. Our dad kept finding whatever we'd hidden so we got better and better at coming up with spots he couldn't find. Take me to Brian's apartment and I'll show you the spot."

"I was there this morning," I told him. "Looked at most of the obvious places plus a few of the not so obvious spots.

Detective Marco gave me a hard smile, "You were there this morning?" he muttered, didn't look too happy I hadn't notified him.

"Yeah," I answered. "Every time we turn around, there's something coincidental happening, I don't trust coincidence. So, I took a look inside the apartment."

I didn't mention my list of other things I didn't trust. I'd been married and divorced once already so I had a long list.

The colonel indicated he knew the way to his brother's apartment. We left the building, the colonel took his rented car and Detective Marco rode with me.

"In a hurry?" Marco asked as I got on the freeway.

"Not especially. You going to write me a ticket for speeding?" I asked as I switched lanes.

He gave me a look that asked, 'who are you?' and tightened his seat belt.

I was about to remind him the FBI stood for 'Full Blown Insanity' but most cops already felt this way so why push it. I love going fast, always have. I ski fast, walk fast, and run fast. It's in my blood. My dad used to take me out on the back roads and let me drive. He'd turn on his siren and let me haul ass. I learned to like 'fast' early on, I still do.

"We're going to need to let the colonel see his brother's letter," Marco told me as I passed a truck.

"I will, as soon as my boss gives me the green light."

I could tell he was scowling, I took the next off-ramp. "This could be tied into the bombing at the White House," I added, "this memory stick might help us find out who did it."

Marco pried his eyes off of the road long enough to glance at me. "I asked the Colonel about the gun his brother had on him when he was shot, the MK 23. He told me he'd given it to his brother when he'd returned from Afghanistan."

We rode in silence the rest of the way to the apartment.

The guys from the fire department were still doing the cleanup. They checked our ID's and let us back into apartment Four.

The colonel grabbed one of the chairs from under the dining table, put it against the door of the guest bedroom, and stood on it. He ran his finger across the top of the doorframe. Didn't find anything. Moved the chair to the main bedroom and did the same thing across the top of the door.

Sam and I watched as the colonel moved the chair around the apartment. Finally, at the bathroom door, he stopped, took out a pocketknife and pried off a small round piece of wood from the top of the door. Prying it loose with the tips of his thick fingers, he pulled out an old film container, popped off the top and pulled out a one-inch memory stick. "Is what you were asking about, agent?" and handed it to me.

"It is," and slipped it into my pocket. My curiosity piqued. Grabbing a chair from the kitchen, I put it next to his and climbed up.

A hole about an inch wide and two inches deep had been drilled into the top of the door. The colonel handed me the wood cover. "Haven't seen this used as a hiding place before," I admitted and put the wood back over the hole.

The colonel gave a half-hearted shrug, "It was my brother's invention. He'd hide his pot in a hole like this at home. Never got caught."

Wish I'd thought of that back in high school.

"I'd like to stay here and look around for a few minutes," the colonel asked, "See if I can get an idea of what I'm going to have to pack up."

"Not yet, Colonel," I had to tell him. "There may be more evidence here. Let me take this memory device back with me to our headquarters and see what we find. As soon as we're done, we'll release this location to you."

He stood, wringing his hands together. "You have your procedures and your orders, that's something I can respect," and handed me his military issue business card.

The letter was coming true.

YANKEY WHITE

Chapter 9

S uspicion times anxiety equals paranoia, at least it does in my profession, which is why I took the memory device straight to the computer analysis department on the eighth floor of the FBI building.

I found Shreya in her office eating a candy bar with one hand, typing with the other. When she saw me, she took a bite and offered me the remainder.

I finished it off and handed her the jump drive. "This is the memory stick I told you about. I've got the encryption code right here."

I handed her the password on a piece of paper. "After you get this open, picture me buying you drinks at the Fat Angel." Mental note, stop at the ATM and pull out as much cash as I can get. This woman can drink like a Russian spy. Extra Strength Excedrin and cash for a taxi ride home would be a smart move too.

"Deal," she grinned and plugged the jump drive into the USB port and punched in the encryption code. The first file contained diagrams, schematics, charts, and a spreadsheet ending with a typed message.

We both leaned in and read the message.

• 1 • Operation: NSPD51 • 2 • Military control • Missing code •

• 4 • congress • 5 • assassinations • 6 • trust no one.

"Is this for real?" Shreya asked, her nose practically touching the screen.

She got the message when I closed her office door.

"Let me see the other info on this drive," I whispered.

Shreya opened the next file, a diagram of the House of Representatives drawn in 3-D with cross sections of each department filling the screen. She kept scrolling. Architectural blueprints for the entire Capitol building were in the following folder.

Sixteen pages of spreadsheets with detailed information on every senator, congressman, and cabinet appointment followed. A chart of the entire United States military command structure existed in the fifth file with detailed materials on weapons research, storage locations and troop deployments in the northern hemisphere.

All of it top secret.

Shreya pulled out another chocolate bar, broke it in half and we chewed in silence, scanning the remaining files.

I barely tasted the chocolate, watching digital files, click by, scroll up.

"Save everything on a new memory stick," I whispered, "And erase everything off your hard drive if it pertains to what we just saw. Give me both memory drives and most importantly, don't breathe a word of this to anyone."

Shreya looked anxious, "I'll reconfigure the root directory and wipe it clean."

'Yeah, ok wipe it clean, use soap and water as far as I'm concerned." I didn't have a clue what the root directory was. Sounded like a place you store vegetables.

"As far as I'm concerned," Shreya replied, "You didn't even come by my office today, but girl you're going have to buy me dinner and cocktails for this one."

I headed to Gilliam's office with both drives in my hand. This was turning into a shit storm. I could feel the adrenaline rush. I like adrenaline rushes. Shit storms not so much.

Gilliam's secretary took one look at my face as I came into the office and pointed at the boss' door, "Go on in."

I guess I wasn't wearing my best poker face.

My boss was on the phone when I walked in, took one look at me and told whoever he'd been talking to he'd call them back.

"You may have to shoot me after you see this," I told him and handed him the memory stick. "A lot of it's top secret and over my pay grade."

"I've already got plenty of reasons to shoot you," he said and plugged it into his USB drive.

When the 3-D plans of the congressional building came on screen Gilliam closed the door. "These plans were on the memory stick?" he asked and zoomed in on the image.

"They're just the beginning," I answered and stepped behind his desk. As each page came across the screen Gilliam moved closer to the monitor. His hands tightened into fists as he poured over the files. When he got to the military command data he turned his computer off and looked at me.

His face turned ashen, "This information is classified 'SCI'. Almost no one see's this stuff. These documents are Compartment X files and are tagged YANKEE WHITE, presidential eyes only."

I'd been working for Gilliam for over two years, I'd seen him angry, sad, surprised, and disgusted but this was the first time he looked scared. He ejected the memory stick and unplugged it from the USB drive, unlocked the bottom drawer of his desk and put it inside, and re-locked it.

"How in God's name did a civilian get hold of this information?" he whispered. "If this guy Mitchell hadn't been murdered, he'd be the most wanted man in the country."

We'd just read the top-secret manifest.

I wonder what that made us?

SHIT-STORM

Chapter 10

G illiam looked up from his computer screen as I walked into his office the next morning with large coffees for both of us. "Is this everything on the original drive?" he asked as he removed the memory device from his computer.

"Yes, sir," I answered briskly.

It was 'yes sir, no sir' time.

"Contact Detective Marco," Gilliam told me, "And have him come to your office ASAP. Let me know if he needs me to contact his commanding officer. Inform him he is not to reveal anything he's witnessed since the murder. Gilliam looked back at the monitor, an idea troubling his brow. "Who else knows about this?"

"Only the detective and Shreya Aswini, one of our computer specialists. I had her open the encrypted files."

"Have her join us in your office when the detective arrives." Gilliam gave me the look that said 'now'.

I nodded and left. No sense in arguing. I headed down the hall, passing Tony's office as far away from his door as I could. I didn't hear a 'Hello, Erica.' Maybe he wasn't in.

When I got to my desk, I called Detective Marco.

"Detective, I'm sorry to do this to you, but the situation with our murder victim has risen to the next level. My Bureau Chief has requested you to come to my office immediately. He's prepared to contact your supervisor, if need be, to make the request directly to him. He also is asking for every detail of this investigation be kept secret. No one, including your boss, should be informed of the details you've been privy to."

"Not a problem," he answered. "Be there in a half hour."

I called Shreya and told her to meet at my office in a half hour.

Alone with my thoughts for the first time this morning, one thing kept buzzing in my brain. Something I'd read in Mitchell's secret files. He'd mentioned Operation NSPD51 multiple times. I flipped open my laptop and dug in.

NSPD51. The National Security and Homeland Presidential Directive 51. Signed into law by President George W. Bush after 9/11. It gave the President full power to run the government for as long as necessary in the event of a "catastrophic emergency".

I re-read Mitchell's letter. 'No one in the government can be trusted. It was starting to feel like a spy novel, and not in a good way.

Restless, I pulled my coffee maker from the cabinet and started brewing some fresh caffeine. Thankfully, I got pulled from my cynical thoughts half-way through the brew.

Shreya arrived first carrying her laptop, a few minutes later, Detective Marco entered. I called Gilliam, asked my two visitors to please sit, offered them coffee.

Gilliam strode through my door moments later, closing it softly behind him. Gave everyone a curt nod.

"The only people who know anything about this are in this room?" he asked.

"Colonel Mitchell knows something." Detective Marco offered. "What is this about Chief, why am I here?"

"The letter we received," and handed it to Marco, watched him read it before saying, "Indicated the first bombing would be on the twenty-fourth. As you all know, a bomb exploded on the White House lawn on that day."

Shreya glanced at me, her eyes glassy, licking her lips, she took several sips of her coffee.

Gilliam continued, "Brian Mitchell's memory stick contained top secret information. We need to pay attention to what he wrote. He claimed 'many lives were at stake'. I've considered bringing in the CIA on this, but the damn letter says 'no one should be trusted'. I'm going to keep this in-house for as long as possible. Only trust the people in this room"

Gilliam let everything sink in. He brought the extended pause to a close with a sweep of his hands across the desktop. "Erica," he told me, "I want you to brief everyone on the Intel we've gathered, get them up to speed"

Gilliam saw the coffee I'd brewed and poured a cup into my favorite mug, added three bags of sugar, half a pound of Coffee Mate, and took a long gulp. He raised his eyebrow at Detective Marco. "I would like you to liaison with us on this investigation. I'll clear it with your supervisor. I need you to look at the evidence collected after the murder - the gun he used, his cell phone contacts, his employment history, you know the routine. Anything which paints a better picture of what he'd been doing."

Gilliam turned to Shreya. "Look into his brother's life. See if there's a military connection between the two brothers, climb into their contacts, who they know in common. Do your thing. Go deep into Mitchell's life, I want to know what he eats for breakfast on the weekends."

I almost gave her a heads-up and said 'Cheerios,' but kept my mouth shut.

I was next on Gilliam's to-do list. "Erica, you're running point on this. Everybody runs everything through Erica and she reports to me. I also want you to get into what happened with the fire at the man's apartment."

Gilliam headed for the door, my coffee cup in his hand. "Nobody talks to anybody about this except through Erica," he said over his shoulder, not looking back, leaving us in my office to get started. Shreya, clutching her laptop to her chest followed him out.

"I'd like to get your opinion, Detective," I told Marco, offering him a seat in front of my computer, "on the information we got from the memory disk we found in Mitchell's apartment." I opened the files on my screen.

"Call me Sam," he said, looking through the information. "Okay to call you Erica?" he asked, glancing at me for an answer.

"Sure," I told him, meeting his eyes. Neither of us looked away. Something about using our first names felt strange. Different. He smiled. "How old are you?"

That caught me off guard, "You want to know my age?" I have a habit of answering a question with a question when I'm flustered. I felt like I was back in 8th grade so I started acting like it. "How old do you think I am, Sam?" I asked.

"Thirty-one years, eleven months, three weeks, and two days," he answered.

Somebody did his homework.

"What's with the birthday question?" I asked.

"Wanted to confirm that you are who I thought you were, so I did a little research on you."

I was curious, "What else did you find out?"

"Your Dad was a cop, a good one. My Pop too." Something in his eyes shifted, a softness. "They knew each other. Worked on a case together back in the day. How's your Dad doing?"

"He's doing great, retired and driving my mom crazy. How about your Dad?"

"Passed away a couple years ago. Cancer."

"I'm sorry, Sam. Did you ever meet my Dad?"

"I did. In fact, I met you and your sister."

"Okay, wait a minute, time out. When was this?"

"About twenty years ago. My dad had a case he'd been working on with your father in Virginia Beach. I'd always wanted to go to the Neptune Festival on the boardwalk so my Dad took me with him. I was seventeen. We made the four-hour drive, stopped at your house and had lunch with your mom and dad. You were there with your sister. She looked like fourteen or fifteen and you were about eleven or twelve. You came into the kitchen for a few minutes before hightailing it upstairs. Didn't see you again before we left but I remember meeting you."

"I don't remember that day." I searched my mind again, drew only blanks. "What a trip," I said, looking back to his eyes. "You were in my house?"

He had a slight smile, "After our fathers talked about their case, my Dad and I left for the festival. When you left my office the other day I remembered your last name and did a little digging. I asked how old you were to see if it was you." Sam smiled. "You became a cop like your Dad, an FBI cop, sure, but that's still pretty cool."

Sam went back to reading the report, the grin still on his face.

I was an 'invisible kid' at eleven, I'm surprised he remembered me.

I gave him more time to finish looking at the files and asked, "What's your opinion? Is this a wild goose chase or a total shit-storm?"

I figured, what the hell, he'd known me for twenty years, we have history, let the swearing begin.

Sam leaned back in the chair, the smile on his face hid deeper concerns. "I'm guessing a shit-storm."

MARIA

Chapter 11

S oon as Sam left, I got in touch with the Fire Chief and made an appointment to meet his arson investigator at the apartment building. My boss had to pull some strings to get it done quickly, but soon the call came in for me to get over there. Nothing like the power of the FBI and a bottle of Johnnie Walker Black to speed things along.

Noontime traffic kept me at the speed limit.

A black SUV with "District of Columbia Fire & EMS logo on the side was parked out front of the building. I pulled in behind it.

A guy in a gray suit opened my door.

You got to love the power of Johnny Walker Black.

He gave me the 'five-second x-ray' look and told me his name was Investigator Ryan Burner.

I almost laughed but told him my name instead, shook his hand.

I followed Burner into the basement. The smell hit me again, but compared to the morgue this was incense at a hippy pad. He flipped on his flashlight, which was bright enough to start the fire again, and shined it around the room.

I had a lot of questions, but the first thing I wanted to know was how does a guy with the last name 'Burner' end up being a fire investigator?

We stepped over to the back wall next to a workbench. The entire bench had been charred black from end to end.

"Here's where the fire started," Burner told me and shined his five hundred million-candlepower flashlight at the wall and up at the ceiling. "The fire spread in this direction and burned through the flooring of apartment number one and two. No one was at home in either apartment so the fire expanded in this direction, toward apartments three and four across the hall. It would have kept going except for this," and shined his eight-inch 'torch of god' up at the wall on the other side of the basement.

Burner held the light in front of his waist with both hands. This guy had a thing for his flashlight.

A bank of hot water heaters lined the back wall, "The water unit right there, where the pipes come down from above," he shined the light on the spot. "The thermal coupler must have been in bad condition. The heat from the fire blew this connector pipe and it sprayed water on the ceiling, along this path right above number four. If it weren't for that, this whole bottom floor would have burned. The water slowed the fire enough for the apartment manager to see smoke coming out of the basement and call 911."

I knew he wasn't going to give it up easy, but I still asked, "Can I borrow your flashlight for a sec?"

He hesitated, but complied. I took it over to the basement window at the back of the room and looked at the latch. It was in the locked position. I turned the lock, it opened inward from the bottom. We were at ground level, I could see a couple of large bushes outside on either side of the window.

"You see anything I can stand on?" I asked Burner.

He brought me a three-step aluminum ladder.

From the second step I could see the fire had scorched the wood around the window but the glass hadn't broken. The window opened easily.

The ground on the outside had been freshly raked. I closed the window and turned the lock. There were several indentations along the bottom of the sill running underneath the latch. I got out my phone and took a photo.

"What started the fire?" I asked Burner.

"Someone left the overhead bench light on, the bulb made contact with one of the oily rags and 'presto' we have a blaze." He shined the light along the burnt bench, all the way to the other side of the room. "The fire moved along the oil-stained wood and up the wall. If it wasn't for the hot water heater blowing, the whole building could have gone up."

Burner decided he was done with his show and tell and walked toward the basement door. I followed him out and asked to have a copy of his report sent to my office. Today.

He frowned, looked me up and down before saying, "Sure." I could tell he felt a bit grumpy that my jurisdiction trumped his. Without a goodbye, he turned and walked back to his car.

"Do you have the name of the apartment manager for this place?" I called out.

"Yeah," and pointed as he walked. "She's right there."

I looked where he gestured and saw a woman in her early seventies standing on the sidewalk directly across the street from us. The woman was five feet-zero and built like a fire hydrant. Her blue dress traveled all the way to her ankles with a white apron tied around her waist.

It turned out the manager's name is Maria. She was a born talker with a unmistakable Italian accent. I barely got my credentials out of my pocket before she had me in her apartment across the street, making coffee and setting out cookies.

She'd been the manager for the last seven years and everyone had to go through her to rent a unit. Her coffee tasted great and for the next hour, I learned about everyone who lived in Mitchell's building.

According to Maria, Mitchell lived alone in apartment four. Never made any noise and paid his rent on the first of every month, even if the first landed on a Sunday. "When I come home from lighting candles for my Giuseppe at Saint Dominic mass," Maria told me, "I find his check in my mailbox."

"Did you ever talk with him?" I asked.

"Only when he had a problem with something inside his apartment. He mostly kept to himself except sometimes several nice looking men, tall and dressed in uniforms would visit. Ai-yai-yai" she added, shaking her hand in front of her.

I always thought ai-yai-yai was a Spanish phrase. Maybe Maria's been watching too much television.

"Did you see the kind of car they came in?" I asked, savoring the aroma of my half-finished coffee.

"They came in a taxi. The taxi would wait, sometimes maybe an hour or so, before they would all leave together."

"Would Mister Mitchell go with them?"

"Sí."

"Maria, can you describe the uniform the men were wearing?"

"I think a... lots of green, like a leaf. How do you say... hiding, I don't know the word?"

"Camouflage? Is that what you saw?"

"Sí. Camouflage."

"How do you know all of this?" I asked.

58

"It's my 'lavoro', you know, my business. I sit by my window," Maria pointed to the large bay window with a view of the apartment across the street. "I talk to my daughter on the telephone and look out my window."

And I thought my job in the mailroom had been a drag.

"So, you saw the fire the other day?"

"Sí. I saw smoke coming out of the basement and called 911."

My heart rate jumped. I had an eyewitness to the fire. I pressed her for more information, finally getting somewhere. "Before the fire did you see anyone go into the basement or come out of the basement?"

"No," she answered, "nobody went in and nobody left."

"Where did you call 911 from? Were you sitting here at the window?"

"No, I used my phone in my kitchen."

"Maria, can I show you something across the street?"

We walked across the street to the side of the building where the window to the basement opened. I pointed out the area right in front of the window.

"This looks like it was raked recently, did the lawn maintenance people come here this week?"

"No, they come every two weeks. They should be here tomorrow." Maria gave me a big smile. "I watch the young boys work. Sometimes they take off their shirts. Molto bene."

This lady needed to get laid. I know this because it's been about a hundred years since I've had any fun and I'm thinking if it's hot tomorrow I might come over and watch the landscape guys with her.

I walked along the side of the building and looked between the other bushes. Most of the surrounding area had leaves and twigs around the bushes. I circled back to the basement window and checked. The ground below the window looked like it had been raked clean.

I couldn't see Maria's apartment from where I stood so she wouldn't have been able to see if someone had been on this side of the building.

"Okay Maria, thank you for everything. Can I have your phone number in case I want to talk to you again?"

She gave me her number, told me to come over anytime for coffee. I thanked her again and walked back to my car.

I sat there for a few minutes, waiting for Maria to go back inside. I got my Swiss Army Knife out of my glove box.

Yeah, I'm a girl scout; I carry a red Swiss Army Knife in my glove box. 'Be prepared' and all that.

I headed back to the window and slipped the long blade between the windowsill and the latch. It took five seconds to unlock the window. I did the same thing in reverse and locked it back up.

The dots were connecting, I took a couple of deep breaths and called Secret Service Agent Decker to see if there were any new developments on the bombing.

"We've digitally enhanced the image of our suspect," he told me. "Come by the office and I'll show you what we've got. Security is still at level three, I'll have your clearance ready at the main entrance."

Apparently, level 3 requires I be scanned again. I was wondering if the operator recognized me.

Agent Decker seemed a little surprised to see me so soon. Obviously, I thought, shaking his hand, he's never driven in a car with me.

I followed him back to the same viewing room and he brought up the image of the suspect. This one looked a lot sharper.

The guy's face, under the hoodie, surprised me.

We could only see a skinny vertical patch of his face, from his forehead to his chin. When I first saw the tape, the perp looked in his early-twenties, but this guy was older. Probably in his thirties. "Can I see the footage of him running away again?" I asked.

Decker pushed a few buttons and the security camera footage I'd seen the first time popped on the screen. This guy ran like an athlete. He was in top condition. I'd have been hard-pressed to run him down.

"We're sending your office a copy of the enhanced photo of our bombing suspect," Decker told me. "The Washington police have put out an APB and we're releasing the photo to the press tonight."

It wasn't the best idea I'd heard all day and told Decker as much, "Can you hold off releasing the photo to the press for a couple of days? We're pursuing several leads that might be connected with this bomber. Letting him know you've got this image might make him go deeper into hiding. Might be something to avoid right now."

Decker crossed his arms and gave me the 'I'm the boss here, Missy,' look and proceeded to mark his territory. I didn't necessarily blame him. Every agency does the same thing when they anticipate their case being commandeered. The FBI does it, so does the CIA, the local cops, the IRS, the FDA, and probably the PTA. Agent Decker was protecting his turf. I took a mental step back and let him speak.

He squared his shoulders, brow stern. "The enhanced images are being released in time for the evening news, the decision's been made."

I considered playing hardball, but shifted tactics, remembering that I'm trying to build relationships here, not vying for a blue ribbon in a spitting contest. "Okay," I said, meeting his stare firmly. A glint of confusion in his eyes, like a dog when it hears a bark off in the distance. Men don't know how to handle the word 'okay' when they're expecting a fight.

At the doorway, I gave a slight pause. "You'll be hearing from me shortly," I added matter-of-factly, heading out the door and out of the building. Just as I got to my car I could have sworn I heard the sound of a dog bark.

PARANOID

Chapter 12

My cell phone was ringing when I got to my office, caller I.D. Indicated it was Shreya. "I've found some Intel on Mitchell, you got time to take a look?"

"On my way," I replied, throwing my purse down with a sigh and headed for the eighth floor.

"Shut the door," she told me as I came in.

"Why? We going to do some drinking?" I could only wish. It felt good to ask.

My quip didn't faze her. She was locked onto her screen. Glued. Techies do that, get so deep into it you can spend half an hour in a room with them and they'll never look away from their screen.

"I thought you should know this guy Mitchell, the one who was murdered, lived a pretty savvy computer geek life." Shreya gestured at her monitor. "His online profile started out so boring I had to drink a Red Bull. It wasn't till I launched Tor, rewrote the rootkit and redirected his servers before figuring out I had to do a brute force attack to compile his IP in the DAT file. That's when I realized this guy might be a legendary Grandmaster coder."

Now I needed a Red Bull. I could have pretended I understood every-thing she'd said, but the last twenty seconds of 'hacker speak' had me in a brain freeze. I shook her jargon out of my head. "Way to geek me, Hotshot, try non-binary English. What did you find?" I asked.

Without looking away from her screen, she exhaled through her mouth and told me, "This guy loves crypto. He's getting paid in Monero but is converting it to Bitcoins, and at today's price he's got over four-hundred and ninety thousand dollars' sitting in cyberspace. I've been checking his purchases, but he's not a buyer, he's a seller."

I knew the dark web used Bitcoin currency for transactions, which keeps the buyer and seller anonymous, but Monero sounded more like a spaghetti sauce than a way to move money from one person to another. "What the hell is Monero?" I asked, leaning forward for a better look at the screen.

Shreya tore her eyes away from the screen and glanced at me, "Ask me when we're drinking at the bar. Trust me, it will make more sense when you're under the influence of a couple shots of tequila. You need to be heavily sedated when you hear the crap that goes on in the dark web." She paused, grinned at me. "It'll also help a lot if you've seen the movie Princess Bride before we talk."

"WTF girl, I love that movie! What does Monero have to do with Princess Bride?"

"Remember the 'Dread Pirate Roberts' character? Well, he..." She didn't finish her sentence, trailing off as the computer sucked her back in. She hammered out a couple keystrokes and turned back to me. "Never mind. But this," she pointed to the screen, the financial accounts spread open, "this is impossible. I can't trace Monero so I can't find out who's pay-ing him. I've run several of our proprietary search engines, but haven't been able to penetrate the Onion Browser. I'm trying to look into Mitchell's life, but this guy knows how to stay hidden. There's some serious social engineering going on here."

I examined the files, scrolled through them. Only some of it made sense. "Can you find out what he's selling?" I asked her, fishing for anything.

"Same thing. No way." She clenched her fists. "Not yet, anyway. This guy worked with black hat hackers in the deepest parts of the web. You don't go there unless you're into some serious shit."

I considered this. Wasn't sure I liked where it was heading. "Let me know the minute you find anything we can use to find out who Mitchell dealt with," I told her.

I left her office and waited for the elevator to take me back upstairs.

The elevator doors dinged open. There was Tony, a smile lighting those beautiful eyes. "Going up?" he asked through his shit-eating grin. I walked in and leaned on the opposite side of the elevator, sizing him up.

"Heard you walk by my office this morning," he told me.

"How come you didn't say hi?"

"Because it freaks you out."

"How do you know it's me?" I asked. "Do you have a camera set up? Seriously?"

"I can smell your perfume. I can smell it right now."

"You're so full of shit your eyes are brown." I turned away, teasing him. "I inspected a burned-out apartment all morning. All I smell like now is burnt toast."

"Smell fine to me," he said, staring through my charade. Against my better instincts, I chanced a peek. Damn, he looked good standing there, all suited up, and smug. The chemistry was coming back to me, a warm wall pulsing in all the right places. Hell, I'm thirty-one and ovulating, give a girl a break, right?

I was 'this close' to forgetting my rule when the doors opened and two women stepped in. I was tempted to pull my gun and order them out, but I'd just gotten out of the mailroom. So I pushed the 'close door' button instead.

We all rode in silence, everyone staring expectantly at the floor indicator lights as if they were lottery numbers.

I needed a distraction and hustled to my office. Anything to take my mind off walking right into Tony's office and locking the door behind me. I played it smart and took out the letter instead, read it several times. One of the phrases kept gnawing at me. 'No one in the government can be trusted, not even the ones who are dead.' What does that mean? I read it again. Not even the ones who are dead. I set the letter on my desk.

I get pissed at mumbo jumbo stuff like this. I can't let it go or understand the point. Say what you mean, don't make me spin my wheels playing word games.

Like I mentioned, I can't let this stuff go so I took out my coffee maker and brewed some 'go' juice. I was good and wired when the thought came to me. No one in government can be trusted. Duh... everyone knows that. It's a trite platitude at this point. But 'not even the ones who are dead'? Maybe he's talking about government personnel who might be dead soon? That might die?

I wasn't sold on my train of thought, but it was sound enough to reserve a ticket. I called Gilliam's office and told him what I'd learned from the arson inspector, the apartment building manager and Secret Service Agent Decker at the White House. I concluded I'd had a hell of a day. Gilliam wasn't crazy about the enhanced image being shown on the news, same as me, but there wasn't much of the guy's face showing. It looked like a million different men if they were wearing a hoodie.

"Bad move for us, but they don't know what we're working on so I can see their logic. Have you talked with Marco yet?" Gilliam asked.

"No, he's my next call.

Detective Marco answered on the second ring.

"Hello, detective," I said, "This is agent ... Erica. I'd like to talk with Mitchell's brother again. You want to be in on the conversation?"

"He's on his way to my precinct right now," Sam told me, you want to join us here?"

"Sure," I answered.

"Okay for me to contact you on your cell phone from now on?" Sam asked.

We exchanged cell numbers.

When I arrived at the station Colonel Mitchell was already talking with Sam in his office. I knocked and ambled in. Both men stood.

Wow, old school. Men who stand when a woman comes in the room or comes back to the restaurant table after using the ladies room are as rare as Siberian tigers. And just as dangerous.

Sam pulled out a chair for me.

They were already in the middle of a conversation, "your brother in the military too?" Sam was asking the colonel.

"No, it's the direction my life took, not his. My brother wanted to be a software engineer."

That got my attention.

The colonel had a haunted look. "In the early '80s my brother decided to learn how computers work. He took apart his Commodore 64 and put it back together, and the damn thing worked."

I figure I'd embed myself into the conversation, "Did he stay with the computer stuff," I asked.

"He learned how to write code early on and turned our bedroom into a computer workstation as soon as I moved out to join the Marines."

The colonel looked away for a few seconds before adding, "I lost track of Brian for a couple of years. First time I came home on Christmas leave I found out he'd gotten a job at a mom and pop computer repair shop and had moved out of our parent's home. I didn't see him for a long while. It wasn't until our parents died that we began to talk again."

"So, you two weren't close?" I asked.

"Not for a while, but about two years ago, he started to come around more. He'd gotten a job in the pharmaceutical industry. It seemed like he was making good money but he didn't talk about it much. He'd come out to my base and visit for his entire vacation."

Sam walked into the hallway and came back with three bottled waters. We all took a couple of sips.

"What did your brother do all day when he'd visit?"

I think the question surprised the colonel. He thought about it before saying, "He seemed interested in everything we were doing here, especially the computer software we used for our communications."

"Were you able to tell him much about the software?" I asked.

"Not me," the colonel answered, "I'd put him in contact with our tech guys and they'd given him the VIP treatment. He loved it, couldn't get enough. They'd disappear and talk computer crap all night."

"When's the last time you spoke with him?" Sam asked.

The colonel got quiet again, took a couple more sips of his water and looked at Sam. "About five days ago. I called to check in on him."

"What did you talk about?" Sam asked.

"The usual stuff, how my kids were doing, stuff like that. But he didn't sound like himself, seemed distant, almost sad. When I asked if he was okay, he claimed to be tired from work. I invited him to take some time off and come out for a visit."

"What'd he answer?" I asked.

"He said 'not right now'."

The colonel glanced at me, his voice had dropped to a whisper, "My brother told me he'd made a mistake at work and needed to fix the problem. Told me he loved me and hung up."

We all sat quietly for a minute, the colonel kept his head down, rubbing his temples. Finally, he looked at us, "I knew something wasn't right, but I let it go. I should have kept him on the phone, found out what was wrong. Damn, I should have called him back."

I gave him a couple of seconds before asking, "Is there anything that might point us in the direction of why your brother wrote the letter?"

Shaking his head, "No," he answered, "but I sure as hell want to find out."

Sam grabbed the file on his desk and opened it. Took out the top page and turned it so the colonel and I could read it. "These are my notes after I contacted your brother's employer at the pharmaceutical company he worked for."

Sam pointed to the third line. 'Mr. Brian Mitchell resigned nineteen months ago. No reason was given.'

"You had no idea Brian quit his job?" Sam asked.

The colonel's body went rigid as he picked up the file.

"None," he stammered. "My brother told me he was on vacation every year when he'd come out to visit me at the base. Now you're telling me he quit his job a couple years ago? What the hell is going on here?"

Sam abruptly stood, "colonel, would you excuse us for a minute while I walk Erica to her car."

I got the hint. It'd be a good time for me to leave and said goodbye to the colonel. As we walked to the elevator, I told Sam, "I've used all my FBI skills and have deduced you wanted to speak with me alone."

"Sorry, but I'm pretty sure you know where I'm going with this. Thought it would be a better idea to say it out of earshot of the colonel."

"You want to talk to the colonel's military tech guys," I said as we got on the elevator. "See what questions his brother was asking them."

"We're on the same page," Sam replied, "I'm pretty sure the colonel's not going to like where we're going with this, but I believe he wants to know what's going on as much as we do."

"You want to ask him, or should I?" I asked.

"I'll do it when I get back to my office. If he says 'yes' we're going to need to make a trip to his base as soon as possible."

The doors opened, Sam stayed in the elevator. "I'm pretty sure with your FBI skills you'll be able to find your own car," he deadpanned.

"You know I'm keeping score," I yelled as the doors closed and walked to my car.

Afternoon commute traffic was heavy so I took the back streets heading to my office. As I waited to turn on Columbus Avenue, I noticed the same cab I'd seen pulling out of the precinct-parking garage still behind me. Ninety-nine percent of D.C cabs have advertising on the roof of their cars. This one didn't.

An electric zinger made a loop through my spine. Paranoid? Maybe. Maria, the apartment manager, told me Mister Mitchell's visitors always arrived in a taxi which would wait, sometimes as long as an hour. That's pretty odd, one without an advertising placard, rare. My distrust of coincidences joined the little paranoid voice in the back of my brain. I don't know what the voice was saying but I wasn't going to ignore it.

I put on my blinker and made the turn. The cab did the same. I felt a tingle in my chest. I don't need a lot of reasons to drive fast so I decided to test my paranoia and made my way onto the Beltway. Nobody in front of me. Good. I cleared out some of the carbon my engine had built up, doing eighty-five as I merged into traffic.

I didn't see the cab in my rear mirror anymore, so I did a couple lane changes and got in front of a truck in the slow lane. Hung there for a couple miles. When the cab didn't show, I got off on Myer Street and parked. Kept an eye out but didn't see the cab. My cell rang. I forced my paranoia out of my head and looked at the caller I.D. "Hello, Detec… Sam,"

"The Colonel agreed," Sam told me. "We're scheduled to fly out with him in the morning. Andrews Air Force Base, seven a.m. in the USO lounge. You'll be there?"

I was caught off guard, but what the hell, go where the evidence points, right? "Sure," I answered.

I called Gilliam, told him where I was going. "I had a thought about the letter," I added. "You know the part where it says no one can be trusted, not even the ones who are dead? Mitchell might have been referring to people who are still alive, but might die soon. Or even if they died recently they still shouldn't be trusted because of something they were hiding or were involved in."

"You're reaching pretty far," He told me. "But if something happens…"

I could tell he was weighing the possibility. He gave a contemplative sigh and asked, "What's your opinion on the fire? Was it arson?"

I'd been mulling over this too, and I wasn't buying 'Mister Flashlight's' opinion about it being an accidental fire. The easy window access had my panties all bunched. In not so many words, I told Gilliam that and added, "Ol' Flashlight's ready to declare it an accidental fire caused by oily rags too close to a light fixture but I'm not ready to sign off on this yet. Like to check a couple of things first, like talking with Mitchell's brother again.

"Do it," Gilliam told me. "Go home and pack. Contact me when you get situated at the base."

I headed home to the same apartment I've lived in since the divorce. Nothing fancy, but its got a good view of the Capitol and my neighbors are quiet.

I threw my shoes in the bedroom and headed for the kitchen. Wine time. I reached for the refrigerator door. Shit, it was already open. I'd left the damn thing open all night and most of today. Idiot. In my defense, it wasn't the first time I'd left the fridge open. The door had a glitch making it sound like it had closed when it wasn't. Every time it's happened before all of the food inside spoiled.

Scowling, I grabbed the half bottle of white wine from last night. It was still cold with a hint of condensation. I checked the milk and the mustard. Everything felt cold. Fresh. My leg muscles tightened as the paranoia hit again.

Images of what-could-be flashed through my mind. I pulled my gun and headed for the bedroom. I flipped on the light, everything looked like I'd left it. Same with the bathroom. There were no signs of forced entry on the front door. Since I was on the fourth floor I didn't bother with the windows.

Two bouts of paranoia in the last two hours, I took a long drink of the wine straight from the bottle. It helped. I took two more.

My room was its usual semi-mess. I live alone, so making my bed isn't too high on my to-do list and my dirty clothes are generally close enough to the laundry basket. I like to toss them from my bed, like shooting free-throws: two points for making it in the basket, one point for hitting the basket before it hits the floor, everything else is out of bounds.

The refrigerator door kept bugging me.

What if...? The two-word question that's never satisfied because it has brothers and sisters all lined up behind it. 'What if' a taxi had been following me? 'What if' I hadn't left my refrigerator open? Everything was still cold, as cold as the paranoia winding down my back.

I wanted to curb my paranoid impulses, and I would have if not for one unwavering final thought.

'What if'?

CELL PHONE

Chapter 13

I t took five hours to fly to Camp Pendleton in the military transport. The colonel sat in the cockpit while Sam and I shared the cabin with about forty military personnel on their way back to base. I've been on more comfortable flights, but couldn't argue about the price.

I told Sam about my two paranoid episodes.

He gave me an understanding nod, "I can't remember seeing a taxi without an advertisement on its roof," Sam acknowledged. "And the refrigerator thing would have freaked me out too. Stuff should have been room temperature after that long. Anything else different?"

"No, how about you? Anything different at your place?"

Sam thought for a moment, "Nothing I noticed, but I wasn't looking either. Playing the 'what if' game can get in your head. Paranoia's not a bad thing to have in our jobs, but sometimes the best thing you can do is have a beer and let it go."

Sam slept the rest of the way to California, but didn't snore, drool, or talk in his sleep. I'm pretty sure I do all three.

A car met us on the tarmac. Life's good when you're the commander of an entire military base.

Our overnight bags were taken to a two-bedroom condo a couple miles from the base in the housing area while we rode with the Colonel to his office.

Everything changed as soon as we stepped out of the car. The colonel transformed from the diminished man I'd seen in the morgue standing next to his brother's body to a man who emanated power. He even looked several inches taller. Everyone we passed saluted as we made our way to his office. He walked with wide steps, but stopped several times to talk quietly with various personnel, many of them offering him condolences for the loss of his brother.

We followed the colonel upstairs to his office.

A mahogany desk sat in front of a large window overlooking the base. A small conference table and chairs were on the far side of the room. A Marine insignia, sewn into the center of the wall-to-wall blue rug, gave the room a sense of power.

A photograph of General Eisenhower, hanging behind his desk, created the illusion that Ike was looking right at you no matter where you were in the room.

"Have a seat," the colonel said, taking his. He gestured towards the two chairs on the opposite side of his desk.

He didn't waste any time. "Who do you want to talk to first?" he asked, tapping his fingers on his desk.

"The highest-ranking tech officer your brother communicated with," I answered. "Then move down the ranking."

Sam walked over to the conference table. "Okay, if we meet with them in your office? And it would be best if you weren't in the room, colonel. They'll talk a little easier outside of your presence."

The colonel nodded, looking grateful for the break. He grabbed his phone and made the call. Six minutes later, Lieutenant Harris arrived, nervously standing as straight as a pencil. He saluted and held his salute until the Colonel returned the gesture.

"At ease, Lieutenant,"

Colonel Mitchell pointed at us. "These two civilian law enforcement officers are going to interview you about my brother and I am ordering you to answer their questions."

"Sir, yes, Sir," Harris replied, eyes forward, shoulders squared. The colonel walked out of the room and we led Harris over to the conference table. Harris was in his early thirties, taller than Sam, wearing a starched and speckless Marine uniform. He didn't look too happy to see us. Nobody is happy when they're about to be questioned by the FBI and the cops.

"Take a seat, Lieutenant. I'm FBI agent Erica Brewer and this is Detective Sam Marco of the Washington DC Metropolitan Police Department. We're investigating the death of Colonel Mitchell's brother. You spoke with Brian Mitchell several times when he visited the base, is that correct?"

"Yes Ma'am."

I was hoping for a 'yes sir'.

"You can call me Agent Brewer," I told him.

"Yes, ma'am," he replied, and looked at me like 'who do you think you are, bitch'?

He glanced at Sam, who let a couple of seconds pass before saying, "You can call me any fucking thing you want, son, just as long as you answer our questions. What did you and Brian talk about?"

"Computer software," he answered and put his hands in his pockets.

I nodded. "Did he seem to understand what you were telling him?"

"Smartest non-military computer nerd I've ever met. He wanted to know how we used encryption software and quantum computing."

"And you told him?"

"As much as I could without giving out classified information."

I leaned towards him, elbows on the table. "I'd like you to give me the same information you gave him."

Harris muttered. "You wouldn't understand what I'm talking about,"

"Try me," I said, pulling out my phone. I clicked the record button and put it on the table.

His nostrils flared, "I'm not talking into your phone recorder."

"Why? You said it wasn't classified," I reminded him.

Harris stared at me incredulously. Not his best idea of the day. I wasn't in the mood to sit there and play catch with this guy. "Lieutenant, you're not giving me the information I'm asking for."

He didn't reply.

I wasn't screwing around. I'd spent the last five hours flying to the left coast in a uncomfortable-as-hell military aircraft. A touch of jet lag had settled in, I was hungry, sore, and not about to do a dick dance with Lieutenant Harris. I didn't try to hide the impatience on my face. I walked out the door and asked his secretary to have the Colonel return to his office.

I sat back at the table and waited till the colonel arrived.

"Colonel, Lieutenant Harris is not interested in cooperating with us. Could you let him know how you'd like this investigation to go. Perhaps tell him how important it is to you?"

The colonel had Sam and I step outside.

With all the money the military spends on hammers and ashtrays you'd figure their walls would have been a little thicker. I couldn't make out every word the colonel screamed, but Harris seemed a lot more cooperative when we were called back in. He spoke loud and clear into my phone while he recalled his tech talks with the colonel's brother.

My brain was going numb as he rambled on for the next half hour about hijacking DNS on the Wi-Fi Pineapple. I never let on I didn't comprehend ninety percent of it. I kept nodding my head and saying 'ah-ha."

Finally, Sam took pity on me and asked Harris if Mitchell had spoken with any other tech personnel.

"He talked with one other member of my staff," Harris replied.

I turned off my recorder, 'Lieutenant do not speak to anyone about our conversation today."

To my surprise, he answered, "Yes, sir."

I was hoping for a salute too, but he got up and left.

After the flight and the interview, I was glad to see our bags sitting inside the doorway when we got to our condo. I took the first bedroom on the left, Sam took the bedroom upstairs.

The fridge was loaded with food, we broiled a couple of steaks and drank several of the Coronas someone had so thoughtfully left for us. On our second beer, I asked Sam, "What's your story? What have you been doing for the last twenty years?"

"Beside becoming a cop?"

I nodded and took a serious swallow of Corona.

"Baseball," he said, setting his beer on the table and leaning back in his chair. "I used to be a pretty good shortstop in high school. Got a scholarship to play for Georgetown, which would pay for my pre-law courses. By the second semester I was bored out of my mind, too much reading and not enough doing. I walked away from my scholarship and transferred to the Metropolitan Police Academy. Met my future ex-wife in one of my classes. We both graduated at the same time, got married, and started looking for jobs."

Sam paused for a second, took a couple of sips of his beer and clasped his hands together behind his head. "Not a good way to start a marriage, she got hired by the Arlington County Police department and I got on at D.C. Metropolitan on the other side of the Potomac. It might as well have been on the other side of the Atlantic. She got the day shift and I got the night, doesn't work too well if you ever want to see each other. After two years of watching each other sleep we agreed to go our own ways. No kids, no house. We just let go. I see her every once in a while, at some of the cop functions. She got married again, I'm happy for her." He swirled his beer around the bottle, watched the bubbles for a second. "After that, I focused on becoming a detective. I bought a house in Edgewood. Play drums in a small jazz band with a couple of buddies, we do some gigs here and there. That's my story and I'm sticking with it." He downed his beer and stood. "You want another beer?"

"Sure, thanks." I watched him walk to the fridge. I could see the jock walk. Shortstops have a look about them, you know? They have a cat-like walk, like they're ready to jump in any direction at the drop of a hat.

Sam opened both beers and handed me mine along with a playful grin.

"I kind of know your story," he told me.

"You mean besides visiting my house when I was a kid?"

"Yeah," he said. "I did some homework on you after I found out we were going to be working together. I won't work on a case with anyone I don't know. I learned it the hard way with my first partner. Almost got me killed. So I'm careful."

"What happened," I asked. I've had bullets fired at me in anger a couple of times so I figured I was a part of the 'almost killed on duty' club.

"My first partner," Sam said, sitting back down and picking up his fork, "had more than a few bad habits. Gambling was one of them and like most idiots who gamble, he didn't do it too well." He speared a sautéed onion, held it at the ready. "Borrowed money from the wrong guys. They weren't too happy about his payback schedule and decided to let their other customers know that everybody, including cops, needed to pay their bills. Unfortunately, they delivered their message while we were on patrol. He died, I didn't, and now I check out everyone I'm working with."

Made sense; every cop has a story. I drank my beer and watched Sam pop the near-translucent onion slice into his mouth, his eyes momentarily growing cloudy with thought before he blinked it off and smiled. "So, I looked into who you are. I knew you've gotten close to getting shot a couple of times when you were in Chicago. I'm betting that wasn't a lot of fun."

I shook my head. It hadn't been fun. But it hadn't freaked me out either. Shooting at another human being who's shooting at you tests you in a way all the training in the world can't prepare you for. When it happens, everything in your life disappears; your mind goes blank except for this need to survive. An instinct takes over and fills you with a new emotion. Predator. That's as close as I can come to giving the emotion a name. It emanates from above your stomach and drives you in a straight line to your jungle instincts.

The person shooting at you is no longer a human. You sense it all the way to your DNA. It's raw survival instinct. The gun becomes part of your hand, part of your brain. You don't fire it with your finger you fire it with your mind. Every shot comes from inside you. The noise, the recoil, the smell, it's all a part of you. When it's over the connection fades fast and the shaking starts. It doesn't matter if it's a hundred degrees out, you shake.

I felt it both times it happened and hope I don't have to experience it again. But if I do, I know I can handle it.

"I know you were married for a short time," Sam added.

"Yeah, wrong time, wrong guy," I said as some of the past memories made a bee-line across my mind. "No kids, no house, same as you."

"I also heard about the stunt you pulled about a month ago," Sam said, holding his beer bottle up to his smiling lips. "The one that got you sent to the mail room." He chuckled. "Where did you get the nerve to do that?"

"My mother," I told him, "is fearless. She'd been a fashion model in New York back in the day. It takes a lot more guts than most people think to be a model. She didn't take crap from anyone. She knew it'd be a short-term

MICHAEL AGLIOLO

gig. Figured she'd get paid enough to go back to school and get the degree that would allow her to do what she wanted to do, teach photography."

We both took long swigs on our beers. Talking about ex- spouses can make you thirsty. Too bad there wasn't anything stronger. Tequila would do.

"What are you going to do with the recording?" Sam asked, gesturing with his head towards my phone.

"Send it to Shreya after we interview our other tech. Have her go through it and see what she comes up with. Did any of Harris' jargon make sense to you?"

"Nope," he answered, "and I'm glad it didn't. Those guys live in a different universe than I do. They speak a different language, keep insane hours and in a lot of ways they run the world right now. We can't live without them and they know it. Politicians assume politicians run things. They don't. It's the folks writing code who run everything. Someone like Steve Jobs is going to be president someday, some techie with their finger on the pulse of the future. Might work out, don't know, but I'm pretty sure we're going to find out sooner than later."

Not sure if it was the Coronas or the conversation, but Sam kept getting better looking by the minute. He was smart, funny, taller than me, and hadn't given me the x-ray look once. All the main food groups.

"I'm going to call it a night," he said, walking over to put his empty beer bottle in the sink.

"Good night," I said, smiling quickly before looking away.

I went to my room, looked in the mirror and asked myself 'what's with all this man passion'? First, it was Tony and now Sam. It came to me, I was finally over my divorce. Two years of painful questions with too many painful answers. We'd both been too young. The clouds were beginning to clear out and my body was starting to remember what my mind had figured out. Being loved was everything.

79

I brushed my teeth, took an Excedrin PM and plugged my phone into the charger next to the bed. Let my clothes fall on the floor and crawled into bed.

I must have been asleep when something clinked in the bathroom on the far side of my room. I listened for a second, but the Excedrin was working overtime and I fell back asleep. I woke again, something wasn't right. I rolled over and reached for my phone to check the time but couldn't find it. Damn, I felt groggy.

The digital alarm clock on the other side of the bed read 3:38 AM. I reached for my cell phone again. My hand hit the charger, but the phone wasn't on it. What the hell? The sound of footsteps in the hallway just past my door popped me out of bed. I thought for a second it might be Sam heading for the kitchen when I saw my bedroom door was ajar, light seeping in through the crack.

I flung open the door just as two bodies slammed into the wall, crashing to the floor. I recognized Sam as he rammed a knee into the guy's back.

"I got this one," he yelled at me. "Go after the one who hightailed it out the front door."

I dashed back inside, grabbed my gun from under my clothes and stepped back into the hall. As I stepped out the front door, I caught a glimpse of a man darting across the lawn.

The streetlight caught a reflection, something shiny in his left hand as he jumped into a newer model black sedan and took off. I tried to catch the license number, but I couldn't see it in the dark. The car sped around the corner with its lights off.

Frustrated and cursing under my breath, I ran back inside. Sam was still on the guy's back. I flipped on the hall light. Sam grabbed the man's hair and ground his face into the hardwood floor before turning his face toward me. There was Lieutenant Harris, his nose bleeding. An anger-laced fear tinted his eyes as he stared at me. I wasn't sure what to make of his expression until I noticed Sam had an equally curious look on his face.

"You look damn good with that gun in your hand," Sam said, a sly grin coming to his lips.

I looked down at my gun and caught on I wasn't wearing anything but a pair of panties. Both men kept looking.

"I bet you say that to all the girls," I said, stepping past them into my room. I love it when my mouth comes out with a spiffy comeback before my brain even has time to think.

I grabbed my sweatshirt, pulled it over my head, pulled on my pants and walked back out into the hall. Sam had Harris in one of the kitchen chairs, standing over him.

"Where's my cell phone?" I yelled at Harris.

He clenched his jaw and wiped the blood from his nose with his sleeve. I aimed my gun at his face and repeated my question. He stared at me, his lips moved, but no sound came out. You could smell the fear, the uncertainty, on him. He turned from me, looked back to Sam.

I hate it when I'm full of adrenaline and no one's paying attention. I cocked my gun.

That worked.

GOOD RIDDANCE

Chapter 14

The President of the United States walked out of the Oval Office, shoulders pulled back, his chest thrust forward, his secret service detail following right behind him.

He knew his agents' names, but nothing about them. Why get personal with people who weren't going to be in your life much longer? By next month he'd be guarded by a new military contingent of soldiers, hand-picked by General Wallace.

As the President walked to the press briefing room, he took out the piece of paper he'd put in his breast pocket and read the name and location of the first reporter he'd call on at the briefing.

'Second row on the right next to the aisle', the note read. Everything had been pre-arranged. The reporter would ask the question he wanted to be asked in exchange for a one on one interview.

The President knew the interview would never happen. The chaos and confusion set to happen the following week would negate any one-on-one interviews. There would be press conferences, but not like this one. The entire world was about to change.

The President headed to the podium. A rush of power surged through his body as every reporter stood waiting for permission to sit.

"I will make a brief statement and take a couple of questions before turning the podium over to General Wallace," the President said, waving everyone to take their seats with a flick of his fingers.

"Our intelligence agencies have uncovered a credible terrorist threat against our nation's capital," the President said into the bouquet of microphones before him. "A new terrorist group based in Iran has taken credit for the bombing which took place in front of the White House on Tuesday. I am raising the Homeland security threat level to 'severe'. All law enforcement personnel are being reassigned to protect major government facilities. We are asking all citizens to be vigilant. If you observe suspicious activity, contact your local authorities. Do not, and I repeat, do not act on your own. Observe and report."

The President stepped back, cleared his throat and let his last statement resonate before saying, "I want to assure the American public that everything is being done to end this threat and to return our nation to peace and prosperity. Foreign intervention in our way of life will not be tolerated. We will find the people responsible for the attack on the White House and bring them to justice." He paused for effect, "I'll take a couple of questions before turning this over to the general."

Every reporter in the room jumped to their feet yelling out questions. The President held his hands for quiet and pointed to the reporter in the second row next to the aisle.

"Mister President, will this impact the British Prime Minister's planned speech to both houses of Congress next week?"

"No, it will not, unless the situation changes this administration will continue to pursue our goals to keep this government open for business. We cannot let a terrorist threat stop this government in its tracks. If we do the fanatics have won."

The same reporter yelled out, "Will you be attending the Prime Minister 's speech?"

"I will accompany the Prime Minister to the chamber but this is his night. I will return to the White House and watch the speech from there."

Another reporter yelled out, "Have the candidates on both sides been advised of this threat and will they be involved in any decisions if it becomes necessary?"

"Both campaigns are being briefed at this moment and will be informed of every step this administration is taking in regards to this situation."

More question were yelled at the President, but he motioned for General Wallace to take over. "I have complete confidence that General Wallace will be able to answer the rest of your questions."

Putting the paper with the reporter's name back in his breast pocket, the President made his way to the sanctuary of his office.

I hate this liberal press core. Most of them will be attending the speech. Two birds with one stone, he thought. Good riddance.

•••

FOUR IN THE MORNING

Chapter 15

"They will kill my wife and kids," Lieutenant Harris pleaded. "I had to retrieve your phone with the recording you made yesterday, I'd said too much."

Harris's nose had stopped bleeding. He sat in the kitchen chair, his wrists handcuffed behind him.

"I had no choice but to come here to get it." Harris kept repeating.

"Who's going to kill your family?" Sam ordered.

"The general's men," Harris hollered. "They'll kill my whole family. I had to come here. I'm sorry, I had to."

My adrenaline had passed, but I kept my gun pointed in his direction. I sat on one side of Harris, Sam on the other.

"Which general?" I yelled back, getting down into his face.

Harris looked at the floor, I could see his body trembling. It was going to be a long night. I got up to brew some coffee. Put a pot of water on the stove and turned on the burner.

The room went black.

Two arms wrapped around my waist and pulled me to the floor just as the kitchen window exploded. My gun slipped out of my hand as I landed on the floor. Two bullets hit the cabinet next to me, then a third. The only sound came from the slugs penetrating the wood. Whoever was shooting was using a silencer. I started scrambling for my weapon. Sam found it first and slipped it into my hand.

The blue flame from the stovetop cast enough light to see Harris's head slumped to one side.

"Follow me," Sam breathed.

I followed Sam into the hallway and up the stairs to his bedroom. "I'm going for my gun by the bed, cover my six," he whispered.

I stood at the top of the stairs rooted to one spot. Nobody was going to come up those stairs without my permission. My ears were pounding, I could almost see in the dark.

"Got it," Sam whispered. We made our way downstairs and scanned the hallway. The front door was still open. Light from the street lamp illuminated the front yard, nothing moved. I felt a surge of heat flushing through my body, I was turning from hunted to hunter.

The silencer had masked the sounds of the gunshots, the neighborhood hadn't noticed. We moved toward opposite sides of the house. I heard Sam whisper 'clear'. I said the same and we both came back around to the front door.

"I saw the breaker box on the side of the house under the kitchen window," Sam told me. "Go back inside. I'll flip the switch and hopefully get the lights back on."

As I made my way inside I saw the silhouette of Lieutenant Harris' body slumped in the chair.

The lights flickered and came on.

Harris had been shot once through his temple. I checked his pulse, the shooter had made a perfect shot in the dark. Whatever Harris knew someone didn't want him telling us.

I dialed the Colonel's cell phone number. He answered, his voice groggy from sleep. "Hold on a second," he ordered. I heard a click and assumed he was turning on his bedroom light. "Agent Brewer," he said, a statement, not a question. Caller ID takes the fun out of everything. "Why are you calling at four in the morning?"

As calmly as I could, I said, "Lieutenant Harris has been assassinated in our kitchen, I thought you should be informed."

"Repeat what you just said, Agent," the colonel's voice suddenly wasn't as calm as mine.

"Lieutenant Harris broke into our condo and someone shot him while Detective Marco and I were questioning him. He's dead. I was about to call in the authorities when I remembered you are the authorities. What are your orders, Sir?" I thought using 'Sir' would be appropriate seeing as one of his soldiers had been murdered in our kitchen.

"I will be there in twenty minutes," he said, "and don't touch anything."

So this is how it feels like to be ordered 'not to touch anything' at a crime scene. I've said it a hundred times and I'll bet Sam's said it a thousand. I didn't like it. I was curious what Sam's reaction would be.

I didn't have to wait long. Sam came into the house and stood next to Harris's body.

"I called the colonel, he's on his way." I said, "He told us not to touch anything,"

"Yeah, right," Sam replied, got on one knee and combed through Harris's pockets. I joined him.

His pockets were empty, no wallet, or keys, nothing. It didn't surprise me. You don't want to accidentally leave anything behind when you're breaking and entering.

I took photos of the bullet holes in the kitchen walls while we waited for the colonel.

"You want some coffee?" I asked Sam. "Not much chance of this evening ending soon."

I guess this is what you call being jaded. Dead body on the floor, shot by a hit man, and Sam and I were brewing coffee. "You want sugar?" I asked.

I could see the snarky response bloom on his lips. Looking at the dead body, though, Sam held it in. Shook his head 'no,' and slid his pistol into the holster under his shoulder.

A.S.A.P.

Chapter 16

We covered Harris' body with a bed sheet and waited for the colonel to arrive. Fifteen minutes later his jeep skidded to a stop in our driveway.

The colonel was wearing Marine fatigues and black boots. The golden insignia on his cap, the only identifier to his rank. He looked exhausted and furious at the same time. "Tell me what happened," he ordered as he looked at the body of the Lieutenant.

Sam spoke first; "I was heading downstairs to use the bathroom, I heard the floorboards in the hallway creak several times. I stopped as the silhouette of a man walked by the stairwell. I jumped the last steps and knocked him against the back wall. We both fell to the floor. As I climbed on his back, I got a glimpse of a someone running out the front door."

Sam paused for a second, "Erica came out of her room with her gun and went after him."

Sam looked over at me, my turn.

"He drove off in a black SUV," I told the Colonel. "It was too dark to get a license plate number. I came back in, turned on the lights. That's when we saw it was Lieutenant Harris."

I left out the part about being naked. Not that I'd forgotten. Pretty sure Sam hadn't forgotten either, it's not often you get to see someone wearing a 40 caliber Glock 22 and a pair of black panties.

"I couldn't find my cell phone," I finished telling the Colonel. "Harris had taken it. Sam and I were questioning him when the lights went out and the shooter fired through the window." I looked over to the kitchen window, the broken glass spread out on the floor. "Harris took a bullet to the head before the shooter turned the gun on us." I pointed out the bullet holes in the kitchen cabinets. "Almost no sound from the shooter's weapon. Must have used a silencer. Sam and I made it to his room, got his weapon and canvassed the outside of the house. That's when I called you."

The colonel took out his phone and walked into the hallway, came back a minute later, "The military police and the local cops are on their way. You are to tell them exactly what happened here, leave out nothing. When asked why you're here at the base, refer them to me. No matter who asks you, refer them directly to me."

We both nodded. It made sense, the last thing we wanted would be the locals climbing into our murder investigation. Better to have one voice, the colonel's, to answer those questions.

Within twenty minutes the house was crawling with cops. We were separated and interviewed by both the city cops and the military police. It was late morning by the time we were done being questioned. We packed our stuff into a waiting van and were driven back to the Colonel's office.

I was getting light-headed from the lack of sleep and being questioned all night. Getting shot at didn't help my mood either. I plopped myself into one of the leather chairs in the colonel's office and tried to turn off my brain. My mind was doing a high wire act with questions when my cell rang. It was my boss.

"Get your butt back here ASAP," Gilliam said.

"Well, good morning to you too, boss," I answered.

"Don't have time for 'good mornings,'" he barked, "We've been put on high alert by the President. All personnel are being reassigned due to the heightened terror threat the President enacted last night. Didn't you see his press conference?"

"No, sir," I answered, "I've spent the night answering questions about a dead body in the kitchen of the condo we're staying in."

"What!" he shouted. "Wait, don't tell me right now. Get yourself on a plane back here as fast as you can, and send me a complete report on what happened from the plane. Report to my office as soon as you get back."

Sam was pacing back and forth, he saw me get off the phone and pulled a chair next to mine, "Have you heard about the President's speech last night?"

"My boss just mentioned it," I confessed, "And told me to get back to Washington immediately. How did you hear about it?"

Sam started pacing again. "I checked the news on my phone. There's been a credible terror alert, the President set the threat level to 'severe'. Every cop in Washington is being re-assigned to safeguard against the risk. They'll be pulling me off of this case and putting me on armed patrol." Sam lowered his voice, "After what happened to us last night it's hard to imagine there's not a connection. We're running this case as a cover with a murder investigation as cover and have kept it a secret at the request of your boss. But it's turning into some kind of conspiracy. We need to have a face to face with Gilliam as soon as we get back."

I agreed, "Let's see if the colonel can get us a flight back."

Too many dots were connecting, it was time to open the door and let Homeland Security in.

The colonel got clearance from the local cops for us to fly back to D.C. He promised he would handle the investigation into Harris's murder while we were gone.

Three hours later we boarded a Gulfstream C-20 for the flight back to D.C.

The difference between the military transport we flew out in and the Gulfstream was like comparing a dump truck to a Maserati.

I'm pretty sure I could get used to white leather seats on beige carpeting, six overhead skylights and Sam and I traveling east at six hundred and fifty miles per hour.

I finished my report on my laptop and slept the last three hours of the flight. Sam fell asleep ten minutes after the plane took off. I was starting to see a pattern.

With the three-hour time difference, it was late afternoon by the time we made it to the FBI building. Sam and I sat in the two chairs in front of my boss's desk watching him read my report. He kept lifting his glasses and looking at us.

"I think we should inform Homeland Security," I told Gilliam and showed him the photos of the bullet holes that hit the cabinets.

"There's a possibility everything that happened in California is connected to the President's terrorist alert."

Leaning forward, "What about you?" Gilliam asked Sam, "You believe they're connected?"

Sam locked eyes with Gilliam, "I think so. The murder of Harris closes the loop. We're getting close to discovering something and someone put a bullet in Lieutenant Harris' head to stop us. They sent a couple of bullets our way before they left." Sam glanced back at me, took a deep breath before looking back at Gilliam.

"I'll make the call," my boss told us, "In the meantime I want you two to stay on this. Sam, I'll make a request to your commander to have you reassigned to our Security Protective Service. Are you okay with that?"

"Someone shot and killed a man we were questioning barely two feet from Agent Brewer and myself. I'm fine with staying on this case."

"Go, you two," Gilliam said, "Find out what the hell is going on."

Sam went back to his precinct. I shook the jet lag and cobwebs from my brain and headed to my office.

QUANTUM

Chapter 17

I'd just sat behind my desk when Shreya walked in.

"He eats Cheerios."

"What!" I blurted out.

Shreya gave me her 'just messing with you look and said, "Gilliam wanted me to dig into Mitchell's life, tell you what he eats for breakfast. Well he eats Cheerios for breakfast and the rest of the time he lives in the deepest parts of the web. Not the everyday, run of the mill deep web. Our murder victim used polymeric derivations which require quantum computer speed to access the Darknet."

"Stop! English girl," I demanded and started massaging my temples.

"Your murder victim was at the bottom of the dark web before he caught a bullet. He'd managed to access the deepest levels. Hackers call it 'the Marianas', named after the Mariana Trench. You know 'the deepest part of the Ocean'. It's also known as the 'Vatican Secret Archives,' where historical documents, government plans, and military secrets are kept. It requires quantum computer speed to hack in but there's one small problem."

"What's the problem?"

"Quantum computers haven't been invented yet."

"Apparently neither has a straight answer," I told her and kept rubbing my head.

Shreya shrugged her shoulders, "The government denies they have a quantum computer. Even our agency geeks say we don't have the technology to build one, but the NSA has been funding research at the Joint Quantum Institute at the University of Maryland."

My head was spinning, "Do we have one or not, and what's so special about a quantum computer?"

"A quantum computer can crack and write encryption codes exponentially faster than any computer ever built."

Shreya looked at me like she wasn't sure if I'd ever heard of a microwave oven. Finally, she cut me some slack and continued, "Somehow your murder victim managed to hack into a database, where he downloaded all of those files on the memory disk. Mitchell even hacked NSA, got military decryption codes and used them to tunnel through the deepest levels of the secret military communications database. I can't tell you how he did it, but he left breadcrumbs along the way. I followed his trail and found this date." She put a piece of paper on my desk with a date written on it.

It was for the following Monday, "What happens on that date?" I asked.

"Not sure yet, but I can tell you it's four days before your birthday."

She was right, Holy shit I was going to be thirty-two.

She rubbed her tummy and said, "It's getting late. Let's get that drink you promised me. I'm thirsty, hungry and lonely. We can talk when we get there."

YOU'RE NEXT

Chapter 18

I f Jesus ever makes it back to earth he's going to find exactly what he's looking for at the Fat Angel restaurant in D.C. Great food and a room full of sinners.

The restaurant was packed when we arrived. We took the last two seats at the bar, ordered gin and tonics and asked for menus. Shreya powered down two tonics before I'd finished my first. I hadn't eaten since this morning and had been running on caffeine. The gin was tickling my brain. We ordered dinner at the bar and started guessing what the other people in the restaurant did for a living. It's a game we play. It's dumb, offensive, and we should be ashamed of ourselves.

I love it.

We saw a couple sitting at the end of the bar looking like this might be their first date. The guy was sporting a Brooks Brother haircut, wearing a black silk shirt with a black tie and never took his eyes off of his date. Two points for him. I had him pegged for a lobbyist, which is minus one point. Shreya guessed sales manager at a Mercedes dealership, which would be worth one point. His date was a cute redhead, wearing a low cut white dress; two points. Her jewelry looked tasteful but her shoes were

Christian Louboutin high heels, which cost a thousand bucks a pair. Four points; she wins.

Being two bitchy brunettes feeling the effects of the gin, we both agreed the redhead worked at the same shoe store the heels came from. We figured she'd talked her boss into letting her wear them out on her date, promising not to scratch them or she would buy them. We both looked at our shoes and laughed.

The rest of the restaurant was full of the usual Washington crowd, lobbyist, political aids, and lawyers. Like I said, Jesus would have been busy.

When our food arrived, we switched to wine and ordered a bottle of Sangiovese.

My credit card was whispering to me from inside my back pocket, "eighteen percent interest on unpaid balance".

I told it to shut up and took a bite of my Italian sausage cannelloni. Neither of us had brought up the case so far, but that was about to change.

"What's the deal with quantum computers?" I finally asked. "What can they do if they did exist?"

Shreya soaked her French bread into the olive oil and vinegar dip, took a bite and washed it down with the Sangiovese, "They're so much faster than even the biggest mainframes NSA has, the speed difference is like comparing the speed of a bullet compared to the speed of light. When it comes to hacking, speed is the king for cracking passwords." She took another sip of her wine before telling me, "Some mid-level hackers can crack a 7-character password in less than a minute, 8 characters about five hours, 9 characters maybe five days, 10 can take three or four months and 11 characters can take a decade. A quantum computer could crack an 11-character passcode in less than a second."

Shreya put her wine glass on the bar and scooted to the edge of her bar stool. This is her world and she wanted me to grasp the meaning of what she'd said.

97

"Access to a quantum computer is a game changer, communication between computers would be undetectable. No matter how deep the dark web flows, everyone and everything would be hackable."

I was about to ask Shreya another question when a voice from behind me said, "You both need to follow me, right now." I recognized the voice and spun around. Before I could ask him anything, Detective Marco put his arms around me and whispered in my ear. "Your boss has been shot. You're next. We have maybe two minutes to get out of here." Sam pulled out a hundred-dollar bill, put it on the counter and gave me a look which said 'right now'.

"Shreya, come with me," I told her and followed Sam. We moved past the couple at the end of the bar, I couldn't help myself and whispered, "nice shoes."

Sam led us into the restaurant kitchen, pulled out his badge and flashed his ID at one of the cooks, "Where's the service entrance?" The guy pointed to the back corner. We made our way past the stainless-steel counters and found the back door. Sam drew his gun and signaled for us to wait. He slowly opened the door and moved out into the dark alleyway before motioning us to follow.

Night had fallen and the alley looked empty except for a delivery truck parked next to the trash bins. We moved to the front of the truck and tried the driver side door; locked, but the window had been rolled down a few inches. Sam tried to reach the lock, but his arm couldn't fit through the opening.

"Let me try," I told him and managed to slide my arm far enough to pull up the lock. The truck looked about the same size as a UPS delivery van. We got in, re-locked the door and crawled into the back. The smell of sourdough bread hit me. We were in an old-style bread truck with shelves filled with bread. No rearview window so I slid below one of the shelves and used the driver's side mirror to look at the front entrance to the alley. Sam did the same on the passenger side.

"You carrying?" he asked me.

"Yeah," I told him, unsnapped my holster and pulled out my Glock. "Talk to me," I said.

Sam's look told me our lives were about to get a lot more complicated. I chambered a bullet and waited for Sam's reply.

"Your boss was shot a couple hours ago getting out of his car in front of his house. He's in surgery, I don't know his condition. I was turning in my transfer papers at the precinct when the call came in about the shooting. I tried your cell, but all I got is your voicemail."

I pulled my phone from my coat pocket and saw I'd gotten his call. The noise from the restaurant must have masked it.

"How did you know we were here?" I asked.

"I drove to your office. The security guard at the counter said you two had checked out together about an hour earlier. He knew you were heading to the Fat Angel."

"That's me," Shreya said. "He's a cutie, I was hoping he'd come by the restaurant after he got off work."

Shreya wasn't a field agent, she's a computer geek. I could see her lips trembling.

"Why would someone shoot our boss?" Shreya groaned.

"It makes sense," I told her. "Every step in this investigation has pointed to someone high up in the government's power structure. Looks like they don't like us digging around. Between the fire at the apartment, the killing of Lieutenant Harris in California, and now Gilliam being shot, someone wants us to drop our shovels."

"It's more than that," Sam broke in. "The security guard told me someone had just been asking for you both. Two guys in military clothes, left in a taxi. Which is why I decided to come to get you. Of the seven people who know something about this case, three of them have been shot. I don't like where this is going."

Sam looked at the rearview mirror, "Headlights are coming toward us, both of you get as low as you can."

"Lay down at the back of the truck," I told Shreya.

Sam and I made a wall of French bread and had Shreya lie behind it.

The car came to a stop behind our truck. Two car doors opened, I heard the sound of footsteps moving toward the back entrance to the restaurant. Another set of footsteps came toward us; someone tried the driver side door.

Sam pointed his gun at the front of the truck. If he pulled the trigger, our eardrums would shatter. I had my weapon pointed at the passenger door, willing to sacrifice my ears if necessary. Whoever had tried to open the door quit and shined a flashlight through the windshield, the light reflected off the back of the truck.

A muffled voice from behind the truck said, "They're not here. I checked the bathrooms, the bartender said they'd left about five minutes ago, didn't see them go, paid cash and were gone."

The footsteps moved back to the car. I snuck a peek at the rearview mirror and saw a taxi backing out of the alley; no advertising sign on its roof. My muscles tensed.

"Stay where you are," I whispered to Shreya, "until I tell you to come out."

I heard a quiet "okay," and looked over at Sam. The alley security light cast enough light to see his face. He looked calm considering we'd almost been in a shootout in the back of a bread truck.

"Good advice," he whispered and kept his gun pointed at the front of the truck. We sat there quietly for five long minutes, trying to come up with our next move when I heard footsteps coming up the alley. Sam looked at his side rearview mirror.

"One guy, on foot, coming this way slowly," He whispered. I took a peak and saw a silhouette moving toward the truck, something in his right hand. The guy stopped about twenty feet from the truck and turned toward the wall.

"I can't see him from my side mirror." Sam whispered, "What's he doing?"

"He's taking a leak on the wall," I told him. "He's got something in his hand, might be a bottle of booze."

"Nice," Sam said, "homeless dude. Let's wait till he leaves."

I kept watching until the guy finished doing his business and walked back toward the street.

"He's leaving," I told Sam, "Shreya, come out of there."

"That wasn't a lot of fun," she said as she moved around the wall of bread.

The sound of metal hitting metal vibrated the back of the truck. A hole, about the size of a dime, let light in from the back door of the truck, right where Shreya had been. Another sound vibrated and another hole opened next to the first one.

I pulled Shreya to my side of the truck, laid her on the floor. "Someone's shooting at us at with a silencer."

Sam climbed into the driver's seat and slammed the back of his gun on the ignition switch.

I jumped into the passenger seat, opened the window and fired two rounds into the ground at the front of the alley. I wasn't using a silencer and whoever fired at us just found out this wasn't going to be a turkey shoot. Sam got the engine going, put it in reverse and stepped on the gas. The bread truck barreled toward the street. I slid as low as I could and still see out the window, my gun aimed straight up. Sam put his weapon on the seat beside him and steered with his right hand, keeping his left on the horn as we barreled out of the alley. As the truck hit the street Sam slammed on the brakes and spun the wheel to the right. All the bread came off the shelves and landed on Shreya as the back end of the truck swerved to the left. The windshield shattered as a bullet lodged in the rear headboard. Sam put the truck in gear and floored it. A loud noise on my side of the truck exploded, the truck swerved as we moved across the empty street.

"They shot out one of the tires," Sam shouted, as he ran the red light and turned the corner. The wind was whistling through the hole in the windshield.

"How the hell are we still going with a flat tire?" I yelled back.

"This old truck has a double set of tires in the rear, we're running on one instead of two."

"You all right," I yelled back at Shreya.

"Yeah, when can I come out from under all of this bread?"

"Right now," I said. "Do you have your phone?"

"Fuck yes," she snapped.

I looked out the window and read the street signs.

"We're going west on P Street in Georgetown heading toward the University. Tell the police Detective Marco is taking fire and requests backup."

I could hear Shreya, her voice trembling as she gave our location.

The wind was blowing through the large hole in the windshield, making a high-pitched whistle, "Are we being followed?" I yelled out to Sam.

"No, and I don't know why. How the hell did they know we were in the truck?" He shouted back.

I took a guess, "The homeless guy doing his thing on the wall had something in his hand; I thought it was a bottle of booze. Could have been a heat scanner. You can buy the damn things for two hundred bucks on Amazon."

I heard sirens in the distance.

"Nothing like a cop being shot at to get the troops motivated." Sam shook his head, "Why the hell aren't we being followed?" he repeated.

"Whoever's after us has all the toys. Might be monitoring the cop radios or they could have someone inside the police department," I answered. The letter said 'don't trust anyone'."

I could tell Sam didn't like my inference. The cops consider themselves brothers. After a few seconds he said, "We can't take the chance, we need to ditch this truck and work this out ourselves."

"If they have us GPS'd they're going to keep following the truck." I reminded Sam, "When it stops they're going to know it."

"I'll keep the truck going," Shreya said from the back. "When I slow down you two jump out. I'll keep going until the cops stop me."

"I'm not leaving you alone, Shreya," I told her. "You're in this thing too."

"Not like you two are," she cautioned, "I'll tell the cops you made me drive before jumping out of the van. I'll keep going, get as far away from you as I can." Shreya's voice was calm, her nostrils flared. "Sam, can you give me the name of a cop you trust? If you tell me what to say maybe he'll help out."

"Jamie Stevens," Sam replied, "And Jamie's not a he; not even close. Have the cops bring you to the station and ask for Jamie. Tell her I'm the one who gave you her name. She'll help you."

"If we're getting out we need to do it now," I said.

Sam looked back at Shreya, "Okay, kiddo, get in here and take the wheel. We're coming up to Georgetown University. Drive straight ahead onto the Copley lawn. We'll jump out and you get back on the street. Go as fast as you can and go left on 37th Street and keep going until the cops are right behind you. Lie to them about where we jumped out and remember Jamie Stevens!"

We hit the curb at 20 miles an hour and landed hard. Sam opened his door as I opened mine. I heard him yell 'now'.

The ground came up to greet me, hard. I tried to inhale but the air wouldn't go past my throat. I kept trying, finally, a tiny bit made it into my lungs. I saw Sam running toward me.

"You got the wind knocked out of you," he said kneeling next to me. "It'll come back, don't try to force it."

I'd have paid every dollar I would ever make for my next breath.

The air gradually made its way into my lungs. God, it felt good to inhale. I took a couple more breaths. "Can you get up," Sam asked.

I nodded and got on my knees. The air tasted good. I took in a couple of deep breaths and looked around. A lighted walking path, twenty yards off the back end of the lawn, led to the university campus. I turned and looked up the street, flashing red lights were about a mile away, Shreya had been pulled over.

Sam stood and held out his hand, "We need to get out of here. You ready to walk?"

I checked to make sure all my parts were still working.

"You know how to show a girl a good time," I told Sam.

I have no idea why stuff like that comes out of my mouth.

"Yeah, I can tell I take your breath away," he said and handed me my gun, "It came out of your holster when you hit the ground."

We cut across the lawn toward campus. It's was a school night, not too many students were out and about. They were all in the library doing their homework…or in their bathrooms smoking a joint with the fan on. I went to college.

"You got an ATM card?" Sam asked me.

"Yeah, in my back pocket."

"We need cash," he said, "As much as we can get. We're going to have to steal a car and ditch our phones. Can't use our credit cards either. We've got to disappear, off the grid. Let me know if you have any great hiding places cause that's where we're going."

We found the campus store. Sam used cash and bought some scratch paper and two pens, we copied all the 'must have' phone numbers from our phones. Then shopped around the store, bought four pre-paid cell phones, some junk food, and a Swiss Army Knife.

We hit the ATM machine on the way out, pulled out as much cash as the machine would let us. Pulled the batteries from our phones and dumped everything in the trash.

"Let's get out of D.C.," I told Sam, "and head for Baltimore, hide out till…"

I stopped talking. 'Till what', I asked myself.

We took a taxi across the 14th street Bridge to one of the big box stores.

"This is a good place to borrow a car," Sam told me as we walked to the back of the building. "Most of these are the night shift cars, these folks will be working all night restocking shelves. They won't know their car's missing until the morning. I hate doing this, but if we don't get out of here we're going to be dead."

"I vote we 'live'," I said and pointed out an American made white truck. "This is the most common vehicle on the road. We'll need to switch plates with another truck before heading to Baltimore."

Sam glanced back at me, gave me the 'look'.

I was tempted to tell him some of my past, but that would have to wait.

The Swiss Army Knife came in handy as I switched plates with another truck. By the time I'd finished Sam had the truck unlocked and the engine running.

The drive to Baltimore took an hour and a half. We parked in the back-parking lot of a motel and checked in. The night clerk noticed we didn't have any luggage and gave Sam the 'nice going smile'. I pretended not to notice.

When we got to our room, Sam hit the bathroom and I called my boss on one of our burner phones. Got his voice mail and disconnected. I could hear the shower going so I downed one of the five dollar bottled waters in the room and turned on the local news. Five commercials later the anchor came back on. The situation at the White House was dominating the news cycle. I kept watching to see if there were any reports on our bread truck adventure. I decided to try a different station and switched to Fox. Nothing except a gorgeous blond reading the teleprompter. I switched back to the local news.

My turn in the bathroom gave me a chance to hit the shower. No toothbrush, no comb, no nothing. I took a deep breath, put on my bra and panties and wrapped a towel around me.

Sam was in the bed closest to the door, watching the news, the last thing we needed to see would be our face's plastered on the screen. The butterflies in my stomach were multiplying until the weather guy came on the air and did his thing. Sam shut off the TV.

"We need to make a plan," I told him as I climbed into my bed.

"In the morning," he answered and killed the lights.

The darkness felt good, for the moment we were invisible.

CELL TOWER

Chapter 19

I woke in the fetal position. Happens to me a couple of times a year; the damn same nightmare. I'm in front of a secret room behind a locked door in some stranger's house. I need to get in the room, but no matter what I try I can't get the door open. I get on the floor to look under the door when I sense someone is behind me. Just as I turn to look I wake up. I hate this dream, gives me the heebie-jeebies.

I felt disoriented. You know the lousy feeling you get when you wake in a strange place and don't recognize anything. I rolled over and looked at the window. The shades were pulled, but enough sun was coming through for me to see Sam putting on his shoes. It all came back to me.

Sam noticed I was awake, "We need to go shopping," he said, "I need new socks and a toothbrush."

"Yeah, I could use some pajamas," I added, and pulled the bed sheet around me, grabbed my clothes and headed into the bathroom.

We put the 'do not disturb' sign on the door and drove to Wal-Mart.

I hate big box stores, but when you're on the run and need toothpaste, pajamas, and ammunition they're your one-stop shopping center. We paid cash and I drove back to the hotel. The parking lot looked empty as I pulled around back.

"Something's not right," I told Sam. "Checkout time isn't until 11 AM. Why are most of the cars gone?"

"Keep going," he said, "Go out the exit and park across the street."

A black SUV pulled into the lot. Sam pulled out his gun and suggested we get the hell out of there. I floored it but the SUV stayed right behind me.

I turned right on Washington Boulevard and headed for downtown. The SUV's windows were tinted and I couldn't make out who was driving. Our Chevy had a big block V-8 and we slipped in and out of traffic. The SUV driver stayed right on my tail. I ran a red light and got on the 95 freeway with the asshole right behind us.

We took the next exit and drove past the University hospital, made the loop under the freeway and got back on the 95 going the opposite way. I was five car lengths ahead of the SUV when I noticed that a UPS truck in the left lane had just passed a U-Haul van. I slipped into the right lane in front of the van and whipped back into the left lane. The UPS driver hit his horn and slowed. Both trucks were now blocking the SUV. I hit the gas and got off on the next exit, saw an auto dealership, pulled in and drove around back. The repair department was open. I parked our truck next to several white vehicles and went inside. The place was humming with activity. No one noticed as we walked to the back of the building and out the rear door. Four auto-detailing areas had crews washing cars. Several of the vehicles were parked next to a gas pump. We climbed in the one furthest away and acted like we knew what we were doing. The keys were in the ignition. No one noticed as we drove off the lot in a brand-new Pontiac Firebird.

Sam was leaning forward, scanning the area. "How did they find us?" I asked, "We dumped our phones, stole a car and changed plates. What's left to track us?"

Raising his eyebrow, "Did you call anyone on your phone?" he asked.

"Yeah, I called my boss on one of the burner phones when you were in the shower last night and left a message. A burner's not traceable. It's not."

Sam leaned back in his seat, "Unless they found out we'd jumped out of the bread truck near the University," he said. "And checked to see if anyone bought a pre-paid phone in the area. With the right credentials, you can get a burner phone's registration code and wait for a cell tower to ping from the number."

I wanted to kick myself. Sam was right, it would have put someone looking for us within the general vicinity of the call. We'd paid cash for our room, which is a little unusual. They had all night to figure it out. We're lucky we'd gone shopping before they closed in.

We were headed north on 295 doing the speed limit.

"We need to find somewhere to hide," Sam said, "Somewhere not connected to family or friends, but first we need to dump these phones and get new ones."

"I know where we can go," I replied and took the next exit. Flipped a U-turn and got back on the freeway going south, back to D.C."

NOTHING

Chapter 20

I n four days it won't matter, General Wallace told himself as he put down the receiver on his Pentagon phone. Pushing his chair back, he walked over to his humidor and took out a single box of cigars. Inside, he pulled out a cedar strip that lined the inside of the box. Using a wooden match to light the cedar, Wallace put the flame to the Cohiba Behike, slowly letting the bottom of the flame touch the tip of the cigar.

'You don't light a hundred-dollar cigar with a one of those newfangled lighters,' he thought to himself. *'This Habanos is one of the few things the damn communist know how to make. Only an idiot would lite it with a torch'.*

His office door was wide open, letting the aroma drift out into the no smoking hallways of the Pentagon. He wasn't worried Who the hell is going to tell a four-star general to put it out?

The nicotine calmed him down. The phone call hadn't been good news. The D.C. cop and the woman FBI agent that he'd ordered captured had gotten away, again. How much Lieutenant Harris had told them before his soldier assassinated him was impossible to know.

Agent Brewer and Detective Marco needed to be found.

The general took a long, slow drag as he dialed the President's private cell phone.

The President answered, "Hello General, hope all is going well."

"Very well, Mister President, wrapping up the final details. It would be beneficial if we could meet tonight, Sir."

"The Oval Office at 10 PM tonight, General. We can talk, then," the President replied.

The General hesitated, "Sir, would it be possible to meet somewhere else, perhaps in the residence?"

"Fine general, be at my private study in the White House at 10 PM." The phone clicked off.

In four days, the world would be stunned by the terrorist attack at the joint session of Congress. The two presidential candidates would be dead. The President would invoke the 51st Directive giving him complete control of the government. The left-wing pussies who permeated congress with their social engineering giveaways and their willingness to slash the defense budget would be gone.

He and the President were not going to let them destroy the country. Not on their watch. The President would appoint him supreme commander of the armed forces. Together they would save the nation from itself.

His phone rang. "Sir, the two suspects stole a car from a dealership," his field commander informed him. "We have the plate numbers and a description. We'll contact you the minute we have them, Sir."

"You do that commander," the general barked and hung up.

Taking two generous puffs on his cigar the general did something he rarely did, closed his office door.

His hands shook as he keyed in the correct code to his office safe and pulled out a red binder. Inside was a list of names, six pages of them. One hundred senators and four hundred thirty-five members of the House of Representatives, listed in alphabetical order.

Some he knew well, others he'd only heard their name in passing. He paused when he came to the Vice President's name. Even he would need to die, he thought to himself. The nation would be better off without all of them. The sacrifice of the few to save the many.

He leaned back in his chair and took a long, slow drag on his Cohiba and thumbed through the remaining pages of charts and architectural drawings. He placed everything back into his safe, opened a small chemical vial and poured the liquid over the file. He took several last puffs before placing the cigar on top of the secret papers. In two hours, every trace of the folder would be an inert puddle on the bottom of the safe. He closed the safe door.

The general turned back and looked at the framed statement on the wall behind his desk.

"The measure of a man is what he does with power."

- Plato -

General Wallace sat in his chair and thought about the power he was about to possess.

"There is nothing I would not do for my country," he whispered to himself.

"Nothing," he repeated and opened his office door.

PASTA SUGO

Chapter 21

"We can't use this car much longer," Sam reminded me. "The dealership is going to call the cops as soon they notice it's missing."

Sam looked out his window as I pulled into the slow lane. "Take the next exit," he suggested, "And turn right, we need to borrow another car. We'll ditch it in a couple of hours when we get to D.C."

It was getting easier to accept the idea of stealing cars, especially when you use the word 'borrow'. Of course, I believed Sam and I were on the side of the angels, trying to get to the bottom of a conspiracy. I'm sure every car thief has a reason. I wasn't looking forward to telling ours to a judge.

I got off the freeway.

Sam pointed to a gas station, "Pull in over there. I'll ask where the closest big box store is around here."

Three minutes later, Sam climbed back into the car.

"Take a left here and a right on Columbus Boulevard, there's a strip mall a half a mile from there."

Several small retail shops sat next to a large discount store. I pulled behind the building and parked next to the warehouse loading area.

Sam pointed to a spot under some trees in the back of the lot. "Let's look for a car with one of the windows open a few inches. Most German cars still use a pull-up lock."

We found a 2008 BMW with its driver side window down about an inch. Sam took off his shoe and removed the shoelace, tied a slip knot on one end and hung it in the window over the door lock and let it drop. It synched around the lock, he pulled upward and the door unlocked.

"Aren't you a piece of work!" I said, torn between kissing him and cuffing him.

"There are more ways to steal a car than there are ways to lock 'em," he replied and did his thing to the ignition switch. We climbed in and headed for D.C.

We were going to need some help. I pulled around the corner from the FBI building and made a call to Ron Collins in the Mailroom. Five minutes later, Ron walked out the westside exit, saw me sitting in the car and headed our way.

I glanced over at Sam, "The only person who knows I know this guy is my boss. Ron's been trying to get the nerve to ask me out for the past couple of weeks. We're about to see how bad he wants a date."

"What the hell's going on," were Ron's first words as he came to my side of the car. He was frowning and kept looking around.

"Ron, I haven't got time or a lot of answers. I need your help."

"I'll bet you do," he said and folded his arms across his chest. "I heard a couple of military guys were here inquiring about you."

"Did they talk to you?" I asked.

"No, not me. How'd you get my private number?" He asked.

"I work for the FBI Ron. Getting your number wasn't too hard. I need your help."

Leaning in the window, he asked "What kind of help?"

"Cash and information."

Ron surprised me when he said, "How much, and what information?

"Two-grand and what's the latest on Gilliam,"

"First, I got to know what's going on," Ron demanded.

He had a right to know, but at the moment we weren't a hundred percent sure ourselves. "Detective Marco and I were attacked yesterday by the same people who shot our boss. We need your help, you interested?"

Ron glanced at Sam and back to me. He wasn't checking me out anymore, he looked scared.

"I'll get the money," he whispered. "Last I heard Gilliam's out of intensive care and supposed to be all right. There's an investigation to see if there's any connection between Gilliam being shot and the terrorist threat the President announced." Ron's voice rose an octave, "How do I get ahold of you after I get the money?" he squeaked.

"I'll contact you, when will you have it?"

"Give me a couple of hours," he said and looked at Sam. "You're both in danger, aren't you?"

"Yeah," Sam answered, "We need to stay hidden till we figure out what's going on. Appreciate you helping us."

"Okay, I'll wait for your call," Ron said and walked back toward the building.

I waited till Ron was back inside the building, then headed toward Parkview. I stayed on Parkview all the way to the residential district. When I turned on Clement Street Sam asked, "Isn't this the same street where Mitchell's apartment caught on fire?"

"Yeah," I told him, "We need a place to stay and I've got an idea."

Calling anyone we knew was out of the question. The motel hadn't worked last time, paying cash was too big a giveaway.

I pulled into an apartment building about a mile from Mitchell's apartment. Parked in the basement garage and left the keys on the seat. As we wiped our prints off the steering wheel and the door handles I kept trying to think of an alternative to where we were going but nothing came to mind. We walked to Brian Mitchell's apartment building and rang the manager's doorbell. Maria answered. "Benvenuto Erica," she said in Italian and hugged me like I was part of her family, "And who's this handsome man?" she asked as she opened the door all the way for us to come in.

I introduced Sam as we walked in.

"It's good to see you again," I told Maria.

"I'm happy you came to visit me again," she said. I could see her smiling at Sam. This woman had a healthy libido. God bless her, there's still life after seventy.

"I make some coffee for everybody, come a-sit down," Maria said and shuffled off into the kitchen.

"I have a feeling she likes you, Sam, be gentle," I said.

Sam chuckled, "No promises, she's a cutie, you better not leave me alone with her." He followed me into the living room, Maria came in with a coffee tray and poured everyone a cup.

"Maria, Sam and I need your help and what I'm about to tell you may frighten you," I said. "When I'm done, you may want us to leave and never come back and that's exactly what we will do."

Maria took a sip of her coffee and in her Italian accent said, "My Joseppi, may God rest his soul, work as a fireman. Every day I a-frightened for my husband. But I get used to the feeling, I no afraid to be afraid. Capisce?"

"Capisce," I replied. "You know I work for the FBI, and Sam is a detective for the Washington police department, we're working undercover on something your renter, Mister Mitchell, was involved in. We believe the fire next door was set on purpose and meant for his unit. Some powerful people don't want us to find out what happened and Sam and I need to go into hiding. We can't go back to our homes or even stay in hotels where we might be found. I'm hoping you will let us both stay here for a day or two, I believe it's the last place anyone would ever look for us."

Maria took another sip of her coffee, "You two like pasta sugo for dinner?" she asked.

BLINK THREE TIMES

Chapter 22

The fluorescent lights were too bright for FBI Bureau ChiefGilliam. He closed his eyes, welcoming the darkness. He tried opening them one more time, but only managed a couple of blinks. He tried to speak, but the tube down his throat prevented his vocal cords from working.

He felt his hand being squeezed and turned his head enough to see his wife smiling down on him. He tried to speak, but it was impossible.

"Don't try and talk," she said to him. Let me tell you what happened and I'll get you something to write with if you have any questions, just blink three times."

She leaned over and kissed him, their faces touched and one of her tears moistened his cheek.

"You are going to be fine," she said. "You were shot as you were getting out of the car in our driveway yesterday. I heard your car pulling up and when you didn't come in I decided to check on you."

Tears were streaming down his wife's cheeks and he squeezed her hand. "You were shot twice, once in your right shoulder and the other grazed your head. The police said the shooter must have used a silencer because no one heard anything. The bullet missed all of your vital organs. The police, the FBI and the media are all over this. They want to talk to you when you can. But I'm not going to let them get near you till you tell me you're ready." She kissed his hand, "I love you so much," she told him. "The doctors said you will fully recover and should be out of the hospital in a few days, but for right now you need to rest."

Gilliam blinked three times.

"You want to write something?" she asked.

He blinked three more times. She left the room and came back with a sheet of paper and a black marking pen. His hand shook, he dropped the pen several times before he finally scribbled;

"You want me to check on Erica, from work?"

Gilliam nodded and held up the pen.

His wife turned the paper over.

"You want Erica to come here?" she asked him.

Gilliam closed his eyes. When he opened them his wife said, "She's in danger, isn't she?"

He blinked three times.

GREEN BANANAS

Chapter 23

Maria's two-bedroom, two bath apartment was painted all white, even the shower curtain in the guest bathroom was white. I was tempted to leave my sunglasses on.

Every two feet a different family picture hung in fancy wooden frames all the way to the top of the stairs leading to the guest bedroom.

A queen size bed. A hand knitted blanket resting at the foot of the bed. A bay window overlooking the apartment building across the street, giving me a clear view of Mitchell's apartment.

The house was so clean I wasn't sure I could ever go back to my messy place. I felt ashamed for about ten seconds and got over it.

Maria was in the kitchen making the pasta sugo for dinner. Sam was helping her chop the garlic.

Why in God's name do they call it pasta sugo? It's spaghetti! This is America, we don't call a hot dog 'wurstchen' we call it a 'dog'.

I had to admit whatever they were making smelled good.

I walked into the living room and called Ron Collin's cell phone. He answered on the first ring. "I've been waiting for your call," he said, talking rapidly. I needed to calm him down.

"Ron, you sound scared. Are you all right?

His voice cracked a couple of times. "I've got the money for you, where should I make the drop?"

'Make the drop'? What the hell, he's talking like this is a kidnap movie. "Ron, no one knows we're in touch with you. You can relax. What time do you plan on leaving work today?"

"Five o'clock," he said. "Should we meet in a public place or should I drive out of town and meet you out in the countryside?"

Please God don't let me be sarcastic. Ron's living out a fantasy that I've decided to play out.

"Okay, here's the plan," I told him. "Leave work at your normal time and drive to Trader Joe's on 14th street, I'll meet you in the produce department next to the bananas. I'll have one of those small baskets with bananas in it. You put a few in your basket plus the money and we'll exchange baskets. Got that?"

"Yeah, Trader Joe's. Perfect," he said. "I'll be there at 5:30. Should we talk or pretend we don't know each other?"

I pushed the 'hold' button on my phone for a second, and caught my breath. This wasn't the best time to laugh.

"No talking," I said, "Just put the money in a paper bag at the bottom of the bananas and take my cart and go through the checkout counter."

"Green bananas," Ron said.

"What about them?" I sputtered.

"I like green bananas," he said. "If I'm going to buy bananas I want green ones."

"Okay," I told him and hung up. I didn't want him to hear me say 'what the fuck'.

When I walked into the kitchen Sam was blowing on a wooden spoon, cooling the spaghetti sauce. He glanced over at me and offered me a taste.

I shook my head and told him the plan I'd made with Ron. I should have waited until he'd finished tasting the sauce before I mentioned the green bananas. I thought the hot sauce was going to come out his nose.

The three of us drank coffee until close to five o'clock.

Maria gave us permission to use her car, her parting words were, "The longer the sugo cooks the better it a-taste."

Sam drove. We got there ten minutes early.

"If we're going to be staying at Maria's house, let's bring some food back with us," I told Sam and grabbed a grocery cart and put one of the smaller hand baskets inside.

We grabbed some eggs and coffee and as we passed the refrigerated area I asked Sam, "You like ice cream?"

"Yeah, I love the stuff," he said and grabbed a pint of Haagen-Dazs Chocolate Chip Cookie Dough and put it in the basket. That's my favorite ice cream.

I don't know what came over me, but I leaned over the shopping cart and kissed him right in the frozen food section. He seemed surprised for a second, but caught his second wind and kissed me back. He knew what he was doing. It took me a second to realize we weren't alone.

We both looked around the store. Either nobody cared or they were being polite. We tried to move closer, but the cart was in the way. The moment passed and I grabbed an espresso chocolate cookie crumble and dropped it in the basket.

Sam headed for the wine section. Smart man.

I was picking through the green bananas when Ron puts his basket next to mine. He tried not to look at me, but I saw him sneak a peek. I was tempted to put a spy novel in his coat, but it was time to get out of there.

I picked up his basket, saw the envelope on the bottom and walked away. I found Sam in line at one of the checkout sections, grabbed the envelope and paid for our groceries with one of the hundreds. We rolled our cart to the car like a married couple.

A note was inside the envelope. 'Gilliam wants you to come to him in the hospital, says it's urgent. Don't be seen.'

"How did your boss know to get in touch with you through Ron?" Sam asked, as he put the groceries in the trunk.

"I haven't a clue. I'm going to have to ask my boss when I see him. Thank God he's okay," I told Sam and handed him another bag.

"Any ideas how we can sneak into the hospital and find out what he wants?" I asked Sam.

"He's going to be guarded 24/7. It'll be your FBI folks at his door. Going to be hard to get in without being seen. I'll give it some thought."

"Me too," I told Sam.

I should have said, 'I haven't a clue'. But we had ice cream and Sam knew how to kiss, so not everything was looking impossible.

THE GENERAL'S SON

Chapter 24

Dinner was waiting for us on the dining room table as we carried the groceries into the kitchen.

Now I know why they call it pasta sugo and not spaghetti. Pasta sugo cooked by an Italian grandmother is like filet mignon cooked by a master chef, compared to a hamburger from a drive thru.

Sam helped Maria with the dishes. I had to lie down for twenty minutes after dinner to stop the pain after eating a third helping of garlic bread dipped in the sauce.

Sam found me massaging my stomach on the couch.

"I've been trying to figure out how to visit your boss at the hospital without being seen," he told me. "Is he close with his wife, will she be at his bedside?"

"They're like soul mates. She'll be sleeping at the hospital."

"There's our way in," he said, looking relieved. "We're going to need her help. Do you know her well?"

"Yeah, I've been to their house for dinner a couple of times. She's a great lady. What do you have in mind?"

"First, we get in touch with her, do you have her cell number?"

"No, I've got my boss's number, but I doubt he's taking calls."

I pulled out a burner and dialed Gilliam's number, got his voicemail and hung up.

"My voice is more likely to be recognized than yours," I told Sam. "You should make the call. Say it's his friend Bill Sterling calling to check how he's doing."

I took out a piece of paper and wrote some additional stuff for Sam to say. "Tell him you'd like to come by for a visit and you'll be sneaking in a bottle of his birthday scotch. He'll know the message is from me. He keeps the bottle I gave him for his birthday in his office. Ask him to call you back on your new number when he's up to it."

I wrote down one of our burner phone numbers.

Sam called and left the message.

Nothing we could do now but wait. We watched TV with Maria until 9 PM, some program about rich people and how happy they were with their indoor swimming pool.

Maria put sheets on the couch for Sam and I made my way upstairs. I got undressed and opened the closet door to hang up my clothes. Figured I shouldn't be my messy self. I flicked on the light and was surprised how large the closet was. Several round boxes were stacked in the corner. They looked like the old style hat boxes from back in the day. The hangers were full of dresses, and scarfs. On the top shelf were two wigs on Styrofoam heads, one brunette and one blond. I couldn't help myself and took the blond wig into the bathroom and slipped it on. I stared at myself in the mirror. With my blue eyes I'd slid right into the look. I've never thought about what I'd look like as a blond and there I was staring at this whole other person. My sister wouldn't have recognized me.

I took off the wig and got ready for bed. I was just falling asleep when I felt a hand on my shoulder. Sam was sitting on the edge of my bed. He had one finger over his lips telling me to be quiet.

I wanted to move his hand and get a clear shot at those soft lips when he whispered, "I just got a call from your bosses wife. She got our message and knew it had come from you. She says there's one FBI agent standing guard at night. Apparently, he sits in the chair next to the door to her husband's hospital room. He drinks a lot of coffee and needs to use the bathroom every couple of hours. He comes on duty at midnight and has a coffee as soon as he arrives. She says the agent will be heading for the men's room sometime around 2 AM. That'll be our chance to get in. We'll have to wait for his second pee break to get out. They're in room 314. We need to leave now and find a place to keep an eye out for the agent's next nature call."

"Give me five minutes and I'll meet you downstairs," I told him.

I got dressed, put on the wig and wrapped a scarf around my neck. Sam stared at me the whole time I came down the stairs. "Wow, where did you find that?" He kept staring. "Talk about a whole new look. I'm in shock."

We needed to take Maria's car but didn't want to wake her for permission, so we took it. That's four vehicles we'd taken without permission in twenty-four hours. A judge would have thrown the book at us. Add, taking the wig and I was a walking crime spree.

Washington Memorial Hospital stands seven-stories high and dominates an entire block in Georgetown. The emergency waiting room was packed. We sat and did what you do in the emergency room… we waited. A little before 1 AM, a man came in with chest pains. Organized chaos ensued and everyone's attention focused on the man.

The police officer on duty put the guy in a wheelchair while the hospital staff peppered him with questions.

Pretty sure they wanted to know what kind of health coverage he had or whether he'd be putting this on his master card. I'm getting cynical in my old age.

Sam and I used the confusion and took the elevator up to the third floor.

"Visiting hours are over at 10 PM," a voice said from behind us. We both spun around and saw a nurse coming our way.

"I'm sorry," she said again, "but only hospital staff can be on this floor after 10 PM."

Sam flashed his ID badge.

"Official business," Sam replied.

"Oh, I'm sorry," she said, "Please check in at the nurse's station." She walked away.

The third-floor sign read, 'Cardiology'. We could see the nurse's station at the end of the hall so we turned the opposite way and walked past several patients' rooms. Their doors were open and most of the beds were occupied.

I always get the same sensation when I'm visiting someone in the hospital. Mostly it's 'get me out of here' followed by 'get me out of here, 'now'. I could feel my stomach starting to churn.

Just beyond the bathrooms, we found a door labeled 'Linens'.

"You be the patient I'll be the doctor," I told Sam as we walked in. "How about you be the patient," he challenged, "and I'll be the doctor."

We both looked around to see who would find the doctor's coat first. There weren't any, only bed sheets, towels, and gowns. I handed him a gown.

We're both going to be patients," I told him. "Get undressed."

He gave me the look that said 'you first' but started taking off his shirt. I stood watching.

"What are you doing?" he asked.

"I'm watching, just like you did at the house in California. Remember all I had on was a gun."

"Yeah, that image is burned in my brain," he said and started taking off his pants. Men in their underwear can look pretty funny. He didn't look funny; he looked good. He had the kind of underwear basketball players wear on the court, kind of long and a little baggy, but not too baggy. He'd spent a good amount of time in the gym and I could see him watching me watching him. The kiss we shared at the store had broken the invisible 'does he like me' game the sexes have played since the beginning of time.

I smiled and undressed. Took off the wig and hid everything under a stack of bed sheets. We decided to go to the third floor separately.

I put on a hairnet and left first. You got to love the way hospital gowns fit. Cover the front, but let the back show as much skin as a Kardashian evening gown.

I made my way toward the elevator. Sam headed the opposite way. I looked back and saw he'd found a walker by one of the rooms and was going the opposite way. The elevator arrived, took me to the third floor. Room 314 was the last room at the end of the hall. An agent was sitting by the door looking at his phone. I could see a thermos bottle and a book on the small table next to him.

Most of the patient's doors were open. I stepped inside one and hid in the shadows, hoping whoever was in the bed wasn't awake.

It was almost 2 AM, things were quiet but it was only a matter of time before a nurse would be coming by to check on their patient.

The room had a soft night-light on and I could see an elderly man sleeping on his back. The bathroom door was closed; I opened it wide enough for me to enter in case I needed a place to hide and glanced down the hall. The agent was drinking from his thermos.

I've done a lot of all-nighters. Time goes by so slowly, it's almost painful. The agent took another swig and grabbed a book off the table, I thought he'd start reading, but he stood, stretched and headed in my direction. I kept thinking about the worst-case scenario and stepped deeper into the room as he walked by. I stuck my head around the corner in time to see him step into the men's room. I made my way toward the Gilliam's room.

A few feet from his door, I saw movement coming from inside. I froze for a second until I recognized it was my boss's wife Rose, coming out.

Rose looked right at me, nodded her head and walked to the nurse's station. She knew what she was doing and blocked the nurse's view.

I walked into Gilliam's room and left the door open. A few minutes later, Sam slid in and stood next to me.

A small night-light illuminated the room; my boss looked pretty good for a guy who'd been shot.

Easy for me to say.

Rose walked in and closed the door. She gave me a strong hug. "You two need to step over to the other side of the room," she told us. "The agent will be looking in the door window when he comes back to make sure everything's okay." And pointed to where she wanted us to stand.

We waited. Rose sat on the chair next to the bed, finally spoke in a soft voice. "The agent's back in his chair. I'll wake David now."

She gently shook her husband's shoulder and whispered in his ear, "Wake up love, Erica's here."

I could see him open his eyes and glance around the room, finally settling on my face. He licked his lips and gave me a smile.

Rose cautioned us, "You'll both need to come closer. He had the breathing tube removed this morning. His voice is pretty soft."

I took Gilliam's hand and squeezed it. He squeezed back and glanced up at Sam.

"They're after you both," he whispered. His eyes flickered back and forth between Sam and me.

"I know," I told him, "we've been playing hide and seek since you got shot."

Rose fed him some water through a straw.

"I ran the photo of the guy who threw the bomb over the White House fence," he whispered. "Our FBI database couldn't identify him, so I called in a favor and had a British agent run the file through their system. I got a match."

Gilliam coughed. He took a couple more sips, it seemed to help.

"One who wouldn't have shown up on the White House secret service files," he added, "or on any known terrorist files. But the British files contain images of almost every important person in the world and their families. We don't, we focus on threat assessment." Gilliam took a few seconds to catch his breath. "Soon as I viewed the name and comprehended who it was, I pulled it off-line. But it must have made it into the cue. I logged off and left the office. I was going to contact you when I got home, but as you can see I must have struck a nerve. The name must have been tagged in the XML database."

"What name did they get off the picture?" I asked.

"The image matches the only son of four-star General Wallace."

"You got to be kidding me!" I said before I could stop myself.

I'd heard of General Wallace, he was a Gulf War hero. I looked over at Sam and back to my boss. "Is this the same general who was at the side of the President at his press conference?"

Gilliam pushed the button on his bed to make it sit up higher. He took a deep breath before saying, "Yes, and I suspect our victim was caught up with something the general was working on. Could be what got him killed."

Gilliam looked tired, but kept talking, "The letter you found was Mitchell's last opportunity to stop it. But he couldn't take a chance someone would find the evidence so he hides it where only his brother could find it. My guess is whoever is behind all of this tried to torch his apartment to keep anyone from finding it."

Gilliam took a few more breaths, clenched his jaw, "They don't know if you and Sam know anything yet, but they're not going to take any chances. You need to stay out of sight."

My boss looked at me, took a deep breath. "The letter," he stuttered, "You, you need to read it again. Something is going to happen soon and it could be coming from inside our own military. You need to…"

The door opened, the night nurse walked in. "What is going on in here?" she demanded, "Do you know these people?" she asked Rose, never taking her eyes off of us.

Before Rose could answer the nurse called the agent.

He drew his gun as soon as he saw us. "How did you two get in here? On your knees," he ordered and pointed his weapon at Sam, and me. "Who the fuck are you two?'

"D.C. Police," Sam said, and pointed at me, "She's FBI."

We both went down to our knees. The agent held out his hand spreading his fingers like a fan, "Let me see your ID's," he demanded.

"They're on the second floor, agent," I said, "Hidden in the linen closet with our clothes. And you," I read his I.D. badge around his neck, "Agent Carter, are about to get fired."

I glanced at Gilliam and back at the agent who had a 'what the fuck' look on his face.

"You're not supposed to leave the Chief alone," I ranted, "We got in here like it was a walk in the park.".

"That's the truth, agent," Gilliam added. "They're both on assignment through my office. I'm ordering you to take them to where they left their identification."

Agent Carter began to lower his weapon, "I'm not letting you out of my sight, sir."

"You're right," Gilliam replied, "put me in a wheelchair and we'll all go to the second floor together."

Carter looked at us on our knees and back at the Chief. This wasn't in the training manual.

Gilliam took over, "Agent, I'm about to wake half the bureau if you don't start moving. Now get me that wheelchair." Agent Carter holstered his gun.

We took the elevator to the second floor. Sam and I came out of the closet with our I. D's.

Gilliam stared at Carter, "Agent, would you please take me back to my room, I'm extremely tired and have a decision to make about how I am going to report this incident."

Sam and I got dressed. It was time we found the general's son, find out why he threw the bomb over the White House fence.

I've always been amazed at what someone will tell you when they have a gun shoved in their face.

Charles Wallace was about to find out.

EUPHORIA

Chapter 25

C harles wanted the money almost as badly as he wanted to find his lover and leave town…forever. He had a decision to make. Let the two soldiers in Army fatigues with a large duffle bag into his house or pretend he wasn't home.

Charles opened the door. The taller of the two soldiers, the one with the crew cut and dead eyes, put the bag on the floor and unzipped it. "Count it" the other soldier ordered.

It was full of cash. Charles got on one knee and pulled out the top three bundles of hundreds, started counting.

"Not here in front of the door. Take it upstairs and count it, you idiot," Mister dead eyes told him.

Charles dragged the bag upstairs and tossed it on his bed. This was what he'd been promised for throwing the bomb over the White House fence, a quarter million dollars cash and safe passage for himself and his lover.

Halfway through his count, he heard the sound of glass breaking downstairs. He'd forgotten about the soldiers, the stacks of hundreds spread out on his bed had him hypnotized. More sounds came from downstairs. He memorized his count before going down to see what had happened.

The living room was trashed. Books, furniture, photographs, everything had been tossed on the floor. He glanced into the kitchen, the contents of the cabinets were spilled out on the counters.

Both soldiers stopped their search, noticed Charles was watching them, ignored him and returned to their hunt.

"What the fuck are you doing?" Charles yelled.

Neither soldier even looked up.

"Stop," Charles yelled. "What are you looking for? Tell me, I'll find it for you." Instinct took over as he grabbed the soldier's arm.

A shock wave of pain ran through his body as he landed on the hardwood floor. Each soldier grabbed an arm and dragged him up the stairs before tossing him on top of the money on his bed.

For an instant Charles thought of using his father's name to stop them. But he didn't say a word. He'd rather die than mention his father's name. The realization that these soldiers were doing exactly what his father had ordered made him shake uncontrollably.

"We were going to wait till you were done counting the money," soldier number one barked at him, "but you're getting on my nerves."

He grabbed Charles shirt and ripped it off him. The other soldier pulled off his shoes and pulled his pants below his knees. Using his knee, he put his full weight on Charles' chest, pinning him to the bed.

His scream was terminated by a bundle of hundred-dollar bills shoved in his mouth.

Charles felt a cold needle enter his left arm. It stung for a second before a rush of euphoria surged through his body.

Oh my God, it felt so good. The elation kept growing. His body relaxed, every muscle surrendered to the ecstasy. He wanted to thank the soldiers. The gift they had given him was… familiar. A fleeting moment of alarm passed through his thoughts as he recognized the heroin surging through his veins. A wave of nausea hit him hard, then another, but it didn't matter. Nothing mattered. The world was fading slowly into darkness. The sound of his heart beating in his chest was the last sensation he felt as a dark shadow slowly covered him from head to toe.

Both soldiers stepped away from his body and put the money back in the duffle bag. One of the soldiers removed Charles pants and laid them on the floor by his shirt and put the empty syringe into the Charles' hand, making sure his fingerprints were on it before putting it on the nightstand. They rolled Charles body onto his stomach before tearing through his room. A black hoodie, black pants, and a backpack were in the corner of the closet. Everything was shoved into the duffle bag with the cash.

"The general's idiot son didn't burn his clothes," the soldier told his comrade as they took the bag downstairs.

"As long as he's dead, Monday nights attack should take care of the problem forever. Let's finish searching downstairs, take the cash and then get the hell out of here."

WHAT DAY IS IT

Chapter 26

"I need an address," I told Shreya. "Guy's name is Charles Wallace. He's the son of four-star General Robert Wallace."

"Give me a bit," she said and disconnected.

The smell of caffeine and pastry, my two favorite food groups, led me downstairs. I followed my nose and found Sam and Maria in the kitchen. Maria put one of her muffins on a paper plate and slid it over to me. "Mangia," she said in Italian, "Eat, such a skinny ragazza."

I took a bite, drank some of her coffee and decided I wanted Maria to be my grandmother.

I told Sam, "I called Shreya a few minutes ago, she's getting the info we need."

Sam nodded and re-filled everyone's cup. He needed a shave and another four hours of sleep.

I finished the muffin and considered another, but opted for a shower.

I was drying off when Shreya called back.

"General Wallace is one of the Presidents closest military advisors," she informed me. "He's second in command in the Situation Room and briefs the President on all military matters. He's been decorated three times for his service in the first Gulf War and again in the Iraq war. I dug deeper in the web and found he has a loyal contingent of high-ranking officers who worship the ground he walks on. His proximity to the President makes him one of the most powerful military advisors at the Pentagon."

"What about his son," I asked.

"His name is Charles Raymond Wallace. He's 34, lives close to D.C. in Virginia. He was in the military for a short time before being discharged. He's openly gay, works as a bartender at a club called Gents. His boyfriend works as a manager at Carlyle's restaurant in Arlington. I'm sending you a screen capture of Charles' driver's license photo. Not much more out there on this guy, I had to dig deep to even get this much info."

"Text me his address with his photo," I asked Shreya, "and destroy your burner phone," I added. "I'm going to dump mine as soon as I get the info you're sending me. Memorize this number, it's Sam's burner. We haven't used his yet and let me know the number of your next phone."

I told her Sam's number. Her text with the general's son's photo attached came through. I dressed and made my way back downstairs. It was looking like we were going to get some answers.

"Do you have a computer?" I asked Maria.

"No, I don't like the interestnet. I don't understand," she said.

'Interestnet', that was a new one, I kind of liked it.

We borrowed Maria's car and as much as it made Sam nervous, I drove.

We parked a half a block away from Charles two-story house. An older model Ford truck sat in the driveway.

"I say we pay Charles a visit," I told Sam, "and put the fear of God in him."

I had a newspaper with the photo the Secret Service had released and Charles driver's license picture on my phone. It's impossible to say they matched, but guilty people will see things innocent folks don't.

We had our I.D.'s out when I rang the doorbell. No answer. I knocked. Nothing.

"He's either not here or not answering. Either way, we're going inside," I told Sam. He shrugged and took out a set of keys. He had a lock-pick on his key ring.

"You're a different kind of cop than my dad," I told him.

He gave me a look as if he knew something I didn't know, shook his head and opened the door.

We stepped inside. The house was totaled. Not like my house, someone had turned the place upside-down. We drew our guns and checked the ground floor. Sam inspected the garage before we both moved up the stairs. Every door on the top floor was open except one. We cleared each of the rooms and stood in front of the last door. I turned the knob and swung the door open. A man's body, wearing only a pair of undershorts was face down on the bed.

We scanned the room before moving over to the bed.

It wasn't easy to tell, but it looked like the general's son. I thought he was dead until he made a groaning sound.

We rolled him over. He was unshaven, hair a mess and made another loud snoring sound.

"He's either drunk or stoned out of his mind," Sam said. "Help me sit him up and see if we can wake him."

We each took an arm and propped him up on the headboard. He mumbled something incoherent and tried to open his eyes.

"Water," I said and walked into the bathroom. I filled a cup with cold water and came back to the bed.

"Hey Charles," I yelled and threw it in his face."

That got his attention for about five seconds. He opened one eye and glared at me before his head slumped back down.

I could tell the third cup did the trick when he yelled, "What the fuck!" And took a swing at me.

"Charles," I hollered, "You're under arrest for the bombing of the White House," and flashed my badge in his face. That's when he threw up.

We got Charles out of the bedroom and downstairs, found a coffee maker in the kitchen and some dark roast in the fridge. Sam cleared off one of the living room chairs, sat Charles down and poured coffee down his throat till he looked semi-coherent.

"We're arresting you for the bombing at the White House," Sam repeated and pulled out the photo of him in the black hoodie running from the scene. "That's you, Charles. We have a video of you running after you threw the bomb. You've been positively identified as the bomber."

He didn't vomit again, which was good. But he was crying and kept repeating, "He made me, the piece of shit made me."

I was about to ask 'who made you' but his eyes rolled backward and I'm pretty sure he was about to have a total meltdown. We needed his attention back on the here and now.

I change the subject, "What happened here," And pointed to everything strewn about the room.

"Soldiers," he slurred, "I've got to pee."

Sam walked him to the bathroom.

He looked a little better when he came back, "When did this happen?" I asked, to keep him talking.

"Yesterday, I think." He mumbled. "Wanted the clothes I'd worn, my computer, my phone. He looked around the room, "Bastards tore my place apart and shot me up with heroin. They were trying to make it look like an overdose."

"Why did you throw the bomb over the fence, Charles, why'd you do it?" I asked.

"Cover," he said between sobs. "For what's going to happen."

Oh shit.

"What's going to happen?"

"What day is it?" Charles stammered.

"It's Thursday morning."

"Monday night, it's going to happen Monday night."

He stopped crying, looked at both of us, "I want immunity," he shouted, "Lawyer, lawyer, lawyer," he kept repeating. "I want immunity or I'm not saying another word."

"You threw a bomb at the White House, Charles," I barked at him, "No one on this planet is going to give you immunity. The only thing you're going to get is the death sentence for a terrorist act. Tell me what's going to happen Monday night."

"Ask my father, he's the one who tried to have me killed," he ranted.

Sam took out his phone.

"Who are you calling?" Charles groaned.

"Your father, just like you asked."

Charles lost it, tried to get out of his chair. We pushed him back.

"We're all going to die," he yelled. "My father's going to come over here and kill all of us. I don't care how many cops you have outside, you're all as good as dead. He'll eliminate all of you."

TOO LATE

Chapter 27

I t took an hour to get Charles dressed, cuffed and in the back seat of
Maria's car without the neighbors noticing. He was still reeling from
the heroin, but awake enough to notice it had only been Sam and I at
his house. It didn't take too long, after we'd put him into the back seat of a
light blue Honda Civic with a crucifix dangling from the rear-view mirror,
before he started asking questions. Sometimes the best way to get a perp
talking is to answer their questions first.

I pulled over next to Arlington Cemetery and let him ask whatever he
wanted. This was it. Find out what he knew or wait for whatever was going
to go down on Monday night.

Sam caught me off guard when he asked Charles, "What branch of the
military did you serve in?"

When Charles answered, "Air Force, just to piss off my Father." I decided to stay out of it and let the boys talk.

"Why'd it piss him off?" Sam asked.

Charles looked at his feet before answering, "He wanted me to join
the Army, but I'd had enough Army crap as a kid. I joined the Air Force
instead. It jerked his chain. I fucking loved it."

Sam nodded in agreement, "Why does your military record go silent after two years?"

"How do you know that?" Charles asked.

I almost jumped into the conversation with my patented 'we're the FBI, dipshit' reply, but this was 'the man zone', a 'guy-to-guy' thing. I sat back and waited for Sam to tell Charles he'd been in the military too. Should get his juices flowing.

Charles didn't wait for an answer and volunteered, "My Father wanted me in the military, then pulled me out. I didn't know it at the time but it was part of the plan he'd been working on. So, he got me out."

It was Sam's turn to volunteer some information and told Charles, "My old man wanted me to make a career in the marines, so I know what it's like to have 'Dad' want to have his kid in the military."

There it was, soldier to soldier. At this point I wasn't going to identify with what they were talking about so I pretended I wasn't in the car.

"You were a Marine?" Charles asked. "Were you in the Gulf?"

"Special Forces, 8th Marine Regiment. Two tours, that was enough," Sam said and turned quiet for a second. I kept my head turned toward the windshield.

"I wanted to stay in," Charles said, "But the old man yanked me out. One phone call and I was home twenty-four hours later."

"Charles, I need to know why your Dad pulled you out, what did he need you for?"

He was sweating, wouldn't look up. Finally, he mumbled, "I was used as a diversion, to set it all up. You can't stop it, no one can, not when the President of United States is behind the whole thing."

"The President bombed his own Whitehouse, what the fuck." Sam yelled. "A diversion for what?

Charles stared out the window.

I started the car, "Where you taking me?" he stammered.

"To turn you over to Howard Decker, the head of the Secret Service."

I stepped on the gas and slid into traffic. Sam reads my mind and turned around and faced the front. I could see Charles in my rearview mirror. He looked a hundred years old. I drove through the city toward the White House.

"Don't take me in there," Charles pleaded, "it'll be too late. It's already too late."

"Hey Charles," Sam grunted, "if it's already too late and were all dead if your father finds out we have you, why the fuck are you not telling us what's going to happen? Seriously, what good is a lawyer if we're all going to be dead."

Sam let it sink in and added, "We have no choice. We either take you to the Secret Service and they do whatever they do to find out what you know, or you trust us and we do our best to protect you from your father and the President.

Charles didn't reply, the White House was coming into view at the end of Pennsylvania Avenue.

"Somewhere in the Capitol Building," Charles whispered. "I don't know exactly where, or what, I just know it's supposed to happen Monday night."

"How do you know?" Sam asked, "Did your father tell you?"

"My Father didn't tell me. He used me to initiate his next move. I heard it from the two soldiers who tore up my house. They figured I was a dead man from the over-dose they gave me, but I heard them talking about Monday night."

"How do you know it was heroin and not some other drug?" I asked.

"I was a heroin user," Charles answered. "I snort it, I don't shoot it. No one knows except my lover and my dealer. My father didn't know until he had to bail me out of jail once when I got busted buying on the street.

The dose they gave me would have killed a non-user but I've been doing heroin since I got out of the military. Built a tolerance."

The floodgates were opened, Charles looked at Sam. "The soldiers who trashed my house said something about 'it would take care of the problem forever'. I was pretty out of it so I'm not sure exactly what they were saying."

"You have any idea what they're looking for at your house?" I asked.

"For anything that connects me to the bombing. Don't reckon it'll look too good on my Dad's resume if they find out his son threw a bomb at the White House."

We had him talking, nothing like caffeine and guilt to make someone tell you their life story.

"Why'd you do it?" I asked him.

"My father hates me. Has since I came 'out'. My Mom passed away when I was in high school. Dad wasn't a ball of fun before that, but once I came out as gay it was seething anger at every look. How could 'mister G.I. Joe' have a son like me? He set out to cure me. Put me in military school, then tried to get me to enlist in the Army. I refused for years. I finally relented. Joined the Air Force instead, which made him hate me even more. My heroin habit was the last straw. That's when he had his henchmen come to my home to force me to do the bomb thing at the White House. I was promised a half a million dollars and ordered to never come back to Washington. If I didn't agree I'd disappear without a trace right after my boyfriend was killed in an auto accident. At first, I couldn't figure out why he wanted me to do his bidding, but it finally made sense. He knew I'd do it to save my lover, knew I'd never go to the police. Hell, he knew I ran track in high school and could still run fast. I was his gay, druggy kid who was too afraid of his father to ever talk. I was perfect for his bullshit. He had one of his soldiers train me how to set the timer. I did as I was told."

Charles stared out the windshield. The White House was a few blocks away. "The same two soldiers came to me a week ago. They knew every detail of my life, where my lover works, where he lives. They gave me the clothes to wear, showed me how to arm the bomb. Told me where to run afterwards to find the escape car. My boyfriend never knew a thing. He stayed at his sister's place for a couple of days. We'd been fighting about my drug problem, which is why he wasn't at my house." Charles looked at the floor, "He would've believed I overdosed."

It was time to dig deeper. "What do you know about what's going to happen Monday?" I asked, "Is it a bomb? Is it the same explosive you used? Do you know anything?"

"The one I threw over the fence was a diversion. It was supposed to divert attention, make it look like there was a terrorist loose in D.C. I don't know what's going to happen, but whatever it is it's going to be Monday night."

I turned the car around and headed downtown. Turning him over to the Secret Service was the last place we wanted him if the President was part of the plot. The Secret Service's job is to protect the President not arrest him. That's when it hit me. Who has the power to arrest the President of the United States. The CIA, the FBI, the military? How the hell do you arrest the most powerful person in the world? And if you did where would you put him? In county lockup?

I drove through DuPont Circle and headed north on Connecticut Avenue. It was time to put Charles in a motel room and find out how the hell you arrest the leader of the free world.

WHERE'D YOU GO

Chapter 28

S am wanted to handcuff Charles to the bed at the motel, but the look on Charles' face said he wasn't going anywhere. His two choices were daytime television or Leavenworth prison. Not an easy choice.

We drove back to Maria's and called Shreya's burner.

"Jeez Loueez," she answered, "scared the shit out of me when this thing rang!"

"Sorry, but I need you to look up something for me." I paused until she said, "what?"

"How do you arrest the President of the United States?"

"Now you're really scaring the shit out of me," she whispered. "You want me to do a search on locking up POTUS? I don't know if it's even possible, I'll call you back."

I walked back into the living room. Maria was sitting with Sam. She'd made lunch and asked me if I'd like some. I took a couple of bites, but what I needed was sleep. I walked upstairs to my room and fell on the bed. I was drifting off when my phone vibrated.

"Sergeant at Arms is the only one who can do it," Shreya stammered into the phone," and added, "but the D.C. police once arrested a President.

I sat on the side of the bed trying to clear my head.

"For what?" I asked.

"Speeding."

"And you're a funny woman Shreya, especially when you've been drinking."

"Unfortunately, I'm sober," she said, "Ulysses S Grant was arrested for speeding on M Street. They impounded his horse and carriage and brought him to the station, charged him a fine and made him walk back to the White House. Swear to God."

"Tell me more about the Sergeant at Arms. Can he arrest a sitting president?" I asked her.

"Only if he's ordered to do so by the Senate. The president isn't considered a person, he's an institution. You can't arrest an institution. You have to impeach him first."

"But you said the Sergeant at Arms can do it," I repeated.

"After he's been impeached it's the Sergeant at Arms who serves him the papers. The Constitution is vague about which branch of the law would arrest him. Without an impeachment, the Secret Service would stop anyone from trying."

This got me questioning the Constitution, which is not necessarily the best idea if you're an FBI agent.

"What if the President grabbed a rifle and started shooting from the balcony of the White House?" I asked Shreya. "Would that be reason enough to arrest him?"

Shreya was silent for a few seconds before saying, "You're killing me girl. That's not a question you'll find an answer for in Wikipedia. There might not be an answer, but I'll see what I can dig up. I'll get back to you."

"Give me a couple of hours," I told her. "I need to get some sleep, my brain's fried."

51st DIRECTIVE

I woke to the smell of garlic, onions, and oregano. The sleep felt great, but now my stomach was taking over. I made my way downstairs and found Maria in the kitchen. I didn't see Sam so I looked in the living room.

"Where's Sam?" I asked Maria.

"He asked to use my car. Said he be back soon."

I looked at what Maria was making. She had several chicken breasts cooking in a skillet with garlic and onions. Bread was baking in the oven and an open bottle of red wine sat on the table.

I heard the back door close, then Sam walked into the kitchen. He looked pretty beat. He signaled for me to follow him.

We left Maria in the kitchen where she makes life worth living and stepped into the living room.

"Where'd you go?" I asked. It was a stupid question. He was about to tell me, but it popped out of my mouth.

"Out drinking with the boys," he answered and waited for another stupid question.

"So, what were you and the boys drinking, vodka, or scotch?"

I'm not the nicest person when I wake from a nap.

To my surprise, Sam walked right up and kissed me.

"You got a quick comeback for everything, don't you?" he asked, but didn't wait for an answer. This time he kissed me all the way to my shoes. Now I was in conflict, my stomach verses my libido. I wanted both, a bite of chicken and another kiss followed by a sip of wine and his hands…STOP!

Maria walked into the living room, saw us making out like two teenagers and said, 'Ah amore, but first sit and eat, love can wait but not my chicken cacciatore."

She was right; I'd forgotten how good home cooking tasted. I love my cheese and crackers with a mug of wine, but this was real food, made by a cook who can really cook.

148

After dinner, Sam and I started in on the dishes while Maria watched TV.

"So, every time I ask, 'where'd you go' you going to kiss me?" I asked Sam.

Sam dropped the dishtowel on the counter, spun me around and leaned me against the counter. This time it wouldn't have mattered if Maria came into the kitchen. We had our soapy hands all over each other. He was happy to be doing dishes with me and every time we surfaced for air I kept asking him 'so where'd you go'?

We did everything you can do standing in a kitchen with a seventy-two-year-old grandmother twenty feet away watching Wheel of Fortune. Finally, we ran upstairs to my room and put the final touches on the dishes. I couldn't remember the last time I'd felt this way. We never made it downstairs for dessert, but I did ask Sam where 'he went again' and found out it was better than Haagen-Dazs chocolate chip cookie dough.

DOCTOR PEPPER

Chapter 29

When I woke the sun was coming through the window. The day had started without me.

Sam was gone.

I heard voices downstairs. Sam and Maria were talking in the living room. They both smiled at me as I came in. I felt like I'd been caught with my hand in the cookie jar.

Perfect metaphor.

"Maria just showed me a newspaper article," Sam told me and held up the paper. "It seems the newly elected British Prime Minister is going to be speaking at a joint session of Congress this Monday night."

"He's a nice looking Englishman, no" Maria added.

Sam kept looking at me. I wasn't sure if it was the news of the Monday night event or the memory of doing the dishes together last night. Either way, I kept looking back.

"Maria," I said, "Can we use your car again today?"

"Si, you can use it all day, my daughter is coming over to take me shopping. "You two hungry?" she asked and gave me the woman-to-woman smile which says - 'you burned a lot of calories last night, you need to keep up your strength'.

I thought of her baked bread and incredible coffee and surrendered, again.

I was taking my last sip of coffee when Shreya called.

"There's no answer on the internet to your question about who can stop a President from committing a crime," she told me. "The Constitution says you have to impeach the President before you can arrest him. But arresting a modern-day President has never been tested. If the FBI tried to arrest the president before impeachment, the Secret Service would pull their guns and it would be the cluster fuck of all time."

"Does the president have the right to carry a gun?" I asked.

"Yeap, he does. And as far as I can tell, he can open fire on anybody and no one has the legal authority to stop him. I'm not saying nobody would stop him," Shreya added. "It's just never been tested. Do you believe POTUS is planning on opening fire on someone?"

"Unfortunately, I'm envisioning him doing something worse."

Shreya was quiet for a second before saying, "Isn't this what presidents do? They put out kill orders on our enemies. They order the military to do it. What if the president wanted to do it himself? I don't know who can stop him."

I drank another cup and drove to the motel.

Charles let us in and jumped back on the bed. The TV was on, Judge Judy was giving one of her victims an earful. An empty pizza box sat on the counter by the TV and five crushed cans of Doctor Pepper were scattered around the room.

"How'd you pay for all of this?" I asked.

"Coupon from the phone book," Charles answered and took a swallow of his soda. "The pizza joint has a deal with this hotel," he volunteered and started bouncing up and down. "They deliver food and put it on the motel bill. It's right here on the room instructions." He jumped up and showed me the paperwork. "I had the delivery guy leave it by the door. Told him to give himself a five-dollar tip. Nobody saw me." He jumped back on the bed and started fidgeting with the TV remote.

"What's with all the soda cans?" I asked.

"Heroin reaction," Sam answered. "Users need the sugar. Goes to the same brain receptors as the drug. Keeps 'em calm, for a while."

Charles kept changing channels, "We may need to get him another six-pack," I told Sam and stood in front of the TV set.

"Hey Charles, we need you to do something today."

Charles waited for me to explain. I let him wait. He wasn't going to like what Sam and I decided on the way over.

Sam jumped in first, "We need you to go to the Pentagon and pay a visit to your Dad."

Charles seemed to take the request pretty well until he threw up in the garbage can next to the bed. The guy can't hold down his stuff very well. Pizza and soda may not be the best combo when you've been asked to visit the person who tried to have you murdered.

We let Charles clean himself up and waited for him to ask the question we knew he was going to ask.

"Why the fuck would I do that?" he said right on cue.

"Because you're the only one who can get close enough to plant a bug," I answered.

"He tried to have me killed. What's he going to do when I walk into his office?"

"Shock and awe," I said. "He's going to have the shit scared out of him for the first time in his life when he sees you're alive. That's when you plant the bug in his office. It's the only way we have a shot at finding out what he's up to. We're sure as hell not going to be able to plant one in the Oval Office."

"And what's going to stop him from pulling out his gun and shooting me in the face?" Charles hollered.

"The noise," Sam said with just enough sarcasm.

Sam pulled one of the motel chairs over by the bed and explained, "You walk into his office, sit in the chair closest to his desk, it's the last thing on earth he'd be expecting. I seriously doubt he's going to ask you why you're still alive. He's going to be stunned, which is when you plant the bug."

"You two are nuts," Charles snapped.

"That's what everybody says when they figure out they're going to have to do something they don't want to," I told him.

I was hoping Charles wasn't going to puke again when I told him someone from the FBI was going to come over to show him how to activate the device. Fortunately, he only turned a shade of red I can't quite describe and stared at us.

Sam and I told him we'd be back and left. Sam wanted to handcuff Charles to the bed again, but we both knew if we dropped him off at the Pentagon, he could walk in one door and out one of the other nine exits. Might as well trust him now if we're going to have to trust him later.

We drove to the Wal-Mart on West 5th and bought three more burner phones and a six-pack of Doctor Pepper. I called Shreya.

"I need another favor," I said.

She didn't hang up on me, which was a small miracle seeing what she'd already gone through with us.

"You know Tony Hayes, the head of the surveillance division, don't you?" I asked.

"The cute guy on the eleventh floor? Yeah, I've ridden in the elevator four floors past mine just to hang out with him."

What's with Tony and the elevator? I asked myself.

"I need you to go to his office, unannounced, and tell him what's happening. Everything from beginning till now, and have him call me on one of your burner phones."

"When?" she asked.

"Now. And next time you're in an elevator with him, don't stand in front of him."

"You're crazy girl. I've already stood in front of him in the elevator. If he wasn't still married, I'd ride up and down with him all day." She made a giggling sound and hung up.

We drove back to Maria's and waited for Tony to call.

Tony sounded pretty normal for a guy who just found out he was about to risk his career and possibly his life for a conspiracy theory based on information from the son of a four-star general and who also happened to be a heroin addict. Of course, Tony didn't know he was about to be asked to bug a four-star general inside the confines of the Pentagon. That'll get his attention.

"What do you need me to do?" he asked.

"Teach a guy how to place a listening device inside an office," I told him, trying to walk him in slowly.

"Which guy, and whose office?"

"General Wallace, inside the Pentagon."

"Right, and we have a warrant to do this?" Tony asked.

"No warrant and not a lot of time to get this done. This general has tried to have me killed twice and is responsible for our boss being shot. So, this is off the books, and I need an answer now. Can you do it?"

I was pleased he was only quiet for a few seconds before saying, "Yeah, I can do it. I'm going to need a couple of hours to get my toys ready," he mumbled. "Where do I go to meet this 'guy' who's going to plant the bug?"

"The guy is his son," I added.

I gave Tony the address and the room number.

Before we hung up I said, "By the way, the general we're going to bug tried to kill his son with an overdose of heroin yesterday. See ya at the motel."

GET ME THE HELL OUT OF HERE

Chapter 30

S am and I hung out at the motel with Charles watching reruns of M.A.S.H. and drinking sodas. We were in our third episode when Tony arrived.

Tony took a look around the room, nodded at Sam and sat in one of the chairs.

Charles and Tony were about as opposite as two people can get. Tony's a straight, suit-wearing FBI surveillance agent. Charles is a gay, heroin-snorting bartender.

Then there's Sam and Tony. Neither one knew about the other in regards to me, but men have a pheromone they radiate when they're in a room with a woman they both want. Then there's me, trying to be 'miss all business' with one guy on one side of the room who I almost let get to second base and on the other side a man I was sure had hit a grand slam.

Charles wasn't looking too good. He'd just come off a drug overdose ordered by a father who wanted him dead, had eaten an entire pepperoni pizza and drunk a gallon of Doctor Pepper while watching daytime television. I'm surprised he hadn't drowned himself in the bathtub.

We all sat in the motel room around the bed, which was kind of weird. Tony unwrapped a stick of gum and popped it in his mouth. "We're not going to be able to transmit a signal out of the Pentagon," he told us.

"They've spent a ton of money on acoustic insulation and technical surveillance countermeasures. Hell, they utilize electronic processing adequate RF attenuation at the inspectable space boundary."

Tony was showing off, trying to be the top dog in the room.

I almost slipped off my chair when Sam said, "I'm pretty sure the PUC would identify an activated sensor if an intrusion was detected."

Tony smiled at Sam and nodded his head.

OMG, they'd just bonded over insulation.

"So how do we do this?" I interjected before the boys made a date to go hunting together.

Tony took out the gum he'd been chewing and stuck it under the armrest on his chair.

"We use this," he said and pointed to the gum, then reached into his shirt pocket and took out a clear plastic box. Inside was a single black speck, no bigger than a grain of rice. Tony took it out and pushed it into the gum.

"This will record any sound made in the general's office for the next forty-eight hours. Since it's a recording device and not a transmitter it won't be detected. Once it's retrieved we'll be able to isolate any conversation made in the room."

"Retrieved," Charles cried. "Are you saying I have to go back in a second time and get it?"

Tony nodded his head.

Charles turned red again and keep repeating "you fucking kidding me", over and over.

Ten minutes later, Tony showed him how to push the recording device into the gum and flatten it under the armrest of the chair.

"The gum tastes like crap," Tony informed Charles. "It's made of a special material which lets sound penetrate the surface."

To be extra careful Tony decided Charles should have the gum, with the device already inside it, in his mouth between his cheek and gum when he arrived at the Pentagon, just in case he was searched or hand scanned.

"Fuck, fuck, fuck and fuck," Charles barked, as the reality of what he needed to do set in.

I felt his pain, "You're right, this is fucked, but this is all we've got," I told him.

Charles had a look on his face that screamed 'why me'? Finally, he asked "and what do I tell dear old dad when I go back to get the device?"

I had no idea; we were making this up as we went along.

"Let's take this one step at a time," I answered. "We need to do this first part now. Will you do it?"

"This could end my father's life, couldn't it?" Charles asked. "Like jail for the rest of his life, maybe even the death penalty?"

"That's a possibility."

"I'm going to take a shower," Charles answered, "Then we'll go."

I looked over by the door where Sam and Tony were talking. I couldn't hear what they were saying, but I'm pretty sure they weren't sharing cooking recipes. I was looking forward to asking Sam what they talked about. Maybe it would get the same response as when I asked him where he'd gone. A trigger's a trigger.

Tony left and Sam and I waited for Charles in the car.

"I'm pretty sure Tony has a 'thing' for you," Sam told me as we got in. "Anything I need to know?" He asked.

"Only that I don't go out with married men, even if they're separated. It's a bad idea. Tony knows how I feel."

We both sat looking out the windshield. One of those awkward moments when the next one who speaks is going to have to reveal how they feel.

Neither of us said anything. We glanced at each other for a few seconds and then 'boom' we were making out in the car like I used to do in front of my boyfriends' parents' house on Friday nights back in high school.

I heard Charles coming out of the apartment and got myself straightened out before he reached the car.

Sam drove. We took South Washington Blvd to the North Rotary exit and parked by the 9/11 Pentagon Memorial.

Charles popped the gum in his mouth and started chewing. I could tell it didn't taste too good by the gagging sounds he was making in the backseat. But Charles had done all the worshiping he was going to do at the foot of the porcelain altar and kept chewing.

Before getting out of the car he put the listening device inside the gum and flattened it against the inside of his cheek.

"Can you tell?" he asked as he opened the door. Sam and I assumed he meant the gum in his mouth and not how nervous he looked. "Nope, can't tell. We'll be right here waiting," I said and watched him make his way to the main entrance.

I'd been to the Pentagon once after I'd completed my FBI training. The place is one of the largest office buildings in the world. Twenty-three thousand people work there on any given day. You could live inside the Pentagon for months and never leave the building. It has a Subway, McDonald's, Dunkin' Donuts, Panda Express, Starbucks, KFC, and a Taco Bell. If you got fat from the food you could work it off at the fitness center, or ask for forgiveness in the meditation room.

Sam turned on the radio and we both laid back in our seats listening to Nirvana. I couldn't escape the irony that some faction of the military was looking for us while we were sitting on their front porch listening to 'Lithium'.

A little less than an hour later we saw Charles walking back to the car.

"It's done," he said as he got in the backseat. "Now get me the hell out of here."

GAME ON

Chapter 31

Charles wept in the backseat all the way to the motel. It took an hour and a two-liter bottle of Doctor Pepper to calm him enough to get the details of what happened.

"My old man was sitting behind his desk when I walked in. He looked like he always looked, pissed. No surprise at seeing me, just a cold stare.

"Did your father say anything about the soldiers trying to overdose you?' Sam asked.

"He said they weren't trying to kill me, only wanted me to be too stoned to go anywhere or tell anyone what I'd done. I almost believed him. Dear old dad said if he wanted me dead, I'd be dead already. I'm to go home and wait for my money to be delivered, tomorrow. That's when I started to cry and spit the gum into my hand. He ordered me out of his office. I stuck the gum under the arm of the chair as I stood up to leave."

Charles sat on the bed trying not to break down.

"When we stop your piece of shit father from doing whatever he's got planned," Sam told Charles, "it'll be your testimony that sends him to prison for treason. You'll be given full immunity from prosecution for your testimony and when you get done writing a book about the whole thing you can disappear and live wherever the hell you want with anyone you want."

"We'll come back tomorrow," I told Charles. "Stay inside, order food to be delivered and pay with this," I gave him a fifty before Sam and I left.

When we got to Maria's we found her doing what God put her on earth to do. And like two puppy dogs we scooted into the kitchen to see what she was cooking.

She saw us, opened the oven door, and took out a rack of cookies. Not just cookies, Italian cookies. She called them 'Nookie', I tried to repeat the name but I was already chewing one and my mouth didn't want to do anything but chew. Sam had ecstasy written all over his face and was looking for the milk when I left the room to call Colonel Mitchell. I used our last burner phone and called his office.

His secretary remembered me and put me through.

"Colonel," I said, "it's Agent Brewer, I was hoping - -"

"It's getting tight out here," he barked. "The assassination of my communications officer has gone up the chain of command. Now I've got General Wallace asking all kinds of questions. Wants to send his own investigators. Bunch of bullshit. Whatever is going on is making waves all the way to the top."

Hearing General Wallace's name had my stomach rolling over, the cookies felt like a rock in my gut.

"What did you tell the general?" I asked. "Is he sending a team to you?"

"I'm doing my best to keep the investigation in-house," he replied. "The Army and the Marines hate each other. Every branch of the armed forces claims the others are beneath them. A lot like the FBI, and the cops."

It was time to tell the colonel why I called, "Sam and I have uncovered a conspiracy involving the President and General Wallace," I blurted out.

It was silent on the other end, so I kept going. "And we believe something is going to happen on Monday night somewhere in the Capitol building. We suspect this is what your brother and your communication officer were involved in and why they're both dead. We can't prove any of this, at least not enough to stop the President and a four-star general from doing whatever they want."

The colonel's voice changed. It wasn't angry anymore, just steady and measured. "How do you know all of this?"

"We have the guy who threw the bomb over the White House fence," I told him. "It's the general's son."

"His son! The general's son? Are you positive?" He exploded. So much for steady and measured.

"He confessed colonel. We have him hidden in a motel room. He's working with us to find out what's going to happen on Monday." I let it sink in for a second then dropped another bomb on him. "We've been able to plant a recording device in General Wallace's Pentagon office."

The colonal snapped, "How the hell did you get a bug into the Pentagon?"

I couldn't help myself and replied, "We're the FBI, Colonel, this is what we do. We had General Wallace's son plant it."

It was silent again. We'd bugged a four-star general inside the Pentagon, which was an act of treason. I waited for his reaction. It was the longest ten seconds I'd spent since being in a shootout. "Son of a bitch," he yelled. "What in God's name is going on here?"

"Whatever it is Colonel, it's connected to something that's going to happen this Monday," I told him and waited for his response.

"How can I help Agent?" he replied. "Tell me your next move."

"Colonel, I need you to hold for one minute." I wanted Sam's opinion and ran downstairs. He was lying on the couch eating an Italian cookie. He had his shoes off and a glass of milk in his hand. We'd been running for our lives the last couple of days and here he was munching on cookies and milk. The man knew how to handle stress.

"I've got Colonel Mitchell on the phone," I told Sam,

"I'm about to ask him to come back out here and help us. You agree?"

He put his milk on the coffee table. I tried not to laugh at the milk mustache under his nose.

"We can use his help getting the recording device out of the Pentagon. I say get him back out here."

I agreed and hustled back upstairs to finish the call.

"We're going to need your help, Colonel. Can you leave the Base and come to D.C.?"

"Hold on a second," he said. The line went dead for a minute before he came back. "I can be there tomorrow at eleven hundred hours, where will I find you?" he asked.

"Your brother's apartment," I told him and disconnected.

Maria was still putzing around the kitchen, which has quickly become my favorite place to see her putzing. I found Sam still in the living room. "The colonel will be here tomorrow morning," I told him. "I'm hoping Shreya can hack into the colonel's brother's web account again to see if there's more info we can use to stop whatever is going to happen."

"It's either that or the listening device," Sam said. "And we're going to need a safe place to meet with Colonel Mitchell. Somewhere we can see him before he sees us."

Sam breathed in a nose full of air. "What smells so good?" he asked.

"Chicken cacciatore, with Parmesan cheese, red wine, and a salad," I told him. "I saw Maria's groceries on the counter and my stomach took over my brain."

"Give Shreya a call and I'll go help Maria," Sam said. "I'm learning how to cook from a master."

My heart was on fire. He didn't snore, could kiss like there was no tomorrow, and was learning to cook chicken cacciatore. More importantly, he could handle stress, which would come in handy if he wanted to hang out with me.

I called Shreya's burner.

"We need to talk," she answered.

"Yeah, that's kind of why I'm calling you," I shot back.

"Me first," she said. "I hacked into Mitchell's email account again. I had to create a new tenet on the DB-servers to access the ACI configuration, but I was able to locate an updated version of the architectural plans, we found last time. This is what I got…"

My phone vibrated with a text message. I opened the file. A diagram of the Capitol building opened on my screen.

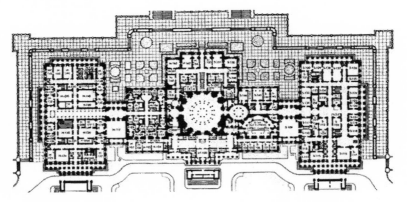

"You're looking at the same blueprint of the ground floor of the capitol building we found when we hacked into Mitchell's dark web account. This time I downloaded the full resolution image and took a closer look. The one on the far-left side, in section H-131, I noticed a mark on the file. When I zoomed in, I found the American flag over the image. Here's a cropped section."

My phone vibrated again and another image came in.

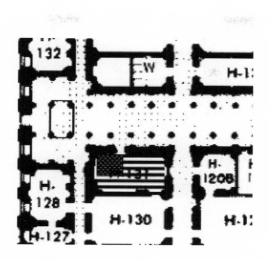

"See the flag over the space?" she asked.

"Yeah, what does it mean?"

"It's the only space that has any unusual marks. I couldn't make heads or tails out of it until I looked at the blueprints on the second floor. That office space is on the first floor, it sits directly below the House of Representatives chamber. I put an X on the spot in the next image."

The third image arrived.

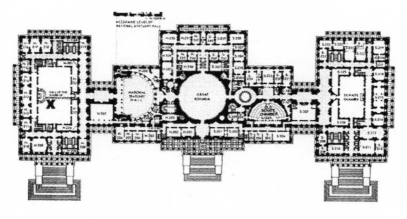

"Give yourself a raise," I told Shreya, "I'll call you right back."

I took my phone downstairs and showed Sam.

"What the hell," he exclaimed and zoomed in on all three images.

"We need to get this to Gilliam in the hospital," I told Sam. "I doubt if the hospital gown thing will work again, we're going to need another way to get in."

I had an idea and told Sam I'd be back in a few minutes to check and see how his cooking lessons were going.

I added, "if I see you wearing an apron, Maria or no Maria, I'm coming after you right here in the kitchen."

"Chicken cacciatore gets you pretty excited" he said, as I turned and walked away.

I know he was watching me go up the stairs. I did my best not to show I knew he was looking, but of course, he knew. It's the game we all play. Men have their own sixth sense, going back to when we were apes. The macho male would watch one of his females climb a tree. She knew he was watching, scratched her butt on the way up. Game on.

I called Shreya back. "Sam agrees. Now we've got to find out if what you discovered on the blueprint means anything. We're going to need Gilliam's help with this. If I can get ahold of his wife I'm pretty sure she'll help you get in to see him."

"Me?" she blurted out, paused for a second and moaned, "I guess it makes sense, he knows we're working together. Want me to try?"

"Yeah, kiddo," I answered. "I do. I need you to go to the hospital, buy some flowers, pretend you're trying to visit your boss. Go today, Okay?"

"I'll let you know how it goes."

The smell of the food was making its way upstairs. I followed it down to the kitchen. Sam was standing in front of Maria chopping garlic. When she stepped away Sam turned around and asked, "How do you like my apron?"

If it wasn't for the knife in his hand, I would have taken him right there in the kitchen between the dishwasher and the kitchen sink. A man who's not shy about putting on an apron and tooling around in the kitchen with a gun strapped to his shoulder gets my vote for 'sexy'.

Good thing I have self-control or Maria would have had an interesting story to tell her daughter.

I WAS NEVER HERE

Chapter 32

We watched Jeopardy until Maria fell asleep in her chair, which Sam and I took as an opportunity to raid the freezer and eat ice cream.

I woke Maria and walked her to her room. Sam grabbed a blanket and slept on the couch. We'd decided getting eight hours sleep would prolong our lives.

The smell of bacon woke me. This had to stop or I was going to eat myself into a fat farm.

My phone rang as I was on my way downstairs.

"I got in to see Gilliam's wife last night," Shreya told me. "She recognized my name and came to the lobby. I showed her the images on the phone and explained our theory. She took my phone to her husband and told me he would call you this morning at 10 AM."

"Were you followed?" I asked.

"Don't think so, I drove to Wal-Mart first and called Uber from inside the store. The driver texted me when he got there and I walked out surrounded by four ladies who believed my story about a man who'd been harassing me in the clothing department. I walked in the middle of the group as they escorted me to the car. I doubt anyone saw me."

"Hey girl, you got some game." I teased her.

"You got another burner phone number for me?" I asked.

She gave it to me and we signed off.

At 10AM Gilliam called. His voice sounded back to normal. "Erica, happy to hear you're still above ground," he said.

"Yeah, same to you Boss. How are you?"

"Better," he said. "A lot better. I'm doing well enough to get out of here soon. I've looked over the images Shreya gave me. It's a pretty big leap to go from a flag on a blueprint to treason, at the highest level. But my gut tells me you're on to something."

"Is this the same gut that has a hole in it?" I asked.

"Yeah, that's the one," he grunted. He wanted to laugh but knew it would hurt.

"You can't take this theory to anyone," he added. "They'll throw you out of their office if you don't have absolute proof and who the hell knows who we can trust."

"Sam and I are safe for now," I told Gilliam and left off the sleeping arrangements. "I have the colonel flying in from California. He should be here in about two hours."

"Ask him to use his contacts to find out if there's been anything unusual at the Capitol building," Gillian suggested. "I've got my laptop here at the hospital. There's a lot I can do here. Be careful Erica."

"I'll get back to you as soon as I find out anything. Take care boss."

There was nothing to do until the colonel would arrive so we ate bacon and drank coffee.

I could get used to living like this - making out on the couch, eating bacon, not working in the mailroom. Did I mention eating bacon?

Sam and I sat by the front window, keeping a lookout for Colonel Mitchell. At 11:35 a car with military plates stopped in front of the apartment building. A man wearing full Marine dress, including the blue service hat with the gold eagle insignia, stepped out of the back seat. Even from the middle of the street the colonel looked in command.

The car stayed where it was with the engine running.

The colonel walked into the apartment building. Fifteen seconds later my phone rang.

"Hello Colonel," I said, "glad you made it safely."

"I'm standing in the hall in front of my brother's apartment. Where are you?" He asked.

"Best not to tell you, sir." I said. "I'm not sure who might be listening or may have followed you."

"If someone is following me or spying on my conversations they better be ready to have a F-16 flown up their backside. I won't stand for any more bullshit. Is that clear?"

I'm sure Colonel Mitchell wasn't talking to me. The idea of a jet fighter doing a colonoscopy was pretty hard to imagine. I did my best to keep it out of my head.

"Do you remember where we first met, Colonel?" I asked him.

"Yes, I do."

"Do you know what direction you were facing when I came into the room?"

"You mean compass direction? Hell no. But I can figure it out."

"Go one mile in that direction. There's a building near there. You'll know you're in the right place because it'll make you laugh. Wait in the lobby."

"I'm not good at this FBI cloak and dagger routine," the colonel told me, "but I'll follow your directions."

Sam laughed when I told him where we were meeting the colonel.

We borrowed Maria's car and left early. We needed to locate a spot where we could see the colonel when he came into the building but not be seen ourselves.

The lobby had hardwood floors with four roped off sections leading to the ticket counters. We bought three tickets and took the stairs to the second-floor gift shop. We could see the lobby from the window. I bought a T-shirt for Maria, 'I WAS NEVER HERE' written on the front.

The colonel walked in at exactly 1 PM. We waited until we were sure he hadn't been followed before Sam slipped downstairs and brought him to where I was waiting in the gift shop.

When the colonel saw me he said, "You were right, I laughed when I found this place; the International Spy Museum', it's definitely you."

I got right to the point "We need your help Colonel," and pulled out my phone. I showed him the blueprint files Shreya had sent me of the Capitol building.

"Can you use any of your military contacts to find out if anything unusual has happened in the building, anything at all?"

I zoomed in on the west end of the building and pointed to the House of Representatives. "Especially on this end," I told him.

"What am I looking for?"

"Our best guess is that something is going to happen Monday night during the British prime minister's speech in front of the Joint Session of Congress. The room with the flag on it is right under the house chamber." I pointed out the flag.

The colonel requested, "Tell me again who you suspect is behind whatever is going to happen,".

"The President and the military," I answered.

He glanced at Sam and then back at me. "I agree something's going on," he conceded. "I suspect it's connected to the death of my brother and the murder of Lieutenant Harris. But the President and the military?"

"General Wallace," I told him, "is part of whatever is going on."

I could see the wheels turning as the colonel stared at me. "Now it makes sense that the general has been trying to stick his nose in Lieutenant Harris' murder!" he exclaimed. Then he asked, "And your source for all of this is General Wallace's son? You said the President is in on this. How do you know?"

The colonel's eyes stayed locked on mine. "This is where your brother comes in," I answered. "Our computer tech at the bureau was able to hack into your brother's deep web content and found encoded data pointing to the President and General Wallace in some form of secret communications. We suspect your brother was trying to get this information out, maybe even blackmailing them. Either way he got caught."

The colonel looked grief-stricken. I added, "Lieutenant Harris must have realized he'd revealed too much in our interview and came back for my phone. When we caught him someone didn't want to take a chance he'd tell us more and ensured his silence with a bullet to his head."

We sat there quietly for a few minutes before the Colonel said, "A four-star general in concert with the President of the United States can do just about anything he chooses. I need to make some calls," he told us and got up to leave.

I handed him a pre-paid phone and asked him to memorize my burner phone number. He repeated it back to me. The grief in his face had morphed into anger as he walked out of the museum. His brother was dead and his Commander in Chief was responsible.

HEAD TO TOE

Chapter 33

Colonel Mitchell made two calls from his burner phone on his way to the Pentagon. The first to his wife of thirty-one years. His next call was to Brigadier General Christopher Jenkins, his flight navigator in the Gulf War back in 1991 and a lifelong friend.

Jenkins answered his phone the same way he always did.

"What?" he growled.

"It's me, Chris," Mitchell answered, "and this is going to leave a mark."

Every muscle in Jenkins' body tensed, the last time he heard Mitchell say those seven words he'd drowned.

*

On what turned out to be their last bombing mission in the first Gulf War, Jenkins was seated behind Mitchell who was piloting their F-14 Tomcat fighter aircraft. On the final pass over their target, they'd taken flak from Iraqi ground artillery and were losing fuel. They made an emergency run back to their aircraft carrier patrolling five miles off the coast of Saudi Arabia. The flak had damaged the hydraulic fluid connector to their landing gear. The wheels were stuck in 'flight position', forcing them to abort the landing. They were ordered to bail out one mile from the carrier and let their Tomcat crash into the Persian Gulf.

Mitchell piloted the plane into position. The procedure called for Jenkins to bail out first. When he pulled the dual levers on either side of his seat, nothing happened. He pulled a second time. Nothing, his ejector seat was jammed. Mitchell circled the carrier twice while Jenkins tried to get the bailout mechanism to function.

Their fuel exhausted, the flight commander ordered Mitchell to punch out on their next pass. A second copter would rescue Jenkins after the plane ditched in the sea.

Both men knew without a pilot the jet would nose dive into the water, killing whoever was left in the fighter.

The colonel disobeyed his orders and flew the plane above the water line, keeping the nose elevated as long as possible. The tail section touched first. The jet skipped once like a smooth rock on the surface before smashing into the water.

Last thing Jenkins remembered hearing before impact was Mitchell saying, "This is going to leave a mark."

The impact knocked both men unconscious, rescue teams had to use a defibrillator to bring the men back to life after their jet sank two hundred feet to the bottom of the Gulf.

Both men stayed in the military rising through the ranks, Jenkins now in command at Quantico marine base in Virginia, Mitchell at Camp Pendleton.

*

"Anything you need brother," Jenkins replied without hesitation.

"Let's talk on a secure line," the Colonel told his friend. "How long till you can access one?"

"Give me twenty minutes," Jenkins told him, "then call me back. How big of a mark is this going to leave?"

"Head to toe," Colonel Mitchell replied and hung up.

MRI

Chapter 34

"The colonel's right," I told Sam after we got back to Maria's house. "A four-star general with the backing of the President of the United States can do about anything he wants, whenever he wants."

"I need a cigarette," was Sam's response as he headed downstairs.

"You smoke?" I asked, surprised by his request.

"Nope, but I used to. I could go for a shot of Scotch too. I could use some calming down right about now. I'm going to ask Maria, she's given us everything she owns - her car, her house, her food, why not some Scotch and a smoke?"

Hell, maybe she has some weed, I thought, as I followed Sam downstairs.

Maria didn't have any cigarettes, or Scotch so we settled for some white wine. And bless her heart, she had a five-pack of Italian cigars her husband had kept in a humidor.

We sat on her back patio and drank the wine. Sam and I shared a cigar and Maria lit her own and told us about her husband.

"My sweet Giuseppe, his heart was bad, he died eating lunch at work. Both of our families came from the same village in Reggio Calabria. We went to the same school, got married and came to America when I just 19 years old. My Angelina was born one year later. We had a good life. My Giuseppe was a good man."

She filled in the rest of her story about moving from New York and settling in Washington, D.C., where her husband worked at Fire Station 11.

"La vita é questa," she said, "this is life."

Maria finished her cigar before going to watch T.V.

It was a warm evening. Sam and I sat on the patio and finished off the wine. I re-lit the last two inches of nicotine left in the cigar and stared at the sky.

I never did ask Maria if she had any bud. My phone rang. It was Shreya.

"Been dumpster diving in the deep web," she announced. "I hacked into Brian Mitchell's account again and followed his breadcrumbs. I was able to open the back door into General Wallace's emails. Looks like he communicated with a few select military leaders, a high-ranking CIA official and several government bureaucrats listed in his database but un-named."

The 'do not trust anyone' was good advice. Whoever's involved in this goes all the way to the top of the food chain.

I took the last puff of the cigar and asked Shreya, "can any of this be proven? Is there any documentation we can use to stop this?"

"Stop what?" Shreya interrupted. "There are no names, only references to positions in the database. And we don't know exactly what's going to happen. These folks are smart. They used the dark web to communicate, but they knew what they were doing. If it wasn't for the colonel's brother leaving enough breadcrumbs for me to follow we wouldn't have anything at all."

"I'm going to get ahold of our boss," I told Shreya, "He's got the contacts we need to stop this. I'm going to need you to pay him another visit and bring him another phone. Go now, we're running out of time."

She agreed and disconnected.

I told Sam what I'd found out and suggested sending Charles back into his father's office to get the recording device."

"It's too soon," Sam said. "We need to wait until Sunday and hope the general says something incriminating."

I couldn't fake any optimism, "This is a long shot, counting on a bug in the general's office."

"Everything about this is a long shot. Let's go inside." Sam said.

We headed back into the house. Maria was in the living room watching Jeopardy. The last category was 'WHAT WOMEN WANT'. Sam got every answer wrong.

He's perfect for me.

Wheel of Fortune was about to start and I was contemplating ways to get Sam upstairs when Shreya called back.

"I just talked with Gilliam," she blurted out. "Says we need to get him out of the hospital, now." She took a breath, "He's been told someone's going to make another attempt on his life. Says he needs to be out of there tonight before the FBI night agent comes on duty at midnight. He gave me the name of his doctor and the doc's phone number."

I looked at my watch, it was 7:44. "We're going to need your help," I told Shreya.

"Where do you want me? The hospital or my office?"

"The office may need you to do your thing online," I told her.

I got off the phone and signaled for Sam to follow me into the kitchen. "Buy a vowel, you idiot," he yelled at the TV as he got up.

"Taking the game a little seriously?" I asked.

"Never watched that show before, I guess I got a little more into it than I should have. What's up?"

"You got any ideas on how we can get Gillian out of the hospital tonight? He believes someone's coming after him again. Needs out of there before midnight."

"Besides pulling the fire alarm, I'm going to have to give it some thought," Sam answered.

I called Gilliam's doctor. He wasn't thrilled that I'd called. I'm pretty sure I could hear 'Wheel of Fortune' in the background. When he heard what Gilliam had told me he agreed to meet us in the hospital parking garage in one hour.

We pulled into the underground lot and parked next to the service elevator. Gilliam's doctor arrived ten minutes later, asked us to wait in our car, and took the elevator. Fifteen minutes later Gilliam and his wife walked out of the elevator. Gilliam was wearing a light blue button-up shirt, two sizes too small and a pair of slacks with the pant legs dragging on the ground.

They saw us and got in the back seat.

"Please, get us the hell out of here." Gilliam requested.

I drove out of the garage and got on the freeway.

"How'd you get away from the agent guarding you?" I asked as I headed for downtown.

Gilliam's wife answered, "He's got a good doctor."

"I've got a great doctor," Gilliam added, "He risked his career getting me out of there. I'm going to need to find a way to make sure he's not fired."

"Your life was in danger," his wife pointed out. "He did what was necessary to save it. That's what Doctor's do."

"Same question boss," I said. "How'd he get you out of there?"

"My doctor ordered an emergency MRI and escorted me to the lab. We switched places. He's the one in the MRI machine wearing my patient gown and I'm wearing his clothes. The agent is still in the MRI waiting room expecting me to come out the way I went in. The agent doesn't know about the doctor's entrance from the other side of the lab."

I had to agree. Gilliam's doctor is great.

I got off the freeway, turned on Connecticut Avenue and drove until we arrived at the motel where we'd stashed Charles. We needed to put Gilliam and his wife where nobody could find them. I parked in the back lot and paid cash for the motel room next to Charles'.

I was breaking one of my dad's rules about putting all your eggs in one basket.

In this case, one of our eggs had been shot twice, the other injected with an overdose of heroin. Our two eggs were now in the same frying pan, just above the flame.

EXPECT THE UNEXPECTED

Chapter 35

"General Wallace, the President is on line two," his secretary informed him.

This was the confirmation call he'd been waiting for.

The general stood behind his desk. He always stood when speaking to the President, even on the phone. Honor, duty, and respect ran deep. He held the phone to his ear and hit line two.

The President's voice came on the line. "Good morning General, I trust you slept well?"

"Yes, sir, six solid."

"The Monday night event, everything in order?" The President asked.

"Yes, sir, everything's in place," Wallace replied. "I will be riding with you and the Prime Minister to the Capitol building and then back with you to the White House."

"Do you anticipate any problems, General?"

"No, sir, but I've made a living expecting the unexpected. It's how I've survived two wars, Mister President. Is there anything else, sir?"

"No, General, God bless you and God bless the United States of America."

Satisfied the general walked over to his Pentagon window and looked out at the light rain falling. A robin, flying too low crashed against the glass. The thud startled the general. He watched as the unconscious bird fell to the ground.

"Always expect the unexpected," he whispered to himself as he watched the bird give its last shudder and die.

•••

GET OUT NOW

Chapter 36

Sunday morning, Maria left for the 8AM mass at Saint Dominic Church. Sam and I skipped church and went straight to taking communion.

I made coffee and we sat outside in Maria's courtyard. I read the front section of the newspaper and gave Sam the sports page.

"Let me know if the Wizards won last night's game," I asked him.

He looked around the edge of the paper at me and shook his head. "You're a sucker for pain," he said. "The Wizards need a point guard who can distribute the ball and a center who can play some 'D'. Until then they don't have a chance.

Sam went back to the paper before he could see the smile on my face.

The plan was… we had no plan. The best we'd come up with was to wait for Maria to return with her car so we could visit our 'two birds in one motel'. Then we'd drive Charles back to the Pentagon to collect the listening device he'd planted in his father's office.

I went up to shower and had just got the hot water going when Colonel Mitchell called my burner. It's time to turn off my phone when I'm about to take a shower.

"I can help retrieve the listening device from the Pentagon," he told me. "We need to meet."

I gave the colonel the address of the motel and the room number. "Let's meet in an hour."

I showered and found Sam talking with Maria in the living room.

"Okay to use the car again today?" I asked Maria.

"Sí," she answered. "My daughters picking me up and take me to visit her bambino."

Sam and I stopped at Wal-Mart to buy a couple more burner phones before heading to our meeting with the colonel. I'd lost count of how many phones we'd purchased. We weren't about to let our guard down.

When we got to the motel we checked in on Gilliam and his wife before going next door to get Charles and bringing him over to their room. We all waited for the colonel to arrive.

Everyone stopped talking when we heard the knock on the door. Sam looked through the peephole and let Colonel Mitchell in. He was dressed in a pair of slacks with a button-down shirt. He had on a baseball cap and looked like your average middle-aged man, not the commander of a military base. Now I know why they say 'the uniform makes the man'.

I introduced everyone. Just your average room full of FBI agents, a cop, a colonel, and a part time heroin user.

"We're going to need you to go back to the Pentagon and retrieve the listening device," I told Charles.

I was proud of him when he didn't puke.

"I know," he answered, "but it's Sunday. My Father may not be there. I won't be able to get in the building."

"I can help with that," the colonel said. "I'll be able to get us in but we'll need some help accessing his office. I've got a friend who can give us a hand."

The colonel looked over at Charles. "Let's go visit your father's office."

I called Shreya after they'd left.

"Can you have Tony on standby to download the listening device?" I asked her.

"I'll call him now," she said, "He gave me his phone number when I saw him last night." She paused. One of those three second pauses which said a lot. If I put it into words, it would go something like... 'I like this guy and pretty soon I'm going to let him know how much and I hope it's alright with you. And yes, I know he's still married, but they're separated which is the only reason I haven't stormed the cotton with him. I'm dying to tell you all the details.'

Not bad for a three second pause.

I said "ah-ha." Then it was my turn to do the three-second pause, which said to her... 'It's okay to like him, but you should wait till he's not married and then you can jump his bones and tell me all the details.'

"Ah-ha," she replied. We both knew the score.

"I'll get in touch with him now," Shreya finally said. "How do you want to get the device into his hands?"

"I'll give it to you to give to him. Don't need any more bodies in this room. I'll be in touch."

It was back to the waiting game. Not my favorite thing to do, but it comes with the job. Seventy-five percent boredom followed by ten percent adrenaline. The last fifteen percent is paperwork.

Sam and Gilliam's wife left to get some food for everyone.

"How you feeling?" I asked Gilliam when we were alone.

"Pretty good for an old guy who got shot. The shooter used a small caliber 22 with a silencer. It's the quietest weapon made. Didn't want anyone to hear. Lucky for me my wife heard me pull in our driveway and when I didn't come in she came out and found me on the lawn. Called 911, told the dispatcher I was the head of the FBI. I heard sirens coming two minutes after she got off the phone. I was going to be released this weekend anyway, but didn't want to find out if someone was coming back to finish the job."

I nodded and asked, "What's going to happen to your doctor? The hospital and the FBI are going to know he was the one who got you out."

"I can take care of the bureau; the hospital is another matter. I'm going to need to prove that my life was in danger and the doctor did what doctors are supposed to do - saved my life by getting me out there."

"Is that true?" I asked him.

Gilliam thought for a second, "Someone left a message on my wife's phone that said, 'They're coming back tonight,' and I needed to 'get out now'. No name, only the message. I wasn't going to wait to find out if it was real."

"Any idea who made the call?"

"No idea. But this 'don't trust anyone' advice seems like it might be working both ways. Do you know what the colonel is planning?" Gilliam asked me.

"Not yet. He's waiting to see what we get from the recording device. Without it, we're dancing in the dark. We have nothing but speculation. Everything is based on a letter and a heroin addict with serious daddy issues."

Gilliam looked angry. "It's no secret the President is fuming over the nation's left turn. The polls show the liberal candidate is going to win in a landslide, giving them a huge mandate. The candidate is running on an open border with Mexico platform, which is the last thing this President wants. The general is one of the President's closest advisors and is as far to the political right as you can get. These two men have been in power their whole lives and are about to be ousted by the liberal establishment they hate the most. History is full of desperate men doing anything they can to stay in power."

"Absolute power corrupts absolutely," I added, and then felt stupid for saying the obvious.

Gilliam sat up higher in his bed and I helped prop a pillow behind him. "We can't just yell out 'conspiracy' and expect to be able to stop whatever shit they're working on," he warned. "We need to find out who's involved and how they intend to do whatever they're planning. So far, the letter's been right. Hell, the closer we get, the more people are getting shot at. This goes to the highest levels of government. Anyone involved will not go down without a fight. And we have no idea who we're fighting. I'm going to take the letter's advice and 'trust no one'."

Sam and Gilliam's wife returned with a shopping bag full of food. I saw a box of espresso chocolate cookie crumble ice cream at the top of the bag.

Sam's a quick learner. Too bad I'd lost my appetite.

SURPRISE

Chapter 37

No one saluted the colonel as he escorted Charles through the maze of hallways at the Pentagon on their way to his father's office.

Saluting a superior officer at the Pentagon would require the lower rank staff to be saluting so much they would never be able to take their hand off their forehead.

General Wallace's secretary was surprised when he saw the colonel standing in front of his desk. "Sorry sir, I wasn't notified you were coming, sir."

"At ease soldier, I'm escorting the general son to see his father. Could you let him know he's here?"

"I'm sorry, sir, the general's not in. He's in a meeting with the President at the White House. I'll contact him and let him know you are here, sir."

"No. It's a surprise visit," the colonel said. "Charles brought his father a gift for his office."

Charles held up the gift-wrapped 11x14 photograph they'd purchased at an art supply store on the way to the Pentagon. It wasn't hard to find a sample image of a woman and a young boy already framed.

"I'd like to hang it in his office as a surprise," Charles said. Would that be okay?"

"I'm sorry, sir. I'm not supposed to let anyone in the general's office when he's not here, sir."

"Sergeant, this is his son. You've met him before, right?"

"Yes, sir. Hello Charles," the secretary said. "How are you?"

"Fine, thanks" Charles answered. "This will only take a second. I'll be right in and out."

A man's voice interrupted them, "Oh, hello colonel," the voice said.

The colonel turned around and smiled at his best friend, who'd arrived right on schedule.

"Charles, I'd like you to meet General Christopher Jenkins. We served together in the first Gulf War. Chris this is General Wallace's son." The two men shook hands.

"We came here to give Charles' father a surprise gift," the Colonel told his friend. "But the general's at the White House. Looks like we're not going to be allowed to go in."

"What did you bring your dad?" Jenkins asked.

"It's a photograph of my mother and me before she died. Here, let me show you."

Charles unwrapped the photo and showed it to Jenkins, careful not to let the general's secretary see the front.

"That's a great shot of you two. Your dad is going to be surprised. He'll love it."

General Jenkins leaned around Charles and looked at Wallace's secretary, "Sergeant, go ahead and let Charles put the photo in his Dad's office. I'll take responsibility. Go ahead and show him in, sergeant.

"Yes, sir, right this way Mister Wallace."

Charles put the picture face down on his father's desk and closed the door. The chair was still in front of the desk. He slid his hand under the armrest. The wood was smooth, too smooth, nothing there. He checked the other armrest, nothing. Fear moved outward from the center of his body. Dizzy, he sat in the chair. His hands shook as he checked again. Nothing. The device was gone. Maybe the cleanup crew had found what they thought was a wad of gum or maybe his father had found it and discovered the listening device. Either way, they were screwed. He tried to catch his breath; he needed to get out of there now. As he stood to leave the general's secretary walked into the office, "Can I get you some coffee?" he asked.

Charles practically leaped the rest of the way out of his seat.

"Sure, yes, thank you, I'm still looking for where I want to hang the picture," he managed to sputter out. "Black please," he added as his heart returned to his chest.

Charles looked around the room. It was full of military paraphernalia. A brass eagle, holding arrows in its claws, sat on a black marble stand by the window. Even the ashtrays had Army insignia embedded in the glass. An American flag hung on a pole to the right of the desk. The clock on the wall, read out in ZULU time. Charles reaffirmed his father had never been his father. He was a four-star general who put God and Country above all else. His mother was dead and he had no brothers or sisters. His uncles had all been military men. That's when it came to him. Both his uncles had retired from the military and taken jobs in the CIA and FBI. This was info he needed to tell Agent Brewer and Detective Marco.

The secretary came back into the room with the coffee in a Pentagon mug and placed it on the desk in front of Charles and left.

Taking the cup, he walked to the window. The office looked into the center courtyard, five acres of trees and manicured lawns surrounding the café called 'Ground Zero'. His father had told him it was the perfect name for the first target the Russians would bomb if war ever broke out.

Charles sat in one of the chairs under the window. All he wanted to do was fill his nose with some brown crystal and sleep for three days. Fuck all of this, fuck his father, fuck the country. Just get out of there. He pushed himself out of the chair and took a half step toward the door, stopped and turned around. Had he felt something with his hand? He looked under the armrest. The gum was right where he'd left it. Someone had moved the chairs around.

With his fingernail, he scraped the gum into his hand and put it in his mouth. He was almost to the door when he remembered the picture sitting on the desk. He grabbed it and walked out the door. Holding it in his hand Charles waved it toward his father's secretary.

"Please don't tell my father, I was here," Charles told him and quickly put the photo back under his arm. "I looked around the room, there's just no place to put it. Probably be a better if I give it to him in person. I'd hate to hang it somewhere he might not like. Thanks for letting me try."

Walking through the halls of the Pentagon, Charles dumped the photo in the last trash bin and walked out into the fresh air. The gum didn't taste as bad this time.

LIE TO HIS FACE

Chapter 38

"Here's what I got from the bug," Tony told the group as he walked into the motel room Sunday night.

"We got close, but it's not enough," he told everyone. "I've edited it down to two of the generals conversations which went beyond the usual back and forth military jargon that flows inside a Pentagon office. The first one is between the general and one of his soldiers. Time record indicates it was the morning after Charles placed the device.

There was a small amount of hiss as the device activated. A voice could be heard saying," Sir, you requested my presence's, sir."

"Lieutenant, were you able to carry out my order? Can I put this matter to rest?"

"No, sir, the target was not at the planned location. We re-conned the area, sir. No joy."

The recording was silent, only the sound of hiss for several seconds.

Tony informed us, "When the unit is activated it leaves a hissing sound whenever there's silence."

The general's voice came back. "Return to your mission this evening at 22 hundred hours and report back to me."

"Yes, sir."

The sound of a door closing. Then the General could be heard saying, "Son of a bitch," and then what sounded like the same door opening. The recording stopped.

I glanced at Charles. His face was ash white, his body trembling as he stared at the floor. I'm pretty sure he was thinking the same thing I was. His father had sent the soldiers out to his house again but couldn't find him. Not sure how I would have taken it if someone in my family was looking to stick a needle in my arm full of heroin for the second time. That would bump them from my shit list to my 'get even' list. Not a good list to be on.

Tony clicked on the second recording. "Good morning Mister President,…yes sir, six solid." A few seconds passed, "Yes, sir, everything's in place," General Wallace could be heard saying "I will be riding with you and the Prime Minister to the Capitol building and then back with you to the White House."

Only the hissing sound for a few seconds, then, "No, sir, but I've made a living expecting the unexpected. That's how I survived two wars, Mister President. Is there anything else, sir?"

A few more seconds of static before, "God bless you too, sir, and the United States of America."

The hissing sound returned, then nothing.

Tony told us, "The last recording took place late yesterday afternoon."

Gilliam looked around the room, "There's nothing we can use to incriminate the President or the general from what I heard. If anyone has an idea of what to do next, now's the time to start talking."

We all stared at each other. A thought wrestled its way into my mind. I finally told everyone my idea. We talked it through till midnight and agreed to meet Monday afternoon at the motel. Come hell or high water we were going to look the President of the United States in the eye and lie to his face.

00200

Chapter 39

I was jolted awake by my re-occurring nightmare. Apparently, my subconscious thought it would be a good time for an encore presentation of my dream with a twist at the end.

Every time I have this dream I'm on the floor trying to see under a mysterious locked door when I sense someone standing behind me. It usually wakes me, but this time I see a man's shoe about two inches from my face coming at me in anger. Scared the crap out of me.

I'm laying here trying to slow my heart down. It's Monday morning and tonight we're going to try and stop the President of the United States from doing … I don't know what. But whatever it is, General Wallace is in on it.

I rolled over and looked at Sam's face, he was sleeping so peacefully it calmed me down.

At 4 PM everyone met in Charles' motel room.

Gilliam got all of our attention, "The President will be escorting the British Prime Minister to the House chamber tonight. Security will be at level three," he informed us.

Sam added, "Officer Stevens, from my precinct, checked to make sure they didn't have an APB out on us. None so far. Our credentials will only give us access to the outside of the Capitol building, Officer Steven's will meet us there."

Gilliam finished off by saying, "keep in mind the Secret Service will protect the President at all costs. They'll shoot to kill if they suspect he's in any danger. All we're trying to do is stir the pot and get the general and the President off whatever plan they're heading toward."

I sensed the metaphorical rope tightening around my neck. My stomach was rolling and my vision narrowed. It reminded me of being shot at. Nothing else mattered. My body was moving toward survival mode. My plan to reveal what we'd learned from the general's son was going to start a shit storm. Good chance it would get all of us sequestered in the Secret Service lockdown facility.

I'd been wracking my brain trying to figure out one more clue, anything we could use to stop whatever the President was planning.

"Shreya, I need one last try." I said into my burner phone, "Can you climb back into the deep web, search Mitchell's logs and see if you can find anything which might relate to what he found out, did we miss anything, anything at all?"

My voice was two octaves higher than usual. I know my fight or flight level was twice as high. There was no hiding this much anxiety.

"I'm on it," Shreya said. "I'll have to hack the registrar again and change the server configuration. Keep your phone nearby."

She hung up before I could say 'what'?

We left the motel and drove back to Maria's. All we could do was wait for Shreya's call to see if she found anything floating in the sludge at the bottom of the web.

Sam and I had decided it was time to stop staying at Maria's home. We weren't going to leave a trail back to her if things went south.

Sam found me in the courtyard smoking one of Maria's cigars.

"I'm going to go inside and talk with Maria. Let her know she can't ever tell anyone outside of her daughter we stayed here."

"I'll wait here," I told Sam, "I'm hoping I hear from Shreya before we need to leave." I pulled him toward me. "I'm scared shitless and pissed off at the same time."

"Ditto," he said and kissed me before walking inside.

The next two hours passed about as slowly as time can move. My nerves were still ping-ponging back and forth as I played out every scenario. None of them ended well.

Hugging Maria goodbye was tough. She cried, I cried. Sam put a good face on it and said he'd be back for more Italian cooking lessons. I called a cab and requested a pick up at a laundromat a mile from Maria's.

Shreya called as we were walking to our pickup spot.

"I only found one thing Mitchell wrote about that didn't mean anything to me when I first saw it," Shreya told me.

"What'd you find?"

"It's a series of numbers on the back of a rootkit sitting inside the server. There was so much data the first time I opened the file I didn't catch it."

"What are the numbers," I asked.

"1 0 0 1 0 0 0 2 0 0 1 0 0 1 0. They were imbedded in the code but it reads as a place holder.

I know a binary code is made of zeroes and ones, but there's this big old number two in the middle of the numbers.

"You have any clue what they mean?" I asked.

"I ran them past Tony. He thinks they're a 15-digit IMEI number. It's a unique identifier number all cell phones have. He tried looking up the number using our internal database, which is supposed to have every IMEI number. He couldn't find that one. There are only two phones that don't have a listed code - the Joint Chief of Staff and the President of the United States. That's all I got kiddo, but I'll keep digging."

"If you find any more numbers, let me know. But for now, go home and sit tight. Shit's going to fly one way or another. There's nothing else you can do."

"Be careful sister," Shreya told me. "I'll be in touch if I find anything else."

MISSING CODE

Chapter 40

By 8 PM Washington was in full swing. The Joint Sessions of Congress were D.C.'s version of the Oscars. Everyone was dressed to the nines, arriving in limos and talking amongst themselves like they were deep in the business of making laws. I was pretty sure they were just trying to figure out who was throwing the best 'after the speech party'.

We'd checked again with Sam's cop friend to make sure we didn't have any warrants out on us. Our credentials got us past the roped off area. We blended into the crowd and looked for Officer Stevens. When she arrived, I had to stop myself from giving her the 'five-second check her out thing'. Jamie Stevens was a knockout even in her cop uniform. Male or female, you were going to stop and look at her.

Sam introduced us as we moved off the steps and into the shadows of the Capitol building.

The protesters were out in force; the usual groups of anti-anything you can think of, holding signs and yelling at the attendees as they pulled up to the main entrance. One of the signs read 'I'D RATHER WATCH SAUSAGE BEING MADE'. I almost laughed.

The local cops were keeping them as far away as the law allowed.

The paparazzi were everywhere, their flash units as welcome as the bathroom light in the middle of the night. The network news anchors were interviewing the lawmakers as they stepped out of their limos. The Capital was in 'party mode'.

I got a call from Gilliam letting me know he was on his way to us. We headed for the rendezvous spot and waited.

My cell phone vibrated. It was Shreya, "I know you don't have time for me to explain," she said. "You asked me if there were any other numbers in Mitchell's files. I sent you the ones I found but I looked again at everything and I found this…" My phone beeped and a text came through:

• 1 • Operation: NSPD51 • 2 • Military control •

• Missing code •• 4 • congress • 5 • assassinations •

6 • trust no one •

I'd already seen this list the first time we downloaded the memory device. I was wondering why Shreya had sent them again.

"When I saw these numbers, I thought they were Mitchell numbering his research areas. But I looked at them again. There's no number 3 in front of 'Missing code'," Shreya told me.

"Why would he leave out the number three?" I asked.

"I figured he'd made a typo, so I let it go as a gaff."

It wasn't much to go on but genius hackers like Mitchell don't make typos. We disconnected.

I called my boss and let him know about the IMEI numbers and the out of sequence numbers Shreya had found.

"Maybe the colonel's brother was trying to tell us something," I told him. "Could be Mitchell's way of giving us the second set of numbers, or it could be nothing."

"I'll be joining you in ten minutes," Gilliam told me and hung up.

We needed to get our hands on the President's phone. I could see it now, "Excuse me Mister President, can I borrow your private cell phone to make a quick call? It will only take a second."

It was almost 9 PM and the crowds were thinning as we moved to the back of the Capitol building where the President was due to arrive.

I saw Colonel Mitchell alongside General Jenkins. Both men in full regalia were coming toward us. My boss arrived a few minutes later.

A presidential motorcade is a choreographed event.

The first limo arrived at the curb; four Secret Service agents stepped out simultaneously. Two moved to the back door of the building the other two waited by the curb. The President's Limo was next, followed by a third.

Four more agents exited the last car and encircled the President's limo. Secret Service Agent Decker stepped out of the President's car, He spoke into his wrist microphone before opening the back door.

The British Prime Minister was the first to step out, The President was next, followed by General Wallace directly behind him. The President straightened his tie as he looked around the area.

My boss approached the agents, never taking his eyes off the President.

"Mister President, I am FBI Bureau Chief David Gilliam, this is Marine General Christopher Jenkins and Colonel Mitchell, Commander of Camp Pendleton. We have reason to believe there is a conspiracy to violently disrupt this Joint Session of Congress."

When the Secret Service agents heard 'violently disrupt', every Agent pulled their weapon and tightened the circle around the President.

Decker recognized me, "What is going on here Agent Brewer?"

This was my plan, and like a lot of desperate plans, it contained a hand full of lies. The ones wrapped in the truth usually work best, mine was wrapped in desperation with a ribbon of truth.

"We caught the man who threw the bomb over the White House fence," I yelled out to Decker.

"Why wasn't I informed?" he barked.

I looked at General Wallace next to the President. He wasn't looking too good. His jaw was clenched and his eyes got smaller as he glared at me. 'If looks could kill'.

"We just caught him moments ago," I lied. "He confessed there's going to be a major disruption during the speech tonight. We pried this information from him a few minutes ago. We're here to protect the President."

Damn, I'm a good liar.

Decker re-opened the limo door, hustled his protectives back inside and slammed the door. The Secret Service detail remained where they were, each agent scanning the area.

Agent Decker spoke to several of his men before turning back toward me, "I want the bombing suspect put into my custody..."

Before he could finish, the back doors of the Capitol building burst open. A stampede of people raced toward us, terror on their faces.

Decker didn't hesitate. "Code Red," he hollered. Tapped on the windshield and shouted 'bunker' to the driver. The limo sped off. Decker ordered his men back into the last limo and sped off right behind the President's car.

I saw Sam making his way through the pandemonium toward the front entrance of the Capitol building. I followed him, Colonel Mitchell right alongside me.

A stampede of panicked attendees raced down the concrete stairs from both sides of the building. Their screams filled the air.

Sam grabbed a man running toward us, "What the fuck are you running from?" he yelled.

"Everyone is dying in there. They're on the ground. Oh God, they're dying." The guy broke free from Sam and kept running.

"He did it," Sam groaned. "I saw the damn president pull out his phone as the Secret Service pushed him into the car."

"Go everyone," Gilliam yelled, "There's nothing we can do here."

I was in shock, my legs were frozen in place. I'd watched General Wallace's face react when I said we'd caught the bomber. He knows we have his son.

"Go everyone," Gilliam repeated. "Go."

•••

From his place on the top tier of the dais, Vice President Bennington had a perfect view of everyone in the room. Which meant everyone had a perfect view of him.

It's good to be king, he thought as he shook hands with the Speaker of the House, *even if it's for only one day.*

Eleven cameras, strategically situated around the House of Representatives stood by ready to broadcast the newly elected British Prime Minister's speech to the Joint Session of Congress.

The American President, not wanting to 'steal the spotlight' had announced he would bring the Prime Minister to the proceedings and then return to watch the speech from the Oval Office. This, the Vice President supposed, would leave him as the most powerful leader in the room.

Spectators lined the back walls and upper level mezzanine in the Chamber. All nine Supreme Court Justices were seated in the front row. On their left sat the top commanders of the Armed Forces and on their right the President's Cabinet.

Behind them the men and woman of both Houses of Congress were taking their seats.

The Vice President glanced at his watch. The Prime Minister would be arriving at any moment.

Straightening his tie, the Vice President leaned back in his chair and relaxed knowing his only job was to applaud when everyone else did and look good for the cameras.

It really was good to be *king*.

A shout rang out from the back of the chamber. "Oh my God, no," someone yelled as a spectator from the upper mezzanine crashed to the floor below. The sound of the body landing on the people seated beneath echoed through the room. The first signs of panic began to ripple through the crowd.

The Vice President climbed to his feet. The shock of what he saw next froze him in place. Bodies, from both sides of the chamber were tumbling to the floor, withering in agony.

A sudden wave of nausea shot through his body, bending him at his knees. The room began to spin. He made an effort to inhale but his lungs burned like fire. The pain dropped him to his knees.

The neurotransmitters in his brain began to overload his nervous system. A violent convulsion knocked him to the ground.

Through blood stained eyes he saw the Speaker of the House collapse to the floor. All his senses began to fade into a gray darkness. His scream, emanating from deep inside his body, went unheard as it stuck in his clenched throat.

The Vice President was melting from the inside out, there was nothing left to do but die.

ONLY THE BEGINNING

Chapter 41

S
ecret Service Agent Decker and three of his men raced the President and the general through the underground passageway to the Presidential bunker in the East Wing of the White House. The door was sealed behind them and the room activated.

Three large-screen monitors lining the back wall flickered to life. A series of communication systems sitting on the large conference table in the back of the bunker was casting a red glow in the darkened room as their tactical systems were activated.

The president stared at the three screens, each one broadcasting the panic taking place in front of the Congress. First responders, wearing HAZMAT suits could be seen running into the building evacuating people from the area. The headline on the bottom of the screen read:

JOINT SESSION OF CONGRESS UNDER CHEMICAL ATTACK

"Raise the volume on that screen," the President ordered one of his agents.

One of the network reporters, standing outside the entrance to the building, filled the screen. "We have just received confirmation both the president and the British prime minister are unharmed. The president has been sequestered in the presidential bunker in the East Wing of the White House. It is not known where the British prime minister was taken. The death toll is impossible to estimate, but the House of Representatives chamber held over six-hundred congressional, judiciary, and military attendees as well as both presidential candidates."

The reporter hesitated, put his hand over his ear to block the sounds of sirens in the background and turned his head to the side. He appeared to be getting new information. Turning back to the camera, he said. "It's been confirmed. Vice President Bennington was killed in the attack. His body is being taken to Washington Memorial Hospital." The reporter paused for several seconds before adding, "A line of ambulances has pulled up to the Capitol steps as first responders are bringing out the bodies of the attendees. There's been no official estimate of casualties, but reports from inside the chamber report that the death toll is staggering."

The reporter was visibly shaken. "This could be the deadliest attack on our nation since 911. The devastation to the governing body of this nation is unprecedented. Our only solace lies with the survival of our President and his ability to lead us back from this disaster."

An aerial view of the Capitol building came up on the screen. The red lights of the responding vehicles dotted the landscape. Television camera lights reflected on the steps of the building highlighting what looked like black spots covering most of the stairs. As the camera zoomed in, the President saw that the black dots were individual body bags waiting to be taken away by the ambulances

The president leaned back in his chair. The sacrifice of the few to save the many, he thought as he turned around to find the general. He'd assumed the general was next to him watching the news coverage. "Where's the general," the President demanded from one of his agents. The Secret Service agent pointed at the entrance they'd just entered. General Wallace was leaning against the concrete-steel reinforced blast door, his hands rubbing his temples, a wild look on his face.

Glancing back at the television monitors the President remembered the encounter at the back of the Capitol building with Colonel Mitchell, General Jenkins, and FBI Bureau Chief Gilliam. How much did they know? And who was the woman agent claiming to have apprehended the White House bombing suspect?

The President continued watching the news. It was critical to know if anyone in the chamber had survived.

This was only the beginning.

TWENTY-FOUR HOURS

Chapter 42

I was in a daze as a human wave poured out of the building, some collapsing on the stairs, others stepping over their bodies, trying to outrun the air itself.

The sounds of the panic invaded my ears. Sam's voice cut through the confusion, "We need to get out of here now," he hollered.

I moved toward him.

Sam called out to officer Jamie, "How'd you get here?"

She pointed to a group of vehicles parked nearby. "Squad car," she answered.

We followed Jamie out to the designated parking area while General Jenkins headed in the opposite direction.

The colonel saw me watching Jenkins, "He's going back to Quantico and I'll be heading back to my base as soon as possible."

Gilliam caught my eye as we made our way through the crowd of reporters and first responders. "I'm going back to the motel," he said. "Then to my office. I'll need every resource at the bureau I can muster; I can do more from FBI headquarters than anywhere else. I'm going to trust no one. I suggest you do the same. Get in touch with me through Shreya in twenty-four hours."

I nodded and kept going.

Sam and I needed to disappear, again.

"Come back with me to my base," the colonel said as if he'd read my mind, "You'll be safe there, while all of this," he pointed at the chaos, "shakes out."

I could hardly see through my tear stained eyes as we climbed in Jamie's vehicle. The loss of life was overwhelming.

It took twenty minutes to get to the motel. Jamie dropped us off and drove back to her precinct. She knew she needed to lay low and say nothing about what she'd witnessed.

I needed to clear my head, figure out what to do next. Going to California with Colonel Mitchell sounded like the right thing to do. But right now, I needed to calm down.

Gilliam's wife greeted us at the door and guided her husband to the bed.

"I've watched everything on the news," she told us. Her eyes were swollen and red.

She handed Sam a set of keys.

"Take our car," she said. "I want my husband to rest. We'll call a taxi tomorrow."

Sam nodded and took the keys. "We need to check on Charles," he said.

"Twenty-four hours," Gilliam repeated to me as we left.

"I want to hear from you in twenty-four."

"I'm sorry," Charles told us as we entered his room. "I am so sorry."

"You did everything you could," Sam told him.

Charles stated the obvious, "It's time to disappear, isn't it?"

"Yes," I replied, "It's time for all of us to stay out of sight. Do you have anywhere you can go?"

"I have friends in California that my Father has never heard of. I can disappear in the Bay Area. I only need a way to get there."

"We can help," I told him. "Stay here tonight and we'll come back to you tomorrow."

Sam asked Charles, "You have any money left?".

"Yeah, I'm good. How about you two, you have a place to go?"

Sam looked over at me, "We'll find a place for tonight," he said, "And be back for you tomorrow."

As we left in Gilliam's car, I laid my head back against the seat and closed my eyes, forcing myself to block out the sound of the screams. I kept my eyes closed and let Sam drive. Fifteen minutes later he pulled over, got out of the car and opened my door.

"Come on, we're here," he explained and led me toward the front door of a small brick house, the porch light was on; Sam knocked. Officer Jamie opened it halfway and said, "I thought you two might be coming back here. Come inside."

DIRECTIVE 51

Chapter 43

"Fifteen seconds. Standby opening, ready one on close-up. Ready two, stand by to roll tape. All mics and cue on my mark... Cue the President in three, two, one...

"My fellow Americans, yesterday's attack, aimed at the heart of our America democracy, was a horrific massacre of this nation's best and brightest. Our prayers are with the families of the fallen who are grasping for answers on this tragic day of mourning. We are gathering the facts."

"Hold, camera one. Stand by to roll tape. Cue tape."

An overhead view of the Capitol building filled the screen. Images from the helicopter circling over the Capitol building showed first responders still dealing with the disaster. Police cars, ambulances, and military vehicles were spread over the entire area. White dots were moving across the steps and in and out of the building. As the camera zoomed in the white dots became identifiable as first responders wearing white protective HAZMAT suits.

The President's voice could be heard over the images; "I've directed the FBI, Homeland Security, the CIA and local law enforcement to identify the perpetrators of this savage attack on our way of life and to bring them to justice. In the face of this catastrophic emergency, I have enacted National Security Presidential Directive 51.

A graphic of the Homeland Security logo appeared on the screen.

The President continued, "This directive authorizes the President to form an enduring constitutional government to preside over the executive, legislative, and judicial branches of the federal government. This constitutional government, under my direction, will oversee the nations day-to-day functions until it has been determined that this crisis has been resolved."

The camera cut away from the video footage and back to the President at his desk in the Oval Office. The camera did a slow zoom backward as the President spoke. "In light of the death of the Joint Chief of Staff, I am appointing four star General Raymond Wallace to command all branches of our military forces. I have ordered all reserve personnel to report to their command stations while we remain at high alert."

The television monitor showed General Wallace standing behind the President. His eyes focused on the President seated in front of him.

"I call on all Americans, to stand together as we face the challenges of the difficult days ahead. We will endure this crisis as we have done since the birth of this great nation. I will leave no stone unturned as we hunt down the perpetrators of this heinous act and bring them to justice. As the facts become known I will broadcast from this office the necessary steps we are taking to protect our citizens. Rest assured we will rise from this assault on our way of life and manifest to the world that America is still the most powerful nation on earth. May God bless you, God bless all of our fallen countrymen and may God bless the United States of America."

"Camera one, stand by for three-second fade to black...cut mic and fade. We are clear. That's a wrap," the control room supervisor called out and removed his headphones.

All the camera equipment was cleared out of the Oval Office, leaving the President alone with the general.

A four-page list of casualties sat on the President's desk.

Ninety-two senators, four hundred and nineteen members of congress, eight of the nine Supreme Court Justices, the Vice President, and every member except one of his cabinet were dead. Every one of his five-star generals had also died in the chamber, along with both candidates for president. The few survivors were hospitalized most in comas.

Leaders from around the world were calling to express their condolences and to offer any assistance the United States might need. The President could hear the apprehension in their voices. Fear of not knowing what America might inflict on the rest of the world in retaliation had the leaders on edge.

The President spun his chair around and looked out the French windows behind his desk. He could see the lush green grass of the South Lawn.

"They're scared shitless," he told the general.

"Every leader in the civilized world is terrified, as they should be. We are about to reinstate this country back to its rightful place as a power to fear. You and I general have saved the greatest nation on earth from a slow spiral march to third world status. You should be proud."

The room was silent, the President circled his chair back around. The northwest door to his office was wide open. General Wallace was gone.

CAPTAIN HOLT

Chapter 44

S am swore at the television and called the President "a piece of shit," before walking outside the temporary housing unit we'd moved into at Camp Pendleton to light a cigarette.

We'd accepted Colonel Mitchell's offer to bring us out to his base. Figured it was our best bet at staying 'out of sight' and alive. Before leaving, we'd scooped up Charles from the hotel and taken him with us to the west coast.

Charles had contacted some of his friends in the Tenderloin district in San Francisco, which pretty much guaranteed that no one was going to find him. We dropped him off at Moffett Airfield in the Bay Area and flew south to Camp Pendleton.

I turned off the T.V. and joined Sam outside. "I'll take a hit of that," I said and took a puff of his Marlboro Red. Sam and I agreed we'd buy only one pack to get us through the first couple of days of the 'post-Washington disaster'. It looked like we'd be breaking that promise; we'd already gone through half a pack on our first day.

Welcome to California, the place to hide from the Feds and start smoking again. Great to be back in the Golden State.

Our two-bedroom condo, located inside the base, came with a jeep, compliments of Colonel Mitchell.

Sam and I hoped no one would be shooting at us like last time. We'd both requested to keep our firearms. Permission granted.

The President's speech had the acid in my stomach churning. We knew he was behind the attack, and now he'd implemented the 51st Directive, giving him complete power over every branch of the government. In one murderous act, he'd eliminated the entire Washington power structure. Without the checks and balances the Constitution provided the federal government, the President was 'King of America'.

I'd studied the 51st directive when I was in training to become an FBI Agent. The President was in complete control of the government until he declared that the crisis was over. Unfortunately, the only person who could decide when the crisis was over and cancel the directive was the President. Someone in the Bush administration didn't think this all the way through.

There was no precedent for this type of disaster. The President now would be making the rules. Special elections would have to be established to replace the deceased members of Congress. The entire Supreme Court would need to be named without a congress to confirm the appointments. Everything was now in under the control of the presidency.

I took another puff and called my boss from a burner I'd bought at the base commissary.

"What are the odds your phone is tapped?" I asked Gilliam when his secretary put me through.

"Zero," he said. I had Tony Hayes from surveillance encrypt my phone with software as secure as the Presidents."

"That's one phone I'd like to tap," I told Gilliam, "In fact, I'd like to 'tap' the President and the general."

Gilliam let me rant for a couple more seconds before informing me the FBI had been put in charge of the investigation.

I let it soak in for a second, "The President's that confident they won't be discovered. No doubt one of our 'Mid-Eastern enemies' will be blamed for the attack. He'll send in the troops and level their capital. The rest of the world will sit by and let it happen. No one wants to mess with the angry eagle when it's revenge time." I needed another cigarette.

"The President believes he's gotten away with his attack," Gilliam said, "If the general's son goes to the press he'll be painted as a gay heroin junkie who hates his father so much he threw an explosive over the White House fence. They'll put him on trial for committing a terrorist act and lock him up forever. The President and General Wallace aren't afraid of us, but don't let your guard down for a second."

Gilliam was right; Charles was damaged goods, easy to vilify. He was the center of our case. If he was discredited, we had no proof.

"Charles is confident he can stay hidden," I told Gilliam. "We need to find a way to prove it was a conspiracy between the President and the man he appointed the head of the entire military. Any ideas about what Sam and I can do to bust this piece of…"

"Hey," Gilliam cut in. "I know how you feel. They tried to kill me too."

Damn, I hadn't even asked my boss how he was feeling.

"How were you physically able to do what you did the other night?" I asked. "Confronting the President?"

"I'm fine. Like I told you the small caliber bullet passed through my right shoulder. I'm pretty sore, but I'm doing alright. Besides, we've got the best medical doctors in the world."

No shit, I thought. Take a body shot and you're back at work in four days. American medicine is the best. Can't live without it, can't afford it.

215

"Sam and I are going to see what we can dig up here," I told Gilliam. "The colonel's investigation of Harris' murder might tell us something. Why are you so confident the President isn't going to go after you? We told him we'd captured the bomb thrower. He's got to know it's the general's son. Why isn't he going to come after you?"

"My guess is he wants Charles dead first. It makes sense. No Charles, just a crazy conspiracy charge. No proof. But it goes both ways. You can't arrest the head of the FBI without cause. He'll play cat and mouse with me, pretend I don't have anything I can prove. And he's right. I've got security 24/7. I'm safe. One hell of a letter you found in the mailroom last week," he added. "Every time I look at my scar I'm going to think of you. Let me know what you find out."

My boss was right. The letter had changed everything. I was smack dab in the middle of a conspiracy, living on a Marine base with a man I was falling in love with. Throw in the cigarettes and you get the bad with the good.

"Let's go see the colonel," Sam said as he walked into our cinderblock accommodations. "We need to dig into what happened when we were here last. Maybe find out who took out Harris and tried to end both of us. If nothing else, I'd like to stick my gun in the 'perp's' face to see how he handles it."

Looks like Sam and I were riding the same motivator. Payback.

On the drive to the colonel's office, I caught a glimpse of an F-22 fighter jets sitting on the tarmac. I'd love to catch a ride in one. Like Maverick told his buddy Goose in Top Gun, 'I got the need for speed'.

As we drove through the base I could smell the ocean. The base practically sits on the beach. Highway 5 separates the 125,000-acre facility from the water. A hundred thousand soldiers occupy this complex along with sixty thousand civilian personnel on a daily basis: Colonel Mitchell's in command of them all.

We parked in front of division headquarters and took the stairs to the second floor. The colonel's secretary showed us in.

"You two settling in?" The colonel asked.

"Sir, yes sir," I said.

Not really… but I did nod my head.

The colonel slid a manila envelope across his desk,

"Here's the file from Lieutenant Harris's murder investigation. Whoever pulled the trigger was a professional from off base, not one of my soldiers."

Sam asked, "What makes you think so, Colonel?"

"Harris was shot in his right temple. You both were secondary targets, the wall separating the dining area from the kitchen saved you two. Ballistics' reports show the shooter was using a modified .22 caliber Ruger. Your statement of 'only hearing the window breaking, not the sound of gunshots' indicates the killer used a silencer. It's not a weapon we use here, not even close. This is an assassin's gun, made to be used at close range without being heard. The gun and the ammunition were brought onto the base from the outside and whoever fired it was trained in its use.

"It's possible whoever shot Harris may still be on my base," the colonel said.

"Is there a way to find out?" Sam asked.

The colonel turned his computer monitor toward us. We could see a live shot of the front gate.

"I've got the video footage of the base's four entrances for a week before and every day since the shooting. It's being scrutinized. Our visitation rules are extremely tight. A visitor needs to be sponsored by an authorized person and have a valid reason for being on the base. Thousands of people come and go every day. We're crosschecking to see who came in but hasn't left the base. No leads yet, but my men are still looking."

"How much authority do we have here, colonel," Sam asked. "Can we question someone without going through you? What's our status on base?"

"I'm assigning you both Marine Corps law enforcement credentials. You both can carry a concealed weapon and make an arrest. You don't need my permission to interview anyone, I'll notify our MP's of your status today."

I asked the colonel, "What's come down the military pipeline about the Washington attack?"

"We're on 'Stand by Alert', with 'Readiness for Action Operations in hand'." The colonel pointed at the top of the monitor, red letters read; 'CONDITION: DEFCON 3.

"We haven't been at DEFCON 3 since 9/11," he told us.

The colonel turned the monitor back and looked at us.

"The general saw me at the Congressional building the night of the attack," he explained. "He knows we're investigating the murder of Lieutenant Harris at this base. Once he gets his bearings, he may turn his attention to me. For right now it's my base but he has the authority to remove me. Knowing what I know I won't let him. That's when we step off the cliff and all hell breaks loose."

This was turning into a bad movie, I visualized Bruce Willis stealing a jet and attacking Washington. Bombs going off everywhere, the music pounding and everyone but Bruce dies.

I couldn't help myself and asked, "What would happen if you refused to step down as commander of this base?"

His phone rang, which startled the bejesus out of me.

The colonel answered, listened for a few seconds before hanging up.

"That was Captain Holt," Mitchell told us, "head of my MP unit. Says he has something on our investigation. You two follow me," he ordered. "And as to your question about refusing to step down... never has happened in the history of our military. So there's your answer."

Three hundred pounds of muscles tucked into an MP uniform was waiting for us as we arrived at the Command Center. Holt saluted the colonel as we got out of the Humvee. The veins in the MP's arms reminded me of tree roots as they twisted their way around the tattoos running from his wrists to the edge of his camouflaged shirt. A Beretta M9 in a drop leg holster was strapped on his left side, a leather Billy-club on the other.

We followed him inside and stopped at his computer station.

Holt pointed to a man's face on the monitor. He was sitting in the driver's seat of a black Escalade, "Sir, this image is from our surveillance camera at the San Luis Bay Gate. He's not regular personnel, sir, nor is he a soldier stationed on this base. We can't find any video footage of this man leaving the base, sir."

"Let me see his entrance pass," the colonel requested.

The MP handed him a sheet of paper. The Colonel placed it on the table where we could all see it.

- DoD Uniformed Service Identification:
- CAC Army Major Franklin Parker.
- Purpose for visit: Observation – Training facility
- Duration: Open

"Where was he housed?" the colonel asked.

"Area 14, top floor of Barrack 19, sir."

"Good work, Captain. Please bring the master key and accompany us to his barracks."

"Is that all the identification this Major Parker needed to get on base?" Sam asked Holt.

"No, sir, he would have had to show his photo identification card which would have been scanned and run through the database before he was permitted to enter."

"Can you access that information, Captain?" I asked.

"Yes, ma'am."

It finally happened. Someone called me 'ma'am' without it sounding like an insult. I almost replied, "good work 'Captain', but let it pass.

Holt printed out the identification card before we left. It had a photo of Major Parker printed in the corner. He looked to be in his mid-forties. No smile, no expression at all, clean-shaven. He looked pretty un-impressive except for his eyes. He had dead eyes, blank like he was a quart low on blood. My Dad used to talk about people with those eyes, said they were the most dangerous. He called them 'deadeyes walking'.

I looked at the ID print out again. He looked familiar. I'm pretty good with faces, but this wasn't someone I'd met. Damn for a second I felt like I'd seen him before.

We drove to Area 14, took the stairs to the second floor of barrack 19. Colonel Mitchell knocked on door G-3, then stepped aside and let Holt open it. I would have normally had my gun out, but this MP was a loaded weapon on two legs.

The room was empty. Clean as a whistle. No one had stayed here, or if they had, they'd put it back together like a hotel maid. Not a dish in the sink. I looked in the bathroom. The toilet paper roll still had a folded V. I looked in the sink and the shower. Not a hair.

"Our Major Parker is either the cleanest human being alive or he's never stayed here," I said.

"Where the hell is he?" The colonel cursed. "Captain, I want this man found and detained. Report back to me the minute he's in your custody."

No one spoke on the drive back. We dropped Holt off at his post and drove back to the colonel's office. We grabbed the file on Lieutenant Harris and headed back to our condo.

"Did you see the guns on that MP?" Sam asked as I drove through the base.

"Those weren't guns," I giggled, "They're grenade launchers with hands attached at the ends."

Sam didn't even laugh, "Seriously, that guy must live in the gym," Sam gushed, "I'll bet he eats raw meat and sleeps standing up."

"Maybe you two should get a room," I suggested.

I'd pretended long enough, "That guy scares me," I said. "And at the same time makes me feel safe. You venture he's hitting the steroids? I mean, how do you get your body to look like that?"

"You mean like this?" Sam said and flexed his muscles. Held the pose as long as he could and started laughing.

"Yeah, just like that," I lied, and remembered Sam saving my life on the kitchen floor a week ago when Harris was killed. I forgot about Mister America's muscles and started remembering Sam's soft kisses. I pushed my foot on the gas and drove like a cop's daughter back to our place.

THOSE EYES

Chapter 45

The clock read 6:42 AM. I could hear the sound of the shower coming from the bathroom. I closed my eyes for just a second, and woke at 8:15.

I put on the bathrobe I'd bought at the base commissary and followed my nose to the smell of coffee.

"Morning," I greeted Sam as I walked into the kitchen. The Harris homicide report was open on the kitchen table next to him.

Sam looked at me in my robe and did a double take.

"You like the look?" I asked.

I could see he was trying not to laugh, "As a matter of fact, I do, especially the big yellow flowers printed on the front. Turn around let me see the back."

I put my hands above my head and did a pirouette.

"Wow, more yellow flowers," he chuckled.

"How about now?" I said and showed a little cleavage then spun around one more time.

"Got to love those flowers," he smiled. "Want some coffee?"

I pointed to the report. "How long you have been reading that?"

He got up and poured me a cup. "About an hour."

The coffee tasted okay, but I was missing Maria's blend. "What do you think?" I asked him.

Sam's mood changed. "We need to speak to Harris' wife, find out if the local law enforcement missed anything. Something on the cell phone recording was damaging enough that they ended Harris' life and tried to do the same to us. Didn't you send the recording to Shreya for her to go through?"

"I never sent it." I told Sam. "After Harris was shot we spent the night being interrogated by the locals. Then we were put on a plane back to Washington. I never got it to Shreya. It was the same phone we trashed after the bread truck chase. How could I be so stupid? Why didn't I send it to Shreya right after we interviewed Harris?"

"Because we were still planning to interview some of the other techs the next morning," Sam reminded me. "Nothing like someone killing your suspect and then trying and kill you to make your brain miss a detail."

I'd messed up and Sam was being easy on me. If he'd done the same thing he'd be kicking his own butt up and down the block. Why didn't I just…?

"Wait a second," I said. "I sent myself an email with an attachment of the recording after we interviewed Harris, right after he left the colonel's office. I do that sometimes so I can run the recording program through a voice translation and not have to transcribe the file by hand."

"Which email, work or personal?"

"Work."

I grabbed the laptop we'd bought at the commissary and logged in to my account. I found the email and opened the attachment. It was kind of eerie, Harris' voice talking to us like he was still in the room talking geek-speak.

"I'm going to get this to Shreya right now and have her take a listen. See if she can find anything." I sent the file.

Sam stepped outside, I thought he was going to smoke a cigarette, but he just sat on the three concrete steps the military calls a front porch.

I walked out front and stood behind him.

"I sent the file," I said, "Let's go see Mrs. Harris."

I drove. Sam didn't say a word on the way over.

Harris' wife answered the door. Her eyes told me the kind of pain she was in. These were eyes you pray you never have to wear.

She invited us into the kitchen. We both refused the coffee, she offered.

"You know who we are, Mrs. Harris?" I asked her.

"I do," she answered. "Please call me Ava."

I nodded.

Ava explained, "I was told my husband had broken into where you were staying. You were questioning him when it happened."

"That's right," I said, "He'd come for my phone. We believe it was because of what we recorded with him earlier in the colonel's office."

I've interviewed the loved ones of victim's before. It comes with the job. But this felt different. I was part of the reason her husband was dead. You're supposed to lock out your emotions, listen to your brain not your heart. I was trying, but her eyes...

"What we're trying to find out now is, why?" I asked, and added "this is one of those times when we have to ask if there was anything, even the smallest thing that sticks out in your mind. Not only the night it happened but at any time did you feel your husband was different, nervous or afraid?"

Ava's hands were shaking. She got up and walked to the window.

"My husband loved his work as a technical analyst. He was considered to be one of the best in the Marines."

"Did you ever see what he was working on? Did he ever talk to you about it?"

"Sometimes. Most of it didn't make a lot of sense at first, but after a while the language started to sound familiar. We've been here almost four years. The first couple of years he'd tell me what he was working on. Then around Christmas time two years ago he started keeping his work to himself. It bothered me and we talked about leaving the Marines and going into the private sector. But he insisted we stay a little longer."

Ava paused for a second, I thought she might cry, but she turned and looked at me. "The night my husband was killed he was scared," she said. "Told me to stay at home, not to open the door for anyone but him."

"Do you know why?"

"He wouldn't tell me. Just repeated not to open the door and left."

"You say it was about two years ago things changed?" I asked. "Is there anything you can remember happening around then? Were there more phone calls? Did he stay at work longer?"

"He got quiet," she answered. "At first I thought he'd done something wrong at work and was too embarrassed to tell me. But he refused to talk about it. Sometimes he'd be fine for months and then back to moody."

"How many months apart?"

I glanced over at Sam. He was taking notes and I could tell he was going to let me do the interview.

"I don't know," Ava answered. "I haven't thought about a time frame." She sat quietly looking at the floor. I let her think. Something was pinging in my memory and I wanted to let it come to the surface.

"Maybe six months," she finally said and looked at the floor again.

"He'd be distant for a couple of weeks, then slowly come out of it. This happened, maybe every six months or so. We have two kids and he loved playing with them, but that would stop when he was down."

"You said he was scared that night and told you not to let anyone in. Was it the same kind of upset he showed every six months?"

"No, this was different. He was scared, scared. Like I told the police, he got a call on his cell and was gone within a half hour."

"You have any idea who called him?"

"No, but he didn't take his phone with him when he left. I gave it to the investigators."

I looked over at Sam, "Anything you want to ask Ava?"

He shook his head and looked at her before saying, "We are so sorry for this tragedy, for you and your children. Thank you for talking with us." We both stood to leave. It's not in the rulebook, but I couldn't help myself and gave Ava a hug.

I re-read the police report as Sam drove back to our place. I found the logs for Lieutenant Harris' cell phone. The last call he'd gotten came from the phone in the mess hall and lasted less than two minutes. I pulled up the calendar on my phone. Ava said it was about every six months her husband would climb into his 'quiet self'. The first time was around Christmas. I looked at the calendar, six months later would be June or July and then six months later Christmas again. I told Sam the interval. "Call the colonel," he suggested and rolled up his window so we'd both be able to hear.

I put the phone on speaker and dialed.

The colonel's secretary put me through.

"How many times did your brother come out to visit you in the last two years?" I asked.

"Three or four I guess, why?"

"You said he came out on his vacations. Was it during the summer?" I asked without answering his 'why'.

"Yeah, and a couple of times during the holidays. Where are you heading with this?"

"Sam and I just interviewed Ava Harris. She mentioned her husband would have mood swings about every six months. Acted like he felt guilty about something, but a couple of weeks later he'd be back to his old self again. She was pretty sure it was during the summer and around Christmas. You said your brother came to visit at those same times. We need to check the visitor logs and see who else came during those dates, starting with our missing Army Major Franklin Parker."

The colonel was silent for a moment. I could hear him take a deep breath, "Give me a few minutes. I'll have the records checked. Call you right back."

"What do you want to bet Major Parker was at this base every time the colonel's brother was here?" Sam asked me. It was time to get Major Parker in an interrogation room.

My cell rang. It was the Colonel calling back. "Major Parker was here every time my brother came to visit."

That did it. I was right in the middle of saying, "It's time to find this Major…" when the colonel interrupted me. "Hold on a second," he said. A minute later he came back on line. "I just ordered an ad hoc emergency base drill. All personnel not at alert stations are required to return to their dorms. My MP's will be waiting for Parker to return to his room."

The sirens were blasting all around us as we pulled up to our condo.

"You're hearing the Mass Notification System," the colonel told me over the phone. "In a few seconds you'll hear a GV over the exterior speakers, then an IV over the interior speakers ordering everyone to their stations."

"What's a GV? I asked.

"Giant voice," he answered. "IV is internal voice. "I'll contact you as soon as we locate Major Parker."

An announcement replaced the sirens, "All personnel report to station one."

No one was going to sleep through this drill.

Sam and I sat on the steps watching the base turn into a flurry of activity. Soldiers moved in double time heading for their posts. The barracks around us were filling up with personnel. The colonel ran a tight ship; everyone was on the move. Ten minutes later everything slows down. It was like a whole city was coming to a complete stop. I wanted to drive over to our missing soldier's assigned quarters and watch Captain Holt scare the crap out of Major Parker. As fun as that sounded the only thing we could do was wait for the colonel to call.

TWISTED

Chapter 46

S am turned on the TV while we waited to hear from the colonel. 'ALERT STATIONS' ran across the bottom of the screen, Sam flipped on the news.

The anchor was a gorgeous blond, looked about thirty-five, wearing a red sweater with just enough cleavage to tease but not enough to complain about. Her red lipstick matched her sweater. She read the teleprompter like she'd been doing it her whole life. I gave the woman kudos for getting the gig and wished I could afford her $600 sweater. A live image of the President came on the large screen behind the anchor.

"Mister President," red sweater said, and turned toward the monitor. "It's been thirty-six hours since the attack. Can you tell the American people the current state of our government? How is the chain of command being handled?"

"Sally," the President replied, apparently they were on first name basis.

"The authors of our constitution barely touched on this possibility. The Bush administration, after 9/11, formulated these protocols in the event our government was decimated. Under the National Security and Homeland Security Presidential Directive 51, this office is authorized a new enduring Constitutional Government. In consultation with the surviving members of the House and the Senate, as well as the judiciary I have begun the process of establishing a new constitutional government. In light of this unimaginable tragedy, I want to assure the American people that our government is up and running. The perpetrators of this attack will be apprehended and brought to justice."

The President's face changed when he said this. His eyes formed two narrow slits and he stared at the screen like he was talking to the perpetrators - and in a twisted way, he was. "My administration is formulating a plan for new nominating conventions to replace the Presidential candidates who were so brutally taken from us. It will take time to put this in place. I will have more information on this in the near future. I believe our nation will endure this crisis and rise up stronger."

Red sweater 'Sally', looked at her desk, like she was fighting back tears. Then she looked at the monitor. "With the loss of your Vice President," she asked, "have you given any thought to whom you will appoint?"

"Yes, I have Sally. It's imperative we have a successor if something should happen to me…"

"Something is going to happen to you," Sam yelled at the television.

"… it is paramount this nation has a strong leader who can take on the task of rebuilding this government. I will make an announcement in the next couple of days."

Sally had managed to not let any tears interfere with her makeup and asked the President, "is there anything you would like to say to our nation, to help us all through this historic moment?"

"Only to pray for those great men and women who as President Lincoln so nobly put it, 'gave their last full measure of devotion'. God bless you, Sally, and God bless America."

"Thank you, Mister President, and we'll be right back after these messages."

"We need to bust this piece of trash," I told Sam, "before he hand-picks a new vice president. Someone needs to stop him, but everyone's dead."

"Not everyone," a voice said behind us.

We turned around, Colonel Mitchell was standing in our open door-way. Probably wasn't too impressed a detective and an FBI agent had just been snuck up on from behind. "We found Parker," Mitchell, said. "Want to go have a chat with him?"

WATCH

Chapter 47

The brig was housed in the same building as Captain Holt's command center. We pulled up in the colonel's jeep and walked inside. Holt stood at attention.

"At ease, Captain," the Colonel ordered. "Bring Parker into interrogation room one."

"Sir, yes sir."

Two guards stood at attention at either end of the green painted cement hallway. They saluted the colonel as we walked past. Every inch of the place was painted the same 'Army' green. A metal table and three chairs sat in the middle of the interrogation room. It was claustrophobic and cold. The walls felt wet.

I looked above the table expecting to see a single light bulb hanging from the ceiling, but instead four florescent light fixtures were bolted to the roof, adding even more of a greenish cast to the room.

I now had a least favorite color.

A one-way mirror filled the back wall. No one can accuse the military of overspending on decorations.

"You two 'do your thing', the Colonel told us. "I'll be watching and listening from in there." He pointed at the mirror and left the room.

Sam and I sat with our backs to the mirror and waited.

The door opened and Holt walked in with his prisoner.

I was surprised Parker wasn't in handcuffs. Then I took another look at Captain Holt and understood no one was leaving the room without his permission.

Parker was wearing standard Army fatigues, his military rank sewn on his sleeve. He looked in his mid-forties. Short hair on the sides, longer on top. Six feet two or three, square chin with eyes that had seen their share of combat. He knew the drill and sat.

I'd seen him before. I don't know where but damn his face was familiar.

Holt stood in front of the door. Like I said no one was leaving without his permission.

I introduced myself, "Major Parker, I'm FBI agent Brewer, this is Washington D.C. Detective Marco. We're investigating the death of Lieutenant Harris. The main gate log indicates you've been on this base for the past six days. What was the reason for being here, sir?"

"Read the gate report," he growled and stared at me.

He didn't know staring back was a hobby of mine. No way I was going to blink. I don't care if my eyes dried out like prunes and my eyelids stuck to my pupils. Without looking away, I said, "observation at the training facility. It also says you were housed in Area 14, barrack 19. Sound about right Major?"

"If that's what it says," he replied. He kept staring, but I was a pro. I could tell he wasn't used to having a female hold his eyes this long. I had him and he knew it.

"Why didn't you sleep there?" I asked."

It was time for him to lie. His eyes gave it away and he shifted his gaze downward.

"Where were you when Lieutenant Harris was shot," Sam asked.

"Who the fuck is Lieutenant Harris?" Parker yelled and looked past us at the one-way mirror. "What is this?" Parker barked, "Crime Story?" and coughed up a laugh,

"What a joke!"

"Answer my question Major, where were you?"

"I don't know anyone named Harris. So if this is about someone named Harris get me the hell out of here." Parker stood up to leave. I could see a tiny smile cross Captain Holt's face. I was pretty sure Parker saw it too because he returned to his chair.

Sam asked again, "Where were you Major, at 2:20 AM five nights ago, and who were you with? If you tell me you were sleeping, I'm going to ask you where, because it sure wasn't in barrack 19. Please stare at me like you were with Agent Brewer. I'm curious what you look like when you're lying. Right here, Major." Sam said, and pointed at his eyes.

Parker looked at Sam, crossed his arms over his chest and looked over at me. He realized that wasn't going to do a lot of good and looked at the table.

"I want my JAG," he hissed. "I'm not saying another word to you ass-holes until my JAG gets here."

I wasn't surprised when Sam leaped over the table and tackled Parker to the ground. The pain in Harris's wife's eyes was still gnawing at me, too.

The two shots Sam landed had Parker bleeding from his nose. I watched him wipe the blood with his sleeve as Holt separated the two men.

The door opened and the colonel came in the room. "No JAG," the colonel told Parker. "You're going to answer the detective's question. We're at DEFCON 3. You get a lawyer when I say you get a lawyer.

Parker's expression didn't change. It was going to take more than a couple of face shots before he'd be giving up his secrets. I'd noticed something on Parker's arm when he was wiping the blood off his face. I needed to check on it before we questioned him any further.

"Colonel," I interrupted, "Let's give the major a chance to jog his memory and wipe the blood off his face while we have lunch. Watching an asshole getting his butt kicked makes me hungry."

The colonel looked at Parker, "Good idea. Keep our prisoner in here until we get back," he ordered Captain Holt. And give him something to wipe his face with."

We drove back to the colonels office.

"Can I see the 'gate report' again?" I asked as we walked up to his office. He handed me the file, then called his secretary. "I want a full dossier on Army Major Franklin Parker as quickly as possible... Yes, I'd like hard copies."

I read the gate report again, then asked Sam, "The night Harris broke in and took my phone, you had Harris on the floor at the bottom of the stairs and told me to go after the guy who had run out the front door."

"Yeah, I'll always remember, you were only wearing your gun."

I'm impressed that he'd noticed I had a gun in my hand.

Sam finished saying, "You told me the guy got away in a black sedan, but it was too dark to get the license number."

"That's right," I said. "But before he made it to the car something shiny on the guy's left arm caught the streetlight. It was too small to be a gun, but I remember the reflection."

Sam asked the colonel, "Does gate security take photos of the vehicles as they check in?"

"We have multiple video cameras running 24/7."

"How long do you hold onto the tapes?"

"180 days."

"We need to check the time Major Parker checked in."

Fifteen minutes later we had the video footage and a dossier on Parker's military background. The colonel handed us each a set of hard copies of the dossier then played the gate video footage of Parker entering the base. A time stamp under the image showed the hours, minutes and seconds as we watched a late model black Chrysler pulled to the gate. An arm came out the driver side window and handed the soldier on duty an identification card. The soldier saluted and waved the car through.

"Stop," I said and pointed to the monitor.

"Can you run it back again," I asked the colonel.

He did.

"Stop right there!"

The image froze as the man's arm came out of the window.

"Zoom in on his arm."

We watched, as the camera closed in.

"He's wearing a watch," I said. "It's one of those extra-large watches. This one looks like it's silver."

"When Parker wiped the blood off his face," I told Sam and the Colonel, "I noticed he had a large white patch, on his left arm, right where you'd wear a watch. Let's see if Parker was wearing one when he was taken to the brig."

The colonel called Captain Holt and asked about the watch.

"Thank you, captain, we'll be back within the hour."

"Oversize silver watch was taken from Parker when he was brought in," the colonel told us.

"If this was the guy who broke into our condo with Harris and drove away in the Chrysler, then who shot Harris?" I asked.

Sam looked at me. I could tell his brain was working overtime. We'd both figured Parker as the shooter.

"He could have doubled back and opened fire," I said. "There was enough time before we started questioning Harris."

"Let me see the dossier," Sam asked.

I handed him a copy and kept one for myself.

Army Major Franklin Parker was an Army brat. His father had been a Lieutenant Colonel in the Army Special Forces. He'd served three tours in the first Iraq war before retiring.

Major Parker attended Command and General Staff School in Kansas, and was stationed at Fort Myer in Arlington, Virginia, the same base as his father. His current assignment was listed as 'O/R military training facilities.

"What is O/R?" I asked the colonel.

"Observe and report," the colonel answered, "It's a standard assignment. The officer travels to several military bases to survey the training methods being used and reports back his findings to his commander. We do the same thing, with Air Force and Navy facilities."

"What's this?" I asked the colonel and pointed at the second page of Major Parkers report.

"That's an itinerary of the major's travel."

I pointed to a travel log. "What does TR-11- C-40 Andrew 3x Rt Pen. stand for?"

"TR-11 is our internal memo for short term travel request. This one was to Andrews Air Force Base aboard a C-40 transport and a return to this base three days later."

What dates were they for?" I asked the colonel.

His face turned dark. "The same date I flew out to the claim my brother's body and the same date I returned with you two on board."

That's where I'd seen Parker. He was one of the soldiers returning on the transport. Just another face among the forty other soldiers on board.

"He was in Washington the whole time you were colonel. What was he doing?" I muttered.

The taxi with no advertising and my open refrigerator popped into my head. Did this shithead break into my apartment? I looked over at Sam. I could tell he was traveling down the same path.

"Can we go one step deeper?" I asked the colonel. "Can we see the military dossier on Parker's father?"

The colonel typed in the father's name. An eleven-page PDA popped up on his monitor.

Skip down to his tours in the first Iraq war," I asked.

There it was. General Wallace had rescued Parker's father from behind enemy lines and saved his life. After the war, both men had been stationed at Fort Myer. The dots were lining up. Grateful soldier becomes indebted to his rescuer. Passes his loyalty to his son. Time to go back and have another chat with Major Parker.

"Did you feed him?" the colonel asked as we walked into the building.

"Yes, sir. Brought it to him in the interrogation room, sir."

"Good. Let's see how fast his digestive system can push the food to its eventual end," the Colonel replied. He led us to the holding cell, Holt right behind us.

"I want to call my jag," Parker said as we walked in. "Want my phone call."

"And I want to come over the table at you again," Sam said. "But were both going to have to live with the disappointment."

"You drove a black Chrysler onto the base. "Where is it?" I asked Parker,

"I'm not telling you shit, bitch," he said and took a sip of his water.

At least he got my nickname right.

Holt wasn't too happy about the way Parker responded. I could tell by the way he smashed the plastic water bottle out of the majors hands and picked him off his chair. The colonel didn't say a thing as we watched his MP slide Parker up the wall.

"Please be more careful with your choice of words when answering Agent Brewer's questions, Major. Am I making myself clear?" Holt asked in a calm voice, which was kind of strange seeing as he had Parker three feet off the ground.

Parker nodded his head.

Major Parker wasn't a small man. His military file said he'd been a soldier for over twenty years. I doubted a detective or an MP had ever smacked him around before.

I was about to ask if he was going to cry and decided to hold my smart-alecky remarks for later.

Captain Holt placed Parker back in his chair and I repeated the question.

Before he could answer I decided to cut the 'slow walk' and speed up the game.

"I saw the wristwatch you were wearing when you ran from the condo where Harris was murdered," I told him, "It's sitting in your personal belongings. You came here in a black sedan, the same black sedan I saw that night. I'm betting if we drag you in front of Harris' wife she'll report seeing you with her husband at some point in the last two years."

I was about to ask him about his three days in D.C. but decided to hold it for later. We had something else.

"We also know your father was indebted to General Wallace and you've been working on a special project with Harris. We know everything Major, including your connection with General Wallace. So, let's cut the crap and end this charade."

Parker flinched when I mention his father. He was looking less and less like a soldier and more like the cat who ate the canary and still had feathers stuck on his face. I'm sure his lunch was trying to figure out which way to go, north or south.

The colonel leaned forward on the table as Holt took a step closer and put both his hands on Parker's chair. "What the fuck were you working on with Harris?" the colonel demanded.

"Computer shit," Parker grunted. "And before you get all 'holier than thou; colonel, your brother was right there working with us the whole time. Hell, he was the mastermind behind everything. So back the hell up, all of you. I was following orders. Tell your dog behind me to get his paws off my chair."

The colonel glanced at his MP and nodded. Holt took two steps back. The colonel was working the interrogation like the FBI. When a perp starts pissing information, you take a step back and give him room to spill everything out on the floor."

"My brother is dead," the colonel shouted. "Major Harris is dead. Over five hundred members of congress are dead. Our country is under attack from within, and you're standing right in the middle of this shit hole…"

A knock on the door caught us all by surprise. Holt opened it, and listened.

"Sir, I've just been informed General Wallace is waiting for you in your office, sir."

For the first time since we'd arrived on base the colonel looked caught off guard.

"General Wallace is in my office!" the colonel hissed.

"Well, isn't this one big happy family. Let's all go have a chat with the general."

MAYBE LESS

Chapter 48

General Wallace was staring out the window when we walked into the colonel's office. He was wearing his full military uniform covered in medals. The largest being the two-inch round insignia of the Chairmen of the Joint Chief of Staff hanging below his left pocket, over his heart.

The general turned around as we walked in, "Why did you order a lockdown on this base, Colonel?" He demanded.

Colonel Mitchell ignored the question, "Why the hell are you here, General?"

"I asked you a question, Colonel," the General snapped. "I'm ordering you to answer it immediately or I'll have you court martialed."

The two men stood face to face. Sam and I were in the back of the room with Captain Holt, all of us listening to the sound of oversized military brass balls banging into each other.

It was the colonels turn to swing. "General, we have Major Parker in the brig. He's being held on multiple charges, including treason. The base was put on alert for the express purpose of capturing him. Now answer my question General, why are you on my base?"

The general adjusted his jock and fired back. "You are one step from being arrested for insubordination, Colonel. I am Chairman of the Joint Chiefs of Staff, appointed by the President. This is not 'your' base, Colonel, it is mine. I am ordering you to release Major Parker to my custody immediately."

"Not going to happen, General, I do not recognize your authority. You were appointed to your commission by a treasonous President and have conspired with him for the sole purpose of remaining in power."

General Wallace's eyes were locked on the colonel's. There was enough heat coming off the two men to melt snow.

"Arrest the colonel," the general ordered. "And throw him in the brig."

Holt stood at attention and didn't move a muscle; his eyes stared straight ahead.

"I just gave you a direct order soldier. Arrest the Colonel."

Holt didn't move.

I wasn't sure how this was going to play out. The highest-ranking General in the military had given an order to a subordinate who ignored him. Holt didn't even blink.

The colonel turned toward his MP, "Put the general in interrogation room two."

"Sir, yes sir," Holt answered and moved toward the General.

"You will be hung for treason if you take one more step in my direction," General Wallace hissed. "Am I making myself clear soldier?"

"Sir, crystal clear, sir. Now please turn around and put your hands behind your back, sir."

The general took two steps backward. Only two thin slits for eyes stared at Holt. His lips were pushed together so tightly they disappeared.

Holt took the last two steps and stopped in front of the general, his voice almost a whisper, "Turn around, General. Now," Holt ordered.

I've never heard a whisper with so much menace before.

You could see the shock on the general's face; he stood frozen in place. It didn't matter. Holt spun the general around like a toy top and cuffed him.

"Gag him," the colonel added. "And have him sit."

Holt walked into the office bathroom. He came out with a towel and stood in front of the General. "Open your mouth, General." This time the general obeyed.

Holt put an inch of the towel in the general's mouth and wrapped the rest around his head, tied it in a knot and put the Chairman of the Joint Chiefs of Staff in a chair in the back of the room.

"There are two soldiers waiting for the general in my hallway," the colonel told us. "They're not going to like seeing their commanding officer being taken to the brig in handcuffs. I need them gone long enough to get the general out of here. I'll be right back," he said and walked out the office, shutting the door behind him. I could see the General flinch when the door closed.

Thirty seconds later the colonel was back. "I sent them to the mess hall to bring back some lunch for the General and myself. We have fifteen minutes to get him out of here. I'll need to be here when the soldiers come back with the food. You three need to take the General to the brig without being seen."

Holt stood the General up and walked him to the door.

"I need one of you to keep the colonel's secretary busy while I walk the General out the back entrance," Holt requested.

"I got this," I told Sam. "You get the jeep. I'll handle the diversion. What's your secretary's name?" I asked the colonel?"

"Private Connor."

Connor was typing on his keyboard as I came out of the office and walked to the far side of his desk where he couldn't see the colonel's door.

"I've got a question," I said and leaned on his desk.

Connor looked at me, and then back to whatever he'd been working on. He couldn't care less I was in the building. Great, now I want a guy to notice me and he couldn't care less. Holt saw I wasn't getting anywhere and moved the general back into the colonel's office. I had to say something so I asked, "Where's the ladies room?" He pointed down the hallway.

My mom had taught my sister and me how to walk like a model. I figured this was a good time to pretend I was at the Paris fashion show and strutted toward the ladies' room. I glanced back, Private Connor hadn't even looked up. Desperate I banged against the wall and fell. Connor saw me sprawled on the floor and rushed over. I glanced the opposite way and saw Holt was almost to the back exit with the general. He needed a few more seconds of distraction. I wobbled to my feet with the privates help and gave him a hug and whispered, "It's shark week."

The general was in the backseat of the jeep by the time I got there. I climbed in the front next to Sam as he drove to the back entrance of the brig. Holt led us to interrogation room two and took off the general's gag and handcuffs. He pointed to the chair behind the table.

"Do you need some water General?" Holt asked.

He nodded. Holt left to get it.

General Wallace sat straight in his chair, trying to look calm as if he was in charge. But he was anything but calm. He had a panic shudder he couldn't hide. He was freaking out about something besides the way we'd treated him. He glanced at the door and shuddered again. He tried to mask it, but I'd been trained to look for 'tells' in interrogation sessions. This one was deep.

"I recognize you two," he blurted. "You were at the back entrance of the Capitol building when the President arrived with the Prime Minister. You were with the Colonel and General Jenkins."

"You're right, General," I answered. "And we're the ones who found your son, almost dead from an overdose of heroin your soldiers tried to kill him with."

His look changed. "My son," the general exploded, "My gay, drug addict son. And what lies did he spew out to you. What bullshit story did he tell you?"

Now it was my turn to want to jump over the table to back-knuckle him. I held the thought. "He confessed to throwing the bomb over the White House fence. Said you forced him or you'd kill his lover. How's that for openers?"

"And you believed him," he cursed. "You took the word of a sissy, queer drug addict? What in God's name is wrong with you? Do you have any idea the hell you are about to experience? The President of the United States has ordered our defense readiness at DEFCON 3, and you are placing its highest ranking general in the brig because of what a drug-crazed addict told you after almost overdosing on heroin?"

"That's exactly what we're doing" I screamed back at him.

The door opened and Colonel Mitchell motioned for us to follow him out into the hall.

"The Pentagon is aware the General is out of communication and has ordered his men to make contact," the colonel told us. "I can't hold them off much longer. When they find out he's missing, they'll notify their commander, and this base will be ordered locked down until the General is found."

"What happens if you refuse the order, Colonel?" Sam asked.

"We'll be in unchartered territory," he said. "If the President orders it, the military will obey. They could attempt to take this base by force."

"How long before an order like that would be carried out?" Sam asked.

"Twenty-four, maybe thirty-six hours," he answered. "Maybe less."

360° SPIN

Chapter 49

My heart was doing a drum solo in my chest. "Calm down," I told myself, 'think'. Which is easier said than done when you just locked up the Chairmen of the Joint Chief of Staff in the brig.

Another idea did a 360° spin around my brain. The last one hadn't worked out so well. I wasn't overflowing with confidence.

I walked outside and thought about smoking a cigarette, decided it was a bad idea and put it back in the pack. "Calm down," I repeated to myself.

"You, all right?" Shreya asked when I got her on the phone.

"No," I heard myself say before I'd had a chance to put on my happy voice. "Good chance I'm not going to be able to take you to dinner until I get out of a military prison in about a hundred years."

"You're not getting out of dinner that easy," she said, "You already owe me a 'make-up' dinner and drinks cause our last meal got interrupted by gunfire."

"Yeah, I remember," I said. "Something about jumping out of a moving bread truck. You got to admit you weren't bored."

"Bored, no. Nervous breakdown scared, yes. What can I do to help?" Shreya asked.

I explained my idea and told her I needed an answer ASAP, "You're either a genius or a nut job. We'll see," she said and hung up.

I told Sam my plan and watched his body language.

"That's crazy enough to work," he said.

Forty-five minutes later Shreya called.

"Your idea is in play. He'll be there in the morning," she told me, "And he'll have what you asked for. Talk with you tomorrow."

"It's a go for 'mission impossible, part ten," I told Sam and took another look at the pack of smokes.

"We've got to quit smoking when this is over."

He laughed, "What makes you think this is ever going to be over?" And fired up the last one in the pack.

You got to love his sense of humor.

HAIR ON FIRE

Chapter 50

The Gulfstream landed at 7:45 the next morning on the base's airstrip. A single passenger de-planed and was driven to the colonels office where Sam and I were waiting.

"Thanks Tony," I said as he walked in and gave him a serious hug.

"I hope to God this works," the colonel said. "Let's see it."

Tony took a small box out of his pocket and put it on the colonel's desk.

I opened the box and took out a two-inch Joint Chief of Staff medal and laid it on the table next to the one we'd pull off the General's coat after he'd been put in the brig.

They were identical. Four gold swords crisscrossed under a red, white and blue banner which attached to a circle of silver wheat shafts. The name Joint Chief of Staff was engraved in black letters on gold ribbons under the banner.

The idea first came to me when I saw General Wallace in the colonel's office. He was wearing all of his accolades on his chest. The Joint Chiefs of Staff medal had caught my eye. This medal signified that general was the second most powerful man in America. My fear factor had my ears' ringing, that's when the idea hit me. This was our way to get into the Oval Office, maybe catch the President and the general incriminating themselves.

Tony pointed to the insignia. "I had our engineers put the recording device under the center banner. It'll record continuously for seven days with an audio pick-up range of ten feet. I still have to make several adjustments before you put it on the general's coat."

Tony reached in his pocket and pulled out two cards. They looked like a couple of credit cards with the Visa logo and the name 'gift card' written on the front. "This is what you'll need to download the recording. Like I said you'll need to be within ten feet of the medal for the information to download. You have to push on the logo to activate it. The logo will change color and turn red when the files have been downloaded. It'll take about five seconds to complete the file exchange. There are two cards, one for each of you, just in case."

Tony looked at us like he was sorry he'd said that. "I'll need the card back when you're done, to download it," he explained. "I'll have the recording in your hands in under two hours."

"What's the impedance value of the interface?" Sam asked Tony.

I rolled my eyes and waited. They'd already bonded over insulation. Now they will have cemented their relationship over impedance. I wasn't going to sit this one out.

Tony grabbed the device, "I'll know after I set the data-byte transfer rate with a second set of signal lines and run a parallel function analysis."

Sam looked at me and said, "He wants to test it."

"Of course, he does," I answered, "What did you suppose he was going to do? Run an envelope-delay past the intermodulation component? Everybody knows that wouldn't work."

They both looked at me like my hair was on fire.

"You're freaking scaring me," Sam said. "Where'd you learn to talk geek?"

"I can hang with the propeller heads," I told him, which is a total lie. But I work for the FBI. A lie is only a lie if you get caught, until then it's a 'useful tool'.

"Whatever needs to be done, needs to happen now," the colonel added. "General Wallace's men have reported their commander missing. I've been instructed to call another base shutdown."

"What happens if you release the general?" Sam asked.

"I get court marshaled," the colonel answered. "And the base gets turned over to another commander. The new commander will have you two arrested for conspiring to commit treason and the country goes back to exactly what the President and the general want it to be."

I visualized myself in prison, my tattooed cellmate smiling at me.

"And if they find out the general's in the brig, what will happen?" I asked.

"My best guess is an army infantry division will be at our doorstep," the colonel answered. "Then it comes down to my soldiers' devotion to me and how badly the President wants the general back."

The colonel took both medals and put them side-by-side. "I can't tell the difference," he said and started pacing around the room.

We all waited while the colonel circled the room. Finally, he said, "I'll release the general to his aides, then escort them off the base with this on his coat," and held up the fake medal. "Then we stand by to see how far the general is willing to go in terms of court-martialing me and arresting you two."

I'm pretty sure the colonel would have preferred locking General Wallace in Guantanamo prison for his part in his brother's death, but duty before revenge was in his DNA.

He handed the medal back to Tony, "Get this ready as soon as possible."

The three of us left headquarters and headed for the condo. No one spoke. Everyone's brain was in overdrive. I figured there would be a good chance the General would meet with the President after what happened here. Whether or not they would say anything incriminating was another story. But we'd never know if we couldn't figure out how to get close enough to retrieve the audio files. I tried to focus, but my brain kept coming back to my future cellmate.

As soon as we got back to the condo, Tony and Sam started working on the listening device in the kitchen. I stayed outside and called Shreya.

"Anything you'd like to share?" I asked her when she answered, my woman instincts were percolating.

"Tony and I worked together last night on the listening device," she answered, "It's my fault he didn't get it finished. We sort of got caught up in something else."

I laughed. Sex 'now' always overrides sex 'later'.

She read my laugh and tried to change the subject. "I found those files you sent me from the Harris interview."

I knew I was in for a 'hacker talkfest'. I tried to open my mind.

"What'd you find out?" I asked her.

"Brian Mitchell had a backdoor on his email, hard coded to a CT domain," she explained. "The onion protocols are not as anonymous as you think, so I was able to get in."

I rolled my eyes and let her get it out of her system.

"Once I rewrote the rootkit I was able to access all his traffic. But my system was too slow. I needed a fiber connection with gigabit speed. Our boss used his connections to get me in to use the computer system at the University of Maryland's Condensed Matter Theory Center. I had to utilize a brute-force attack with their fastest interface to get me in long enough to download several files before one of the guardians crashed the host."

I glanced at my watch, that was enough 'hack speak'.

"What'd you find?" I interrupted.

"The general was paying Brian Mitchell to hide his communications with several high-level government personnel. The general also made several 'deep web' purchases using Mitchell as a buying agent."

"Do you know what they bought?" I asked.

"Not yet. The purchases were reconfigured, but hackers love attention and I'd bet Mitchell hid an access code in one of his servers. I'll keep looking."

I thought for a second, then asked, "What can you tell me about the general's communications?"

Shreya was quiet for a second. I could tell she was trying to tell me in words I'd comprehend.

"First off, the general paid the colonel's brother over four hundred thousand dollars in crypto for his work. Second, he must have had help getting the secret passwords from the military. Third, I'm pretty sure the government has successfully built a secret quantum computer."

"Thought you said it wasn't possible?"

"You can fill a dump truck with the things I'm wrong about," Shreya admitted. "There's no way they could have secretly commanded this much bandwidth without nanospeed throughput. I only got a glimpse before I got cut off, but the access level they were communicating at was at the bottom of the net."

"What do you mean 'bottom'?"

"That's the only way to describe it. Envision it like the ocean. Ninety-five percent of the world's internet users access the top eight inches of the water. The rest of the web goes all the way to the bottom. Picture how much information is down there. The deeper you go, the harder it is to access. The general, with the Brian Mitchell's help was scraping his belly in the sand at the bottom. The computing power necessary to go that deep is quantum level. There's no way I can hang with them. Beside that's where the deep-sea guardians are monitoring the bottom.

"Deep-sea guardians, what planet are we living on?" I babbled. "So, we either get you on a quantum network or we get squat?" I asked.

"Bingo," she answered.

"So, the government has one?"

"It must. The general got down there."

I thought about it for a second, "You said the colonel's brother had help getting the secret passwords from the military. I'm pretty sure he got them from someone on this base. Keep looking at the Harris interview I sent you, and I'll see what I can figure out from here. Thanks kiddo, I'll get back to you later."

I walked back into the kitchen. Sam and Tony were tinkering with the listening device.

I got Sam's attention, "Remember when we interviewed Harris in the colonel's office when we first got here?"

"Yeah," he answered and took out his note pad. "What do you need?"

"Didn't you ask Harris if the Colonel's brother had spoken to other members of the computer staff."

Sam looked over his notes, "Yeah, said he'd spoken to another member, but he didn't give us the name. We were going to interview him the next day, but Harris was murdered and we were ordered back to Washington."

"Bet I know who knows the name of the other tech Harris was working with," I told Sam.

"Me too," Sam answered. "You drive, we'll get there faster."

<u>KANO</u>

Chapter 51

P arker was in his chair in interrogation room one, Captain Holt by the door.

"One question, Major. Who else met with the Colonel's brother when he visited the base?" I asked.

"Why the hell should I tell you?"

I'd noticed Parker flinched when we mentioned his father's name in our previous 'chat'.

"Your dad looks to be a co-conspirator in this plot," I deadpanned.

Parker stood up slowly. "My Dad had nothing to do with any of this, leave him the fuck out of it." Parker growled.

I'd obviously struck a nerve. I was a little shocked. Figured Parker was dead inside, but there it was a soft spot.

"No, Major, we're not going to leave him out of it," I threatened. "No one is going to be left out of it. I don't care how far down your family tree we have to go. You're going to answer my questions."

Like I said earlier, 'a lie is a lie only if you get caught'. I was more likely to be thrown in jail than the asshole in front of me. Parker didn't know I was spewing bull and I sure the hell wasn't going to tell him.

"Get the colonel in here," Parker growled, "If I'm going to make a deal it's going to be with him, not you two ass….." Parker didn't finish his nickname for us. Good chance he remembered what Holt did to him last time he was rude.

I stepped out into the hall and called the Colonel, told him what was happening.

"Be there in ten," he said.

When I stepped back into the interrogation room Captain Holt had Sam in one hand and Parker in the other. Both men were two feet off the ground with their backs pressed against the wall. I thought about asking what happened, but it was such a display of physical power I just sat speechless in my chair and waited for the colonel to arrive. My guess would be that Sam and Major Parker had another difference of opinion. It didn't appear Holt was going to let either guy down until the colonel arrived so for the next ten minutes we sort of 'hung out' together.

As soon as the colonel came through the door, both men were allowed to stand on their own two feet. My money's on both men behaving for the rest of the interrogation.

"I want my family left out of this, Colonel," Parker demanded and looked at me. "I will answer her questions, but I need your word colonel that my family will be left out."

"You have it, Major. Tell us who else was working with my brother."

Parker glanced over at me, "Kano was the only other computer tech who met with the colonel's brother."

This was the first time I'd heard that name, "Who's this Kano tech? Does he work on base?" I asked.

"He's one of mine," the colonel answered. His voice revealed disappointment that another one of his men had conspired with General Wallace.

"I worked with him a couple of times," Parker added. "Smart technician knew his stuff. Computer Specialist, Lieutenant Kano."

The colonel looked back at Parker. "Why you?" he asked. "Why did General Wallace come to you?"

"The general saved my father's life in the first Gulf War. My dad believes he walks on water. The general came to me, told me how he risked his life to save my dad. Slowly brought me into his inner circle."

"Tell me about my brother. Why did the general want him?" the colonel asked him.

"Your brother was known in the hacker world as SG-3. The same designation is given to the deepest hole ever dug in the earth. Your brother was one of the first hackers to write an encryption code when the deep web was forming. Nothing on the web is deeper, which is where the nickname came from. It's the ultimate hacker handle. Your brother memorized his entire code then destroyed every trace of it. He was so far ahead of everybody else he became a legend, but he never revealed who he was. SG-3 was the legend without a face. But like every hacker, he left a backdoor."

"What's so special about an undetectable encryption code?" I asked Parker, and added, "Why'd the General want access to it?"

I'd already figured out it was to cover for what the President and the General were planning, but when a perp is talking you keep him talking.

Parker looked back at me. I tried to wipe the 'I hate your guts' look off my face. There might be something he'd say I could pass to Shreya to help her access the hidden files.

"Cipher communications," he answered. "The military has been throwing billions of dollars at making a fully capable quantum computer. They succeeded two years ago."

Shreya was right.

Parker continued, "The President assigned the general to oversee its implementation. Using the quantum computer, they were able to hack into your brother's deep site and followed the backdoor back to him. When the general found out you were his brother, he put large amounts of money in bitcoins into a secret account in your brother's name and blackmailed him into coming out to this base to install the system. Your brother didn't know what the general was planning. His job was to embed his encryption code into a secret military database. The people who had access to your brother's source code would be able to communicate without being caught. That's when your brother realized he was no longer needed. He figured you could be easily framed for being his accomplice in stealing government secrets from your base, Colonel, which would have gotten you court-martialed and sent to prison. Your brother chose to die before he'd let that happen."

The colonel kept staring at Parker, finally got up and left the room. Two minutes later he opened the door and signaled for us to join him.

"Time to let General Wallace go. We're going to let Major Parker leave with him."

I could see Sam's body tense. He still wanted Parker for Harris's murder and like me, couldn't get Harris' wife's eyes out of his mind. Letting either of our prisoners go was the last thing I wanted, but it was the colonel's turf and his call.

"We need the listening device in place before we let them go," I said.

"Your agent is bringing it here now," the colonel replied, "He's done testing it. As soon as it's on the General's coat, I'm going to release them both and escort them off the base."

Sam asked, "What are you going to tell them about why you're letting them go?"

"I'm not going to tell them anything. I'm going to put them in a military transport and let their paranoid egos fly back to Washington. If we're lucky the general and the President will communicate in person and we'll get an incriminating conversation."

A door at the end of the hallway opened, I could see Tony coming toward us. He had the General's coat under his arm.

"All set Colonel," Tony said as he arrived, "The device is activated and live for the next seven days. We used the same pinholes in the coat."

"Put the general's coat back in the holding room and return it to him as he leaves," the Colonel told his MP.

I knew the colonel's plan was necessary, but letting them both go felt like a kick in the stomach. Sam didn't look too happy either.

"Why both of them?" Sam asked. "I get the point why you're letting the general go, but we've got Parker as our number one suspect in the murder of one of your men."

"We still need more proof," the colonel replied. "And the general came here to bring Parker back with him. If we hold Parker here I'm pretty sure the general will come back for him and he won't come alone. I don't want a shooting war with our own armed forces. My men will defend this base if I order them to. The Civil War was the last time American soldiers turned on their own brothers and sisters. I don't want it to happen again."

"Can I have one more 'chat' with Parker before you release him?" I asked. "Maybe get a few more answers out of him."

The colonel nodded his head, "Do it now, agent, before I go back in to see the general."

"He's going to try to court-martial you colonel, for detaining him," I reminded him, "And I'll bet he'd like to put Sam and me in front of a firing squad."

"I will not let that happen. I will do whatever's necessary to protect you both. I won't fire the first shot, but no one is coming on this base without my permission. No one."

HAMMER-71

Chapter 52

"I didn't sleep worth beans last night," I told Sam as I sat up in bed. "Yeah, I noticed," he answered. "You got up three times."

"You heard me? I was as quiet as a mouse." I said. "I'm sorry I woke you."

"You didn't wake me," Sam replied, "I was awake most of the night. I'm still pissed we had to let Parker go. I want him in my Washington interrogation room. He not only killed Harris, but he also tried to get rid of us too. I get in a bad mood when someone is shooting at me and the woman I'm falling in love with."

He was about to say something else but I didn't give him a chance.

"I was checking my phone," I told Sam over coffee. "That's why I was up so many times last night. I wanted to see if Shreya had texted me. She does her Internet thing at night. So, I turned off the ringtones on my phone so they wouldn't wake you, and kept checking my phone."

The irony didn't escape me. Sam and I were drinking our coffee, lying in bed on a Marine base. The President of the United States was about to order us both eliminated to hide his treasonous attack on our country, and all I could think about was how much I was falling for a Washington detective. Crazy how things get put into perspective.

I checked with the colonel. He had nothing new to report after releasing the general and Major Parker so Sam and I took the half-mile walk to the ocean. The sun was out. The seagulls were riding a five-mile-per-hour ocean breeze. There were only a few people walking along the shore. Welcome to the Left Coast.

We headed south and came to a pier some creative city councilman decided to name 'Ocean Pier'. It traveled straight out to sea for a quarter mile.

We walked to the end and ate at Ruby's restaurant. Sat out on the deck and had a beer with lunch. I almost forgot I was an FBI agent. We didn't talk much as we looked out over the water, finished our lunch and kept going south with our shoes slung over our shoulders and our pants rolled up. Right out of a date movie.

So, this is California. I get it. I was tempted to keep walking till we hit Mexico.

My cell phone rang.

"I got something," Shreya said. "I found Mitchell's back door. But I keep crashing the host. You said Harris worked with another Marine tech?"

"Yeah, Computer Specialist, Lieutenant Kano."

"I need to talk with him," Shreya said, "as soon as possible. He might know which access port will get me in."

"I'm on it," I told her. "Get back to you as soon as I have Kano in a room."

We got off the beach and took a cab back to the base.

"We need your Lieutenant Kano to talk with my FBI computer tech," I told the colonel when we got to his office. "And he's going to have to answer her questions about what information he gave your brother, even if it's classified."

"If he gave out classified information," the colonel told us. "He'll know he's going to be court-martialed, so he's not going to be cooperative."

"We don't have time to mess around waiting," Sam said, "Kano needs to talk."

The colonel told his secretary to get Lieutenant Kano to his office and then made another call before hanging up.

Two MP's escorted Kano into the office and stood at attention in front of the colonel's desk.

Kano was a short man, maybe five-five, or five-six. His head was shaved and he had the biggest nose I've ever seen. The Colonel let him stand there for a full minute before looking at him.

"Lieutenant Kano, you are under arrest for disseminating classified information and for treason."

The blood drained out of Kano's face, except his nose, which turned bright red. His shoulders slumped, and I thought he was going to pass out.

The colonel called his secretary, "send in Captain Holt."

Now I knew who the second call had been too.

Holt looked bigger than the last time I saw him. His arms barely fit in his shirt. His six foot eight body towered over Lieutenant Kano as he stood at attention and saluted the colonel. The two MP's were sent out of the room.

"Captain Holt, Lieutenant Kano is being charged with treason, and I want you to lock him in the brig and stand guard over him in his cell. Do you understand what I am asking?" the colonel said, his eyes never leaving Kano's face.

"Sir, yes sir," Holt answered. The edge in his voice sounded like sandpaper rubbing over broken glass.

"We know everything," the colonel barked at Kano, "and I personally hold you responsible for my brother's death."

The Colonel came out from behind his desk and stood two inches from Kano's face.

"I'm going to give you one chance to do what I ask before I lock you in the brig with Captain Holt."

Kano was visibly shaking. At first, I thought the Colonel was just trying to scare Kano into doing what we needed, but the vibe in the room was so full of menace I could almost taste it. All of the fury and pent up emotions of the last couple of days had brought the colonel to the point of no return. He wanted blood for his brother's death and Lieutenant Kano was catching the full force of his anger.

"Sit," the Colonel ordered and pointed at a chair in the back of the room.

"What do you want me to do, Colonel?" Kano asked.

"You're going to talk to a computer expert and you are going to answer every question she asks. Even if you think it incriminates you."

Kano put his head on the table. We could all hear him sobbing.

"Are you ready to make the call?" the colonel asked.

"Yes," he whispered between breaths. "Colonel, I want you to know that when I realized that FBI Bureau ChiefGilliam was in danger at the hospital, I was the one who notified him to get out."

"That was you?" I asked.

Colonel Mitchell stared at Kano, and didn't say anything for a few seconds.

"You may have saved yourself a lot of grief, Lieutenant."

I called Shreya and handed Kano the phone. They talked for twenty minutes before handing the phone back to me.

"Did he give you what you needed?" I asked Shreya.

"I've got the key to the back door, it's going to take some time to read through what I find. I'll call you tomorrow."

"Hawaii," she told me before signing off, "Daiquiris with little umbrellas in them. That's where I want to go for drinks."

"Deal," I said and hung up.

I nodded to the Colonel.

"Captain Holt, escort Lieutenant Kano to his quarters and post a guard at his door," the colonel ordered. "You are confined to your room until notified. You will stand trial for your actions, but I will testify at your hearing about your co-operation. Dismissed."

I could see the relief in Kano's face as he was escorted out of the office.

"That went easier than I thought it would," I told the Colonel.

"Captain Holt commands a lot of respect around here. I thought his presence might speed things along."

"What would have happened…" I was asking when the windows started to rattle. A half second later a thundering roar, coming from straight above us, dropped me to my knees. For a second I thought a bomb had exploded. The rumble kept growing. We all stared at the ceiling.

"That's a fighter aircraft below a thousand feet, "The colonel yelled above the noise.

The colonel's secretary burst into the room.

"Sir, General Wallace is at the main gate, demanding you turn over control of the base. He has a full Army battalion with him, sir."

"You two follow me" the colonel ordered and ran out the door, Sam and I right behind him. We followed him out the main doors, across the street to the command center. We could still hear the roar of the fighter jets.

Two armed guards saluted as the colonel led us in. The two-story structure looked identical to the Colonel's building until our eyes adjusted to the darkness.

The entire room was full of personnel sitting at monitoring stations. The front wall was covered with several high-definition screens. The center one displayed a close-up image of two-fighter jets backlit against a blue sky.

"Those are the two F-18 Hornet's that buzzed the base," the colonel told us. "Show me the front gate," the colonel ordered. A live image of the front gate came on the screen to our left. I could see several Marines standing at the entrance, blocking an Army jeep from moving forward. The Marines had their hands next to their sidearms, which were still in their holsters.

"Pull the camera back and give me a wide angle of the gate," the colonel directed.

As the camera zoomed outward we could see at least a hundred vehicles spread out around the perimeter of the base.

"Show me the rest of the gates."

The screen switched to a view of the remaining entrances. Each gate had several of the colonel's Marines blocking the entrance. One of the outer screens switched to a super-wide-angle view of the entire base, including the area outside of the fences. A full regiment of Army soldiers in battle gear surrounded the base just outside the fences.

"Commander," one of the techs called out, "the two Hornets are about to make another pass, sir."

"I want four 1-Z Vipers air born in two minutes, and stand by to launch two F-22 Raptors," the colonel ordered as he moved over to one of the command stations.

"Have Delta company report for perimeter guard duty. Live ammo, double time," he ordered.

"What's a Viper?" I asked Sam.

"An attack helicopter," he said never taking his eyes off the screen.

The sound of the two Hornet F-18's shook the room as they flew over the base.

"Give me a direct com to General Wallace at the main gate," the colonel barked, as the roar of the jets died down.

"I have the general, sir"

"What in God's name are you doing General?" The colonel hollered.

I recognized the general's voice.

"Colonel," came the reply over the loudspeaker, his voice in total control.

"I am relieving you of duty. This is a direct order from the President of the United States. Comply with this order or I will take this base by force and arrest you myself."

"Not going to happen, General," the colonel warned. "Do not set foot on this base. I am in command of this facility and I am ordering you to remove your men."

The room was silent. Every face was looking back at their commander. They'd all heard a direct order from the Chairmen of the Joint Chief of Staff being countermanded by the colonel. I sure as hell was glad I didn't have to choose sides. I also knew that if the colonel didn't hold the base, Sam and I would be taken into custody and placed somewhere deep within the military prison system or most likely be dead.

"Terminate communication," the colonel ordered.

His officer complied.

"Vipers are airborne, sir, and the F-22's are standing by on the tarmac. Delta company is moving into position around the parameter. What are your orders, sir?"

The colonel didn't hesitate, "Launch the F-22's and order the Vipers to take a fixed position over gates one and four. Instruct ground forces to shoot anyone who attempts to breach the fences."

*

General Wallace's hand rested on his sidearm, a flash of rage passed through him. He gave the orders in this military. It was going to be a pleasure handcuffing the colonel and his oversized MP and locking them in the brig. The FBI agent and detective who interrogated him in the brig were not going to see the light of day for the rest of their lives.

"Breach the south gate," Wallace ordered. "Use deadly force if necessary."

The army commander at the south gate raised his M4 Carbine and stepped in front of his Jeep. "I've been ordered to proceed onto the base, step aside."

Three Marine guards at the gate raised their weapons in response.

"No one moves past this gate without a direct order from Colonel Mitchell," the gate commander replied. "Lower your weapon and return to your vehicle."

A single gunshot rang out from behind the Jeep, hitting the gate commander square in the chest, ending his life before he hit the ground. The Marines returned fire, killing the sniper.

"Colonel, shots fired at the South gate, sir." The tech commander reported.

"Give me eyes on that gate," the colonel responded.

The main monitor screen flashed once and displayed his men in a firefight. Several bodies lay on the ground, the army ground forces began moving forward toward the perimeter fences. The grass berms fifty yards from the boundary line were spitting dirt into the air from the return fire.

"Order Viper Delta two-niner to secure the gate," the colonel ordered.

The camera stationed above the Viper's cockpit popped on the second screen as it descended toward the southern gate. Several soldiers were rushing through the gate firing as they ran. The Viper opened fire with its

50 caliber guns. The ground erupted in a moving wall of bullet holes. The Army units began falling back beyond the fence line.

"Give me General Wallace," the colonel ordered.

"General, your men are dying, pull back now."

"Surrender the base,"came the response.

The Colonel gave his station commander the signal to cut communications.

The monitor on the far right showed the two F-22 Raptors on a simultaneous takeoff from the base airstrip. The camera followed them as they circled out to sea. The Hornets turned back toward the base. Both F-22's responded, falling in behind them. All four jets were heading for the base, the sound of their engines filling the room. The voice of one of the colonel's pilots came over the speaker.

"Hammer-71, radar contacts 15 miles southeast, request voice com with inbound aircraft."

Flight control reported back, "Hammer-71, bandit at 12 miles angels 2, still negative com with the aircraft."

"Hammer-71 Roger, bandit now 2 o'clock low 9 miles. Permission to engage at 5 miles."

As the fighter jets closed in the communications officer told the colonel, "The F-22's have locked all four AIM-9 air-to-air missiles on the Hornets, sir, awaiting orders."

Colonel Mitchell nodded his head, "On my order, Lieutenant."

"Hammer-71 flight, Strike, stand by to engage."

I was holding my breath. I looked over at Sam, he looked back at me and mouthed the word 'holy shit' and turned back to the screens. I turned and looked at the colonel, his eyes were locked on the main screen. His body language said he wasn't going to change his mind.

The room pulsated from the roar of the fighters as the jets approached the base. I covered my ears. This was thunder at the front door. Sam put his hands over mine and we both stared at the center screen. Suddenly the two F-18's broke formation, one veering left the other right.

"Hold fire!" the colonel ordered.

Five seconds later the room stopped shaking. I took a breath.

The soldier manning flight control reported: "Commander, all gates reporting the general's vehicles are pulling back, sir."

"Tell all stations to cease fire and stand by their posts. I want the F-22's to remain airborne and the Vipers are to hold position two hundred yards off the coast."

"Yes, sir, anything else, sir."

"I want a casualty report, priority one."

"And get me General Jenkins at Quantico Marine base in Virginia. Patch it through to my office."

CLOSED DOORS

Chapter 53

E very instinct in General Wallace's body was screaming 'go back'. His skin crawled while every bite of food he'd had in the past twenty-four hours was burning a hole in his stomach. He'd spent a lifetime defeating the enemy, now he was running from a fight. He hated himself at this moment, hated everything and everyone, but he was a soldier given an order to 'retreat' by his Commander in Chief. He'd almost disobeyed the President's order, but that would be impossible for him. The command structure came first.

Colonel Mitchell, his giant MP and the two civilians who arrested him were going to face his wrath. But for now, he needed to control his anger. Never show your emotions to your men or they'll realize you're human and then the real trouble starts. His anger moved to his hands, trembling with desire to strike out, hurt someone. He looked at his driver. "Step on it," he barked, "and radio ahead, I want a transport standing by to return me to Washington as soon as we're back on base."

As much as he hated the Oval Office it's where he'd demand answers from the President. He visualized the room with all the doors closed. His hands continued to shake, but now it was for a different reason.

I STILL AM

Chapter 54

"**I** wouldn't want to be riding in the same Jeep as the general right now," the colonel told us as we made our way to his office. "No doubt he's chewing out someone's ass. I'm keeping this base on high alert. Something must have happened to Wallace to cause him to back down," the Colonel added. "General Wallace was born in a bad mood; he never backs away from a fight. The President must have been monitoring the live situation and ordered the general to call off the attack. He's the only one who could give that order."

As we walked into his office the colonel directed his secretary to notify all senior staff to report to the command center in thirty minutes.

"You have General Jenkins on line one, sir." His secretary told him.

"Please wait here," he told us and stepped out to the hallway to take the call.

"There's nothing left for us to do here," I told Sam. "It's time for us to go back east. We're going to need to get our hands on the recording and see what Shreya finds. Everything's back in D.C."

"You ready to go into hiding again?" Sam reminded me.

The colonel came back into the office. The lines in his face gave away the stress he was under.

"I just got off the phone with General Jenkins," he explained. "You both remember him?"

"Yes, sir," Sam and I said at the same time.

"I've made arrangements for both of you to land at his Marine base at Quantico. You two are not safe here, the general may try again."

"We were just talking about that," I acknowledged. "Maybe it's time to go back to Washington."

"Good, we're all on the same page," he replied. "Go pack your things and I'll make arrangements to have you flown back east."

The colonel took out a large cell phone from his desk drawer, "Here's the best way to communicate with me," he said and handed me the phone. "This is a secure satellite phone, it will only attenuate with my phone." He paused for a second, then asked, "You two have the retrieval cards Agent Hayes gave you to download the General's recording?" Sam and I pulled them out of our pockets and showed them to him.

"General Jenkins just informed me all hell is breaking out at the Pentagon over this confrontation. Good luck, you two."

Sam saluted the Colonel. I did the same.

We packed what little we had at the condo and drove to the airstrip on the north end of the base. The same Gulfstream we'd flown out in was waiting for us on the tarmac. Nice to have a plane waiting for you forty-five minutes after you decide you need to be somewhere else. Our American tax dollars at work.

Sam and I were too jacked up to sleep for the first hour, but finally the adrenaline wore off and I fell asleep.

I woke as the Gulfstream was landing in Virginia. Sam was awake, messing with the satellite phone.

"You figured it out?" I asked. The sleep had calmed me down.

"Just getting the feel for it, trying to figure out what all these buttons do." He pointed to the screen at the top of the phone, "Maybe we can log on to Netflix and watch a cop movie, or an FBI flick," he said.

"Maybe it gets porno," I chuckled and started pushing buttons.

Sam added, "I already tried while you were asleep. It doesn't."

A car was waiting for us on the tarmac. It took us to the base commander's headquarters.

"That was one hell of a shit storm at Pendleton," General Jenkins said as we walked into his office. "Don't know how this is going to play out, but it's best you both aren't there to find out."

"Does the outside world know what happened?" I asked.

"The press was told it was a military exercise that went bad. So far they're buying the story, but it's not going to last." the general answered. "This incident will reverberate through our military for a long, long time. Things are spinning out of control."

"It was close to being a lot worse," I said. "Can you give us transportation get off the base, General?"

"Of course, but you can stay here," he offered.

"I think we need to keep moving," I told him. "Trouble seems to be following us. We'll disappear into the Washington background."

"Not a problem, I'll have the car brought around for you to use but it's got military plates. I suggest you ditch it as soon as you can."

We put our stuff in the car and drove into downtown Washington. Suddenly we were back in the world. Now the only saluting going on was from drivers giving each other the finger. No place like home.

We drove to the closest store and bought several more prepaid cell phones. We should have bought stock in the burner phone business.

This was getting old. I wanted to get in my own car, drive fast to my own dirty apartment, throw my shoes in my bedroom, pour a mug of wine and watch my basketball team lose. The only difference was I wanted to take Sam with me. But going there wasn't even in the realm of possibility.

"How's this for irony?" I asked Sam. "We're the law enforcement agents and we're the ones on the run. The chasers are being chased."

I looked at Sam, "If we hit the seedy motels and pay cash we might get away with it?"

"Why not the penthouse suite at the Regency Hotel?" Sam asked, his voice trailing off.

He was as sick of hiding as I was.

"We're on a tight budget, Mister Warren Buffett," I said. "I'm going to call my boss, see what's happening on his side of the country."

I used one of the new burners and called Gilliam's office. His secretary put me through.

"How are you feeling boss?"

"Lucky. I'm doing better than I should, all things considered. You heard what happened at Camp Pendleton today?"

"Yeah, I almost wet my pants," I told him.

"You were there?"

"I still am," I lied.

He knew I wasn't at Pendleton anymore. Gilliam's been an FBI man his entire career. He knows his phone could be tapped. We were going to have to play the 'I lie to you, you lie to me and we'll figure it out later' game.

"We're going to lay low and stay at the base. Nothing left for us to do."

"Good idea," he answered. "Your job in the mailroom is still available when you come back."

This was his way of saying he knew I was back in town.

"Thanks, boss. You know how much I miss the mailroom. I'll call you when I'm back."

I was glad to hear I'm still on the payroll. I've got to pay Ron Collins back the two grand he lent us and if I survive I'd promised to take Shreya to Hawaii and let her drink as much rum as she wanted. I should have asked for a raise.

BIGGER PICTURE

Chapter 55

General Wallace's dread of the Oval Office never diminished. Being surrounded by enemy troops was preferable to a round room with two closed doors. Diagnosed with Entomophobia when he was in high school. Similar to claustrophobia, any room with the doors closed made him frantic. He would sweat, his heart would race and his hands would tremble. The only cure was to open the door or get out of the room. He'd kept it a secret his entire military career; learned how to manage the fear. Mind over phobia.

As he sat in the Oval Office he let his anger at being called off the takeover of Camp Pendleton override his anxiety.

Seated in front of the President's desk, facing the windows he'd managed to avoid looking at any of the closed doors.

"You're not happy with me are you General?" the President asked.

"No, sir, I'm not." He replied. "Colonel Mitchell and his men would be in the brig right now if you hadn't ordered me back to Washington."

The general tried, but couldn't help himself and glanced around the office. His heart rate spiked. Who the hell designed this damn room?

"I was gagged and forced into an interrogation room and held against my will, Mister President. The colonel should be put in front of a firing squad."

The President let the general vent his frustration, but he wasn't going to take much more.

"I understand, General," the President acknowledged, "But there's a bigger picture here, one which overrides your mistreatment. Besides, it was you who said the colonel would obey your order to relinquish command of the base without a fight. You were wrong, General. Taking Camp Pendleton by force would have sent a signal to the country that we were coming apart, just when I need this nation to believe we are coming together. So far, we've managed the press, but those bastards will eventually dig their way in. You will have your justice, General, but not until I've secured a new government."

The doors behind Wallace were closing in on him. He wanted to run out of the room, but his anger kept him in his seat.

"Tomorrow night I will appoint a new vice president," the President added. "And set in motion the process of forming an entirely new Congress with members who believe in the values you and I hold. We will set this nation on a path that will last for generations. The bigger picture, General. We need to focus on the bigger picture."

"Yes, Mister President."

As uncomfortable as the general felt in the room, the power of the Presidency permeated the space. This hallowed ground was the center of the world. The speech the President was going to give the following day would be delivered from here. The General forced himself to stay in his seat.

"Who are you appointing as vice president?" he asked.

"Loretta Erin Anderson," the President responded.

General Wallace gasped. "An ultra-liberal Democrat! Sir, are you serious? Why in God's name would you appoint her?"

"The same reason I called off the attack at the Marine base, General - perception. We need the country to believe we are bringing in a bipartisan government. This is the right move at the right time."

General Wallace got to his feet. "If something should happen to you, Mister President, she would be in charge of forming a new government. How can you take the chance?"

The President opened the top drawer of his desk and handed the general a file marked top secret.

A photograph of two women, both naked, lying on a king size bed, sat inside the file. Several candles were set around the room providing enough light to see two lines of white powder on one of the women's breasts. The general recognized the other woman as Loretta Anderson. She appeared to be snorting the white powder.

The general turned the page and read the rest of the report.

"I'd like you to keep a copy of this file, in case something does happen to me. Then you'll be in a position to make sure this country remains on course."

General Wallace sat back in his chair, the doors temporarily receding into the background, as he wondered if the 'bigger picture' the President had referred to was the 8x10 photo of the future vice president of the United States doing a line of cocaine.

BLACK MUSTANG

Chapter 56

It was time again for Sam and me to blend in with the nineteen million tourists who visit Washington DC every year. Sounded easy enough. But we'd been found once before, so we weren't about to take anything for granted.

I parked the military car General Jenkins loaned us in the mall parking lot with the keys locked inside and called a cab. I'd let General Jenkins know where we'd left it once we settled into our next hiding place.

We had a cabbie drop us off a couple of blocks from the Motor Inn off Grant Road and walked the rest of the way to the motel to check in. Paid cash, which was risky. But we didn't have much choice.

"We need a car," I told Sam, which he already knew, but I couldn't help myself from stating the obvious.

"We're not going to be able to rent one without a credit card," I said, as I continued stating the obvious. "Stealing another car is pushing our luck. All we need is to be pulled over for a stolen vehicle." That rounded out my verbal dive into the self-evident.

Sam kicked off his shoes, laid on the bed and put a pillow over his face. "So, we can't rent a car, or pilfer one. Doesn't leave us a lot of options," he said through the pillow.

I joined him on the bed.

"It's time to go back to the well and call Ron in the mailroom. Lets see if he needs more bananas."

For some reason, Sam knew what I was talking about but it was his turn to state the obvious, "So you're going to use Ron's lust for you to get what you want."

I reminded him that men and woman have been doing it that way for a million years with great success. What could possibly go wrong?

I left Sam under the pillow and used one of the new burner phones to call Ron's office number.

"Agent Ron Collins," he answered.

"Hi agent Ron Collins," I said. "You recognize my voice?"

"Yes, I do," he answered and was silent.

"I need to ask you another favor."

He hesitated. I didn't blame him. Everything was turning to shit and he knew I was involved.

"What can I do for you?" he finally asked.

"How's your supply of fruit?" I answered with a question.

"My what? Oh yeah, um, my fruit supply is running low."

I could tell Ron liked believing he was in a spy novel, which is what your mind will do after spending a third of your life in the basement at the FBI.

I know I was taking advantage of his imagination and his libido, but he worked for the FBI. In some way, he was duty-bound to get involved. At least that's what I told myself to help with the guilt. It worked.

"Meet me where we met before at the same time as last time. Can you do that?" I asked.

The phone went dead.

"What the hell," I said to Sam. "He hung up before saying yes or no."

"That's a yes," Sam said. "It's what FBI agents do in the movies. Hanging up first means 'I'm cool', let's do this."

"No, it's what cops do in the movies," I said.

We were drawing our boundary lines, FBI versus cops. He didn't have a prayer.

"What time do we meet Ron at Trader Joes?" Sam asked.

"Five-thirty."

"What time is it now?"

"Almost four," I answered.

"So, what do you want to do for the next hour?"

I laughed and crawled under his pillow.

We took a taxi to the store and arrived at 5:35. I could see Ron in the produce section next to the bananas as we walked in. I couldn't help wondering how long he'd been thumbing through the pile, trying not to look like a banana molester.

"Come shopping with me," I said as I walked past him. He didn't look at me. He was in spy mode, so I played along. "Did anybody follow you?" I whispered.

"No," he whispered back and trailed behind me as I pushed my cart toward the wine section. "I took about ten side streets and never saw anyone following," he said.

"Good, I need you to rent a car for me and to bring it here. I need you to go now and come back as soon as possible. Can you do that for me?"

"What kind of car? he asked. "A minivan, a sedan, what kind do you want?"

"Something fast, in case I need to outrun someone."

"I understand," he whispered back.

I handed him a bottle of white wine.

"You should buy this as you leave the store. Look's better that way."

He took the bottle and grabbed a second one. "I'll be back. I'll look for you next to the bananas."

I didn't want to laugh, but hearing him say, 'I'll look for you next to the bananas', put me over the edge. I put my hand over my mouth and tried to muffle the laugh. It came out sounding like a sob. Ron thought I was crying and put both arms around me, a bottle of white wine in each hand, and hugged me. I hugged him back.

"There's a car rental place about a mile from here on Fairfax Drive," I whispered to him in the middle of the hug.

He never looked back as he moved to the checkout stand. He was doing the 'cool thing' again.

Sam and I hung out in the store putting stuff in the basket trying not to look like we were killing time.

Ron was back in less than an hour. Sam came with me to the fruit section and the three of us acted like we were old friends saying hello.

"Well, nice seeing you two," Ron said, gave me another hug and whispered in my ear, "Black Mustang, back of the parking lot, keys are on the top of the driver side back tire".

I hugged him back and told him, "If your cell phone rings several times, then stops and rings again, it's me asking you to meet me outside the office, the same place as before."

Ron shook Sam's hand before going back to the wine section where he grabbed another bottle of white wine as he left.

Sam and I put half of the groceries back on the shelves and ended up with a bag of apples, some French bread, Cheddar cheese, a bottle of red wine and two bags of almond chocolate bars in our cart. All the food groups a man and a woman need when they're on the run.

"Nice looking car," Sam said, as we put the food in the trunk of the black mustang. "Ron knows your taste in automobiles."

"I told him to get us 'something fast'," I said as I got behind the wheel. Sam gave an extra tug on his seat belt as I drove back to our motel.

NUMERO UNO

Chapter 57

Everyone should have a best friend who's computer literate, someone who has the answers on how to fix all of your computer problems, usually by telling you to restart the damn thing. That's Shreya, except she loves making me feel like a blockhead.

'Restart it, girl'! she's told me fifty times.

Shreya was still sifting through all the files she'd hacked when I got ahold of her in the morning.

"Can you get me General Wallace's home address?" I asked.

"Not available, classified. I'd have to hack into the Pentagon register for it. Not sure it's a good idea right now."

"I agree, how about the kind of car General Wallace drives. She found the answer while we were still on the phone.

"Government issue black Ford Bronco, license number AR00916. Why you need it?"

"Time to retrieve the recording Tony put together. Call me when you get something from those other files."

Sam was eating one of the apples we'd bought for breakfast and watching the news, "We're going to need to go back to the hornets' nest at the

Pentagon and try to find General Wallace's Ford Bronco."I still had the laptop we'd bought at the base commissary and used it to get an aerial view of the Pentagon complex. I counted sixteen open-air parking lots with the potential to hold over nine thousand cars. Twenty-three-thousand employees come and go on any given day around a building, that's bigger than ten football fields. Talk about finding a needle in a haystack!

"No doubt there'll be cameras focused on the parking areas. So, we can't drive through every lot looking at plates. We need to narrow this down." Sam reminded me.

I googled 'parking for generals at the Pentagon'. The second page showed a reserved parking area.

What a surprise. The higher the rank, the closer the parking space to the building. No doubt this General gets 'spot numero uno'. I looked up the lot number, VIP 3 south entrance.

We typed it into the Mustangs GPS and drove to the entrance.

The VIP 3 south entrance had a guard post manned by several MP's. We parked in the visitor's lot adjacent to the south entrance where we could see anyone coming or going. We had no idea if the general was even there, but this was our best chance for downloading the recording.

We sat there for several hours watching black SUV's, Lincoln Continentals and even a Humvee painted in camouflage green come and go. Finally, at 1:44 the general's car drove out of the lot followed by an Army security vehicle. We waited a few seconds before following them onto the 395. I stayed a couple of cars behind as they took Pennsylvania Exit. Drove a couple of miles before turning into a high-end residential area. He finally pulled into the driveway of a two-story colonial house in the middle of the block. I drove past the house and parked at the far end of the street and watched his security detail enter the house. Five minutes later the detail opened his car door and the general went inside. The security detail drove off. An hour later they were back, escorted him to his car and left.

We waited ten minutes before walking to the house.

I guess not too many nut jobs try to harass high-ranking generals. We walked right up to the door and rang the doorbell. If someone had answered we would have used our ID's to make up a reason for being there.

No answer, so Sam used his handy tool kit and we were in. The house looked like the lobby of a five-star hotel, spotless.

"This guy's a psycho clean freak," I whispered to Sam.

Upstairs, none of the bedrooms had doors. Made sense, I'd detected the general's phobia when we had him in interrogation room two.

"Looks like you're right about the guy's anxiety," Sam acknowledged. "Never heard of that one before."

There were two bedrooms on our left, a bathroom sat between them. At the end of the hall, a double doorway led into the master bedroom. The king size bed didn't have a wrinkle; nothing was out of place. This was as opposite from my apartment as you could get.

I told Sam, "I hate this guy even more now that I've seen this place."

He looked around and replied, "Not me, it's not possible to hate this guy more than I already do."

A single door at the back of the bedroom opened into a walk-in closet. I flipped on the light. The closet looked like a 'Stepford Wife' on steroids had cleaned it. Several military uniforms hung evenly spaced apart. Eight pairs of the same type of shoes were in a straight line under the back clothes rack, the closet light reflecting off their high gloss polish.

Above the shoes hung the coat we were looking for. It was adorned with all of the medals the general had accumulated. I wanted to light it on fire, better yet with the general in it.

An inch below the breast pocket hung the insignia of the Joint Chief of Staff we'd bugged. I took out the credit card down-loader and pushed the logo. About five seconds later the logo turned red like Tony said it would.

We both heard the sound of the front door opening downstairs. I put the card in my pocket, took out my gun and cocked a bullet into the chamber. I heard Sam do the same. We waited.

What sounded like a vacuum cleaner came from downstairs.

"Is that what I think it is?" Sam whispered.

"Good chance it's a housecleaner vacuuming the perfectly clean rugs," I whispered back. "Among other things, our General is a paranoid clean freak."

"I'll be right back," I told Sam and crawled on all fours toward the balcony. A woman was pushing a vacuum over by the couch. I watched for about a minute and didn't see anyone else.

"It's one woman," I told Sam. "She's doing her 'cleaning' thing. If she comes upstairs we've got a problem. If she goes in the kitchen we can make it out the front door."

We both un-chambered our guns and waited. Ten minutes later the vacuum stopped. We'd gotten our wish; the sound of dishes being washed came from the kitchen. We made our way downstairs. I had this overwhelming desire to turn a potted plant over and spread the dirt all over the floor, but I decided not to act like a ten-year-old and followed Sam out the front door.

We drove back to the FBI building, parked around the corner and called Ron in the mailroom. I let the phone ring twice and hung up. I did it one more time.

Five minutes later, Ron walked out of the building carrying a brown bag. He took a seat on one of the park benches which form a semi-circle outside the FBI headquarters, reached in his bag, pulled out a banana and peeled it.

Sam glanced at me, "What in the hell is he doing?"

"He's eating a banana," I answered. "I'll bet it's code for 'all clear'."

"How about I go this time," Sam suggested.

I agreed and gave him the retrieval card and one of our burner phones for Ron to give to Tony.

They sat on the bench talking for longer than it would have taken me. Sam was smiling when he came back to the car. "He's going to take the card to Tony's office after he rides the elevators up and down a couple of times to make sure he's not being followed. He's in spy mode."

We drove back to the motel to wait to hear from Tony. It was almost midnight before he called.

"We've got some incriminating conversations on here," Tony told me. "A lot of it's about the general's anger at being locked in the brig at Camp Pendleton. And there's some disparaging remarks on the candidate being appointed to vice president, but they never mentioned their involvement in the attack. It's two old men being their disgusting selves, but no evidence connecting them to the attack. I'm going to send you a text of the conversation. Check it out. I'll get this to Gilliam."

My phone chirped with an incoming text. Tony was right, it was two assholes being assholes. Close again, but no cigar.

"I, LORETTA ERIN ANDERSON"

Chapter 58

F our tungsten lights bouncing off parabolic white umbrellas gave the President a shadowless lighting effect, making him look five years younger. Two television cameras, set up directly behind the teleprompter, were focused on his face as he sat motionless behind his desk in the Oval Office.

Loretta Erin Anderson stood behind the President alongside General Wallace and two of the senators who'd survived the attack. The lone surviving Supreme Court Judge sat in a wheelchair out of the camera's view.

Looking into camera one the President began, "My fellow Americans, I invite you today to witness the swearing-in of my choice for the vice presidency of the United States; three-term Democratic congresswoman from the state of Colorado, Loretta Erin Anderson."

The camera panned to the right of the President and focused on the smiling face of the vice-presidential appointment. The camera zoomed inward as the President continued, "I believe it is imperative that both political parties be represented under these unprecedented circumstances. A bipartisan government represents the highest ideals of this nation. All points of view must be included in the rebuilding of our nation. Loretta Anderson has dedicated her professional life to the service of this country, she has the leadership qualities this wounded nation can call upon to help rebuild what was so cruelly taken from us."

The President stood and shook his nominee's hand.

Turning back to the camera, "Today I have set in motion the Emergency Election Act. One year from today each of the fifty states will convene a special election to replace their representatives in Congress to fulfill the constitutional duties of that legislative body. Until then, under the mandates of Directive 51, the Office of the President will appoint the necessary personnel to the State Department, the military, the executive and the judicial branches of the federal government."

The camera did a slow outward zoom on the President's face. "Our nation has sustained a tragedy of momentous proportions. We must all come together as Americans to rebuild what has been taken from us. When Congress has been re-established, its first order of business will be to propose a date for the election of the next president. It is a new day in America. We will find the perpetrators of this attack and will bring them to justice. Our constitution is our map for the future. We will follow what our founding fathers established and rebuild this nation stronger than ever before."

The President turned and faced the Supreme Court Judge who was wheeled forward with a bible in his lap. His vice president appointee placed her hand on the Bible and repeated after the judge. "I, Loretta Erin Anderson, do solemnly swear I will faithfully execute the office of Vice President of the United States, and will..."

HIT THE FAN

Chapter 59

"This hypocrite of a president makes me sick," I told Sam and threw my pillow at the television.

Sam didn't say anything; he sat at the edge of the bed and stared at the screen. I thought for a second he might pull his gun and shoot it.

We knew the truth. The President was a traitor, and a psychopath and here he was appointing a vice president without congressional oversight.

I turned off the TV and re-read the transcript from the audio files we'd pilfered from General Wallace's coat. There wasn't enough incriminating evidence to remove the President. It would take indisputable evidence to take down this presidency.

They say 'the truth will set you free'. I'm pretty sure the truth can also get you locked up, shot or just made to disappear. We needed irrefutable evidence. The voice recording didn't have it.

Shreya called. "We need to meet," she informed me, "I need to show you what I've found. Too much to text over to you."

"Where?" I asked.

"Library of Congress, second floor, woman's bathroom in an hour."

"Let me check with Sam, see how he feels about going in the women's bathroom."

"Funny," she said. "See you in an hour."

Sam and I had been stuck in the motel room for most of the time. It was hard to know who was after us. Our faces weren't on television; Sam's friend Jamie confirmed there wasn't an A.P.B. out on us. We were being hunted, we just didn't know by whom. On the bright side, there are worse things in the world than being stuck in a room with someone you're falling in love with, a king size bed and a mini bar.

We headed for our meeting with Shreya. Parked a half block from the entrance and walked the rest of the way.

A bronze statue of Neptune sits in the middle of the fountain at the front entrance of the library. I couldn't help but notice Neptune's statue is ripped. Captain Holt has muscles; this statue has more and is twelve feet tall and naked. Two Triton statues stand on either side of Neptune looked even more dangerous, but the giant snake in the front, with water shooting out of its mouth, made me believe the library wanted to scare the crap out of kids before letting them inside. Maybe a subliminal trick to keep the little ones from making any noise.

We made our way up the concrete stairs through the main double doors. The polished marble floors were shiny enough to do my makeup. Gold-plated tiles lined the arched ceiling. In the center of the ceiling, a giant skylight with blue tinted stained-glass windows lit up the vast interior.

We made our way to the second story and found the ladies room at the end of the hallway. Sam took a seat at one of the reading tables. I went inside.

Two women were using the sinks to wash up. One of the stall doors was closed. I used one of the empty sinks and washed my hands, trying to look busy. After the two women left I softly called out Shreya's name.

From the closed stall, I heard "Erica?"

"That's me," I said. "We're alone in here."

She came out of the stall carrying a briefcase, put it on the counter and gave me a hug.

"Let's find a secluded part of the library and I'll show you what I've found," she said and led me out the door.

Sam had already found a secluded table at the back of a row of bookshelves and waved us over.

"Last time I saw you both you were jumping out of a bread truck," Shreya told Sam.

"My knees remember it, too," Sam said.

Shreya took out a stack of papers from her briefcase. "This is what I found after I accessed Mitchells' backdoor CT domain."

A legal size sheet of paper rested on top of the pile. Illustrations filled the page from top to bottom, looking like a cross between a genealogy chart and a schematic of a computer chip. None of it made sense to me.

Shreya pointed to a box at the bottom of the page.

"This is where the rabbit hole leads. The colonel's brother was a genius. He hid his communication in gaming cyberspace. Gamers want to communicate with each other, but only with a few select people in the industry so they invented their own secret code called 'Leet Speak'. It started simple, but grew more elaborate as hackers figured it out. Mitchell was one of the first to invent his own LEET converter. It was impregnable."

"What does the symbol you're pointing to mean?" I asked Shreya.

"It's the Cypherium Blockchain the general used to communicate with his accomplices. Basically, it's a list of names of people who received payments. Here's a catalog of the people involved."

Sam and I read the list.

"Can you find any information on any of these people?" Sam asked.

"I already did," Shreya answered. "And they're all dead. Either killed in action in Afghanistan, car accidents, heart attacks. You get the picture. The general didn't leave any live witnesses; no one's left to talk."

"Were they all soldiers or ex-soldiers with a military link to the general?" I asked. "

Shreya nodded.

"What did these soldiers do in the military? What did they train in?"

Shreya pulled her laptop out of her briefcase, "Hang on a sec and let me log into the database I hacked."

Two minutes of typing later she said, "Three of them were from the Army Corps of Engineers, three more were from the cyber branch, two were Special Forces bomb experts and one was a warrant officer specializing in chemical, biological, and radiological operations."

"And they're all dead? When?" I asked.

"All of them over the last six months."

"Were any of them stateside within the last three months?"

"Let me take a look," her fingers glided across the keyboard. "The three Army Corp of Engineers were here on a furlough five weeks ago, the others were in Afghanistan for over a year."

"When was the general last in Afghanistan?"

"His last visit was eight months ago. He made an inspection tour on combat readiness."

"Can you do a cross-reference on the location and the dates the engineers were in proximity to the general," I asked. "And see if they were ever in the same place at the same time. See if the Special Forces soldiers were ever in the same location at the same time, too."

"For one day," Shreya explained, "they were all at the regional command center in Kabul."

We were getting closer. Soldiers, all connected to the general had been together in Afghanistan and were no longer among the living.

"Everything else in this stack is a breakdown of this top sheet," Shreya told us. "I put the information you asked about on a memory stick for you."

Can I hold on to everything you showed us today?" I asked. This was tangible evidence; something that could corroborate our theory.

Shreya nodded, put everything in the briefcase, then handed it to me.

"If the dots connect do you have a plan to get the info out?" she asked.

Sam answered, "The Washington Post or New York Times. One of their writers can help put all the pieces together."

I looked over at Shreya, I could tell she was going to say something geeky.

She didn't disappoint.

"That's when the excrement makes physical contact with a hydroelectric powered oscillating device," she deadpanned.

"The shit hit the fan a long time ago," I reminded her. "Lucky us, we get to go in first to clean it up."

TONYA LIGHTSOUT

Chapter 60

Sam and I drove back to the motel, where we spread everything Shreya gave us out on the bed and organized the time line. It was 3am before it made any sense. Everything went back into the briefcase and we passed out on the bed.

The next morning Sam and I set out to one of the few places we trusted, the restaurant across the street from our motel. There, you could get the "all American breakfast, the all American lunch and the 'all American dinner'.

"Who do you know at the Washington Post?" I asked Sam between sips of his 'all American coffee'.

"I've been interviewed a couple of times by one of their reporters for a few of my stories. She knew her stuff, asked the right questions."

"You remember her name?"

"Yeah, her name was hard to forget," he said, "Tonya Lightsout. Say it fast three times and you won't forget it either. Want me to get a hold of her?"

"Let's give her what we've got and see what she wants to do." I answered.

I handed Sam my burner phone and headed for the ladies room.

"She's on her way," Sam told me, when I got back to the table.

"Now?" I asked.

"She knows I'm not a bull-shitter. She'll be here in forty-five minutes."

We ordered pancakes, sausage, and orange juice and finished eating as Tonya walked in the door.

She recognized Sam and came over to our table.

I could smell the cigarette she must have just smoked, I wanted one, but we'd kept our promise.

Tonya's hair was as short as Sam's, which let the long earrings with feathers on the ends hypnotize me as they swung back and forth. She was maybe fifty, give or take a few thousand packs of cigarettes and wore eye glasses Elton John would have been proud of. I liked her before she said a word.

Sam introduced us.

"Ain't this one a beauty?" she said and slid down on the laminate seat next to me. "Okay, you two, tell me a story. Start at the beginning and end it with me sitting here at this table; go."

She listened for an hour without asking a question. Finally, she said, "Show me these papers you got from Shreya."

We walked across the street to our room and laid out the whole thing. When we were done, she said, "I'm going to call my editor," and walked into the bedroom.

"He wants a sit down with you two," she said five minutes later. "He doesn't think it's a good idea to have you come to the paper for obvious reasons. He suggested you follow me to the Embassy Suites and we book a room under my name. I'll text my editor the room number and he'll meet us there."

Tonya looked around at our surroundings, "You two can check out of this lovely establishment and stay in the hotel room I book. We'll toss you out when we're done, but till then you'll be on our tab. Room service included. Sound good?"

I was already grabbing my things, which took less than a minute. We put all the papers back in the briefcase and checked out.

The lobby of the new hotel looked like we'd landed in Hawaii. Palm trees, ferns and green plants were spread throughout the entire interior. Sam and I sat in a remote corner of the main floor, out of view of the public. Tonya checked in and led us into the glass elevator for the ride to the sixteenth floor.

The suite was at the far end of the hall. Our door opened into a large living room furnished with a white leather couch, a large glass coffee table and two high backed chairs facing a flat screen television. A few feet past the television two French doors opened to a peach colored bedroom with two king size beds covered with snow-white comforters. A sliding glass door led out to a balcony overlooking the city.

As much as I missed my apartment, I could get used to this place.

Tonya said she was going to wait out front for her editor and would see us 'in a few'. Which is journalist talk for 'I needed a smoke'.

Sam and I put what little stuff we had in the bedroom drawers and spread the contents of the briefcase on the coffee table.

I snuck a peek at the adult TV guide, saw we could watch 'Buffy the Vampire Layer', and 'For Your Thighs Only' as a double feature. Yeah, we were back in Washington DC.

Tonya came back with her editor, who turned out to be the Editor-In-Chief of the Washington Post. Apparently, we were getting the big guns on this one. We sat around the coffee table and ran the story past our host. It felt like an interrogation; times, dates, names, what happened, what caused it to happen? Then the question we didn't have an answer for; could they use our names and credentials as the source of all the info?

Tonya suggested, "We can identify you as 'reliable sources' inside the FBI and the Washington Police department, but the nature of these accusations is going to start a relentless search by the media for the sources."

I told her I'd check with my boss and see what he wanted me to do. Sam said he needed to do the same.

"We're going to confer with our lawyers," Tonya told us. "Sit tight and we'll meet tomorrow. In the meantime, you can check in with your superiors."

Sam and I nodded our approval.

"If what you've told us today goes to press," Tonya said, "your lives and the lives of everyone in this nation will never be the same. You need to ask yourself if you're ready for that."

Her boss added, "This country is in the most serious crisis since the Civil War. We're in uncharted waters here and these accusations will test the Constitution like never before. We all need to sleep on this and meet tomorrow morning." Tonya and her boss headed back to their office, leaving all of our documentation on the coffee table. No one had committed to publishing the story.

Sam grabbed the TV log and glanced at me before asking, "Do you want to watch 'Buffy the Vampire Layer' now or later?"

DECKER

Chapter 61

The President arrived back at his office from the residence, the list of cabinet appointees he'd announce in the morning sat on his desk.

Doing it on television appealed to him; it would give the country a sense of being involved. His approval ratings were in the mid-eighties, higher than any president in modern history. Before the crisis, they'd dipped below forty percent, but the American people look to their leaders when their backs are against the wall.

He'd saved the country from itself. And as much as he wanted the nation to know of his courage it would have to remain a secret. Like Lincoln and Roosevelt before him, history would judge him for having the courage to send men and women to their final resting place for the sake of their nation.

The cabinet appointee list would have to wait. He needed to check on something first and opened his top drawer. A dossier with the name: FBI Agent Erica Linda Brewer sat inside. Her photo and several pages of her personal history followed. He stared at her image before reading the entire file. He did the same with Detective Samuel Marco's dossier.

The President closed the files and had the head of his Secret Service detail sent in.

Agent Decker knew what was coming as he walked into the Oval Office and stood in front of the President's desk.

"What is the current status of your investigation into the whereabouts of FBI agent Brewer and Detective Marco?" the President demanded.

"Still at large, sir."

"That's it, still at large?" the President fumed.

"Yes sir, our office is still looking. Since neither one has been accused of any illegal activity and only reported as missing we've been unable to use any other law agencies to locate them. I've contacted both of their supervisors here in Washington about any communications they may have had. They are off the grid, sir. Without placing a nationwide APB they will be difficult to locate. Do you want me to go public with our search?"

"No, Chief. I want to keep this in-house," the President answered. "You indicated Agent Brewer came to the Secret Service office shortly after the first bombing on the White House lawn?"

"Yes, sir."

"What was your impression of her? Did she have any concrete evidence or was it only a fact-finding mission?"

"She was sent by Washington FBI bureau Chief, David Gilliam, to liaison with our office. I briefed her on what we had at the time. She was allowed to interview the witnesses and review the footage of the bombing. She asked the right questions and appeared to be a competent agent, sir."

Decker could see the report on the President's desk and added, "She was also at the curb as you arrived on the night of the attack on Congress. Agent Brewer claimed to have identified the first bomber. I was about to question her when the attack happened inside the building which set in motion your evacuation to the bunker. During the chaos that followed, I was unable to secure the name of the suspect. Agent Brewer has not been seen in public since the last encounter. I've been in contact with Chief Gilliam, he has not heard from her. All available FBI agents have been tasked to protect other government buildings from further terrorist strikes. I do not have the jurisdiction to order Gilliam to re-assign any of his agents to locate her. The order would have to come from the Justice Department, sir."

"I'll look into that, Chief," the President replied. "What have we learned about the attack? Are we any closer to finding the perpetrators?"

"Yes, sir," Decker answered, "I'll have a report on your desk by the end of the day. The chemical agent used in the attack was manufactured in Afghanistan and smuggled into Washington by agents we believe were of Iranian descent. The repairs done to the leaking roof in the congressional office was the point of entry for the chemical agent and all personnel involved in the installation are under investigation. Preliminary reports indicate that an enemy RPG, detonated under their transport in Afghanistan, killed three members of the Army Core of Engineers, who were involved in the repairs. Their personnel files will be included in our report. Is there anything else, sir?"

"Yes, Agent Decker, there is. Find those two missing law enforcement agents and bring them to me.

RIP YOUR HEART OUT

Chapter 62

S am ordered breakfast while I took a shower. Nothing like room service when you're trying to lay low.

Couldn't help but wonder what might happen to us if our story broke in the Washington Post. We both knew the President and the general would lie, deny, and come after us hard. This wouldn't be the first time a president had gone after his adversaries.

Identifying us in the newspaper would put our lives under a microscope. Divorces would be unearthed, our families would be dragged through the media machine. This would be the mother of all investigations and I've got a lot of potholes in my past. It's not going to be fun running over them again.

Tonya called wanting to know if she and her editor could come by.

They arrived an hour later and took a seat around the coffee table.

"Who wants to go first?" Tonya asked.

I volunteered, "Sam and I know we're going to get jammed up pretty bad when the President comes after us. Neither of us has been an eagle scout in the past. The media will have private investigators looking up my dress."

The two guys exchanged the 'hidden man smile' at my remark.

Tonya and I rolled our eyes.

"What's the paper's position?" I asked. "Are you folks ready to have the government come after you with lawsuits and injunctions?"

"Been there, done that," Tonya replied. "Expensive in more ways than just money." She added, "So without you two coming forward we don't have enough evidence. An anonymous source won't cut it in a story this big."

"What happens next if we say 'yes'?" Sam asked.

"We go to work for the next couple of days and dig out every bit of corroborating evidence we can find. Run through every detail and match it with the timeline. We're going to need Colonel Mitchells' account. We can keep your co-worker's names out of the story, but Erica's boss will need to step-up. This will take days to work out, and you'll both need to stay hidden until the story breaks."

Sam looked at me and smiled. I could see that he saw some positive aspects about being locked up with me. I smiled back.

"So it's all in or all out?" I asked.

"I'm afraid so," Tonya replied.

"Give Sam and me another hour or two and we'll let you know."

Sam showed them out while I rubbed my neck where the proverbial hangman's rope was brushing against my skin.

After the door closed I suggested, "How about we rob a bank, steal a car and head for Canada?"

"Which bank?" Sam asked, "We're going to need a lot of cash."

"You pick the bank," I told him, "I'll pick the car."

"We're going to do this, aren't we?" I asked Sam. "We're going to bust this general and his boss."

"Yeah, we are," Sam answered. "I need to check in with my precinct captain."

"I'm going to run this by Gilliam and Colonel Mitchell," I told Sam, "They're in as deep in this as we are."

I called my boss. His secretary put me through.

"Need your opinion and your blessings, boss," I said to open the conversation.

"Before you ask," he interrupted, "I need you to get in touch with Shreya. Now. She didn't show up for work today and I can't reach her. She has some time-sensitive intel I need asap and she's not answering her cell."

"Okay, I'll get in touch with her and call you back. What is she working on?"

"Something which concerns you and Detective Marco," he said, "I'll explain after I talk with her."

"I'll try her now on her burner and get right back to you."

Shreya's phone rang four times before I heard a click but no 'hello'.

"Ahoy sister," I said. "Why aren't you at work today?"

"Because I'm all tied up," a man's voice answered. "I've been expecting you to call."

The pit of my stomach tightened. I couldn't breathe.

"Who the fuck is this?" I yelled and put the phone on speaker.

"Listen closely, you'll recognize my voice. I sure as hell recognize yours."

"Yeah, I remember you," I said. "I'm pretty sure Sam remembers you too. He's still cleaning off his shoes after kicking your ass in the interrogation room."

"We'll get back to Sam in a minute," Parker said. "Right now, we need to talk about Shreya."

My stomach felt like I'd swallowed a brick. Every movie cliché I'd ever heard popped in my head. The kidnapper says, 'do exactly what I tell you and she won't be harmed', and the good guy says; 'If you hurt her I'll rip your heart out with my bare hands," and he says "blah, blah, blah."

The brick moved into my throat, but I wasn't going to do some bullshit movie dialog with this asshole.

I did the only thing I could think of. I hung up.

"Breathe," Sam told me.

I tried, but the brick had moved to my lungs. I tried to slow everything down in my mind. I took a small breath first and then two bigger ones. I've read there are seven stages of grief. I journeyed through the first five in the next three breaths.

Major Parker had Shreya. My guess was he wanted me and Sam. Trade us for her and she... she what? This was the general's right-hand man. He could do anything he wanted. I called Shreya's phone again.

"Good of you to call back," Parker goaded. His voice sounded confident. He was in charge. "We know what you're planning. Do not release the newspaper story you're working on."

How the hell did he know?

"Tell the Washington Post you're not ready. Tell them you'll publicly deny anything they claim you said. It's the only thing that will keep Shreya alive."

Someone had leaked the story, Parker knew about it and held Shreya, now what?

"Fuck you, Parker," I said. "I'll have them publish everything in tomorrow morning's paper. Everything! You, the general and the President are going to take the fall. How's that, you piece of shit."

"We thought you'd say that," Parker whispered. "I suggest you call your parents, your sister, and Sam should call his ex-wife. Ask them to look out their windows and describe the kind of car sitting out front of their houses. Should I go on, Agent?"

I couldn't help myself and yelled, "I'm going to rip your heart out with my bare hands," and hung up.

I'd been reduced to some lousy movie dialog.

JONI MITCHELL

Chapter 63

The duct tape around Shreya's wrists had cut off the circulation. Her hands tingled like a swarm of ants were running in circles around her fingers. Add the terror of being awakened in the middle of the night with two men at the foot of her bed, and it made sense she was scared to death.

Alone since being blindfolded and driven to an unknown location, she felt the handcuffs around her ankles binding her to a metal chair.

She'd been breathing the stale air of her own fear for what seemed like forever. As the hours passed, the terror had retreated to despair, but dread of the unknown still lay under the surface waiting to slip into the pit of her stomach.

Don't panic. Breathe. Think of some lyrics to a song, hear it playing in your mind. Don't try to guess what's coming next. Focus on the song.

Shreya heard footsteps approaching, a door opened and a man's voice whispered, "You have one chance of getting out of here. Tell agent Brewer not to go to the press, she'll know what it means. If she obeys your request you will be released, if she doesn't you're going to disappear. It's that simple."

The sound of the door closing brought back the terror.

She started to sing her moms favorite song… *'Don't it always seem to go, that you don't know what you've got till its gone. They paved paradise and put up a parking lot.'* They were the only lyrics she could remember. *Shooo bop bop bop…*

THIRTY-TWO

Chapter 64

S am couldn't remember his ex-wife's phone number, but I knew my sister's and gave her a call. "Look outside your front window and tell me what you see," I asked her.

"There's a black sedan with tinted windows parked across the street," she told me, "Want me to bring them some coffee?"

Not much freaks my sister out. She's a cop's daughter too.

Then there's my mom. She would have taken a dozen eggs out of the fridge and plastered the sedan. I decided not to call her.

I told my sister to check again in 15 minutes. I'd explain later.

No way Sam and I were going to risk our family's lives. We had to kill the story; Sam agreed.

"Call Parker and demand to talk to Shreya," Sam told me. "Make the deal, agree we won't talk to the paper if Shreya is released. Acknowledge our families are in danger and could be put in harm's way if we don't stick to the deal."

I called the number again. I was surprised how quickly Parker agreed. I insisted he put Shreya on the phone.

At first, all I could hear was her breathing, then she said, "Erica, is that you?"

"Yeah, sweetie, I'm right here. Are you hurt?"

"No, just scared. I could use a drink."

"Me too," I told her. "Soon as we get you out of there. I'm guessing they've told you to tell me not to publish the story, right?"

"Yeah, publish and I disappear," She whispered.

"I'm going to do what they are asking," I told her.

I could hear the sound of relief in her exhale."

"Happy birthday," she said.

She was right, today's my birthday. Like I gave a crap.

"I'm so sorry this is happening to you," I told her.

"I'm Okay," she said, "You're the one who's turning thirty-two."

I almost laughed.

Parker came back on the line.

"Don't talk with the newspaper. Are we clear, Agent?" Parker demanded.

"When are you going to let her go?" I yelled.

"Maybe after the President's televised speech, until then you keep your mouths closed."

The phone went dead.

'Happy birthday to me,' I thought.

I'd gotten my best friend kidnapped.

I NEVER WILL

Chapter 65

"The President is on line one," Gilliam's secretary informed him.

"I hope you're kidding me," Gilliam said.

"No sir, line one."

Gilliam hit the blinking button on his phone, "This is FBI Bureau Chief David Gilliam."

"Chief Gilliam, this is the White House switchboard. I am transferring you to the president's office, please hold."

He heard several clicks and then the President's voice.

"Chief Gilliam, I need you to come to the White House to meet with General Wallace and myself.

"Yes sir, when do you want to schedule this meeting?"

"Right now, Chief. A Secret Service car is waiting for you in front of your office.

"Yes sir, I'm on my way."

This wasn't the first time he'd been ordered to the White House. But the request had never come directly from the President himself. The Director of

Homeland Security had always handled it. But that was before the Director of Homeland Security was killed in the attack on Congress.

Gilliam told his secretary he'd been summoned to the Oval Office to meet with General Wallace and the President and to push his next appointment to the afternoon.

Grabbing his coat, he took the elevator to the parking garage. Agent Decker was waiting with the limo door open. The ride took less than ten minutes. He felt like he was walking into the lion's den as Decker escorted him to the Oval Office.

General Wallace, in full uniform, waved him in. The President shook his hand and offered him a seat next to the general who sat in his chair staring straight ahead.

"Good to see you've recovered so quickly from the attempt on your life Agent Gilliam," the President said and took a seat behind his desk. "I was surprised to see you the night of the terrorist attack."

"Thank you, sir, I felt it was necessary to return to work as quickly as possible in light of our current situation." Gilliam glanced over at the General, who was sitting on the edge of his chair looking uncomfortable.

"I've asked you here," the President said, "to inform you the CIA has found evidence that the Iranian Government was involved in the attack on Congress."

The President glanced at General Wallace and then back to Gilliam. "We've also discovered information suggesting that one of your agents may have collaborated with the Iranians. The Secret Service is requesting your help in finding this ..."

"One of my agents," Gilliam interrupted. "Who do they suspect?"

The President wasn't used to being interrupted; didn't like it either. "Special agent Erica Brewer," he snapped. "She claimed to have obtained information about the attack a few moments before it happened. She has not been seen since. We believe she has gone into hiding with a Washington Police officer." The President put a pair of reading glasses low on his nose and looked at his notes. His voice grew irritated as he read, "a Detective Sam Marco." The President looked over his glasses at Gilliam. "Agent Brewer had advance knowledge of the attack and has now disappeared. I want her located and turned over to the Secret Service."

Gilliam knew he'd moved from the lion's den to the lion's mouth. He wasn't going to give up his agent or Detective Marco.

"Mister President, agent Brewer is not in any way connected to the attack on Congress. She is in hiding sir, because of what she learned from the man who threw the bomb over the White House fence. She believes that both her and Detective Marcos lives are in danger."

The President stood, his face contorted into an angry expression. The general stood as well but didn't look at either man.

"Mister Gilliam," the Presidents voice grew louder, "Are you aware your agent was involved in an illegal attempt to hold General Wallace against his will at Camp Pendleton?" The President didn't wait for an answer. "I am giving you a direct order to disclose her location, immediately."

"That's not going to happen, Mister President. She is my agent and is doing her sworn duty to find and apprehend the people responsible for the death of over five hundred members of Congress. Furthermore, I believe the perpetrators of this attack are also responsible for the attempt on my life."

The President pushed his intercom. "Send in my Secret Service agents," he ordered.

Two agents rushed through the door. Gilliam could see the general flinch as the door opened.

"Arrest Chief Gilliam," the President ordered, "And place him under guard at the Washington Navy Yard. He is charged with collaborating with the subversives involved in the attack at the House of Representatives. He is to be held in isolation until further orders from me."

Gilliam was whisked out of the room.

"He knows who orchestrated the attack," the general whispered. "He did everything but come out and say it."

"I know," the President acknowledged and stepped around his desk to sit on one of the two couches in the center of the room.

The general didn't move, stared straight ahead.

"We're this close to going public with our accusations against the Iranians," the general reminded the President. "We need to contain Gilliam and his agent. Colonel Mitchell is also a threat. If they discover that the colonel's brother's murder is connected…"

The President interrupted the general, "They don't have hard evidence or it would be out already. You deal with Colonel Mitchell, my Secret Service detail will handle Gilliam, his agent, and this DC Detective. Come join me, General," the President said. "I'll pour you a drink." He walked over to the cabinet.

The General didn't move, kept looking forward.

"What's wrong, General? You've acted strangely every time you're here. Do you want bourbon or scotch?"

"I can't be in this office, Mister President."

"What are you talking about General. Why can't you?"

"Too many closed doors," was all the General said and kept staring straight ahead.

The President knew the Oval Office had intimidated many of its occupants. President Harry Truman called it 'the crown Jewel of the federal prison system'.

But too many closed doors. Now that's a new one, the President thought. Hell, I never want to leave this place. If this goes as planned I never will.

FIRE WITH FIRE

Chapter 66

S am was wearing out the carpet. "Fire with fire." He finally said. "We fight their bullshit fire with our own bullshit fire."

"Explain," I asked.

"They've kidnapped Shreya and threatened our families in order to stop us from publishing the story. That's their fire. How about we do the same to them?"

I wasn't sure what Sam was getting at but I took a guess, "Kidnap and threaten someone they care about! Is that what you're saying? You're kidding me, right?"

"No, I'm not kidding. We've been hunted, chased, and shot at. Now they've kidnapped Shreya. We fight fire with fire. I'm not kidding."

I was as sick of what was happening as Sam was, "Okay," I said, "I'll take this idea for a walk with you, who are we going to kidnap?"

Sam stared at me, "You're not going to like this."

I was about to say, 'Don't count on it', but I let Sam speak.

"When we were at Camp Pendleton and had Major Parker in the interrogation room, he confessed that he was loyal to General Wallace because the General had saved his father's life in the Gulf War. Then he got all puffed up when we threatened to arrest his dad for collaborating. That's who we take, his father."

"Sam, we can't take an old man. We can't. He's not a part of this. We were bluffing," I insisted.

I couldn't believe what Sam was saying. Kidnappers are the most despicable criminals out there.

"I'd love to scare the crap out of Parker," I added, "but not by putting an old man at risk."

"You just said it," Sam replied, "Scare the hell out of Parker. Don't kidnap his father, make him think we have him."

"How do we do that?"

"With help," he said and handed me his phone. "We get Tony on board. Tell him our idea, see if he wants to help."

Sam's idea started to have legs.

I called Tony. Told him Shreya was missing and what we had in mind. He was at our hotel in less than an hour.

"Where does Parker's father live?" Tony asked as he came in the door.

I used the satellite phone and contacted the colonel to have him access the address from the military database. He didn't ask me why I needed it. Pretty sure he had his own problems to deal with.

"I need to get direct access to his phone system," Tony told us, "This has to be a 'hard wire connect' to intercept all his calls. But first, we need to record the father's voice, make him say things a kidnapped person would say."

"How?" Sam asked.

"Interview him. Record the interview and I edit what he says to make it say what we want."

"Parker's dad is 350 miles from here, how are we going to rewire his phone system?" I asked.

"We'll get one of my surveillance agents in the Akron office to take care of what we need in Parker's father's house. After we interview Parker's father we have to get him out of the house so my guy can access his phone system.

I took out a pad of paper and started throwing ideas around. The list was short. The keywords we needed were, 'I'm okay', 'do what they say', 'I'm scared', and 'hurry,' we also need him to say his son's name.

I volunteered to make the call.

We used Tony's phone as a recording device and I called the number the colonel gave me. The phone rang several times before a man's voice finally answered.

"Is this Lieutenant Colonel Parker?" I asked.

"Speaking."

"Colonel Parker, this is Rebecca Johnson from Gulf War Magazine. We're doing a story on the first Iraq war and your name came up as a possible interview candidate. Do you have a few minutes for us to ask you some questions about your experience's during Operation Desert Storm back in 1991?"

Turns out Colonel Parker loves talking about the war. It took about a half hour before I'd gotten all of the buzzwords we were going to need. I made an excuse to get off the phone but first made an appointment to meet him in person to finish the interview. I asked him what his favorite restaurant was and promised to buy him lunch. We agreed to meet there in an hour. I wasn't too happy about stiffing Parker's father, but we needed him out of his home to access the house wiring. It was better than kidnapping him, I told myself.

Tony took the recording back to his office and ordered the re-wiring of the house.

We had a couple of hours to kill and flipped on the TV in time to see the president standing next to his cabinet appointees as each one was sworn in. After the ceremony, the President took a reporter's question.

"There are reports, Mister President that the CIA is close to declaring Iran responsible for the attack on Congress. Do you have a comment, sir?"

The President expression changed. His jaw clenched and with just the right amount of anger in his voice he replied, "We are close to announcing our finding, but have received information that there may have been domestic involvement in the attack, possibly from within our own intelligence services. Arrests are imminent. The Justice Department will brief you later this afternoon. In the meantime, I'd like to present my new cabinet members. On my right are…"

I clicked off the T.V.

Sam said, "We might want to keep an eye on the Justice Department briefing. There might be a couple of photos of you and me, with a message running underneath that reads; 'Wanted dead or alive'."

Sam was right, "It would be the fastest way to catch us. I'm going to call Gilliam. He'll know what's coming down the pike."

"He's not here," Gilliam's secretary told me. The shake in her voice told me she was worried. "I haven't heard from him since he left for the White House this morning." Her voice cracked again, "He was summoned by the President this morning and ordered to come to the Oval Office to meet with General Wallace and the President. He had me push his appointments to this afternoon, but I had to cancel them when he didn't return."

"What time did he leave for the White House?" I asked.

"At eight this morning. He wasn't too happy he'd been summoned."

"Okay," I told her, "if he shows up, tell him I called."

I looked over at Sam. "My boss got called to the Oval Office this morning and never made it back. His secretary sounded nervous. Didn't we just hear the President announce they suspect domestic involvement in the terrorist attack? Do you think they'll try and aim their conspiracy at Gilliam?"

"Nothing is out of the realm of possibility, nothing," Sam answered. "We need to expect the unexpected."

My hands were shaking. It wasn't fear, it was the adrenaline pumping through my anger.

"Shreya's been kidnapped, my boss is missing, and we're being hunted," I said. "We've been running as fast as we can to stay ahead of this shit and it's not working."

"I agree," Sam replied. "If they release our photos to the media accusing us of being involved with the gas attack we're toast."

My neurons were firing, "We need to get Shreya back before anything else happens, I'm calling Tony, he needs to know what's going on."

Tony answered on the first ring. "It's done," he told me. "Five more minutes then contact Shreya's kidnappers. My agent is at Parker's house, we're ready now."

"There's more," I told him. "Our boss was called to the Oval Office this morning to meet with the President and the general. Gilliam hasn't been heard of since. The news conference, a few minutes ago, had the President claiming there were domestic personnel involved in the attack. It's possible they're holding Gilliam as a suspect. Sam and I think we might be seeing our pictures on TV as accomplices."

There was long silence before Tony spoke, "You sure Gilliam met with the President and the General this morning?"

"Yes."

"Hold on a second," he said. I heard him put the phone on his desk, then the sound of fingers tapping on a keyboard. "There are nine hours left," he said, "until the battery dies."

"What battery?"

"The one in the recording device the general has inside the Joint Chief of Staff insignia on his uniform."

I was floored, "It's still active!"

"It records until it runs out of power. According to my calculations, it still has nine hours of battery life. If the general was in the Oval Office with Gilliam and the President, the recording device would have picked up what they said. Get me that recording in the next nine hours and I'll be able to download its contents and find out."

I asked, "Does it have to be within the next nine hours?"

"The battery dies in nine hours and all digital data dies with it. Do you still have the second recovery card I gave you?" Tony asked.

I passed the question to Sam. He pulled it out of his wallet and showed it to me.

"Got it," I told Tony and asked, "Where are you going to be in nine hours?"

"Wherever you need me to be," he replied and hung up.

"First things first," Sam stressed, "We need to call Parker and tell him we have his father. That's the only way we're going to get Shreya freed."

I made the call.

Fire with fire.

DEAD GIRL WALKING

Chapter 67

Hiding in plain sight, it's what I kept telling myself as Sam and I parked our car around the corner from the general's house. Getting the recording device before the battery ran out was our last chance.

We sat there for an hour. My cell rang, it was Shreya.

"He let me go, she told me, I could hear the relief in her voice. I'm going back to the office. It's the safest place for me."

"I'm so sorry I got you involved in all of this. Are you okay?

"I was pretty scared but you don't need to apologize to me. The only thing I need is for you to take these traitors down and let me help."

"Sam and I are about to bust into the general's house to do just that. I got to go, I'll call you as soon as I can.

I told Sam that Sherya was safe. We sat there and let the night close in. By 7:30 the inside of the house was pitch black. No cars out front. The place looked empty.

"Let's go inside and wait for the general to come home," Sam suggested.

Locks are overrated. Sam jacked open the back door faster than some-one using a key.

As we went through the laundry room, I opened the dryer. It was just large enough for me to curl up in a fetal position and fit inside. Sam handed me a towel for my head to rest on. "I'll find a place to hide in the garage," Sam told me. We agreed to meet upstairs in the guest bedroom as soon as we hear the general's security team leave. Sam closed the dryer door and my world went pitch black. I wasn't sure how long I could stay curled up. My yoga class was coming in handy. I knew from the last time the security team checked the house that they were in and out in less than five minutes. The general had waited in his car until they were done, so we had about two minutes to get upstairs before the general would pull into his garage.

Claustrophobia is not one of my problems, but twenty minutes inside this thing was testing my limits when I heard two men enter the house. I could hear them yell 'clear' as they made their way through the house. When I heard the front door close I was about to push the dryer door open when it opened on its own and Sam reached in and helped extricate me from my hiding spot.

I was pretty cramped up. Sam helped me upstairs and into the spare bedroom closet.

A few minutes later we heard the automatic garage door opening, then someone rustling around in the kitchen. It was another half hour before we heard footsteps coming up the stairs and walk pass our hiding spot. It was getting close to our drop-dead time, at best the battery would last another hour, maybe two.

Sam whispered, "We may need to download the recording at gunpoint. We're running out of time."

We gave it another twenty minutes before we took out our guns and stepped into the hallway. We moved to the front of the master bedroom entrance and listened. The only thing I heard was my heartbeat. I pointed to my watch and signaled to Sam to wait ten more minutes. At this point, I was ready to shoot the general and be done with it, but we waited. The ten minutes were almost up when I heard a low rumble coming from the bedroom, it got louder as we waited. The General was snoring, it got louder with each breath. This guy needed a C-PAP, but it was music to my ears.

A small night-light in the master bathroom was bright enough for us to see the closet door was open. We crawled on our hands and knees into the closet and shut the door behind us. I turned on my cell phone flashlight and shined it where the coat had hung the last time we were here.

There it was, the same coat sat on a hanger right in front of us. Sam took out his wallet, removed the recovery card and pushed the activation spot; nothing happened. He tried several more times before handing it to me. I did exactly what I'd done the first time, but still nothing happened. "What the fuck," Sam whispered and moved next to the coat, unhinged the medal and put it in his pocket. It was time to leave.

I opened the closet door a few inches and listened. The snoring had stopped. I opened it a little more and glanced over at the general's bed. My heart stopped. He wasn't there. The covers were pulled back, the bed was empty.

There are two sounds you never want to hear next to your face, a pissed off rattlesnake or a shotgun being cocked.

I hate snakes, but I'd have preferred it to the sound of General Wallace cocking both barrels of his 12-gauge. The gun was so close I could smell the oil he'd used to clean it.

"Don't fucking move," he growled and flipped on the light. "Lie face down right where you are, hands straight out in front of you," he ordered. "Fucking move a muscle and I end your lives right here."

The general stood over us, the gun pointed at my head. "What the fuck are you two doing in my goddamn closet."

Neither of us replied.

He held the shotgun against my head and frisked me. Did the same to Sam, took our weapons and threw them on the bed. When he found the Joint Chiefs of Staff medal in Sam's pocket, he grunted, "What the fuck you want with this?" Then put it in the pocket of his robe. "You two have been a pain in my ass for the past week. Let's take a walk downstairs," he suggested, his voice calm as a priest in confession.

"Stand up as slowly as you crawled in here," the General advised. "And you, Detective, lock your hands behind your head. If they come down one inch I will shoot her first."

Sam did as he was told and glanced over at me. I tried to hold his eyes, but the general put the barrel of the shotgun on the back of my head and ordered, "Go."

Sam led the way out the bedroom door.

The general had me turn on the lights as we moved through the house into the kitchen. I could feel the air against my skin. I knew these were the last sensations I'd ever experience. It was surreal. My feet were touching the ground, but I seemed to be floating. It was like being half asleep and half awake, hard to tell what was real.

It flashed through my mind, this must be what it's like for a death row prisoner to take their last steps into the gas chamber. My vision narrowed, it was like looking through a pair of binoculars turned backward. All I could hear was the blood pumping through my veins.

"Get down, both of you, face down on the kitchen floor," Wallace ordered like he'd done to his recruits in boot camp.

The room was large with white tile floors, Sam lay down with his head facing the sink and I started getting down on the floor next to the open door to the attached garage. The thought crossed my mind to run into the garage, but it would have ended badly for Sam first and then me. I slid down on the tile face down. I could smell the air from the garage. It was the sweet aroma of life.

"Your little show in the brig is coming back to haunt you," Wallace hissed.

My head was turned toward the general, he saw me looking at him. He pulled his Joint Chiefs of Staff medal out of his pocket and waved it at me. "Is this what you two are going to die for? Someone tell me what the hell you wanted with this. Now!"

As usual, my mouth wasn't going to make matters any better. I could hear the words leave my lips, "It's got a recording device in it," I blurted. "Figured you would want to keep your voice for posterity. Long live the asshole traitors."

He walked over to me and put the shotgun against my head, "You're a real smart-ass bitch, It's a shame I'm going to make a mess of you two in my kitchen." He let that tidbit of information spin around in my head. "Who's waiting for this device? I want names, right now," he demanded.

Sam was looking at me from his side of the kitchen. His eyes kept moving from my face and up the wall behind me. Wallace saw Sam looking at me and moved over and straddled him. He had the shotgun aimed at the roof, in a holding position. Sam was still looking at me, his eyes moving from my face to the wall behind me. I turned my chin to see what he was looking at. There was nothing there just an open door to the garage.

The fog swirling around my brain cleared for a second. I reached out slowly and put my hand on the edge of the door and looked back at Sam. He smiled. I smiled back.

"I'll tell you who's waiting for the recording general," Sam announced.

Wallace stared down at Sam, "I'm listening."

Sam slowly rolled onto his back and looked up at Wallace. "Everyone, General, everyone in the whole world."

I took a breath and slammed the door shut as hard as I could. The general spun around at the sound. He saw the closed door and froze for a split second. His eyes stared at the door, his chest caved slightly as if the air had just left his body. He started to lower the shotgun toward me. Sam, still on his back, drove his foot straight up the generals groin and rolled onto his left leg. Wallace started to fall, the shotgun still in his hands exploded. The general hits the ground hard. He still had another shell in the second barrel. He tried to aim it at Sam, but Sam was rolling across the floor away from the sink. I leaped at the general, my knee landing hard on his chest. I grabbed the barrel of the gun and pushing it toward the refrigerator. I heard the second explosion and felt the heat from the blast. My knee must have knocked the air from the generals lungs. He was gasping for breath, but still struggling to get away from me. He must have gotten a breath because I heard him scream. As I rolled off him Sam had his foot grinding down on the general's trigger hand. Sam twisted the gun out of Wallace's hands and we both stood over him.

I could feel my mouth moving, but I couldn't hear a thing. The shotgun blast had my ears ringing louder than my voice. Sam caught on I was deaf and moved me a few feet away, bent down and grabbed the general by the lapels, raised him off the floor and punched him back to the ground. The general lay still, semiconscious. I got Sam's attention and made my hand into the shape of a gun and pointed at the staircase. He nodded and I ran upstairs and brought down both of our guns and my burner phone. I heard my own footsteps as I came back into the kitchen.

"My hearing is starting to come back," I hollered as I handed Sam his gun.

"Watch him," Sam yelled. "I'm going to see if I can find something to tie him up with. We need to get this," Sam held up the Joint Chiefs of Staff medal, "into Tony's hands."

In my rage, I'd forgotten everything. I'd gone from 'dead girl walking' to 'raging bull' in a two-minute span.

Sam came out of the garage and handed me a roll of duct tape. I started binding the general up while Sam called Tony. I used two pieces over his mouth. We dragged him through the house to the stairs and duct taped him to the railing at the halfway point. If he managed to get free he'd roll down with his hands and feet bound together. Probably kill him. He wasn't going anywhere.

The ringing in my ears was dissipating. We ran to our car. Sam knew I needed to drive, "Show me what you got before this battery dies," he said and put on his seat belt.

Tony had agreed to meet us halfway to the FBI building to save time. He was bringing another downloader to save any data left on the medal. We stayed on the phone and kept updating our location.

We pulled into the parking lot of an all-night gym and flashed our lights. Tony flashed his and Sam handed the medal through the window without stopping. It was close to 11 o'clock and we had no idea if the batteries were dead.

I called Colonel Mitchell at his home, told him everything. I think he liked the idea that General Wallace was duct taped to the stairs. He confirmed he'd get ahold of his friend General Jenkins at Quantico and have his MP's put the general in a holding cell back at his base.

The adrenaline had taken its toll and my body was shutting down. We made it back to our hotel room and collapsed on the couch. We both stared at the TV even though it was off. At 1:39 AM Tony called.

All he said was, "We got him."

IF I HAD A NICKEL

Chapter 68

Secret Service Agent Howard Decker answered his phone at 3:30 AM like he'd been awake for hours. Maybe it's true, 'the Secret Service never sleeps'.

"Agent Decker, this is FBI agent Erica Brewer," I said, "you remember me?"

"Not easy to forget," he replied. "Been trying to find you."

"I bet you have," I answered and got right to the point. "The President is going to be served with articles of impeachment by the Sergeant at Arms of the Senate as soon as I release the evidence of his involvement in the attack on Congress.

"What are you talking about?" Decker demanded.

"The President was behind the attack on the House of Representatives. He's going to be served with articles of impeachment. You need to notify your men they will have to stand aside."

"Not going to happen, Agent Brewer. No one has direct access to the President except for the National Security Advisor and the President's Chief of Staff."

"That's why I'm calling you," I told Decker, "Both men were killed in the attack. There is no clear-cut mandate for how this is to be done under the 51st Directive."

Decker's voice got louder, "Agent Brewer, no one is getting anywhere close to the President without my approval. Meet me at the White House and show me your evidence."

My phone was on speaker, Sam shook his head 'no'.

Walking into the White House was equivalent to diving in a shark tank with blood in the water.

I told Decker, "I'm not getting anywhere near the White House as long as the president is still in control. If the President decided to go out on his balcony with a rifle and started assassinating tourists, who could stop him?" I demanded. "If someone started shooting back wouldn't you be obligated to defend him? Until he's impeached he's untouchable. He could take your gun, Decker, and shoot you. Your men would be obligated to keep you from defending yourself. So, I'm not coming to the White House. I'll meet you somewhere else, only you and me. I'll show you everything."

He hesitated before asking, "Where?"

Sam handed me a note, "On the steps of the Lincoln Memorial in thirty minutes," I answered. "We both know what's at stake here. I will show you unimpeachable evidence"

"Unimpeachable," Decker said. "Interesting choice of words. Meet you in thirty minutes."

"I don't like this," Sam groaned when I disconnected.

Sam held up the recording Tony delivered to us, "Are you going to let Decker hear the whole recording?"

"Yeah, and the first recording we got from the general's son. Tony made copies of both recordings and sent them to five secure locations so if something happens..."

Sam looked worried, "Why not let the Post come out with the story and let nature take its course?"

"I don't trust 'nature' in this situation," I told Sam, "The President has more power than at any time in U.S. history. He could declare martial law, shut down the press. He has complete control of the military and can drop a bomb on whatever country he claims is behind all of this. Too many possibilities. We need the Secret Service on our side."

Sam knew I was right and said, "I'll be watching from the Vietnam memorial. It's right next to the Lincoln Memorial."

It was 4:15 in the morning when we got to the memorial.

I sat on the steps and waited. Behind me, a hundred- seventy-five tons of Georgia white marble carved in the likeness of Abraham Lincoln stared down at me. I felt tiny, and dangerous at the same time. The man behind me had saved the nation, the recording I had in my hand might destroy it.

The view of the Capitol Mall was breathtaking. The Washington Monument was mirrored in the reflecting pond and set against a cobalt night sky. I stared at the view, knowing we were right in the middle of one of its greatest crisis. The beauty and the beast...

It didn't take too long before Decker arrived. He was alone, but I'd bet my government pension there were agents spread out all around us.

He was all business. "Show me," he said and sat down on the steps next to me.

I pushed play and handed him my phone.

He listened without saying a word, but his expression changed as the tape played.

"How long have you had this?" he asked.

"Long enough to have the original put into our lawyer's safe and multiple copies made and spread out to people I trust. The recording has been authenticated by the FBI, but I know you'll have to do your own tests."

"I will," he said as I handed him a memory stick with both audiotapes saved in digital format.

"You lied about the Sergeant at Arms delivering the articles of impeachment," Decker told me, "But I get why. You're right about the President being able to do whatever he wants and the Secret Service being obligated to protect him until he's officially impeached. But don't lie to me again," Decker said and stood. "If this tape is authentic the President will be charged with sedition, General Wallace with conspiracy and this country will be running on fumes."

I was explaining myself, "Fumes are better than these two murdering pieces of...."

"I get it," he said, cutting me off. "I'll have this tested and if it's authentic I will..."

This time I cut him off, "What will you do?" I asked. "What can anyone do? There's no congress to impeach him, no system in place to arrest him. He's an institution with a four-star general at his command. This is why I came to you, Decker. The Secret Service might be the only way to stop him. This is going to hit the newspapers," I said and looked at my watch, "in less than twenty-four hours. "It's anybody's guess what he's going to do when it does. Here's my burner cell phone number. When you find out this tape is real, I'd like to know what you're going to do."

"I was planning on arresting you tonight," Decker told me, "I've got four agents waiting for my signal if I decided this was some kind of scheme."

"I know," I said, and held up my phone, "I would have done the same thing. That's why I have five special unit Marines from Quantico spread out around us waiting for my signal."

Decker gave me a nod and walked down the steps. At the bottom, he turned around and said, "If we all live to see this through, come see me about becoming a Secret Service agent."

I was flattered, but my wise gal mouth said, "If we all live to see this through, come see me about becoming an FBI agent."

Decker spoke into his wrist microphone, ordering his men to stand down as he walked out of the area, I would have done the same thing but I didn't have anyone to call.

I wrapped my sweater around me as I approached the Vietnam memorial to find Sam. Whoever designed the monument understood how to elicit emotions. As you start down the brick path the wall is only eight inches off the ground. The names of the soldiers who died in combat are engraved into its black marble surface.

The 250-foot brick path descends as the wall rises higher. At the center, the wall stood ten feet high over my head. By the time I exited I'd walked past 59,000 names, all of them had died for our country.

"Someday they'll build a memorial for the lives lost in the Middle East," Sam whispered and put his arm around me as we walked back to the street.

My teeth were chattering as we approached our car.

"They sure as hell aren't going to build one for this President," I stuttered and got in the passenger's side.

We drove back to the hotel and used the satellite phone to call Colonel Mitchell. "It's done," I told him. "We've given the recording to the Secret Service, they're going to verify it and then contact me."

The colonel was quiet before telling me, "They've got General Wallace in the brig at Quantico, but it's only a matter of time before he's going to be reported missing. This needs to be resolved before the whole military establishment unravels."

I reminded him, "We can't do anything without the Secret Service on our side."

"Agreed," he replied. "You stay on the Secret Service and I'll handle the military. Call me when you have anything."

We needed sleep, but I wanted to talk with Shreya first. Find out how she got away from her kidnappers.

It was 6 AM when I called her burner, she wasn't too happy I'd woken her, but nobody's happy answering the phone at 6 AM unless it's the lottery telling you you'd won forty million bucks.

"How'd you get away from Parker?" I asked.

"He let me go. Wasn't too happy about it. Said you two had an agreement."

I thought about it for a second. "Yeah, we came to a mutual understanding. We tricked Parker into believing we'd kidnapped his father and would let him go when you were released. Thank God he cares about his dad."

Shreya's voice cracked, "You abducted his father! You wouldn't do that, I know how much you hate kidnappers."

"I do hate them, which is why we only made it look like we abducted him. It was Sam's idea to fight fire with fire. We bugged his dad's phone line and when Parker called, Tony used the edited recording to make Parker believe we had his dad."

"Parker let me go a couple of hours after I talked with you," Shreya said. "He only said only one thing, 'I'm going to kill your bitch friend'."

"If I had a nickel… I've got to get some sleep," I told her. "The story about the Presidents Oval Office conversation with the general should break in the Washington Post tomorrow. I mean today, whatever. That's when we find out how well the Constitution was written. I have no idea what the President will do or who can stop him from doing anything he wants. If you can find out anything else online about what the Constitution says about presidential powers, or what chatter is going on in the deep web, let me know, but give me at least four or five hours to sleep first."

Sam was already heading for bed. He didn't bother taking off his clothes, just his gun, and his coat. I did the same and set the phone to block all calls until noon.

The last thing I remember was how good the pillow felt.

The sound of my phone vibrating on the nightstand pulled me out of my dream. Sunlight was streaming through the window. The phone vibrated again, I let it go to voicemail and looked at the clock. It was 1:45 in the afternoon. I'd been out for almost eight hours.

Sam's bed was empty; I made my way to the bathroom in my bare feet. The mirror above the sink was in a bad mood. My hair was hanging in my face like Sarah Connor's in the Terminator. I wasn't wearing any makeup, my eyes were bloodshot and I had a deep wrinkle where my pillow had left a mark. I splashed water on my face, dried off and walked into the living room. Sam saw me and screamed.

Just kidding.

He smiled and said, "The story broke in the paper about an hour ago. So far there's been no comment from the White House."

Sam raised the volume on the TV. A reporter, standing in front of the Capitol building was saying, "Latest reports indicate the President is hunkered down in his residence. The reporter paused, turned to his right, head down, listening to his earpiece. "I've just been told the President is stepping out to the Rose Garden to make a statement. We're going to live coverage."

A tight shot of the 'Seal of the President' on the front of the podium came up on the screen. The camera panned over to the steps where the President and several Secret Service agents were approaching, Agent Decker leading the way.

The president looked directly into the camera as he stepped in front of the microphone. He leaned forward and put his hands on the podium.

"My fellow Americans, we have all heard the accusation, based on a recording made in the Oval Office of General Wallace and myself discussing the catastrophic attack which took the lives of the great leaders of this nation. Our words have been twisted and taken out of context. This is a desperate attempt by the perpetrators of this attack to buy more time to undermine our investigation. It is beyond comprehension that your President would have anything to do with the attack on our Capitol. I ask the American people to wait for the facts to be released before coming to any rash conclusions about who was behind this violation of our sovereignty." The President crossed his arms over his chest, never taking his eyes off the camera. "The events of the past week have struck at the heart of our country. Make no mistake. Our Nation is again under attack by the fabricators of this alleged conspiracy. I am declaring a National Emergency and placing the Nation under marshal law. In times such as these all Americans need to renew our pledge to come together as one nation, under God, indivisible. May God bless you and God bless America."

The President turned and walked back into the Building. The camera stayed on the empty podium as the press shouted out questions at the departing president who ignored them and kept walking, surrounded by his Secret Service agents.

"We're going to be subpoenaed to testify, there's no way around it," Sam told me. We are going to have to prove the President is behind the attack or he will find a way out of this."

I thought about it before telling Sam, "I don't know if Agent Decker realizes it, but he holds the keys to the kingdom. If he protects the President no one can get to him. If he goes the other way someone is going to have to arrest the President. Probably the FBI, but it's up to Decker to decide how this goes."

NOT YET

Chapter 69

I was thinking of contacting Decker again to find out if he'd authenticated the tapes, when my phone rang.

"Agent Brewer, this is Agent Decker we need to meet again."

"Your ear's must have been burning," I told him, "I was just about to contact you."

"The tape is real, but I can't act on it," he told me. "The President declared marshall law when General Wallace was found bound and gagged in his home. I need more information on how this tape of the President was made and by whom. Will you meet with me again at the same place, in two hours?"

"I'll be there," I told him.

He hung up and I looked at Sam. "What do you think? Should I go or do we abandon ship and head for Iceland."

"Iceland's not far enough. The North Pole, maybe. You and me in an igloo for six months, that should test the relationship."

We both laughed for a second. "We probably shouldn't bring our guns," I added.

Sam brought us back to reality, "Let's see what Decker has in mind," he said. "I'll be in my same spot as before."

I got to the Lincoln memorial twenty minutes early and sat on the steps. Huge white clouds were passing overhead playing a game of hide-and-seek with the sun.

Decker looked pretty burned out when he showed up.

"The President wants you arrested," he told me as he rubbed the back of his neck.

"Yeah, and I want him hanging by his thumbs in a dungeon. Someone's going to be disappointed."

"He's still the President, and until he's impeached he's running the show."

"So, you here to arrest me?

"Not yet. How'd you get the recording in the Oval Office?"

I told him the details, ran the whole scenario by him, step by step.

He wasn't buying all of it. "I've heard the tape. It's not a solid admission of guilt. The closest the Oval Office tape comes to incriminating the President is when General Wallace told the President, 'Gilliam knows who orchestrated the attack. He did everything but come out and say it'." Decker stared at me, "That isn't enough."

I reminded Decker, "why are you leaving out the part when the general said, 'we need to contain Gilliam and his agent. Colonel Mitchell is also a threat. If they discover the Colonels brother's death is connected'."

Decker didn't look convinced, "The colonel's brother is dead, can't testify, can't prove the connection. Sounds incriminating, but it could be spun in ten different ways."

Decker looked away, I could see the strain. Finally, he said, "You heard the President's televised statement. He claims the recording's been taken out of context. We need evidence, not innuendo. This isn't a situation that's ever been contemplated."

Decker was right, the recording wasn't ironclad proof. It wasn't until you put all the evidence together that the conspiracy became real.

"We need a face to face," I told Decker, "with the President. We lay out everything we have in front of him. You decide who's telling the truth."

"I'm not the fucking judge and jury," Decker shouted, and looked around to make sure we were out of earshot of the public.

"Yes, you are, Decker. Under Directive 51 there is no established path to impeachment, not when ninety-nine percent of Congress is either dead or incapacitated. No one foresaw this possibility. The President is untouchable. The only thing between him and a jury is the Secret Service, and you're the head of the Secret Service. The FBI can make the arrest, but it's up to you Decker." I took a deep breath. I was making up shit as we were standing there. "Put us in the same room, hear both sides and decide where the Secret Service's loyalty lies."

"Yeah, that's not going to happen. The President wants to have you arrested not have a sit-down." Decker stood up. "I'm going to take the next twenty-four hours to figure this out. In the meantime I'm going to let Gilliam go as a show of good faith."

"We're not meeting at the White House," I called out to him as he walked down the steps. "If we do all meet, it's got to be somewhere else. Same reasons as before," I said.

Decker raised one hand above his head as he walked away. At first, I thought it was his way of saying 'I heard you' and then I came to my senses and realized it was a signal to his men not to shoot me.

TWO CENTS WORTH

Chapter 70

Everyone met at General Jenkins office at the Quantico marine base in Virginia. Unless General Wallace was going to attack another marine base, it was the safest place for us to be. Colonel Mitchell had flown in the previous night.

Sam and I had moved out of the hotel and were given living quarters on the marine base. Room service consisted of dinner at the commissary with fifty thousand marines.

"If the President refuses to meet with us," Gilliam announced, "we'll need to have a plan B. I imagine it will involve the media again."

I threw in my two cents worth, "The President has the power to shut the media down. Hell, he could shut down the Internet if he decided to. Unless there's an open rebellion and the population attacks the White House, it's just accusations verses denials."

Sam started pacing the room, "Only reason he's going to be willing to meet with us is to have us taken into custody."

I agreed, but my mind did one of its reversals. "If it's the only way he will come, maybe we can use it to our advantage. Anyone know where we can get a copy of the Constitution and someone who knows how to explain it?"

TIME STOPPED

Chapter 71

Decker stood in front of the President's desk, and repeated his statement. "That's what they're requesting, sir," he finished.

The President looked at his head of security and smiled. "Set up the meeting, agent, at the Navy Shipyard, and notify General Wallace and Major Parker to accompany me there. I want the counter assault team on the premises. When this charade is over I want these conspiracy fanatics arrested. Are we clear?"

"Yes, sir."

Decker left the Oval Office and headed for Secret Service headquarters. A face to face with the President's accusers was going to be a logistical nightmare. If the decision was going to be made to arrest the head of the FBI, along with the rest of his team, then the President was right, the 'C.A.T.' team would be necessary.

•

"Agent Brewer, this is Agent Decker, your face to face meeting with the President is scheduled for tomorrow at the Navy Shipyard in building 126 at 9 AM."

"So, is this when you're going to arrest all of us, agent?" I asked him.

"That's a possibility. Make your case, agent and if it doesn't stick it could very well happen. This was your idea. I'll have a C.A.T. Team there to protect the President. Do not attempt anything. Unless the President is impeached, I am legally mandated to protect him. Are we clear?"

"As a bell," I told him and hung up.

I'd already decided to stop doing the 'run and hide the rest of my life' thing. This disappearing act stops now.

I called Gilliam and repeated what Decker had told me. I told Sam the deal. He wasn't any happier than I was but he was done with running, too. I made one last call to Colonel Mitchell and asked him to do me a favor.

•

At 9 AM the following morning Sam and I arrived at the Navy Shipyard. Colonel Mitchell and my boss were waiting in the parking lot.

Building 126 is a two-story warehouse used as part of the Washington Navy Demonstration Project and once served as the Navy Police Station. It had been cleared of all personnel.

I'd notified Decker to expect four additional men, all over the age of sixty, to attend the meeting. I gave him the names.

The six counter assault team members, in full battle gear, had been strategically spread out around the room as we went inside.

There was no doubt whose side, they were on.

When the President arrived, Decker came in first, followed by four Secret Service agents in a tight circle around the President.

General Wallace and Major Parker came in next. Parker tried to stare a hole in me. The hate in his eyes didn't escape me. Both soldiers were in full military gear like they were heading to the front lines of a battlefield.

The President wasted no time before he pointed his finger at Colonel Mitchell. "You disobeyed a direct order from your Commander in Chief to relinquish control of Camp Pendleton to General Wallace. You are relieved of your command, Colonel."

General Wallace stood in the back of the room with a shit-eating grin on his face. He wanted the colonel in his brig.

Mitchell replied, "Mister President, I do not recognize your authority. You have committed treason against this nation. I fully expect you will be impeached and put on trial for your crimes."

Gilliam spoke next. "Mr. President, the FBI has uncovered evidence that you and General Wallace conspired to circumvent the Constitution of the United States for the sole purpose of remaining in power. Your treasonous action resulted in the death of over five hundred citizens. I am advocating that you be stripped of your presidency and tried in a court of law."

The President scoffed. "Chief Gilliam, the only people in this room relinquishing power are you and your cohorts."

Decker stood in the middle of the room, his men surrounding the President.

I pointed at the catwalk on the second floor and said, "Mister President you need to hear what this man has to say. Everyone looked at where I was pointing. A short, gray-haired man stepped up to the railing. He had a piece of paper in his hand and started to read.

"Mister President, I am the Sergeant at Arms of the United States Senate. Article II, Section 4 of the constitution stipulates that the House of Representatives must pass, by a simple majority of those present and voting, articles of impeachment." As he spoke a man in a wheelchair rolled himself into the room. Speaking with a hoarse voice the man identified himself, "I am Steven Sheppard a duly elected representative of the State of New York and the only surviving member of the House of Representatives', which under these circumstances constitutes me as the 'majority'. I have seen the evidence collected by the FBI and hereby vote to impeach you, sir, for acts of treason."

As he wheeled his chair out of the spotlight, the Sergeant at Arms spoke again, "After an impeachment vote by the House, a two-thirds majority of the Senate is required to convict the President."

Two men, both in their late 60's stepped forward. "I am William Stratten, senator from California. This is Senator Joseph O'neal from the state of Nebraska. We have seen the evidence collected by the FBI and do hereby vote to impeach you, sir, for acts of treason."

"You have been declared a citizen of the United States," the Sergeant at Arms announced. "And now stand accused of Treason. Before you can be removed from office a trial must take place before the Chief Justice of the Supreme Court."

"Is this some kind of a joke?" the President yelled. "I do not recognize their authority under the 51st Directive. Agent Decker, arrest them all, immediately."

Decker looked at the President, then at me.

The President repeated his command. I could see the confusion in Decker's eyes as he tried to wrap his head around who to obey.

The four agents surrounding the President tightened their circle, their sunglasses covered their eyes, but I'd bet all eyes were on Decker and me.

I took a step forward. "Agent Decker, it's in your hands," I said. "It's up to you to decide if he's still in command or not. It's a rotten deal, but your men will obey you."

His look told me he hadn't made up his mind. Every day for the last eight years he'd made sure this President was secure. Now he had a decision to make, and the Constitution under the 51st Directive was unclear. A lot of people were about to go to jail, and Decker knew it.

A voice from the back of the room shouted, "Arrest that bitch." Everyone turned toward the sound. Major Parker had his gun out, aimed at me. "She's a traitor to this country. You heard the President, arrest her or I'll end her, right here myself."

Two of the Secret Service agents grabbed the President and took him to the ground. The other two agents pulled their weapons and pointed them at Parker. A blur of motion passed in front of me. I heard Parker's weapon discharge.

I felt nothing. The room exploded in gunfire. Major Parker's body lifted off the ground, his gun flew out of his hand as his body landed on the cement floor.

Sam was down on one knee, right next to me, his gun still in his hand. He looked at me for a half second before falling face first to the ground. I could see the blood pooling underneath him.

I went to the ground beside him, Decker right next to me. Sam was face down, I could hear him moaning softly.

Decker and I rolled him onto his back, the entry wound was on his right side just below his ribcage. I put my hand over the wound and applied pressure. Decker ordered his men to stand down, then spoke into his wrist microphone. "Code blue, man down, an emergency medical team to building 126." He looked at me, "They will be here in under two minutes."

Sam opened his eyes. He was looking right past me at first until his eyes finally settle on me. "Damn, you're a beauty," he said. He coughed twice before asking if anyone else had been hit."

"Just Parker," I answered.

"He was aiming at you," Sam whispered.

I could see Sam's eyes start to flutter and heard the sirens in front of the building. He looked down at where he'd been shot and then back at me.

Two paramedics arrived and knelt beside me, "You can remove your hands," one of them told me.

As I let go the medic placed a sheet of clear plastic over the wound followed by an eight-inch patch of gauze and used a large adhesive tape to cover the whole site. They put Sam on a gurney. I followed them into the back of the ambulance. Before the doors even closed, they had an I.V. in one arm and were starting a second one on his other arm as the ambulance started to move. Sam's eyes opened and closed as he drifted in and out of consciousness. I think I saw him smile at me as they put the oxygen mask over his nose and mouth.

Time stopped, everything disappeared in my life except Sam. By the time we got to the hospital, he was unconscious. They wouldn't let me follow as they wheeled Sam into the trauma unit. As the doors closed behind them, every part of the last two weeks, the deaths at the Capitol building, the attack at the Marine base, and finally Sam being wheeled out of my sight, hit me. I loved him at that moment, more than I can say. I got down on my knees somewhere in the hallway and prayed. I couldn't stop asking God to save Sam. I was still praying when a nurse came out of the trauma room and helped me to my feet.

"We may have got to him in time," she told me and held me in her arms like my mother would have. "The bullet hit him just below his lungs on the right side of his body and lodged itself in his pelvic bone. They are removing it right now. No vital organs were damaged."

I held on to her for longer than I should have, but she never pulled away. Finally, she walked me down the hall and sat me down in the hospital chapel. I tried to stop crying, but my body kept surrendering to my heart.

LOCKED DOWN

Chapter 72

G illiam's wife arrived at the hospital and walked me to the waiting room. She told me what happened after I left in the ambulance. "My husband says the standoff ended as soon as Sam was shot. Looks like he stepped in front of you when Parker pulled his gun. Major Parker died at the scene."

This was the second time Sam had come between me and bullets flying.

"What about the President?" I asked. "What did Decker decide?"

"He had his agents take the President and the general back to the Oval Office and ordered his men to stand guard. No one is allowed to enter or leave. The vice president was called back to Washington. She is in route from Chicago, due back in two hours. The press has no idea what happened. Until the vice president arrives the country is without a leader."

Gilliam's wife went with me back to the trauma ward. I was told Sam was in recovery and would be moved to intensive care. I could see him as soon as he was stable. I found the nurse who had helped me earlier. She gave me another hug. "Give me your cell phone number and I'll call you as soon as he can have a visitor," she told me.

I gave her my burner cell number and got a ride to FBI headquarters. I figured since the President was in custody and Major Parker was dead, it was time to quit hiding.

I took the elevator to the eleventh floor and went straight to Gilliam's office. He wasn't there. His Secretary told me he was at CIA headquarters in an emergency meeting with the director.

"Please have him contact me when he can," I asked and walked back toward my office. I stopped at Tony's door and waited for him to recognize my shadow.

It took him about five seconds before he said, "Erica, get in here."

He told me Shreya was at home, needed some time to put her nerves back together.

I know the feeling.

I brought him up to speed on everything before going to my office and brewing some coffee just for the smell. My office phone rang. It was Gilliam.

"I heard Sam is in intensive care, but should be all right, thank God. How about you?" he asked.

"Right this minute I'm okay, I'll be a lot better when I see Sam."

"The President is locked down in the White House till the vice president arrives," Gilliam told me. "The powers-that-be are in meetings to determine how to proceed. There's no playbook for this scenario. They have the top constitutional experts in a room, trying to come up with an answer."

"When that's done, maybe we get to arrest the President and General Wallace?" I asked.

"I've spoken with the CIA director. He agrees, arresting the President and the general falls under the purview of the FBI, if the impeachment sticks. If that happens, the Vice President officially takes over the Presidency and we can arrest him. You want to be there?"

This was a no brainier. The President of the United States was a mass murder and I definitely wanted to be there. "Just tell me when and where, boss. I'll be at the hospital. Call me."

Everything felt different: my personal life, my job, my belief in the integrity of the federal government. I was at a crossroads. I could smell the coffee brewing, something familiar to help center me. I tried to imagine what was going on in the Oval Office. Thought about it for a second and gave up. There were only two things on my mind: Sam and handcuffing the President.

SHOES

Chapter 73

The Oval Office was dark. The shades had been pulled, the curtains closed. Only one light was on at the far end of the room, which was fine with the President. The darkness fit his mood.

The general, however, did not appreciate the darkness as he paced back and forth leaving tracks in the carpet. The walls were closing in on him.

This was the first time the Oval Office was being used as a 'holding station', with guards keeping the occupants locked inside.

The President was almost done with his second scotch and getting irritated, "Sit down, General," the President demanded, but it seemed as if Wallace didn't hear him. He kept pacing around the office like it was a maternity ward. Finally, the President had had enough. "Sit down, General, that's an order."

General Wallace hesitated for a second. The thought crossed his mind, this might not be his Commander in Chief anymore. Was he required to obey? Was he still the Chairmen of Joint Chiefs of Staff? Could he still give orders? Would military personnel obey him? Or was he just like the man on the couch, a US civilian who was about to be put in prison? He should have taken a bullet, like Parker did. Died like a soldier, fighting for what he believed in.

The outer door opened. Agent Decker walked in, saw the President on the couch and General Wallace pacing the floor.

"Sir, would you and the general please accompany me."

Decker held the door open for the two men.

"Whatever the hell is going on here, Agent Decker?" the President growled as he got to his feet. "Some heads are going to roll. My leadership is what's holding this country together. If any of this impeachment crap leaks out to the press there's no telling what the public will do."

"Please follow me, Sir," Decker replied and pointed toward the hallway.

General Wallace was the first to walk out the door, followed by the President. Members of the President's staff lined the halls. It was eerily quiet as the procession walked out of the West Wing.

Four Secret Service agents led them to the presidential motorcade for the two-mile drive to the steps of the Supreme Court.

Flanked on all sides by the Secret Service, the President was escorted through the marble hallway and into the Great Hall. The red curtains behind the dais swayed back and forth so gently no one noticed. The clock above the center chair read 4:14. The only surviving Supreme Court justice sat in the center seat and stared straight ahead as the President and general entered. The gallery section of the room was filled with the few surviving members of Congress and the newly appointed cabinet members. The press had been kept in the dark.

No one stood as the President entered. The only sound was that of the White House contingent's footsteps on the marble floor.

The vice president was sitting at the long table in front of the dais, facing the Justice. Beside her sat the Sergeant-at-Arms of the Senate. The vice president's hands were leaning on the table, a file folder in front of her. It was so unusual for the President to be standing while others sat that he felt compelled to sit down himself. He hurried to the far side of the table and took a seat, the general beside him.

Slamming his fist down on the table, the President broke the silence. "What in the hell is going on here? I am in the middle of putting this country back together and our traitorous FBI has manufactured a conspiracy, accusing me of being responsible for the attack on our Capitol. This is outrageous."

The justice took a long look at the President before hammering his gavel twice. The echo bounced off the back wall.

"Mister President you have been accused of treason. This court has been convened, under the rules set forth by the Constitution, to determine your legal right to occupy the presidency. There are no guiding rules under Directive 51 for impeaching a sitting President," the justice said. "But under these dire circumstances and the evidence presented, the remaining congressmen plus the newly appointed Cabinet members have convened this hearing to determine your culpability in this crime."

The justice sat stoically, his hands in a prayer position.

"Please bring in FBI Bureau Chief David Gilliam and Agent Brewer," he announced. "We have been notified that our third witness, Detective Marco of the Washington Metropolitan Police, has been seriously injured and cannot give his testimony."

•

I was looking around the hallway for an antacid vending machine. Figured if ever there was a place that needed stomach relief, this was it. Coming face to face with the President wasn't my idea of feeling safe. If the President wasn't stripped of his powers we were going to get to see parts of Washington D.C. nobody knows about.

A security guard led us into the chamber. No one spoke as we approached the long table.

"Chief Gilliam," the Justice requested, please present your evidence."

Gilliam adjusted the microphone. "Mister Justice, may it please the court, I am Washington F.B.I. Bureau Chief David Gilliam. We wish to present today evidence implicating the president and General Wallace as co-conspirators behind the attack on the House of…" The President interrupted Gilliam, "How dare you accuse me. I was just entering the House of Representatives as the attack happened. Do you think I was trying to commit suicide? This was perpetrated by an Iranian terrorist organization…"

"You are out of order Mister President," the Chief Justice said and slammed his gavel hard enough to make me jump out of my seat. I caught myself and slid back down.

The President was still acting like he was in charge. It was unclear under the 51st Directive, whether Article II, Section 4 of the constitution had been properly implemented at the Navy Shipyard. The Constitution called for a determination by the Supreme Court, but there was only one justice alive. The Senate and the House of Representatives had been decimated.

The rule of law was hanging by a thread. And then there was the question of who enforces it?

The only law enforcement in the room was the Secret Service and their job was to protect the United States President. At the moment my best guess would be the one's with the most guns. As of now, that was Decker's agents and his C.A.T. Team.

"You sir," my boss responded, "are the responsible party and I have the evidence to prove it." He looked back at the court clerk and said, "Bring him in."

The door opened and General Wallace's son Charles was brought into the room.

I was looking directly at the general. His eyes were so full of hate when he saw Charles I thought he was going to come over the table at him.

Charles made his way over to the dais and glared back at his father.

"This is Charles Wallace, son of General Wallace. He has a statement to make," Gilliam said and sat down.

This was the favor I'd asked Colonel Mitchell to do for me. Find Charles and have him testify.

Charles never stopped staring at his father as he laid out everything he'd been forced to do. His testimony lasted fifteen minutes while he spelled out every encounter chronologically he'd had with the soldiers sent by his father.

When he was done, the general was no longer staring at Charles. His head was bent, his hands covering his face.

Shreya was brought in. Her testimony about her kidnapping and what she'd learned of the General's deep web activity was presented. She laid what she'd found concerning the three Army Core of Engineer personnel who performed the repairs on the water damage under the House of Representatives and their subsequent deaths upon their return to Afghanistan.

Colonel Mitchell followed and explained the attack on his base and the murder of Lieutenant Harris. Lieutenant Kano stood beside him and admitted his involvement in the deep web communications.

I was the last to speak.

"From the letter I received from Colonel Mitchell's brother on May 3rd, to the recording we recovered from the Oval Office, Detective Marco and I have followed the evidence as it led us to the actions we are testifying about today. I submit this written report detailing all of the actions we took in regard to this crisis." I handed the file to the Sergeant at Arms. "It's the conclusion of the FBI that the President and General Wallace conspired to attack the House of Representatives for the sole purpose of enacting the 51st Directive and the power it gave them over this nation."

When I was finished, we were taken down a spiral staircase to the Supreme Court basement.

From the basement of the FBI to the basement at the Supreme Court, go figure.

The impeachment vote, conducted by the remaining Senators, was unanimous. Vice President Loretta Erin Anderson was sworn into office right there in the Supreme Court chamber by the only justice still alive.

I heard later that Agent Decker had the honor of placing the ex-president under arrest.

•

The country was stunned by the news, the sentencing trial of the President and General Wallace would be televised. Everyone in the country would witness justice on their 50-inch flat screen TV.

It was going to take years to put the nation back together. But the founding fathers knew the future would be unpredictable and gave us a Constitution with the ability to adapt. Its enduring concept was that no one was above the law. No one.

As for Sam and I justice would take a different course, definitely a much better path.

Sam got out of the hospital ten days after being shot. We've been staying together at his home while he recuperates.

This morning Sam had taken off his shoes. They were sitting on the floor next to the couch. I stepped inside them and walked around the room. They were big and warm and felt good on my feet. Sam was about to say something when my phone rang. It was my boss.

"When are you coming back to the office?" He asked. "You still owe me a week in the mailroom."

"Yeah, and I owe Ron Collins a couple thousand dollars and a bunch of green bananas."

It was quiet on the other end, and then Gilliam started laughing. You know how some people's laugh can make everybody laugh? He had one of those. I put him on speaker and Sam and I joined in.

I looked down at my feet and thought about the ex-president. I'm sure as hell glad I wasn't in his shoes.

———————————

Made in the USA
Lexington, KY
24 November 2019

57613736R00219